A Daughter of Fire and Flame

Book Two of the Fire and Flame Series

K.J. Johnson

K.J. Johnson Books

Copyright © 2024 K.J. Johnson First published by K.J. Johnson Books 2024

All rights reserved. No part of this publication may be reproduced, stored or transmitted in any form or by any means, electronic, mechanical, photocopying, recording, scanning, or otherwise without written permission from the publisher. It is illegal to copy this book, post it to a website, or distribute it by any other means without permission.

This novel is entirely a work of fiction. The names, characters and incidents portrayed in it are the work of the author's imagination. Any resemblance to actual persons, living or dead, events or localities is entirely coincidental. K.J. Johnson asserts the moral right to be identified as the author of this work.

ISBN: 978-1-7636825-3-5

Contents

Dedication	VII
Content Warning	VIII
Map of Aetherian	IX
Pronunciation Guide	X
A Quick Recap...	XII
Chapter One	1
Chapter Two	7
Chapter Three	12
Chapter Four	17
Chapter Five	21
Chapter Six	27
Chapter Seven	32
Chapter Eight	36
Chapter Nine	40
Chapter Ten	43

Chapter Eleven	48
Chapter Twelve	54
Chapter Thirteen	58
Chapter Fourteen	62
Chapter Fifteen	66
Chapter Sixteen	70
Chapter Seventeen	75
Chapter Eighteen	80
Chapter Nineteen	85
Chapter Twenty	91
Chapter Twenty-One	96
Chapter Twenty-Two	101
Chapter Twenty-Three	105
Chapter Twenty-Four	110
Chapter Twenty-Five	114
Chapter Twenty-Six	119
Chapter Twenty-Seven	123
Chapter Twenty-Eight	128
Chapter Twenty-Nine	132
Chapter Thirty	137
Chapter Thirty-One	144
Chapter Thirty-Two	150
Chapter Thirty-Three	154
Chapter Thirty-Four	160

Chapter Thirty-Five	165
Chapter Thirty-Six	170
Chapter Thirty-Seven	175
Chapter Thirty-Eight	182
Chapter Thirty-Nine	187
Chapter Forty	191
Chapter Forty-One	195
Chapter Forty-Two	200
Chapter Forty-Three	205
Chapter Forty-Four	209
Chapter Forty-Five	214
Chapter Forty-Six	218
Chapter Forty-Seven	223
Chapter Forty-Eight	231
Chapter Forty-Nine	236
Chapter Fifty	241
Chapter Fifty-One	245
Chapter Fifty-Two	249
Chapter Fifty-Three	255
Chapter Fifty-Four	259
Chapter Fifty-Five	263
Chapter Fifty-Six	267
Chapter Fifty-Seven	271
Chapter Fifty-Eight	276

Chapter Fifty-Nine	280
Chapter Sixty	284
Chapter Sixty-One	288
Chapter Sixty-Two	294
Chapter Sixty-Three	299
Chapter Sixty-Four	303
Chapter Sixty-Five	307
Acknowledgments	311
About the Author	313
Also by K.J. Johnson	315
Social Media Links	316

Dedication

To my real-life Emmerson,
Thank you for making the good times better and the hard times easier. If the zombie apocalypse ever hits, just know, that I'd totally watch your back while we save your book collection.
Priorities!

Content Warning

This story is intended for mature readers only and contains controlling behavior by the MMC towards the FMC, explicit sexual content, dubious consent, sexual assault, drugging, profanity, depictions of violence, and other topics that may be triggering for some readers.

Reader discretion is advised.

Map of Aetherian

Pronunciation Guide

- Valoren: Val – or – ren
- Netheran: Neh – thuh - ran
- Pyrithia: Py – ri – thee - ah
- Vidyaa: Vid – ee - ah
- Zarinia: Zah – reen – ee - ah
- Elysara: Eh – lee – sah - rah
- Aetherian: Uh – thir – ee – an
- Cathal: Kah - hal
- Cian: Kee – an
- Cillian: Kill – ee – an
- Fionn: Fee - on
- Misneach: Mish – nahh

- Caolán: Kway – lawn

- Oisín: Uh – sheen

- Rónán: Roh - nawn

- Niamh: Neev

- Fórsa: Fohr – suh

- Grainne: Grawn - yaa

- Saoirse: Seer – sha

- Drakkon: Drak – kahn

A Quick Recap...

A Heart of Fire and Flame

A Heart of Fire and Flame is set in the realm of Aetherian. The citizens of Aetherian are all connected to the realm by the magic it offers, fórsa. Their connection to the realm allows them to enjoy long lives, with those who can manifest fórsa into a weapon, living the longest.

When Harlowe was an infant, the Kingdoms of Pyrithia, Zarinia, and Vidyaa attempted to overthrow her father, the King of Valoren, and conquer her kingdom. The citizens of Valoren were able to wield fórsa more freely than other kingdoms, and many speculated it was because of the land itself.

With help from the Kingdom of Netheran, Harlowe's father was able to hold off the attacks, and peace returned to the realm.

Unbeknownst to Harlowe, the aid her father received from Kieran, the King of Netheran, came at a steep price: her hand in marriage. Since Harlowe was an infant, Kieran hadn't acted on the marriage agreement.

Twenty-five years after the war, Harlowe is yet to come into her power, despite most people being able to manifest fórsa by their twentieth birthday.

As Harlowe's twenty-fifth birthday approaches, a visiting delegation of Cathal (dragon riders) arrives on Harlowe's doorstep. Harlowe is surprised to discover the delegation is from Pyrithia, as the kingdoms have not interacted since the war. Despite her mistrust of the foreigners, Harlowe can't help her growing attraction to the sexy-as-sin General of the Cathal, Silas.

Intrigued by the man who has been invited to reignite the practice of dragon bonding within her kingdom, something that was outlawed centuries prior because of the risks involved, Harlowe grows close to Silas.

Strange occurrences begin to happen around Harlowe, and unknown assailants attack her kingdom. Silas and Harlowe work together to protect her kingdom, which draws them closer together.

Kieran arrives to attend Harlowe's birthday celebrations and disrupts their budding relationship by announcing his intention to court her.

Harlowe senses Kieran is not the gentleman he pretends to be. Rather than allowing Kieran to court her, she sneaks out of her kingdom, accompanying Silas when he leads the Valoren soldiers in their search for dragons.

Encouraged by her curiosity and her best friend Emmerson, Harlowe sneaks after the soldiers to watch as they seek their potential bond mates.

Silas warned Harlowe and Emmerson not to follow, as it was too dangerous. So when they hear the Cathal flying overhead, they hide out in a nearby cave.

Harlowe and Emmerson realize they are not alone when a dragon, Misneach, speaks to Harlowe, telling her he feels a pull towards her, and that they were destined to meet. Misneach offers his bond to her and Harlowe accepts. They then return to her kingdom with the others.

When they arrive back in Valoren, Kieran shows his true nature, which culminates in him attacking Harlowe at her birthday celebrations and informing her of their betrothal.

Harlowe, injured and feeling betrayed, confronts her parents who confirm Kieran was telling the truth.

Kieran apologizes to Harlowe, and her father insists she fulfills the marriage contract. When she refuses, Harlowe's father locks her in her chambers while they undertake the wedding preparations.

Kieran visits Harlowe in her chambers, revealing his unique powers and confessing to tricking her father into accepting his marriage proposal. Kieran tells Harlowe that he had witches spell the monarchs of Vidyaa and Zarinia to encourage them to invade Valoren. When Netheran offered aid to Valoren, Pyrithia, fearing the outcome of the war and a more powerful Netheran, joined the war to push Kieran back.

Kieran reveals Harlowe was prophesied to wield great power, and he wanted to secure her hand in marriage so he could control her powers.

On the eve of her wedding, Harlowe's mother sneaks into her chambers and gives her the key so she can escape.

Harlowe, Misneach, and Emmerson flee the palace and head towards the Forest of Nightmares, where the last truth-sayer, the Lost Witch, is rumored to be hiding out.

When a group of Cathal spots them, the trio separates, with Misneach serving as a distraction while Harlowe and Emmerson flee.

Inside the forest, the monsters of myth and legend lurk, and Harlowe and Emmerson narrowly avoid falling victim to them when Harlowe releases a torrent of flames, decimating the creatures.

Harlowe and Emmerson locate The Lost Witch, and she confirms Kieran has unique abilities that disrupt the balance of power within the realm. To counter this imbalance, the fates created Harlowe and bestowed her with the ability to call upon dragon flames. This allows Harlowe to have a unique bond with all dragons and not just her bond mate.

The Lost Witch also informs Harlowe that her power is the only thing that can stand in the way of Kieran and his nefarious intentions. However, the Lost Witch also warns Harlowe that should she join forces with Kieran, her power will amplify his, and together they would be the ruination of the realm.

Armed with the knowledge they sought, Harlowe and Emmerson make plans to leave the forest. On the way, they reunite with Silas and his group of Cathal and decide to stay with them for the safety they offer.

However, the next morning, Harlowe wakes to find herself cuffed to the inside of Silas's tent. When she demands to know what's going on, he only tells her he is trying to protect her.

Emmerson discovers that the King of Pyrithia sent Silas and his Cathal to Valoren, pretending they were training the Valoren soldiers. However, their real aim was to abduct Harlowe and bring her back to Pyrithia.

The King of Pyrithia learned of the impending marriage between Harlowe and the King of Netheran, and feared what a stronger alliance between the two kingdoms would mean. He instructed Silas to bring Harlowe to Pyrithia in the hope he could persuade her father to join forces with Pyrithia rather than Netheran.

Upon the group's arrival in Pyrithia, Harlowe discovers Silas is the second-born son of the King and the Prince of Pyrithia.

Silas also learns that his father's plans have changed during his absence. The King now plans to wed Harlowe to his first-born son, Silas's older brother. The King hopes they will produce an heir to strengthen any alliance between the two kingdoms.

Harlowe refuses the match and Silas makes plans to flee with her. However, before they can get away from Silas's father, Kieran arrives and disappears with Harlowe back to Netheran.

Chapter One

I watched in horror as shadows wound their way up Harlowe's body. Our eyes locked for a moment before the darkness completely encased her.

One moment she was there, not twenty feet away, and the next, she was gone; disappearing before my very eyes.

"Fuck!" I bellowed, my breathing ragged. "FUCK!"

"We'll get her back," I heard Cillian say. I wasn't sure if he was talking to me or trying to soothe Emmerson, who was screaming Harlowe's name into the now-empty space she had just occupied.

I raked my hands through my hair, tugging on the strands as I tried to calm myself. I needed to get a handle on my emotions, or I wouldn't be any use to Harlowe.

"**Caolán, can you still feel her?**" I asked, my desperation leaking into my tone.

"I can't... it's like..."

"Don't you dare finish that sentence, Caolán."

My Little Menace wasn't dead. She was a fighter. She wouldn't lie down and let Kieran end her.

"**If you'd let me finish, it's like my connection to her is numb, but I somehow know she is still alive. It's difficult to explain, as I have experienced nothing like this before.**"

An intense heat brushed past my face, and I jumped back. As I turned, I saw Misneach roaring toward the heavens, unleashing his fury with his flames.

When he was done, Caolán growled at the other dragon, the threat clear in the sound. Misneach clawed at the ground as though he was preparing to charge, but Niamh snapped her powerful jaws at one and then the other, seemingly playing the role of intermediary.

"Make no move against Misneach," I warned Caolán. "If anything happens to him, it will only hurt Harlowe."

"He could have incinerated you with his recklessness," Caolán snarled.

"He didn't, so let it go."

Caolán growled again, but this time it sounded more like a grumble.

As I took in the surrounding scene, I saw Emmerson wrapped tight in Cillian's arms and a crippling pain hit me right behind my ribcage. How long would it be before I held my Little Menace in my arms again?

Fionn and Teller crouched over Cian, who seemed to be injured from the fighting. Marching towards them, I stalled when I saw the expression on Fionn's face. It was pure agony. The kind only sparked from unimaginable grief.

"Teller?" I asked hesitantly.

"He's gone," he said without looking away from Cian's unmoving form.

My chest tightened, and it felt as though the air in my lungs had been replaced by burning flames as I sucked in a pained breath.

Cian was gone.

My brother was dead.

How the fuck had this happened?

Moisture gathered behind my eyes, and I closed them, willing the tears away. I inhaled deeply, shutting down my emotions.

I couldn't fall apart.

Harlowe needed me.

Fionn buried his head in his hands and his shoulders shook as he wept silently. Cian had taken Fionn under his wing and had become a brother of sorts to the young Cathal. This was Fionn's first loss, and he would feel it acutely.

We all would.

I worked to lock down my grief, my jaw clenching as I let the General take over.

"Take his body to the healers and have them prepare him for burial," I instructed. Teller turned to face me, nodding his head once in acknowledgment of my orders.

Fionn leaned back on his haunches and let gravity pull him down as he wrapped his arms around his knees and dipped his head.

I placed my hand on his shoulder as I crouched before him and waited for him to lift his gaze to meet mine. Unshed tears shone in his eyes and the sight threatened to drag me under.

I cleared my throat roughly. "We will make Kieran answer for what he has done to our brother," I promised.

Fionn nodded his head, the desperation to channel his grief into something tangible evident in his pained expression.

"But right now, our priority is to bring Harlowe home. Can I count on you to help me, little brother?"

Fionn's eyes widened at the endearment, and I watched as determination settled over him, straightening his shoulders.

"Yes, Silas. You can count on me. Harlowe has become important to me too. To all of us."

I dipped my chin, acknowledging the sentiment, and reached down to pull Fionn up.

Striding towards Cillian, I flicked my head to the side, beckoning him to follow me. Cillian nodded and whispered something to Emmerson before breaking away from her and heading in my direction.

I planted my feet and crossed my arms over my chest to stop myself from pacing. I was barely keeping my shit together, and I didn't want it to show.

"What do we know?" I barked as soon as Cillian was within hearing distance.

"Not much," he sighed. "Teller came to our chambers and told us Cian instructed him to bring Emmerson to Harlowe, who was waiting out by the storage unit. Neither one of them seemed to know what was going on, only that Cian had issued the order."

"You don't think Cian betrayed us, do you?"

Cillian's throat bobbed at the mention of our fallen brother. "I don't think so. Whatever happened here tonight, Cian paid for it with his life."

Cian had challenged me on multiple occasions about my intentions for Harlowe. He wanted me to stick to the plan set out by my father before we left for Valoren. It made no sense for him to betray my father and give Harlowe to the King of Netheran now.

"Whatever Cian's intentions, they aren't what's important right now. The King of Netheran has Harlowe, and we vowed to protect her. So, tell me what our next move is, Silas," Cillian said, pulling me from my musings.

"Don't you dare think about leaving me out of whatever it is you two are planning," Emmerson hollered at us as she marched across the clearing.

"Em," Cillian started.

"Don't you fucking patronize me, Cillian," she spat. "Harlowe is MY Queen," — she jabbed a finger at her chest — "and I'll be the one to get her back. I'll take my last breath before I let you endanger her again."

"The last thing any of us want is to endanger Harlowe, Emmerson," Cillian said gently.

Emmerson lifted her brow in a challenge as she crossed her arms over her chest. "No, it just happens organically whenever you lot are around."

She kind of had a point, and that irked me.

A harsh wind rushed past us as the sound of beating wings cut through the stillness of the night air. I expected to see Oisín flying overhead, but when the giant beast settled across from us, it was Rónán that met my gaze.

"Zeke," Emmerson breathed as she rushed towards her friend.

Zeke slid off the back of his dragon and held his arms wide as Emmerson slammed into him. Cillian growled low in his throat beside me as he watched the pair embrace.

"You came," Emmerson said, the relief unmistakable in her tone.

"Of course I did, Em." Zeke paused and looked around him. "Where's Harlowe?"

A small sob escaped Emmerson before she took a steadying breath. "Kieran came for her," she said, her voice strained against the emotion.

"What?" Zeke asked, not willing to believe what he'd heard. I knew that feeling well.

"Kieran found us and he... he took her... I was right there, Zeke, but I couldn't stop him." Emmerson sobbed freely now, and Zeke clutched her tighter against his chest.

"Shh, Em," he said as he pattered her hair. "We'll get her back, I promise." Emmerson nodded her head against his chest as she tried to calm herself.

"How are you here, exactly?" Cillian asked, interrupting their moment.

When Zeke's eyes locked with mine, the promise of retribution gleamed back at me.

Zeke released Emmerson and prowled towards me, hatred emanating from his every pore. He didn't break his stride as he swung his fist at me, connecting with my ear. I toppled backward and didn't even attempt to defend myself as he continued to pummel me with his fists.

"This is your fucking fault!" Zeke yelled. "She trusted you and you betrayed her."

Cillian gripped Zeke around the waist as he attempted to pull him back, but Zeke broke free and continued pounding his fists into me. Fionn ran over to join Cillian and the pair of them were able to pull Zeke off me.

I sat up and wiped at the blood trickling down my face. Zeke broke free from Cillian's hold and stalked back to Emmerson.

"What's going on?" Teller asked, confusion drawing his brows together as he made his way toward us.

Jumping up from the ground, I moved over to where he stood. "Why were you bringing Emmerson here to meet Harlowe?" I asked, diving straight in.

"Cian told me to. He didn't give me any more information than where to meet him. I assumed the order came directly from you."

Teller looked between me and Cillian, who had since joined us.

"What exactly did he tell you?" Cillian demanded.

"Just that I was to bring Emmerson here and that Harlowe would be waiting."

"You didn't think that was strange?" Cillian growled.

"Why would I?" Teller responded.

"Why the hell would you be meeting Cian and Harlowe with no one else around?"

"I didn't know that none of you would be here. I thought we were all leaving," Teller defended.

"Enough Cillian," I said. "It's not helping." I raked a hand down my face as weariness started to set in.

Teller moved away from us and headed in Fionn's direction. He wrapped his arm around his shoulder and whispered something to the young Cathal, which had him nodding in agreement. I was thankful that Teller was stepping up to guide Fionn through his grief because the gods knew I wasn't capable of thinking of anything beyond my Little Menace right now.

"What about him?" Cillian asked, pointing towards where Zeke stood with Emmerson.

"Let's find out, shall we?"

Zeke watched our approach with a predator's precision.

"How did you know where to find Harlowe and Emmerson?" I asked without preamble.

"I told him," Emmerson said, raising her chin.

"What do you mean, you told him?" Cillian snapped.

"I mean, Cillian," she drawled, "I sent word with Misneach. I knew Zeke would be out scouring the realm for us and that Misneach could get a message to him via Rónán," Emmerson finished, lifting her shoulder nonchalantly.

"When the hell were you able to sneak out to Misneach?" Cillian asked incredulously.

"I didn't sneak," Emmerson snorted. "You all were so busy trying to imprison my Queen that none of you were paying close enough attention to me," she stated smugly. "The first chance I got, I broke away and conspired with Misneach."

"How did you know that your message was received?" I asked, my curiosity getting the best of me.

"Please," Emmerson scoffed. "Some of us are evolved enough that we don't need every little thing spelled out for us."

Misneach chortled from behind her, and Zeke smirked.

That fucking asshole was getting on my last nerve.

"Well, thanks for making a monumental mess of things," Zeke rebuked. "We'll take it from here."

Zeke lifted Emmerson as he mounted Rónán, and the dragon launched into the sky with the pair holding tight to his back. Misneach followed behind them without hesitation.

"Fuck," Cillian shouted, and I turned towards my friend.

I understood his anguish.

"We've all got the same objective here, Cill. You'll be seeing Emmerson again."

My best friend inhaled deeply before saying, "Then let's get to it."

I couldn't agree more.

Chapter Two

Kieran dragged me down a dark passageway; the only light coming from the flames dancing in the sconces. My skin was prickling with the tension permeating the air, as though every shadow concealed a hidden threat.

Kieran hadn't said a single word to me since we'd stepped inside the palace and the eerie silence was unnerving. I wanted to demand he tell me exactly what he had planned for me, but I couldn't trust my voice not to betray just how terrified I was.

We reached a door at the end of the passageway and when Kieran opened it, light flooded the dim interior, temporarily blinding me. I squinted before stepping into a large waiting area with an intricately carved staircase that wound its way toward the upper levels of the palace. As I peered to the side, I saw the front entryway to the palace. When I glanced back over my shoulder, I could no longer see the door I had just stepped through.

Kieran had led me through a hidden entrance to the palace. My mind immediately turned to the possibility of other secret passageways and the thought of finding them.

"My King," a sultry, feminine voice sounded from the staircase. Swinging my gaze toward the sound, I spotted a beautiful woman descending the stairs from the second level. She was tall, with a slender frame and jet-black hair that hung in loose curls around her shoulders. Her porcelain skin was flawless, and a deep shade of purple decorated her plump lips. Her eyes were a stunning shade of blue with flecks of green, which only served to enhance her beauty.

"I'm so glad you're home," the woman purred. Her narrowed gaze then fell upon me, and she asked, "And who might this be?"

"Lucinda," Kieran growled in warning.

Lucinda failed to heed Kieran's warning as she approached me with interest. A perfectly manicured finger ran the length of my face from my temple to my jaw, and I had to resist the urge to recoil from her touch.

I could not show weakness within the Kingdom of Netheran. Doing so would be tantamount to a death sentence. These people were vicious and cruel. Their ruthlessness mirrored their kings, and the gods knew Kieran's cruelty knew no bounds.

Before I could object to Lucinda's touch, her hand was ripped away from my face by a snarling Kieran.

"You forget your place, Lucinda," Kieran barked. "Do not place your hands on what belongs to me."

Lucinda's eyes widened, and she whispered, "So this is the infamous, Harlowe."

A shiver of unease ran up my spine at the way her eyes narrowed and assessed me anew.

"Harlowe," Kieran snapped, reclaiming my attention. "I will show you to your rooms."

Kieran gripped my elbow in a bruising hold as he led me up the staircase and away from Lucinda. I could feel Lucinda's gaze following me, but I refused to glance back over my shoulder.

We walked in silence until we came to a stop outside a pair of double doors. The black wooden frame of the doors had snakes carved into it, similar in design to the carvings on the staircase.

Kieran pushed the door open and led me through a large antechamber that connected to a bedchamber. The biggest bed I'd ever seen stood proudly in the room's center. The four posts framing the bed had sheer black curtains draped over them, each tied to a post with a golden tassel. Black and gold were the color schemes for the entire room. The room's furniture and bedding were a matching midnight shade, while a beautiful golden rug graced the marble floor by the bed.

The room was stunning, yet equally oppressive; the darkness enhancing the gloom that encompassed the space.

"The Queen's rooms," Kieran declared.

I stepped further into the room and immersed myself in the space.

"That door,"— Kieran pointed to the wall behind the bed — "leads into the King's rooms."

Unease washed over me, and bile crept up my throat at the thought of Kieran being so close to me when I was asleep and vulnerable.

As if sensing my unease, Kieran stepped up behind me and wrapped a hand around my waist, pulling me against him.

"If you are a good girl, you have nothing to fear from me, Little Bride," he purred against my ear.

His fingers caressed the side of my face. The gesture could be mistaken as affectionate, were it not for the merciless man behind it.

An involuntary shiver ran through me, and my body trembled.

Kieran chuckled darkly. "Do I frighten you or arouse you, Harlowe?"

"You disgust me," I said with venom.

Kieran tsked. "Behave yourself, Harlowe. I'd hate to be forced to punish you before you've settled into your new home."

"This will never be my home," I hissed.

"Not with that attitude," Kieran mocked.

I spun in his grip and leveled him with the full weight of my fury. "This isn't a joke, Kieran," I yelled, pushing against his chest.

He didn't move an inch.

Kieran's eyes widened and his nostrils flared as he gripped my wrists tightly in his larger hands. He pushed me backward, causing me to stumble and fall as the back of my knees connected with the bed.

He followed me down, pinning me to the bed under the weight of his body pressing into me.

Kieran ran his nose along the side of my throat, and growled, "I think you misunderstand your position here, sweet Harlowe."

My pulse hammered wildly, and I tried to calm my racing heart as it fought to break free from my chest.

"Perhaps that is my fault. Perhaps I have taken it too easy on you," he mused.

Panic threatened to swallow me whole as I recalled the way he had wrapped his hand around my throat, cutting off my air supply. I had worn the bruises for over a week, being reminded of what I had survived with every strained word I uttered. Was that his idea of 'taking it easy' on me?

"Does my father know I'm here?" I asked, trying to divert his attention.

"Your father won't be coming to save you, if that's what you're thinking. He was the one who traded you to me, after all," Kieran taunted.

"What am I doing here Kieran?"

"You already know," he chuckled sinisterly.

"We are not married," I challenged.

He lifted himself so he could look into my eyes. "Not yet, but I will rectify that soon, Bride. I can't have you running away on me again, can I?" Kieran's eyes sparkled with mirth.

The sick bastard was enjoying this.

"I won't marry you, Kieran," I said, with far more confidence than I felt right now.

He lifted a brow in amusement as if my defiance was cute.

"I think you'll change your mind once we get better acquainted."

"I. Will. Not. Marry. You." I snarled.

Anger flashed in Kieran's cold blue eyes as he brought his face an inch from my own.

"Do not think for one moment that you have a choice here, Harlowe," he bit out.

I flinched, not prepared for the viciousness of his reaction.

"If I frighten you now, then I would caution you against testing me further. I can make your life here extremely pleasant... or extremely unpleasant. It's up to you."

Tears filled my eyes and as hard as I willed myself not to let them fall, my body betrayed me as moisture traced its way down the side of my face.

"Your fear excites me almost as much as your rebellion," Kieran mused. Then he leaned in, licking my tears away with his tongue. I could feel his erection growing as he pressed his hips against mine.

"I can't wait to taste every inch of you, Bride," Kieran whispered huskily.

I didn't dare move as I tried to repress the bile threatening to come up.

Kieran studied me for the longest time, and then a wicked grin spread across his cruel face.

"So you can be trained," he chuckled. "I look forward to breaking you, Harlowe."

With that, he stood, strode towards the door connecting our rooms, and disappeared behind it.

I tried to fight off the avalanche of emotions threatening to drown me, but a sob broke free, unbidden. I couldn't stem the flow of tears even if I wanted to.

So much had occurred in such a short time.

Losing Cian was the most devastating.

He had died trying to protect me, and I would forever carry the guilt of his death with me.

So I let the sobs free.

For Cian.

For Misneach.

For the friends I'd left behind.

For my kingdom.

For the life, I thought I could have, but now, I would never know.

I grieved it all. I cried until no tears remained.

Tomorrow, I would need to figure out a way to survive in this pit of snakes. But for now, I allowed the darkness to swallow me and drag me into the sweet respite of nothingness.

Chapter Three

The next morning, I woke to a scratching sound inside my chambers. My eyes flew open, and I reached for the dagger under my pillow, only to find it missing.

Then I remembered this was not my bed, and I was no longer in the safety of my home.

I peered around the room, trying to locate the source of the noise.

A woman stood with her back to me just inside the bathing chamber. Her blonde hair was in a tight bun, and she seemed to be about my height. She was humming quietly to herself as she went about her work cleaning and tidying the space.

Her eyes lifted and as they did, she caught sight of me watching her in the mirror above the basin.

"Oh my," she exclaimed, as she placed her hand over her heart.

Turning around so she was facing me, she said, "I apologize, my Lady. You startled me."

"Harlowe," I croaked out.

"Pardon?"

I cleared my throat and tried again. "My name is Harlowe."

"Well, it is a pleasure to meet you, Harlowe."

"Likewise..." I trailed off, realizing I had no idea who this woman was.

"Everly," she said, introducing herself.

"It's a pleasure to meet you too, Everly."

I may have been kidnapped... again... but I would never abandon my manners.

Twenty-five years of conditioning can have that effect on someone.

"Well, now that you're awake, shall we draw you a bath and get you ready for the day?" Everly smiled kindly, and I already knew this woman would be my lifeline in this otherwise miserable place.

"That would be lovely," I said.

Everly turned back to prepare the bath, and said, "The King has requested you join him for breakfast this morning."

"Has he now?" I muttered.

Appearing back in the doorway, Everly gave me a sympathetic smile.

"The King also sent you several outfits to choose from. I placed them in your dresser while you were sleeping."

Curious, I crawled out of bed and wandered over to the dresser. I almost cringed when I opened the doors and saw that it was filled with nothing but gowns.

"Any pants and tunics amongst that lot?" I asked, jutting my chin towards the open dresser.

"I'm afraid not, my Lady," Everly answered gently.

"Harlowe," I reminded her.

"Harlowe, of course."

Everly disappeared inside the bathing chambers once again, and I looked over at the clothing choices Kieran had provided. Every gown was exquisite; elegantly cut, the softest fabric adorned with jewels and intricate embroidery.

They were fit for a queen, I thought derisively.

"Your bath is ready, Harlowe," Everly said, appearing in the doorway.

Sighing, I closed the dresser doors and meandered to the bathing chamber. Once I settled in the warm water, I felt slightly better as it worked to undo the tension coiling throughout my body. I couldn't help the sigh that escaped me as Everly began washing my hair.

While Everly massaged my scalp, I mulled over my existing knowledge and the information I still required to survive in this place.

Kieran's shadow powers were not of this realm, I was certain of it. His shadows had transported us from Pyrithia to Netheran in the blink of an eye.

I'd never heard of anyone doing that.

The way he wielded his power was also different. With fórsa, the wielder could only generate orbs of energy. The orbs were deadly, but they could not take a specific shape or be directed with the kind of precision that Kieran wielded his shadows. When Kieran had snapped Cian's neck — the memory assaulted my senses without permission, and I inhaled a steadying breath —

it was as though his shadows had been an extension of his own hands. I had never seen anyone use fórsa in such a way.

There was also the fact that whatever his power was, it could numb my bond with Misneach. I hadn't been able to connect with him once since Kieran's shadows had enveloped me fully.

I had hoped that my bond with Misneach had grown strong enough to withstand his power. Back in Valoren, I hadn't been able to sense Misneach from the moment Kieran had entered my bedchamber. But later, as our bond had strengthened, I was able to speak with Misneach when Kieran had first accosted me in Pyrithia.

My hopes had evaporated, however, as soon as Kieran's shadows had swept me away.

I also didn't understand the full extent of Kieran's plans for me.

He wanted me for more than marriage and an alliance with my kingdom. He had told me I was integral to his plans for his kingdom, and the Lost Witch had confirmed he wanted to use the power I housed within me. A power I had no idea how to use or control.

There was also the issue of whoever betrayed Silas by alerting Kieran to where I was. It wasn't luck that had led Kieran directly to me. Someone within Silas's inner circle had told him how to find me.

I had my suspicions about who that person was.

For the first time in my life, I felt truly directionless.

I needed a plan to get myself out of this situation, but that was usually Emmerson's domain. She had a brain geared for warfare, both physical and psychological, and I feared I would be a poor imitation.

She wasn't here, but I was.

I couldn't take on Kieran directly, at least not yet anyway. He had the home-field advantage, and he had fully mastered his powers.

He had already shown he was quick to temper and delighted in his cruelty. Perhaps my father had been right. Meekness and obedience may be the tools most likely to secure my survival.

I could play a part if that's what it took to survive this.

"Are you ready to get out, Harlowe?" Everly asked, drawing me from my musings.

"Yes, thank you."

Everly helped me dry off and wrapped a silk robe around my shoulders.

As she led me towards the dresser, she asked, "Did you have a preference?" gesturing towards the gowns.

"Not really," I muttered. "You pick," I said, blowing out a breath.

Everly rifled through the gowns, and I took a seat at the vanity while I waited for her. Everly returned with a beautiful floor-length black gown that shimmered in the light as it moved. Upon closer inspection, I could see it had hundreds of tiny diamonds sewn into almost every inch of the bodice and sleeves. The gown belonged in a ballroom, not a dining hall.

"Is there anything less..." — I paused, not knowing what I was looking for exactly — "that?" I said and waved a hand over the diamonds.

Everly chuckled. "The King has exquisite taste, Harlowe. But I will do my best to find something... less," she said as she shot me a smile over her shoulder, and I grinned back.

A few minutes later, Everly had replaced the black ball gown with a light green day dress. The quality and make of the dress were no less impressive than the gown, but at least this one didn't sparkle. It had a ruched bust and fitted bodice that tapered off into a flowing skirt at the waist. The dress had sleeves made from a sheer material that ran the length of my arm, from my shoulder to my wrist.

The dress was simple, yet stunning.

Everly began brushing out my tangled strands as she hummed quietly to herself. It was relaxing, and I realized this was the first time I had felt relaxed since I had left my home in Valoren. The irony of that sentiment was not lost on me, however.

"Will anyone be joining the King and I for breakfast?"

Everly's eyes met mine in the mirror of the vanity. "I assume Lucinda will join you," she said in a clipped tone.

"Who is she? To the King I mean?"

Everly hesitated, and I said, "I'm just trying to get a sense of who the key players are," hoping to reassure her.

"Lucinda won't be pleased with your presence, Harlowe. Especially now that you have been given the Queen's rooms. You must be careful around her."

"So she is with Kieran, then?"

"She warms the King's bed, but he has never shown more interest in her than that."

I got the impression that Everly was taking a risk telling me this, and my heart swelled in gratitude for the woman.

"Thank you Everly. I appreciate your honesty."

"I imagine it can't be easy for you being thrust into a new home without a familiar face to help settle you in. I hope I can ease your burdens, even if only a little," she said warmly.

Tears swam in my eyes at the genuine warmth Everly displayed.

I rose from my seat and cleared my throat before saying, "Well then, we shouldn't keep the King waiting. Lead on Everly."

Chapter Four

Anxiety knotted my stomach as I rounded the corner of the corridor that led into the dining hall. As Everly had predicted, I saw Lucinda seated on Kieran's left when I entered the dining hall. The pair were engaged in what appeared to be an intense discussion.

Hearing my approach, Kieran glanced in my direction and a smirk played on his lips as our eyes met.

"I see you received my gifts," he said as he looked me over from head to toe. "I must say, you look even lovelier than I had envisioned."

"Thank you," I said without the contempt I was feeling.

As I drew closer, Kieran stood and pulled out my chair for me, seating me on his right. I sat opposite Lucinda, who was currently scowling at me.

I settled into my seat and glanced around, only to be surprised by the dozens of soldiers lining the walls on either side of the hall.

How had I not noticed them earlier?

"Pay them no mind Harlowe," Kieran said, following my line of sight. I glanced behind me and realized Everly had disappeared while I had been fixated on the soldiers.

I had to fight the unease sinking into me, knowing I was alone with Kieran and Lucinda.

"Sleep well, Princess?" Lucinda asked in a saccharine tone.

"I did. Thank you for asking," I said as I filled my plate with fruit.

Out of the corner of my eye, I could see Kieran studying me, his smirk still in place on his sensual lips. As I popped a strawberry into my mouth, I tried to pretend I was unbothered by his lingering gaze as I chewed.

"I could understand if you were feeling homesick, what with this being your first time away from your kingdom, and being such a tender age," Lucinda continued with false sympathy.

"Thank you for your concern, but there is no need to worry. This is not the first time I have been outside of my kingdom." I countered. "I recently spent some time inside the Forest of Nightmares," I finished and bit into another strawberry.

Lucinda choked on the liquid she had just consumed, and satisfaction rolled through me knowing she underestimated me.

That's right, I thought smugly. Do not mistake me for a weak damsel you can intimidate with ease. I've survived worse things than whatever you can throw at me.

"Now that is interesting," Kieran purred.

I swallowed and internally cursed myself for getting caught up in a pissing contest with Lucinda when the real threat sat beside me. Not that I didn't want Kieran to know that I had been to the Forest of Nightmares, but telling him anything about my time away felt like I was conceding ground in a fight I was already losing.

"And tell me, Harlowe," Kieran purred seductively, "what in the realm drove you to venture inside that particular forest?"

The question felt like a trap.

I suspected Kieran already knew the reason for my visit, but he wanted to see if he could catch me in a lie.

I shrugged, trying for nonchalance. "Got lost," I said as I popped another strawberry into my mouth.

Kieran chuckled darkly. "Is that so?" he said as he leaned closer to me. His thigh pressed against mine under the table, and I felt a familiar heat pooling low in my stomach.

What. The. Fuck.

Apparently, my body didn't get the memo that we don't get aroused by psychopaths.

I took a large gulp of my water, trying to conceal my body's reaction to him. If the coy smile playing on his lips was anything to go by, he was well aware of what I was doing.

"My King," Lucinda said huskily. "There are several matters I need to discuss with you this morning." She feigned an apologetic smile, and I wanted to roll my eyes at her antics. "You understand, of course, Harlowe."

"Please, don't let me keep you," I said, and I meant it. I intended to search the palace for any more hidden doors I could use to escape undetected.

Kieran turned and glared at Lucinda. The look was one I would never want aimed in my direction; utter contempt combined with fury and a promise of retribution.

Lucinda lowered her gaze and opened her mouth as though she would say something, but nothing came out. A second passed, and I realized with a sickening awareness that it wasn't so much that she wouldn't speak, but that she couldn't.

Kieran's shadows had spilled from his palm and snaked their way up Lucinda's body to wrap around her throat. Lucinda clawed at her neck as her face turned crimson and her lungs tried but failed to draw a breath.

"I warned you last night, Lucinda, not to forget your place," Kieran said in an eerily calm tone. "You let your petty jealousy rule you, and you might find the cost is more than you're willing to pay."

"Kieran," I whispered, and he snapped his head to me. "Please," I pleaded.

While I didn't like Lucinda, I didn't want her dead for simply being an inconvenience.

Kieran tilted his head as though I surprised him. "Interesting," he said as he observed me. I fought the urge to wring my hands together under the intensity of his gaze.

Without breaking eye contact with me, Kieran released Lucinda and his shadows withdrew. The woman gasped and sucked in air greedily.

I dragged my eyes away from Kieran and returned my gaze to Lucinda, who was shooting daggers at me as though I had been the one who almost choked her to death.

"You see what kindness gets you, Harlowe?" Kieran chuckled sinisterly. "Lucinda wouldn't think twice about slitting your throat if she thought she could get away with it."

The look on her face right now confirmed that Kieran wasn't lying.

As I looked around the dining hall, I saw the servants going about their duties, unperturbed. It was as if Lucinda's near murder was nothing out of the ordinary and not something to be bothered with.

This is a common occurrence, my subconscious snickered.

The room felt suddenly stifling, and I tugged at the bodice of my dress as though I could remove the vise I felt clenching around my chest.

I stood from my chair abruptly and took an unsteady step back. My body immediately collided with a muscled chest.

"And where do you think you're going?" Kieran growled against my ear as he wrapped his arms around me, holding me in place.

I hadn't even seen him move.

"I... I just need some air," I stuttered.

Kieran chuckled against my throat, and the vibration sent a shot of pleasure racing through me.

What the actual fuck was wrong with me?

I hated this man. He was repulsive and cruel and was holding me prisoner inside his kingdom for his own nefarious purposes.

Why did I react to him in this way?

I was seconds away from hyperventilating when Kieran released me and stepped back.

"Then please, allow me to give you a tour of the grounds," he said, offering me his hand.

I didn't want to take it both out of revulsion and fear of my body's reaction to him.

Kieran narrowed his eyes on me, and I placed my hand in his, completely overwhelmed by whatever was happening to me.

Kieran interlocked his fingers with mine and ran his thumb up and down my own. The soothing gesture only intensified my unease. The contrast to the cruelty I came to expect from Kieran was so striking that I could only stare at where our hands were joined.

I shook my head to clear it and took a deep breath as I fought to get myself under control.

Once I was settled, Kieran headed towards the dining hall doors.

We walked in silence for a time; the sound of our footfalls was harsh in the surrounding quiet. As we reached the front entrance, Kieran leaned in close to me and whispered, "I think you just might enjoy what the palace grounds have to offer."

Kieran pushed open the large, double doors that led outside, and I sucked in a sharp breath at the sight before me.

Chapter Five

We'd traveled through the night, following the path set by Emmerson and Zeke when they'd left us behind. Exhaustion was taking over, and I knew we would have to stop soon. As it was, we'd left before making arrangements for Cian's burial.

My chest tightened at the thought of my friend.

Cian had been by my side nearly as long as Cillian. I'd thought of him as my brother; more than the one I shared flesh and blood with. Cian had always been the voice of reason within our group. Not afraid to call me out and challenge my decisions. He'd saved our lives more than once.

And now he was gone.

Now wasn't the time to grieve my friend, however. I needed to focus so that I had the best chance of getting my Little Menace back.

I would get her back. Failure was not an option.

"How far ahead are they?" I asked Caolán.

"They've stopped just up ahead."

I relayed the information to Cillian, who had been wound tight ever since Emmerson had fled with Zeke. He grunted in acknowledgment.

The sky was beginning to lighten as the sun peeked over the horizon, but it was still dark enough that it was difficult to make out exactly what I was looking at.

At first sight, it appeared to be a pile of rubble. The longer I stared at it, however, I made out several spires breaching the surface of the ground.

"What is this place?" Fionn asked no one in particular.

"I don't know," I admitted.

We had crossed the border of Pyrithia into the Mountains of Dragonia some time ago, but I wasn't familiar with the terrain before me. It was possible we had also crossed the border of Elysara.

Directing Caolán to land, I decided I was going to find out.

I walked around the spires until I found a small opening in the center. As I crouched down, I peered through the opening and saw what appeared to be the interior of a castle buried beneath us. Vines and moss grew wildly, but the stonework was visible underneath it.

I lowered my legs into the opening and grabbed a nearby vine. I tested the strength of the vine, and once I was satisfied it would hold my weight, I swung out and descended into the ruins below.

"Silas," Cillian hissed from above. "What the fuck are you doing?"

Almost at ground level, I released the vine and jumped the last couple of feet.

"For fuck's sake," Cillian muttered before he too grabbed a vine and followed suit.

Once everyone had made it inside, I headed towards a staircase that led to some sort of hallway beyond.

"Be vigilant," I commanded my men as I climbed the steps.

"Rónán and Misneach are close by," Caolán informed me.

"Looks like you'll be seeing your Little Viper sooner than expected," I told Cillian.

No sooner than I said the words, movement up ahead caught my attention. I tipped my head to the left, giving the signal for everyone to span out. We created a ring around Emmerson, who was busy riffling through something up ahead.

I disappeared in the shadows as Teller and Fionn did the same. Cillian, however, was making a beeline straight for his Little Viper.

Cillian unsheathed a dagger as he slid up behind Emmerson and wrapped his hand around her chest. He placed the tip of his dagger to her throat and said, "It's poor practice to leave your back exposed, Em. You should know better."

"Hmm, that would be true," Emmerson said in a sickly sweet tone, "if I hadn't been the bait."

Just then, Zeke emerged from the darkness, Fionn in front of him, hands raised, and a dagger to his throat.

"I would lower your weapon, Cillian, if you intend to keep your balls that is," Zeke said.

Peering down, I could see that Emmerson had a blade pointed directly at Cillian's groin, the tip catching the small ray of light peeking into the chamber.

Emmerson smirked, before saying, "Just keep underestimating me, Cillian. I very much enjoy playing this game."

"Fuck Emmerson," Cillian swore, before lowering his weapon and taking a step back.

Emmerson whirled on him and pointed her finger directly at his chest as she snarled, "Stop fucking following me. I told you I would be the one to bring Harlowe home and you assholes will not fuck this up for me."

"Emmerson," I started, trying for diplomacy rather than losing my shit like I wanted to. "We both want the same thing. Let's work together to bring our girl home."

I flicked my gaze to Zeke and added, "You can lower your weapon now. We've all put ours away. We aren't going to do anything. We just want to talk."

Zeke shot a glance towards Emmerson, who nodded her head once in agreement. He lowered his blade and released Fionn before marching to her side.

"Problem is, I don't trust you, Silas," Emmerson said.

I probably deserved that.

"Be that as it may, I'm still going after Harlowe," I gritted out.

"You realize that this whole situation is your fault, right?" Emmerson challenged.

"Em," Cillian said, but he shut his mouth immediately when Emmerson glowered at him.

"You lied to us," Emmerson said, returning her gaze to mine. "If it weren't for you, Harlowe would never have been taken."

"I fucked up, all right!" I said, throwing my hands in the air. "Is that what you want to hear?"

"No Silas, I want to hear that you're done interfering. That you'll step aside and let me handle this."

"I can't do that, Emmerson," I said, frustration leaking into my voice.

"I won't stand back and let you walk right into the snake pit, Emmerson," Cillian added.

When Emmerson narrowed her eyes on him, he said, "Glare at me all you like. I'll be guarding your back regardless of whether you want me to."

Zeke chuckled, and we all turned our attention to him.

"What?" Cillian growled.

"It's just refreshing to see Em going after someone else for a change."

"You're supposed to be on my side, Zeke," she scowled.

"I am," Zeke defended. "But I'm going to enjoy the show while I'm at it."

Emmerson huffed and then returned her gaze to Cillian. She studied him for a moment, and he straightened under her scrutiny, folding his arms across his chest in a challenge.

Emmerson then turned her glare on me. "You going to be a problem?" she asked, raising her chin.

"Not if you don't try to stop me."

Emmerson laughed without mirth, and a small smirk played at the corner of my mouth. We were about to become one big happy family.

"I'm in charge," Emmerson declared. "I don't care that you're some besotted princeling. Harlowe is my Queen, and I won't allow anyone to put her life in danger. You follow my commands, or you can leave now."

I had no intention of leaving, but I also had no intention of following Emmerson's commands if they deviated from my own plans. If I saw an opening to get my Little Menace back, I'd be taking it.

"You're in charge?" Zeke asked, offended.

"Yes," Emmerson said, raising an eyebrow in challenge.

"I outrank you, Emmerson," Zeke argued.

"You've worked with my father for far too long. We can't afford to be predictable. It's why the Queen drugged you if you recall."

Zeke muttered something unintelligible but didn't argue further.

"Great," Teller said, clapping his hands together. "Now that things are settled, what is this place?"

Everyone peered around the space. There were no distinguishing marks or symbols that would identify the ruins.

"Given the state of decay, it's got to be hundreds of years old," Zeke muttered.

"I don't recall any landmarks in this area on the maps my father has stored in his office," Emmerson added.

"My guess is that it's a remnant from one of the great wars; the War of Witches or even one of the earlier ones," Cillian mused.

"It's creepy is what it is," Teller said, and Fionn nodded in agreement.

I couldn't disagree with them. There was something... off... about this place.

"It's irrelevant," I stated. "Let's get some rest before we plan our next move." I headed back in the direction we came from and found the vine I had descended to reach this place. Climbing back up would be a pain.

Fionn was the last one to emerge from the opening and Teller thrust his hand out to pull him out.

"The dragons are in the forest," I said, pointing to the dense greenery behind me. "I suggest we make camp for a few hours before we're back on our way."

There was mumbled agreement and then we all stalked towards the forest, fatigue weighing heavily on all of us.

Before we made it to the tree line, Saoirse — Cian's dragon — appeared and planted herself in front of Emmerson. Her large, black form eclipsed Emerson's, and I heard her sharp intake of breath as the dragon tilted its head close to hers.

"What's going on?" I asked Caolán.

"**Saoirse wants to help rescue the Princess. She is saying that Cian gave his life to protect her, and he would have wanted her to help get Harlowe back.**"

"What? Why didn't she tell us that from the beginning?"

"**She says no one asked her.**"

I rolled my eyes. Dragon logic.

"What is happening?" Emmerson spluttered.

"What *is* happening?" I asked Caolán.

"**She is offering Emmerson her bond.**"

Well, shit.

"**Saoirse wants to bond with you,**" I told Emmerson.

"What?" Emmerson's voice filled with panic, and I couldn't help but let out a chuckle.

"It's not funny," she seethed. Turning back to Saoirse, she said, "I'm flattered and all that, but I don't think this is the best idea."

The massive dragon growled low, and Cillian took a step forward.

"I don't think Saoirse is asking, Em," he advised.

"I don't want to be a Cathal," she snapped. "I don't particularly like flying and the last time I flew on a dragon, well before Rónán, he threw me done the side of a mountain." She glared at Misneach, who only snorted at her accusation.

"Think about Harlowe," Cillian encouraged. "With Saoirse by your side, you'll be in a far stronger position to help her."

Emmerson seemed to think over his words before she sighed and dropped her head. A moment later, she raised her chin and squared her shoulders.

"Okay, how do we do this thing?" she asked.

"Place your forehead against Saoirse's and she will do the rest," I instructed.

Emmerson leaned her head against the dragon's much larger one and waited. She gasped a moment later and every Cathal in the clearing was remembering the feeling of the bond forming. The sensation of lightning crackling all over your body before a sense of peace settled over you.

Emmerson took a step back and inhaled a deep breath.

"Well, fuck me," she breathed. "I have a dragon."

And then a massive smile split her face.

Chapter Six

I stood at the entryway, frozen in place, as my mind tried to process what I was seeing. How did I not see the colossal labyrinth that now stood before me when I arrived last night?

It was dark, and you were distraught, I told myself, trying to pacify my racing thoughts.

Despair threatened to cripple me as I peered at the imposing hedges standing between me and any hope I had of escape.

The vertical hedges, which were at least ten feet tall, enclosed the entire palace as far as the eye could see, standing as fortifications against anyone who might attempt to enter the grounds... or escape them.

Ahead of me was a small opening, and beyond it, I could see a path leading deep into the maze, where the light of the day was quickly consumed by darkness.

I could see that the path diverged abruptly, with two more passageways emerging from the shadows. I did not doubt that the deeper one traveled into the maze, the more complex the system of passageways became.

The intention was clear; there was no escaping the palace of Netheran.

Well, fuck it! I'd die before giving up on escaping this place.

"Do you like it?" Kieran purred from beside me.

I had almost forgotten he was there; I'd been too busy tormenting myself with my spiraling thoughts.

"It's certainly... unique," I said, trying to hide the despondency I was feeling. Kieran merely chuckled, telling me I had done a poor job of concealing my emotions.

"Would you like me to show you inside?" he asked, tilting his head towards the maze. I hesitated for a moment, not wanting to be alone with him, with no one around to help me.

Who was I kidding?

Everyone else seemed as wary around Kieran as I was. It was unlikely any of them would risk their lives to help me if Kieran did try to harm me. I couldn't blame them, though; everyone was just trying to survive in this kingdom ruled by an unhinged King.

I decided I was better off having Kieran reveal at least part of the way through the maze, so I nodded my head and took his extended arm when he offered it.

"How long has this been here?" I asked.

"Since before the War of Witches," Kieran replied. He turned left at the first junction where the path split. "This maze is over five hundred years old," he continued.

"And what purpose does it serve?"

"Isn't it obvious, Little Bride?" he answered, amusement prominent in his tone.

I repressed the need to scream that I was not his bride as we continued navigating the endless twists and turns designed to confuse and disorient those who wandered inside.

"Does it encircle the entire palace?" I asked, changing the subject.

"It does indeed," Kieran said knowingly.

We continued traipsing through the warren of hedges, all of which were uniform and unchanging, making it impossible to keep track of the endless turns we had taken. I resigned myself to the fact that I would need ample time to map my path out of here.

As we moved further into the maze, the light seemed to diminish, struggling to penetrate the greenery standing tall above us. The darkness created an ominous feeling as if every dark corner concealed a threat that tracked and monitored us as we passed by.

I swallowed and tried to rid myself of the lump forming in my throat. One problem at a time, I reminded myself. I had enough to contend with already, without inventing further obstacles.

"I would like to discuss plans for our upcoming nuptials," Kieran said, pulling me from my thoughts.

I snapped my eyes to his and narrowed them when I saw the challenge brimming there.

"I have already told you," I said through gritted teeth, "I am not marrying you."

"I think you'll find you have little say in the matter."

"Why is marrying me so important to you?" I asked, exasperated. "Whatever your plans are for me, surely you don't need to marry me to use me."

"Do you know of the marriage traditions in Netheran?" Kieran inquired.

I shook my head, almost embarrassed that I didn't.

"Netheran is the only kingdom that still readily utilizes witches," he said.

I already knew that he had witches here. He'd told me himself when he'd boasted of how he'd used them to trick the other kingdoms into attacking Valoren in the Skirmish of Power.

Rage flooded my veins anew at the reminder.

"Your point?" I asked, anger permeating my tone.

"The point, sweet Harlowe," he said as he pulled me to a stop to face him. "Is that witches oversee the marriage rites."

Unease prickled my skin as I waited for the noose to tighten around my throat.

"Marriage is for life in Netheran, and it is sealed with a blood oath."

I could feel the blood draining from my face as Kieran invaded my space, running a hand down the side of my throat as he buried his face in my hair.

"You see," — he continued, as his tongue darted out to lick the shell of my ear — "the blood oath binds the couple in undying loyalty and devotion. Once the ritual is performed, you'll be unable to lift a pretty little finger against me."

"Nor you, me," I spat.

Kieran reared back until his gaze met mine. The viciousness in his eyes almost made my knees buckle.

"That all depends on the wording of the vows, Bride," he said as a victorious smirk pulled up the corner of his mouth.

Leaning back in until his lips met my ear once more, he whispered, "So if I were you, I would behave myself. You will not like what happens if you continue to press me."

Kieran took a step back as he assessed me. I failed to hide the trembling currently coursing throughout my body. Satisfied with the fear he had inspired within me, he gave me a coy smile and extended his arm out, gesturing for me to continue down the path. My heart was beating rapidly as I tried to make sense of everything he'd just told me. Was that even possible?

Admittedly, I was no expert on the magic possessed by witches. This could all be some elaborate ploy to keep me in line.

Or it could be very, very real, a sinister voice inside me, taunted.

"Without my consent, the marriage would be illegal," I whispered, stealing a glance at him.

Kieran chuckled darkly.

"Man-made laws mean nothing to the blood oath, Harlowe. It will be binding all the same."

Shit.

"How exactly am I to help in realizing your vision for your kingdom?" I asked, trying a different angle.

"All in good time, Bride," Kieran said as he patted my hand affectionately. This man was giving me whiplash, but I surmised that was entirely by design.

I wondered if he knew about the power I housed, but I couldn't risk revealing that information to him if he didn't. I feared what he would do with me if he found out.

I had been unable to wield that power since it exploded from within me in the Forest of Nightmares. Yet Kieran wasn't the type to wait for me to figure it out.

"When," I began, but stopped as my voice came out sounding hoarse. Clearing my throat, I tried again. "When is the wedding to take place?"

"Eager to become my Queen, are you Bride?" Kieran chortled.

Fuck no!

"So, I would be your Queen then? Not your Consort?"

Kieran glanced at me, curiosity playing on his features.

"You are a born queen, Harlowe. Don't ever settle for anything less than your birthright."

What. The. Fuck.

Was Kieran... praising me? No, that couldn't be it. It was most likely his ego talking. A man like Kieran wouldn't settle for less than a queen.

"To answer your question, the ritual is strengthened when performed under the blood moon," Kieran said. "The next blood moon is in one month. That is when our marriage will take place."

We walked in silence for a time, and I couldn't contain my sigh of relief as the opening leading out of the maze appeared up ahead. I basked in the glow of the sun, having been denied it while exploring the labyrinth.

"I have some things to attend to this morning, Harlowe," Kieran said matter-of-factly. "You are free to explore the palace and its grounds."

I turned towards him, trying to find the trap in his words.

"When you say free..." I trailed off, but from the glint of amusement in Kieran's eyes, he understood my meaning.

"I have every confidence that my maze will contain you," he chuckled. "Try if you must. It's always fascinating to see what you'll do next. That mind of yours is its own warren, and I can't wait to unravel its secrets." He leaned in and placed a chaste kiss on my forehead before he headed inside the palace.

Warmth washed over me at the tender gesture.

Fuck.

Why was I reacting like this? Logically, I knew that I detested this man. He was brutal, cunning, and dangerous. Everything he did was to further his agenda, and he didn't spare a thought for the consequences.

Physically, however, I was unable to stop the way my body responded to him. Kieran was messing with my head. He was adept at psychological warfare, and he was pulling my strings like a master puppeteer. He made me feel both safe and threatened simultaneously.

I couldn't afford to lose sight of the danger he posed and the devastation he intended to unleash on the realm.

An unwelcome memory rose unbidden to my mind.

"Have you ever heard of twin flames, Princess?" Arabella's sweet voice filled my mind, and I physically recoiled from the idea.

She had been speaking of Silas, but what if... no.

I refused to believe that Kieran was my twin flame. Because if that were true, then there would be no salvation for the realm.

If Kieran was my twin flame, I would be the realm's ruination.

Chapter Seven

As I made my way through the palace towards my rooms, I noticed how every servant and soldier alike averted their gaze whenever I looked in their direction. It was unnerving and only highlighted how utterly alone I was here.

Needing the solace that my chambers provided, I darted inside and shut the door. I closed my eyes and inhaled a deep breath before slowly releasing it as my fingers traced the grooves of the wooden door at my back.

"Rough morning?" Everly asked, her voice cutting through my anxiety.

I looked around, finally noticing her. She was standing on a ladder, dusting the corner of the roof where a spiderweb hung.

"Why won't anyone make eye contact with me?" I asked, pushing away from the door.

"Don't take it personally, my Lady. The King can be... unpredictable... so we have all learned to keep our gazes to ourselves, lest we invite his displeasure," she explained.

Knowing Kieran as I did, I couldn't blame them.

"Over time, it extended to anyone whose station exceeded our own," she finished, shrugging.

"You haven't treated me like that," I pointed out. "And please, call me Harlowe," I reminded her.

"I don't fear you biting my head off if I glance your way," she grinned.

"Why not?" I asked, curious.

"I can sense your authenticity. Your kindness radiates from within. Your compassion and decency are effortless," she said.

"Huh." I had not been expecting that.

I tried to be a good person — flawed, but well-intentioned all the same. The way Everly spoke about my goodness with such authority had me standing taller, wanting to be worthy of her praise.

Everly tilted her head as she examined me. "I saw how you defended Lucinda," she said hesitantly.

My lips thinned into a tight line at being reminded of Kieran's casual cruelty.

"Forgive my intrusion, but you must tread carefully where she is concerned. She will do whatever it takes to undermine you and see you separated from the King. Be careful your compassion is not misplaced," she said gently.

I knew Everly was only trying to help. However, I doubted I could ever stand by as someone else was mistreated. It didn't matter to me if the person was worthy of my sympathy or not.

"Thank you, Everly, for your sage advice."

She nodded her head in acceptance of my thanks.

"I have a few tasks left to do before I can come back and help you get ready for tonight's festivities."

"Festivities?" I asked, confused.

"The King is hosting a celebration of sorts, to welcome you to his kingdom."

"Like a ball?" I groaned internally at the prospect.

Everly shifted her weight from foot to foot, obviously uncomfortable.

"Not exactly."

"What aren't you telling me, Everly?" I pried.

"Well, the King's events have a bit of a... reputation..." she said tentatively.

"Reputation?" I asked, my eyebrow raised.

"They are known for their," — she paused as if trying to find the right word — "libertinism."

A knot formed in my stomach as I envisioned the display that would be put on for my benefit. I was by no means prudish or chaste. However, the stories I had heard about the debauchery of Kieran's court gave me pause.

"And what exactly is expected of me tonight?" I figured it was better to be prepared than completely shocked upon entry.

"Expected?" Everly asked, confused.

"Will I have any formal obligations during the evening?"

"Oh, no, nothing like that Harlowe." I exhaled a sigh of relief before recalling that might have been the least of my worries.

Everly continued to potter around my chambers as she cleaned, and I tried to distract myself from the impending festivities by reading, but the pages failed to hold my attention. By the time Everly returned to assist me in getting ready for the evening, all I had achieved was to pace aimlessly as I stared at the maze from my window.

Everly selected the black ball gown I had rejected earlier in the day, and I no longer had it in me to care about what I wore or the impression it made. The delicate midnight slippers I wore matched the gown to perfection, and it was almost a shame that they were hidden beneath the hem of my dress.

I sat at the vanity as Everly's skilled hands deftly twisted and braided my hair into an elegant and sophisticated updo. I begrudgingly allowed her to apply makeup, choosing to see it as a different type of armor.

Once she was done, Everly retrieved a black onyx crown from the satchel she had brought with her. It had been crafted with meticulous attention to detail, with polished black onyx making up the base of the crown. Encrusted on the onyx base were intricate designs and patterns that arched up towards the pointed peaks. Small black diamonds were woven throughout the design, and the crown sparkled with a subtle yet captivating allure.

It was a crown fit for a queen.

"Where did that come from?" I asked, already knowing the answer.

"The King sent it for you to wear tonight. It is a match for his crown."

The crown curved around my head as Everly placed it in my hair and secured it in place with tiny, ornate pins nestled into the folds of my up-do.

It was surprisingly light atop my head.

"There," Everly said, delighted with her work.

"You look perfect."

I had to admit that Everly had created a true work of art. I hardly recognized myself. Every skillful brush of my hair and swipe of kohl had served to enhance my features, while the velvety black hues of the crown commanded attention.

There would be no hiding in the shadows tonight.

As I took a deep breath, I nodded my head at my reflection and prepared to join the festivities in the belly of the palace below.

"I will escort you, Harlowe," Everly said as she extended her elbow to me.

"Thank you," I said and gave her an appreciative smile.

We walked in silence for a time, as I mentally prepared to enter the hall. I had always hated these types of events. People watched your every move either hoping that you would fail somehow or waiting for the opportune time so they could ingratiate themselves with you.

It was disingenuous and insincere.

Of course, I usually had Emmerson with me to fend off parties from both camps, making the event far more tolerable.

I blocked out the pain I felt at the thought of my best friend. She was safe, away from here. That was all that mattered.

We reached the exterior doors that led into the hall, and I thanked Everly for escorting me. When I turned back towards the door, I took a steadying breath and readied myself to enter alone.

I straightened my spine and pushed the doors open as I stepped inside.

Chapter Eight

Soft, sensual music pulsed throughout the room, and the dim lighting created an atmosphere of secrecy and intrigue. Couples danced intimately all around, their bodies moving in sync with the seductive rhythm of the music.

Plush velvet settees, in rich hues of varying shades, sat around the room, enhancing the intimacy of the atmosphere. Conversation flowed, and the sound of laughter blended seamlessly with the sultry melodies in the background.

I scanned the room; a group of people sprawled across the settees clinked their glasses, toasting to something only they were privy to.

The occasional gasp filled the air, and when I looked closely, I could see that the writhing bodies on the dance floor were intertwined far more closely than I first thought. Desire alighted their eyes as hands slipped beneath the sensual fabrics and daring styles preferred by the partygoers.

The heady scent of pheromones and perspiration was thick within the confined space, and I felt the need to move before I suffocated.

A server passed by me, and I grabbed a drink from his tray as I headed into the mix. People mingled freely while wearing coy smiles that hinted at shared secrets and possibilities. All eyes turned to me as I made my way through the throng of people, and I studiously ignored them as I continued to scan the room.

I raised my glass to my lips and took a deep swallow as I surveyed the area, seeking the only person in the room who truly unsettled me. At the end of the hall, sitting on his throne atop the raised dais, was Kieran; his dark blue eyes locked on me, tracking my every movement like a predator waiting to strike. He was indeed wearing a crown, the exact match for my own. Lucinda stood beside him, her hand draped over his shoulder, trying, and failing, to gain his attention.

I drained the rest of my glass and grabbed another from a server standing nearby. All the while, Kieran watched me with an amused smirk on his beautiful face. After I had finished the second, I felt more relaxed, and a mild sense of euphoria settled over me. I swayed my hips to the music as I felt my anxiety evaporating.

I closed my eyes and allowed my hands to wander; my fingers grazing the soft flesh of my throat in a gentle caress. I lifted my hands above my head and traced delicate patterns through the air, biting my lip as I struggled to recall why I had been apprehensive about being here.

When I opened my eyes, I clashed with vivid, blue ones that reminded me of cerulean pools on a warm summer's day. Kieran placed his hands on my hips, pulling me close against him.

Kieran leaned down, his hot breath fanning my skin as he whispered in my ear, "Was that little dance for me?"

"No," I responded huskily. Realizing how I sounded, I tried to shake my head to clear it.

Kieran gave me a third glass he snatched from a woman passing by.

"Here, you seem to enjoy my wine," he chuckled darkly.

"What," I started, but Kieran silenced me by placing the glass to my lips and tipping its contents into my mouth.

I drank greedily, and before I realized we were moving, Kieran had taken my hand in his and was pulling me toward the dais.

Kieran retook his throne and pulled me into his lap. I had to wrap my arms around his neck to prevent myself from falling.

"What is in the wine?" I tried again.

Kieran's thumb drew circles on the side of my thigh as he looked out over his subjects; the king surveying his kingdom.

"Perhaps you should have asked that before you drank three glasses," he purred.

"I only drank two glasses; you forced-fed me the third," I defended.

Lucinda snorted beside us, and I heard her mutter, "Unbelievable."

"Leave us," Kieran ordered. Lucinda cast a glare in my direction before sauntering off into the crowd.

"The wine is enhanced with an elixir brewed by my witches," Kieran said.

"What does it do?"

It fleetingly occurred to me I should be more upset over the situation. However, I was unable to protest too much as my body hummed with energy.

"It stimulates the pleasure centers of your brain, stripping you of your self-doubt and reservations, allowing you to become... uninhibited," Kieran said roughly as he ran his nose up the column of my throat.

We were seated on the dais, the focal point of the room, and Kieran was running his hands all over me as I sat nestled in his lap. My brain was trying desperately to communicate something to me; something important. But I did not know what.

Kieran shifted me so I was straddling him, my back facing the crowd, and his lips only inches away from my own.

"Should I fuck you right here, on this throne, as my subjects watch? Would you like that?" he asked huskily.

Would I like that?

Kieran sensed my indecision and continued, "Do you want my stiff cock sheathed inside you and pulsing with need, my Little Bride?" He thrust upward, his hard erection pressing against my core as he emphasized his point.

"I-I don't know," I gasped.

Kieran chuckled and a tingle of apprehension spread from the base of my skull all the way down my spine.

What was I worried about? For the life of me, I just couldn't remember.

Kieran nibbled on my earlobe before leaving a trail of kisses down the side of my neck.

"More wine, my King?" a server said as he bowed low, the tray of glasses balanced with ease on his outstretched palm.

Kieran reached down and grabbed a glass from the tray before passing it to me.

"You're not having one?" I asked.

"No," he smirked. "I am enjoying myself far too much already," he whispered.

As I lifted the glass to my lips, I hesitated for a moment before tipping the contents inside my mouth. My taste buds danced with excitement as the different flavors swept across my tongue. The humming in my body intensified until it reached my ears, blocking out the rest of the partygoers.

I watched the crowd and spotted a handsome male trying to entice a young woman with his charming smile and his lingering touch. She laughed when he spoke and leaned into him. The man ran his fingers down her arm, clasping her fingers in his when he reached them. As he leaned in, he whispered something in her ear, and she blushed before nodding. They headed towards the door and departed together into the night.

I continued to watch the partygoers mingling and seducing one another before leaving in pairs or even groups of three and four as the night wore on. I had shifted my position, so I was no longer astride Kieran, but he remained at my back, stroking and touching me continuously.

My eyes grew heavy, and I struggled to hold my head up as I tilted backward, finding purchase on Kieran's shoulder. I thought I might fall asleep right then and there until a tingle of awareness moved across my skull. My eyes flew wide, and I sat up, peering around the room, suddenly alert. A man stood in the corner, his face shrouded in darkness, with his glowing amber eyes trained on me.

I didn't dare blink, fearful that if I did, he would disappear, and I would be unable to determine who he was.

He just stared at me, unmoving, while I fought against the burning sensation in my eyes. But I couldn't fight it. My eyes lowered in quick succession and by the time I cleared my vision, the man was no longer there. I searched the room wildly, but there was no trace of him anywhere.

Trepidation unfurled inside me, weighing me down as my mind began to clear. I glanced over my shoulder to see Kieran looking back at me. Confusion filled me as I looked down and realized I was sitting on Kieran's lap.

"What the fuck?" I began, but Kieran placed a hand against my temple and whispered, "Sleep, Harlowe."

Shadows obstructed my vision, and before I could resist or move away from Kieran, darkness engulfed me.

Chapter Nine

The throbbing inside my head woke me and I peeled a reluctant eye open, taking in the morning light streaming in through the window. I groaned and tried to sit up, but abandoned the idea when my vision swam.

I lay on the bed, unwilling to move, as I struggled to breathe through the nausea churning in my stomach. A large, rough hand gripped my upper thigh, and I jerked back, ignoring the way the room spun around me.

Kieran lay sprawled out on the bed next to me, naked, wearing only a wicked smile as he watched me. I glanced down and noticed that I wore a sheer nightgown that failed to conceal my own nakedness underneath.

I scrambled off the bed, swaying on my feet as I tugged the sheet up to cover my body.

"What the fuck did you do to me?" I screamed at Kieran in accusation. He arched a brow but said nothing.

Memories from last night flooded my mind. The enhanced wine, the debauchery, the man who had studied me with hate-filled eyes.

"What did we do Kieran?" I asked in a whisper.

He snorted. "When I take you, I want you very much aware of what's happening so I can savor your submission," he said icily.

"Then why am I dressed like this?" I hissed, motioning to my nightgown.

Kieran shrugged. "Just because I didn't fuck you doesn't mean I should abstain from looking at what's mine."

Hot fury scorched my veins as I rounded on him. "I don't know how many times I have to say this to you Kieran; I am not yours. I will never be yours. I don't care what you do to me, I will never submit to you," I spat venomously.

In one fluid motion, Kieran jumped up from the bed and was striding towards me. I stumbled backward and my knees hit a chair that had not been there yesterday.

As I glanced around me, I realized I didn't recognize the room.

To my horror, it occurred to me that we must be in Kieran's chambers.

Kieran leaned down, so he was caging me in with his arms. He ripped the sheet away from my body, exposing me to his hungry glare.

"Such supple flesh," he mocked as he tugged on my nipple through the sheer material.

He ran a single finger down my abdomen until he reached my apex, locking eyes with me.

"Despite what lies you tell yourself, Harlowe, you are mine," he said with an eerie calmness. "And I'm getting fucking tired of you continuously challenging me on the point."

"Well, get used to it because I will never stop fighting you," I seethed.

Kieran chuckled darkly. "I think I might believe you," he said, unperturbed.

"Tell you what," he said as he straightened. I had to crane my neck to look up at him from this angle.

"Let's play a little game." I shifted in my seat, refusing to shrink away from him under his scrutinizing gaze.

"When we first met, you asked me where my powers came from." He glanced at me, and I nodded my head in agreement.

"I will give you three chances to guess at their source, and if you guess correctly, I'll let you go. I will not require you to fulfill the marriage contract your father entered on your behalf. You will be free to leave Netheran and live your life however you desire."

My eyes widened in disbelief, and Kieran smirked savagely.

"But," he said, holding up a finger, "if you do not guess correctly by the third time, you will surrender to me. You will not fight me, you will marry me and you will serve as my obedient Queen in the ways expected of you."

I suppressed a shudder. I had a pretty good idea of what his expectations would be.

There had to be a catch. He wouldn't strike this bargain if the odds weren't in his favor.

But what choice did I have here? I was already at his mercy. I lost nothing by trying to win my freedom. And I wouldn't give up on trying to escape this place; either through the maze or figuring out a way to contact Misneach.

"Are there any other rules?" I asked carefully.

"Clever fox," he grinned.

"You are forbidden from seeking the assistance of any member of my staff," he clarified. "You must unearth the truth on your own."

I deflated slightly. Everly had been the first person I intended to interrogate. Maybe I couldn't flat out ask her about it, but surely I could tease information from her or others and piece it together myself.

That would count, right?

After a moment, I said, "Okay, we agree."

Kieran smiled widely. And it was anything but friendly.

"You will seal the deal with a kiss," he purred.

"A handshake," I countered.

Kieran growled low in his throat and stalked towards me. He gripped my throat in his hand as he yanked me up and smashed his lips against mine. His tongue invaded my mouth, and I had no choice but to hold on until he pulled away.

Kieran pushed me back into the chair and snarled, "I am going to enjoy breaking you, Little Bride. Your submission will be even more satisfying when I do."

Turning on his heels, he stalked out of the room, slamming the door on his way.

It took me a moment to compose myself and when I did, I retrieved the sheet Kieran had taken from me and wrapped it around myself as I headed towards the door that led to my adjoining chambers.

The small hallway between the rooms was dark, only illuminated by the light shining beneath each door. I wrenched the door open as I retreated to the relative safety of my room.

I quickly busied myself bathing and dressing for the day; not wanting Everly to see me in my current state.

Crossing to the dresser, I rifled through the outfits Kieran had provided me. They were all far more stylish than I would ever wear back home, preferring my practical tunic and pants for daily use. I settled on the least ostentatious dress I could find and pulled it over my head. I ran my brush through my hair as I hastily worked out the knots.

Now that I was ready, I needed to start searching for answers. I headed out of my rooms and stopped the first servant I saw and asked for directions to the library.

Chapter Ten

"I heard you the first fucking time," Emmerson snarled at Cillian, who hovered behind her as she attempted to mount her dragon.

Given Saoirse's larger size, I could understand the difficulties she was facing. Emmerson lacked any training in the ways of the Cathal, and she wasn't excited to start. To say that she was frustrated with her lack of progress would be putting it mildly.

Zeke chuckled as he leaned against a tree, watching Cillian attempt to give Emmerson her first official flying lesson.

A flash of silver flew in front of my vision and landed with a *thunk* in the tree right beside Zeke's head. He swallowed audibly and moved away from the spot he had been occupying.

"Point taken, Em," he said with his hands raised in a pacifying gesture.

I smiled to myself and continued observing their antics. The problem was that Cillian was so smitten with his Little Viper that he fussed about her and treated her like she was something delicate.

Emmerson was anything but delicate. And it pissed her off he would treat her in that way.

"**Saoirse is pleased with her choice of Cathal,**" Caolán chuckled.

"**She would be! She's a fiend herself. The bloodthirsty little vixen couldn't have bonded better,**" I snickered.

"**Perhaps you should intervene before your second-in-command loses his head,**" Caolán said pointedly.

At that moment, Emmerson reached behind her back and withdrew her twin short swords. She extended them before her, the sharp tips catching the rays of the sun as she took her stance.

"If you doubt my skills, Cillian, why don't we spar and see who draws first blood," Emmerson said in a sweet tone that belied her lethality.

"Whoa, Emmerson," I said, jumping between them. "Let's all take a breath and calm down, shall we?"

Emmerson glared at me for a moment before she took a step back and re-sheathed her blades. I nodded once, and she returned the gesture.

I then turned my attention to Cillian. "How about I take over for a while, Cill?"

"It's not me that's the problem. She's the one who won't listen to a damned thing I tell her!" he complained, utterly frustrated.

"Be that as it may, you're not getting through to her, so let me see if I can help."

I gave him a pointed look, and he glared back at me. "Cillian," I pressed.

"Fine," he snapped back. I had to stifle a laugh. This woman was turning him inside out.

I fixed my attention back on Emmerson and stepped towards her, closing the distance between us. "Do you mind asking Saoirse if she will allow me to accompany you on your flight lesson?"

Emmerson turned towards the massive, obsidian-colored dragon and tilted her head in that telltale way that indicated she was conversing with the beast.

"She agrees, as long as you acknowledge there are multiple ways to reach a goal and what works for you may not work for everyone else."

Emmerson gave Cillian a pointed look, and he scowled back at her.

Fucking hell, these two.

I gave a curt nod in agreement with Saoirse's terms.

"The most important lesson you can learn as a Cathal is trust. Trust is vital. If you trust Saoirse to keep you safe, she will. If you don't, you will overcompensate and put yourself at risk."

"It might be easier to trust her if Misneach hadn't thrown me down a freaking cliff," she mumbled.

From behind me, Misneach chortled, unperturbed by the venomous glare Emmerson shot him.

"Focus on Saoirse," I encouraged. "She chose you, remember? She wants you to be her Cathal. She will protect you with her life, should it be called for."

Emmerson took a measured breath and then released it.

"Now, get acquainted with the feel of your dragon."

Emmerson reached out and placed a trembling hand on Saoirse's muzzle. It was the only sign of just how terrified she was. Emmerson ran her hand along the dragon's neck and continued over her shoulders until she reached the middle of her back.

"Good," I said, reassuring her. "Do you feel the ridges between each scale?"

"Yes."

"You can use them to climb onto her back."

"You mean I don't have to make a death-defying leap onto her back straight from the ground," Emmerson said in mock astonishment.

"A dragon as big as Saoirse will always be a challenge to mount, so why not make it easier for yourself?"

Emmerson lifted her foot to the dragon's foreleg and tucked the tip of her boot into one of Saoirse's scales.

"Good, keep going."

Emmerson continued to climb, finding footholds between the interlocking scales as she made her way higher. As she reached Saoirse's shoulder, she paused, uncertain.

"Take your seat between her wings," I called up to her.

Saoirse remained remarkably still while Emmerson settled atop her, allowing her to find her center of gravity on the dragon's broad, sturdy spine.

Once Emmerson was in place, I took a few steps back and made a running leap onto Saoirse's back behind her.

"Show off," Emmerson muttered, and I grinned.

I took Emmerson's hand in mine and moved it to where I could feel the steady rhythm of Saoirse's heartbeat.

"You feel that?" I asked.

"Yes."

"Saoirse's heartbeat is steady, which means she's calm. Spend a moment connecting with your dragon. Slow your heart rate so it beats in time with hers."

Emmerson closed her eyes and took several deep breaths.

"Feel the way her body moves beneath you. Focus on every shift of her muscles and identify how your own body responds and compensates for the movement."

A low rumble reverberated from Saoirse, and Caolán chuffed.

"She approves of your methods, a chara," Caolán said with pride.

"You realize I've been training Cathal for the better part of a

century, right?"

"**I was merely relaying a compliment. No need to get cocky,**" he chided.

"Are you ready, Emmerson?"

"I think so," she said with a shaky exhale.

"I'm right behind you. It's no different from the other times you have been on a dragon's back."

"Except this time it's my dragon, and I'm leading from the front."

"You've got this. Now squeeze your knees together to let her know you're ready."

"Can't I just tell her, you know, in her mind?" Emmerson asked.

"You won't always have time to speak with your dragon and relay every instruction. Sometimes you will need to communicate with touch or a simple gesture. Your bond, it's intuitive, and one day the slightest movement will save your life."

Emmerson nodded her head and settled into position. With a gentle push, Saoirse unfurled her wings and launched skyward.

I could see the death grip Emmerson had on the ridge along Saoirse's back.

"Having a powerful grip is important, but don't let it come at the expense of your adaptability. If you focus all of your energy on your hold, you'll miss the subtle movements of Saoirse's form in flight. You'll need to be able to pick up on her cues so that you can shift with her. Try to relax and just... feel."

Emmerson's grip loosened as Saoirse leveled out.

It was always a rush to be soaring high in the sky; the world becoming a blur of colors and shapes as we sped by. The feeling of being weightless was exhilarating. It was the closest I ever came to feeling truly free.

Saoirse banked left, and I noticed Emmerson shifting her weight to accommodate the move.

"Good. That's really good, Emmerson. You're a natural."

We glided effortlessly on the currents of the wind, trying various maneuvers until Emmerson was instinctively moving with Saoirse; the hellcat, and her dragon becoming one.

"What's that over there?" Emmerson asked, pointing off into the distance.

Craning my neck to peer over her shoulder, I could make out what appeared to be a contingent of soldiers marching in the direction we had made camp. I couldn't make out any crest or other identifying feature from this height, but given we had crossed the border into Netheran, it wasn't a stretch to conclude they were Kieran's soldiers.

"I'm not sure. We'd better get back and warn the others. They're headed straight for our camp."

"You think Kieran knows we're here?"

"I don't know, but I'm not willing to bet my life on the assumption he doesn't."

Saoirse banked right, pivoting mid-flight, and headed back in the direction we came.

Chapter Eleven

Saoirse landed gently and crouched low to allow us to dismount. I jumped from her back and reached up to help Emmerson climb down. Saoirse truly was a massive beast. She rivaled Caolán and Misneach for size.

Looking around the group, I observed Teller as he led Fionn through an exercise with their blades, the young Cathal matching him blow for blow. Teller had been spending more time with Fionn since Cian's death. He was moving seamlessly into the role of his mentor and was filling the void Cian had left in Fionn's life.

"Good Fionn. Your footwork is improving," Teller praised.

Fionn moved in, curling his boot around Teller's ankle, and pulled. Teller hit the ground with a loud *thud* and Fionn wasted no time in pinning him in place with the tip of his sword; a broad grin lighting up his face.

Teller laughed boisterously, before saying, "Very good indeed!" He thrust his hand up to Fionn, who clasped Teller's hand in his and yanked him to his feet.

"Thank you, brother," he said as he thumped Fionn on the back.

I darted my gaze away from the pair, seeking Cillian, who was sharpening a blade as he glared murderously in Emmerson's direction. Emmerson had joined Zeke and was speaking in hushed tones to her friend.

"That look on your face is certainly going to endear you to her brother," I joked. Cillian turned to face me and scowled, before returning his gaze to the pair.

"We need to move camp," I said, all joking leaving my tone.

This drew Cillian's attention back to me as he asked, "Why is that?"

"Emmerson and I saw a contingent of soldiers heading our way while we were in the air."

"How far away?" Cillian asked, forgetting about his staring contest with Emmerson for the time.

"I'd say half a day, but they're headed right for us."

"Do you think Kieran knows we are here?" Cillian asked, his eyebrows furrowing.

"I can't be sure, but I think it's safest to assume he does."

Cillian nodded his head in agreement.

"So what's the plan?" he asked. "Do we move camp and avoid them, or do we remove the threat?"

"Seeing as everyone agreed I would lead this merry group until Harlowe was returned to us, shouldn't you direct your question to me, Cillian?" Emmerson asked from behind me.

My second snarled at her and I had to take stock of the fact that Cillian had very much lost control of his composure. A rare feat during the years I had known him.

He really did love her, I thought, chuckling.

"And what's so funny?" Emmerson demanded.

I turned to face the hellcat standing behind me. Her hands rested on her hips and her mouth formed a thin line, denoting her displeasure. Zeke stood a few steps behind her, his arms crossed over his chest as he watched the discussion unfold.

"Nothing, Emmerson. You're right. We did agree. What are your plans?"

Emmerson relaxed a little with my answer.

"I agree it's safest to assume they are Kieran's soldiers." She paused for a moment before continuing. "We're taking them out," she replied without hesitation. "They may have already seen us in the skies," she said in my direction, "so, at the very least, we should stop that information from reaching Kieran. Keeping him in the dark about our movements is the best defense we have against him thwarting our plans. And if we capture one, we get whatever information we can out of them regarding Harlowe and how to breach the palace. Failing that, we end any potential threat against Harlowe while we have the chance."

Fionn and Teller, who had wandered over to us, grunted in agreement. I had to admit that I was impressed with Emmerson's strategic mind. Harlowe had not been kidding when she said Emmerson was every bit her father's daughter.

"All right, Emmerson, where and when?" I asked.

She grinned before saying, "We'll ambush them further up the path they were following. We will fly a way out and you, Zeke, Cillian, and I will conceal ourselves within the tree line, while Teller and Fionn fly further ahead and circle behind them. When they are close enough, we will surround them from both sides. We leave as soon as our camp is packed."

I glanced towards Cillian, who was looking at Emmerson as though he had never seen her before in his life. The awe was clear in his expression, and I caught Zeke chuckling at him in my periphery. I couldn't fight the wide grin that spread across my face.

"Let's get to it," I ordered.

It was nearing dark when the first sounds of the approaching soldiers sounded nearby. The methodical rhythm of boots meeting the hardened ground spoke of a disciplined group if they could maintain such rigidity for an extended period.

From what I had observed earlier, there were about twenty to thirty soldiers headed our way.

I liked those odds.

My eyes darted towards Cillian, who was sheltered in the darkness offered by the imposing trees that made up the forest. We were all but invisible to those passing by. I inclined my head towards the impending delegation, and he nodded his head at my silent instruction before disappearing further into the shrubbery.

I glanced towards Emmerson, who was already holding her two short swords, eagerly anticipating the fight that was about to come. Zeke was crouched low, not far from her. I watched as he silently unsheathed his sword from his back, and then reached into his boot to retrieve his dagger.

My eyes returned to the empty pathway up ahead as I waited for Cillian's return. Moments later, he appeared next to me; a silent shadow moving undetected through the darkness that was shielding him.

"Two hundred feet and they will reach the top of the path," he murmured.

I nodded and then inclined my head towards Emmerson. "Let them know."

Cillian disappeared once more, re-emerging at Emmerson's side. She listened intently and then nodded in understanding. Cillian whispered something in her ear before placing a soft kiss on the side of her throat. Emmerson squeezed his hand in response before returning her attention to the path.

Not for the first time, the memory of what had been taken from me caused a small jolt of pain to erupt behind my ribcage.

But I would get her back. There was no scenario I was willing to accept where my Little Menace did not find her way back to me.

The glint of metal pulled me from my darkening thoughts as the first soldiers came into view. The last remnants of light reflected off their armor, making them easy to track.

Emmerson raised her arm and made a fist with her hand, telling us to hold our positions. When the rest of the soldiers had come into view, she opened her hand and signaled for us to move forward.

We blended into our surroundings as we moved towards the soldiers who were now standing about, removing their packs as they peered around, looking for the best spot to set up camp.

Emmerson could not have timed this better.

Zeke broke through the tree line first. He didn't make a sound as he slid up behind a group of three soldiers and ran his blade across the throat of the one closest to him. The soldier slumped in Zeke's hold, and he lowered him to the ground. The remaining two soldiers had not yet detected the lethal threat amongst them as they continued to banter back and forth.

Zeke didn't hesitate as he ran the next soldier through with his sword, and before his companion could raise the alarm, Zeke's dagger had found purchase in the man's throat. A soft gurgling noise sounded before the soldier fell forward, ending any resistance.

Out of the corner of my eye, I could see Emmerson leaning down to retrieve her sword from the midsection of one soldier, while another lay lifeless at her feet. His dead eyes reflected his surprise at the demise he had never seen coming.

Moving towards my own target, I gripped my sword tightly in both hands and raised it in the air. As I brought it down in one swift movement, my blade met with a slight resistance before it sliced through flesh and came to a stop at my side, the steel glistening crimson.

Before me, the soldier staggered before dropping to his knees as his body met the earth. His head slid off his shoulders as blood flowed freely from what remained of his neck, while small fountains erupted every so often as the last of his life essence escaped his severed artery.

I didn't even see his face before I ended his existence. That fact didn't bother me, however.

The clank of metal meeting metal sounded to my left, and I was brought back to myself as the remaining soldiers finally noticed our presence and attacked.

I ran forward into the thick of it as my blade struck down one man after another. Two soldiers circled me on both sides, and my lips curled up at the corner of my mouth in a wicked smirk.

"Eager to die?" I taunted.

"Do you know whose soldiers you're attacking?" the first man spat.

"Your life is forfeit," the other added.

"Do you intend to fight me, or is your intention to stand around and chat?" I curled my fingers towards myself, beckoning them forward.

Both men charged me at once, their swords held high and their battle cries disturbing the night. I dropped into a low crouch and impaled the first soldier with an upward thrust of my sword. Spinning on my heel, I darted out of reach of the second and tugged my blade free from the first.

The remaining soldier snarled and charged forward again. I parried, deftly dispensing his attack. He roared in frustration and allowed his anger to drive his movements. He charged at me again, seemingly lost to his bloodlust as he slashed his weapon towards me. I feigned right, and he followed, leaving his left side open and vulnerable. I stabbed my sword deep into his side, feeling the warmth of his blood flow down my hand.

It took the man a moment to recognize he was mortally wounded. As I yanked on my sword, realization assaulted him and he fell to the side, his lips parted in a gasp.

Something whizzed past my head, clipping my ear as it flew through the air. A sharp stinging sensation erupted at the site, and I could feel my own blood making its way down my neck.

I summoned fórsa to my fingertips and turned in time to see a hulking giant of a man as he lifted an axe to finish what he started.

Without hesitation, I pushed my palm flat against his face and released the power I had called to me. The man's head erupted, no match for the force I wielded, before he crumpled to the ground.

"Nice," Teller said, looking down at the remnants of the man beside me.

I glanced around, and realized all the soldiers were dead, save for the one clasped in Fionn's iron grip. Upon closer inspection of the man, I saw they were, in fact, Netheran soldiers.

"How many did you get, Em?" Cillian asked as he looked over Teller's shoulder, taking in the man at my feet.

"You first," Emmerson purred.

Cillian turned to face her. "Five," he declared proudly. Smug satisfaction was the only word to describe the look on Cillian's face.

Emmerson pumped her fist in the air and hooted in celebration.

"How many?" Cillian demanded.

"Eight," Emmerson beamed.

Fuck me. Even I'd only managed seven.

Cillian swore under his breath, his smug satisfaction quickly evaporating.

"Zeke?" I asked, cocking a brow.

"Six," Zeke said with a shrug, his tone bored.

Turning to Teller, I asked, "And you?"

"Three," Teller grumbled.

"How about you, Silas?" Emmerson simpered.

I scrubbed a hand over my face before answering. "Seven."

With another hoot, Emmerson jumped up and down in victory.

"We'll never hear the end of this," Cillian muttered.

"Aren't you going to ask me?" Fionn said, offended.

All eyes turned to him, and I gave him an expectant look. At that moment, realization dawned on him, and he attempted to backtrack on his previous demand.

"Well, you see," he started, rubbing a hand over the back of his neck. "I was performing another, equally important, task," he said, gesturing to the man he had bound in front of him.

There was a moment of silence, then laughter erupted. Fionn grumbled about how his role was the hardest because he had to keep his target alive, which only caused the group to laugh harder.

Fionn thrust the man in my direction, and I pointed the tip of my sword at the hollow of his throat menacingly.

"You will tell us everything we need to know, or you will suffer the consequences."

Chapter Twelve

I had spent most of the week scanning every single tome in the library, trying to find some clue that would lead me towards the origin of Kieran's powers.

So far, I'd come up empty-handed.

Kieran had even goaded me into wasting one of my guesses during dinner one night, and I hated myself for falling into his trap. When I suggested he was cursed, he laughed in my face and proceeded to mock me, claiming that being the most powerful person in all the realm was hardly what one would consider a curse.

So, I sat in a dimly lit chamber on the second floor of the ancient library, going over everything I'd read in the days prior. I was unwilling to give up on finding something, anything, that might help me.

I closed a leather-bound book and trundled over to the rows of shelves. As I replaced the book on the shelf, I felt a slight resistance when I tried to push it in further. Abruptly, the resistance dissipated, and a cloud of dust burst toward me, making me cough and squint my eyes. A noise echoed beyond the shelf as something hit the ground.

I walked to the next row and saw a large, weathered book covered in dust and cobwebs lying on the ground. I leaned down and flipped the book over, its spine creaking in protest.

"Okay, so you're barely holding it together. Noted."

No title or identifying features adorned the cover. Instead, runes covered the book, some of which I recognized, but most of which I couldn't decipher. I grabbed the book and returned to my table.

As gently as I could, I turned to the first page, trying to avoid damaging the book further. It was yellow and withered from age, the smell of decay clinging to the pages.

"The history of the Aurora Stone," I murmured to myself.

I skimmed a few more pages and discovered an illustration of the stone. It was about the size of my palm and had brilliant, iridescent colors dancing across its translucent surface.

"The Aurora Stone, known for its captivating display of colors, including hues of blue, green, yellow, and purple, can shift and change as viewers observe it from different angles. The spectacular visual effect of the stone is what often draws people to it. However, the true power of the stone lies in its ability to amplify the power of the individual who possesses the stone."

I scanned the rest of the page until a single word caught my attention; nightmares.

"While the stone's augmenting properties are alluring, it is the protective wards generated by the stone that led to its use in sealing the Forest of Nightmares. The stone's ability to deflect and contain negative energies made it instrumental in establishing the wards that trapped the monsters, who had been plaguing the realm for centuries, within the forest, now appropriately named the Forest of Nightmares."

I let out a breath. Well, that explains why the Minotaur Army hasn't been pursuing us since we fled the forest.

How could nobody have known about this?

Why had it never occurred to me to question why all those creatures remained dormant within the forest?

"Unfortunately, the stone was lost within the forest at the time the wards were set, and the witch responsible for putting them in place has not yet reemerged. It is this historian's belief that she was lost to the creatures that dwell within the forest."

Is the Lost Witch the one who set the wards to begin with?

I let the idea churn inside my head for a time, trying to remember if the Lost Witch had indicated when she first entered the forest. But then I remembered she had supposedly fled to the forest to escape retribution following the War of Witches, which had taken place after the forest had already been established.

The passage concluded that they did not undertake any further expeditions to retrieve the stone because they feared it was the only thing keeping the monsters at bay.

"Interesting, but not exactly helpful, my friend," I muttered to the book as I closed it. Another plume of dust escaped, spiraling straight into my nostrils. The musty stench of old parchment assaulted me, and I decided it was time to get some fresh air.

I exited the library and made my way towards the doors that led outside and into the maze. The lights overhead barely illuminated the hall in front of me and I cursed the dreariness as the toe of my slipper snagged on a crack in the foundation.

Everything in the palace was dark and gloomy and I wondered if this was by design, so that Kieran could always draw on nearby shadows. I wasn't sure if he needed physical shadows to draw on his power, but it made the most sense to me.

I darted forward into the maze and set about undertaking the other task I had given myself at the beginning of the week; mapping the maze.

While I had gotten lost many times, I had also successfully navigated a series of turns that led to a small glass greenhouse I used as a landmark to track my progress.

From the window of my chambers, I could see that the greenhouse sat halfway between the palace and the rest of the maze. I couldn't see the end of the maze, but I was hopeful one existed.

It was always unsettling how the light seemed to evaporate the further into the maze one traveled; the height of the hedges casting long shadows in the twisting passageways. As I walked deeper into the maze, I sensed that the unease I felt was more than the usual anxiety I experienced whenever I entered the labyrinth.

I picked up my pace, continuing along the path I had memorized. My heart rate increased with the adrenaline flooding my system.

"Keep your shit together, Harlowe," I growled to myself. "Don't let your mind trick you into seeing threats where there are none."

As much as I tried to will myself to listen, it didn't work. I felt my muscles tensing as if preparing to run and my every sense was on high alert.

I hurried left down a passageway. I became hyper-aware of my surroundings, my eyes darting in every direction, searching for danger. Fear tightened my chest, and I chastised myself once more for my foolishness. My thoughts were becoming scattered and if I didn't concentrate, I would end up allowing my unease to drive me in circles and I'd never find a way out of this place.

I paused, took a breath, and closed my eyes. Drawing my abdomen tight, I exhaled slowly, controlling my breath as it left my body. I wiggled my toes inside my slippers as I ground myself to the earth and the present. I took another deep breath and repeated the process until I cleared my head and got my bearings.

"Okay, not too bad. I still know where I am at least," I mumbled to myself. "Four more turns and I'll be at the greenhouse."

Headed in the greenhouse's direction, I stalled as a prickle of apprehension erupted at the base of my skull. The hairs on the back of my neck stood to attention, and I strained my ears, trying to detect any source of disturbance around me.

I couldn't hear a single sound. The world around me was eerily silent, as if it, too, sensed something was amiss. My intuition screamed at me to run, but I stood rooted in place, unable to move until I identified the source of my unease.

A sound caught my attention. It was barely above a whisper, but I detected it all the same. The sound of dirt shifting under a boot, as someone or something, moved infinitesimally as they shifted their weight.

That was all the confirmation I needed to listen to the voice inside me screaming at me to run.

Pivoting on my feet, I sprinted down the passageway without looking back.

Chapter Thirteen

My breathing was ragged as I pushed myself harder, sprinting down the narrow passageways. I made a sharp left turn and skidded to a stop as an imposing and formidable wall of greenery prevented my escape.

"Fuck."

Backtracking, I ran in the opposite direction, only to slam into another wall of immovable shrubbery. I was becoming disoriented, and the claustrophobic environment was only amplifying my sense of urgency and fear.

"Come on, come on, come on," I begged anyone or anything that might be listening.

I could hear my pursuer's footsteps reverberating off the ground as they no longer worked to conceal their presence.

I darted right and tried to retrace my steps, but I found myself completely turned around. Every time I thought I knew what lay ahead, something else entirely greeted me. My muscles protested the continuous exertion as I sped through the twists and turns that seemed to taunt me.

I ran my fingers along the wall of hedges and my hand slipped into an open space. I paused to study the greenery. A hidden alcove appeared inside the lush foliage, concealed from those passing by the emerald leaves of the hedges. Chancing a quick glance over my shoulder and seeing that I was still alone, I crawled into the space and held my breath.

One second. Two seconds. Three seconds. Four seconds. Five seconds.

The sound of boots hitting the ground grew closer, and I froze, not willing to move an inch lest I alert whoever was chasing me to my hiding place.

Large, black boots slowed and stopped directly in front of me. My pursuer was a male, judging by the size. I flicked my gaze higher and black leather pants filled my vision and what appeared to be a cloak that swung with the man's movements. My vantage point concealed his face from my view, and I couldn't risk moving closer to discover his identity.

He remained fixed in place, and it felt as though he was staring right at me.

Panic threatened to seize me, but I refused to make the first move. If he was so desperate to kill me, he could drag me out kicking and screaming.

The air crackled with tension around me, and a bead of sweat trickled down my spine.

This was it. I was going to die today. Right here, in a fucking hedge. I wanted to scoff at the absurdity but refrained from doing so.

The man shifted his feet, the toe of his boot pointing away from me.

What was he waiting for? I was right here.

Unless he doesn't know.

Hope is such a fragile thing. I clung to it all the same, knowing my life depended on it.

He took a small tentative step forward and I could tell he was leaning his weight on his front foot.

What was he doing? Wait, was he straining to hear me?

A small snuffling sound started up somewhere close by and the man ran toward the noise.

Fucking hell. He didn't know. He was standing right in front of me, and he didn't realize.

I let out a slow, shaky breath. Conscious not to make a sound, I let my lungs expand with air as I steadied my breathing.

The sound of my pursuer's footsteps had fallen away, but I remained hidden in place, not wanting to tempt the fates.

When I could no longer hear anything, I tentatively crawled back out of the hidden alcove. I was covered in scratches when I finally emerged from under the hedge.

As quietly as I could, I began walking down the passage and turned left.

There was no one there.

At the next juncture, I darted left again and paused before peering around the corner.

The space was empty.

I took the next right turn and almost cried in relief when I recognized the surrounding setting.

"Thank the fucking gods," I muttered to myself as I hastened my pace, muscle memory kicking in as I took one sharp turn after another.

I was getting close now.

I knew the way out. I just needed to...

I slammed into a wall of solid muscle and stumbled back from the impact. Before I could careen to the ground, I threw myself against the hedge wall for balance and straightened in time for my eyes to clash with glowing amber ones.

"You," I breathed.

"Me," the man answered in a deep, masculine voice.

I caught the glimmer of steel in his hand, and my eyes widened in shock. He really was trying to kill me.

"Who are you?" I asked, stalling.

I was completely defenseless. Kieran had relieved me of my weapons, and I still couldn't wield any of my power.

His face was hidden by the hood of his cloak, making it difficult to see him clearly. Only his amber eyes stood out. He smirked, the corner of his mouth lifting with the movement. A tiny scar was visible at the edge of his top lip, and I stored that scrap of information away should I live long enough to make it out of here.

"Are you stalling, Princess?" he asked, amusement coating his tone.

So, he knew who I was.

He took a step closer, the dagger he was holding now on full display.

"Hold up," I said, raising my hands. "There's a better way to handle whatever issue you have."

I was talking shit. This guy wouldn't back down. But the longer I stalled, the longer I had to assess my opponent.

He leaned heavier on his right foot, which meant that was his dominant side. The first attack would almost certainly come that way. I also took an inventory of the six other daggers he had sheathed about his person. If I got close enough, I might be able to withdraw one to use against him. He had no other weapons that I could see, which meant he preferred a stealth attack.

Maybe he was an assassin. But who sent him?

Done waiting, he lurched forward on the right, and I threw my forearm up to block the incoming attack. I gripped his wrist and allowed myself to be drawn into him as I reached down and extracted a dagger from his thigh holster.

I palmed the dagger in my hand before I drove it into his knee. The coppery tang of his blood permeated the air, and he loosened his grip, allowing me to dart out of his hold.

He chuckled darkly. "You're just full of surprises, aren't you, Princess?"

"Come closer and see for yourself," I taunted.

He didn't hesitate. He lunged for me, using the dagger in his outstretched arm to slice through the air toward me. The tip nicked my palm as I defended and parried, slashing my dagger across his forearm. He let out a grunt of frustration, and I quickly resumed my stance, preparing for the next attack.

This time, when he charged at me, I dropped low and swept out my leg, catching him off guard and sending him to the ground. Not wanting to waste my advantage, I leaped up and went to straddle his waist, but the skirt of my dress got in the way.

One moment I was pressing my advantage, and the next he had recovered, flipping our positions with him now astride me. He raised his hand, his dagger dripping with the remnants of my blood, as he plunged it toward me with calculated precision.

At that moment, I thanked the gods for my quick reflexes as I bucked my hips and rotated my body to the side, sending the dagger into my shoulder instead of my chest. At the same time, I lashed out with my dagger, thrusting it into his side and hoping like hell I had speared a kidney.

The man roared in pain above me, which triggered my own body's awareness of the injury I had sustained. Fiery agony radiated from my shoulder and I cried out as I gripped the dagger and pulled. Blood flowed freely from the site, and I placed my hand against the wound, trying to stem the flow.

I bucked my hips once more and dislodged the man from above me before I scooted away from him. No longer in any condition to defend myself, I scrambled to my feet.

The man hunched over, his glowing amber eyes glaring at me with unadulterated hatred. Quickly retrieving the dagger I removed from my shoulder, I spun on my feet and ran.

"I'll be seeing you again, Princess," he bellowed after me, and I prayed to the gods that my hit had been fatal.

Chapter Fourteen

Stumbling out of the maze, I forced my legs to carry me up the stone steps and into the palace. As I crossed the threshold, my legs buckled, and I fell to my knees on the unforgiving, cold, marble floor.

My knees flared in pain, and a stinging sensation erupted at my hip. Peering down, I saw crimson liquid staining my dress. I tentatively placed my hand on the spot my blood had soaked through, and a sharp, pulsing pain greeted me.

When did he stab me in the side? And how the fuck did I not realize this sooner?

"Well, well, well, what in the realm is going on here?" Lucinda drawled from above me.

My head swiveled in her direction as I craned my neck and peered up into her cold, blue eyes that were alight with smug satisfaction.

"One wrong turn too many," I croaked, unwilling to share anything that may give her an advantage over me. If Lucinda knew that someone from within Netheran wanted me dead, she was just as likely to join forces.

The sound of her laughter told me she was enjoying this far too much.

I tried to stand, but the injury to my hip meant I couldn't bear my weight. Slumping to the ground I said, "Summon Kieran."

Lucinda crouched down next to me; her mouth twisted in a cruel smirk. "And why would I do that?" she rasped.

"My Lady," a soldier stationed at the foot of the winding staircase that led to the living quarters, said nervously. "I think His Highness would want to know about the state of his betrothed."

"Did I ask for your fucking opinion?" Lucinda spat.

Shadows began to pool right behind Lucinda's crouched frame, sparing the soldier from answering. A moment later, Kieran appeared.

The look in his eyes was pure wrath.

Lucinda noticed the change in my expression and stood abruptly.

She turned toward Kieran and said, "My King. The Princess has been —"

Kieran cut her off when he gripped her throat in his hand and dragged her to him.

"If I find out you had anything to do with this," he said, tightening his grip, "You. Are. Dead."

He tossed a wheezing Lucinda away as though she weighed nothing, and then leaned down to scoop me up into his arms.

I moaned in pain as the movement jostled my injuries.

"Shh, Harlowe," he whispered. "I've got you."

His tender tone was in stark contrast to the ruthlessness he had just displayed towards Lucinda, and it left me reeling.

Kieran climbed the staircase and proceeded down the hallway that I knew led to my chambers. Once outside, he kicked the doors wide, and a soft gasp sounded from within.

Everly had been in the process of tucking in the corners of my bed linen when Kieran startled her.

Kieran placed me down in the middle of my bed and barked, "Heal her of all injuries or you will pay with your life."

"Yes, my King," Everly responded automatically.

"By the gods Harlowe," she gasped, "what happened?"

"Attacked in the maze," I replied between hisses of pain.

"I need to remove your clothing for a closer look. Is that okay?"

My eyes darted to Kieran. "Some privacy?"

He raised a single brow, and a small smirk played on his lips. "It's nothing I haven't seen before, Harlowe."

"Still," I said as I looked pointedly toward the door.

Kieran chuckled but retreated.

Everly began removing my gown to assess the damage. "What the hell happened out there?"

"I was wandering through the maze," — I winced as Everly pulled the fabric away from the blood that had dried around the wound — "and someone ambushed me."

"Who? Who would be so brazen as to attack the King's betrothed in his own kingdom?"

"I don't know. I didn't see their face."

Everly's brows furrowed. "I will need to retrieve my supplies. You'll be all right for a bit?"

I nodded, but she hesitated. "Everly, I promise I won't die on you. I'm far too stubborn for that. Now go." After giving me a quick look, she left.

I closed my eyes and swallowed against the nausea churning in my stomach. The man who attacked me was the same man I saw at Kieran's party. I was certain of it. His glowing amber eyes were distinctive and hard to forget.

But who the hell was he? And more importantly, why did he want me dead?

Unless Kieran's subjects were displeased with his choice of bride, I hadn't been in Netheran long enough to make any enemies. Even if they were, no one would oppose Kieran without a good reason.

Maybe the threat wasn't about Kieran, and the attacker wasn't from here.

Not everyone will sit by idly and allow you to choose your path.

The Lost Witch's warning danced to the forefront of my mind. Before I could pull on the thread, however, Everly returned.

She settled in beside me and started rifling through a basket full of vials.

"What is all that stuff?"

Everly ignored me as she continued hunting through her supplies.

"Ah-ha!" she grinned triumphantly.

Everly uncorked the bottle and pressed it to my lips, then ordered me to drink.

I parted my lips and let the liquid spill into my mouth. A bitter taste swept over my tongue, and I resisted the urge to gag. Everly gave me an apologetic smile.

Once I was done, she took my hands in hers, bowed her head, and started chanting.

"You're a witch," I gasped.

Everly's eyes flashed to mine, and a mischievous grin spread across her face.

"You're an observant one, Harlowe," she teased. "Now shush, I need to concentrate." She lowered her head again and continued chanting.

The skin around my injuries prickled, and I glanced down to see my flesh knitting back together.

"Holy shit," I whispered.

When she was done, Everly lowered my hands and stood, retrieving a bowl of water. She dipped a small cloth into the water and cleaned away the dried blood.

"How does that feel?" she asked gently.

"There's some slight discomfort, but nothing I'm not already used to." I'd experienced more painful injuries during training back home.

"That's to be expected. While I have repaired the damage, the mind has yet to catch up. It'll fade in an hour or two."

"That was incredible. I had no idea witches could do that sort of magic."

"After the War of Witches, a lot of our histories got destroyed," she said sadly. "Few of us remain to recount the tales."

"Can all witches do that?"

"I'm sure others can perform healing spells, but a witch's magic is unique to her."

"So, you can do similar things, but the process is different for every witch?" I clarified.

"Exactly," she grinned.

I nestled into the pillows, suddenly feeling exhausted.

"I'll get you a fresh nightgown and then you should rest."

I nodded my head as I closed my eyes. Everly returned a moment later and helped me into the silk nightie.

By the time she had exited the room, I was already asleep.

Chapter Fifteen

I was teetering on the edge of consciousness and dreaming when I felt the bed dip beside me. My body felt heavy and lethargic, making it difficult to grasp coherent thoughts.

"Silas?" I asked in my dazed state.

Cold blue eyes full of menace greeted me when I finally pried my eyes open. Kieran growled and bared his teeth at me.

My thoughts began to crystallize, and my memories came flooding back. I was no longer in the Kingdom of Valoren, or even the Kingdom of Pyrithia.

No.

Kieran had taken me captive and dragged me back to the gods' forsaken Kingdom of Netheran.

"This is your first and only warning, Harlowe," Kieran said in a tone that sent my heartbeat racing in fear. "You will not say his name inside my kingdom again. If you do, your punishment will be swift and unforgiving. Do I make myself clear?"

When I failed to respond, he barked, "Answer me!"

"Yes," I spat.

Kieran studied me intently for a moment and then smirked. "Good," he purred and nuzzled my neck.

"How are you feeling?"

I just gaped at him, still reeling from the rapid change in demeanor. Kieran truly was unhinged.

"I'm fine," I finally managed. "Everly is an exceptional healer."

"She is," he agreed. Kieran rolled away from me, taking the place at my side, and tucking one arm under his head as he settled against the pillows.

He returned his gaze to me and said, "Tell me who attacked you in the maze."

It wasn't a question. He was demanding an answer, and he had every expectation that I would comply.

"Honestly, I don't know." He narrowed his eyes suspiciously.

"What do you know?" he pressed.

"It was a man. I could tell by his size and the sound of his voice," I supplied. Although, that may not be entirely accurate, as I thought back to how the Lost Witch had changed her voice when in her trance.

"How can you be sure?" Kieran asked as if reading my thoughts.

"I can't. Not for certain. But my impression was that they were male."

"What else can you tell me?" Kieran asked.

I was hesitant to reveal that my attacker had been at the party inside the palace for reasons I could not explain. It's not like I had let him in or anything. And yet, I hesitated.

"He had glowing amber eyes," I finally said.

"What aren't you telling me?" he probed.

Well, fuck.

"I think I saw him at the party you hosted when I first arrived."

"And you didn't think it pertinent to tell me?" he challenged, glaring at me.

"He didn't do anything when I first saw him. How was I supposed to know he would end up coming after me?" I snapped.

Kieran studied me for a moment longer before releasing me from his gaze.

"So they are hunting you," Kieran mused. "I wonder, Little Bride, what do you have that they could be after?" He gave me a knowing look, and I shifted uncomfortably.

"I don't know what you mean."

"I think you do," he said, grinning. "It's the same thing I want from you."

"I'm not even sure what it is you want, Kieran. You haven't exactly been forthcoming," I huffed.

"I know you've come into your power Harlowe, I can feel it. It is the twin of my own, after all."

I reared away from him, sitting up as I put distance between us. Kieran just smirked.

"The question is," he continued, ignoring my reaction, "do they seek to use you themselves, or do they simply want to prevent me from having you?"

"What do you know Kieran?" I growled.

"I know the fates created a counter to my power," he said, looking at me meaningfully. "But I also know that if you choose to stand beside me, our power will combine and nothing in this realm will be able to stand against us," he said, greed glinting in his eyes.

"How do you know I'm the one you seek?" I asked quietly.

"Aside from the fact that I feel a pull towards you like my power is calling to your own?" he arched a brow, daring me to argue it. There seemed little point.

"I already informed you about the prophecy that foretold your birth soon after I gained my power," he continued. "I was told to await the birth of the Daughter of War and Peace. That she would be my equal in every way. And with her by my side, my vision for my kingdom would be realized."

"What if the Daughter of War and Peace is something less literal? Just because my father hails from the Kingdom of War and my mother, from the Kingdom of Peace does not mean I am the one you need. Prophecies are usually more ambiguous, are they not? Maybe it's a metaphor."

Kieran chuckled darkly. "I can tell that even you don't believe the words spilling from your mouth."

Changing tact, I asked, "What is your vision for your kingdom?"

"I seek to regain what was lost to me during the War of Witches," he said vaguely.

"And what was that?" I asked tentatively.

"All in good time," Kieran murmured.

"And if I choose to stand against you?"

"That, I would not advise, Bride. You may have the ability to enhance my power, but if you threaten my plans, I will remove you from existence."

A tendril of fear bubbled up inside me as I saw the promise brimming in his eyes. Until now, I had never considered the possibility that Kieran might kill me.

Hurt me, yes, but not kill me.

I had been foolish to think his need for me to help him with his plans was paramount. I had never stopped to think about what he might do if I outlived that purpose.

"How is it you can move through shadows?" I asked, changing subjects.

"You tell me, Harlowe. Care to chance another guess?"

I licked my lips nervously. Despite my best efforts, my perusal of the tomes in the library had yielded no results. I was no longer confident that I would find the answers I needed. With no other options available, I had to rely on guessing.

But if I guessed wrong...

Kieran's body was tense with anticipation; eager to be one guess closer to my submission.

I exhaled a shaky breath and said, "Do you possess an ancient artifact or some sort of relic that acts as the conduit between you and a shadow god?"

Kieran's face split into a wide grin, and my stomach dropped.

Sitting up, Kieran reached out and grabbed me, flipping me until my body was lying flush with his own, beneath him.

"One more chance to get away from me, Bride," he said huskily. "One more chance before your submission is mine."

The absolute hunger burning in his gaze made my body heat with desire. Kieran seemed to recognize this as he lowered his lips to my own and tugged my bottom lip into his mouth.

"Careful, Harlowe," he warned. "If you keep looking at me like that, I might not wait for your final guess."

Kieran lifted himself off me and strode towards the door.

"I look forward to hearing your third and final guess," he called out over his shoulder as he exited my chambers.

Now that the moment had passed, my body trembled violently. I had been lusting after Kieran. The man who had promised to destroy me if I stood in his way.

What the fuck was wrong with me?

I shook myself out of my spiraling thoughts, letting determination settle between my shoulders.

I had one guess left.

That one guess was my escape from this nightmare.

Chapter Sixteen

I had been sitting in the armchair beside my bed for hours by the time Everly entered my chambers. When her eyes met mine, she smiled, and guilt whirled in my stomach at the thought of what I was about to ask of her.

"I brought you breakfast, seeing as you slept through dinner last night," she said, setting the tray of food down on the small side table next to me.

"Thank you, Everly. That was very thoughtful of you."

"How are you feeling this morning? Any lingering discomfort should have subsided by now."

Murmuring my thanks, I took a sip to conceal my grimace.

"I feel good. You are an exceptional healer, Everly," I praised. She smiled again and then started straightening my bedspread.

"Everly," I said cautiously.

"Hmm?"

"I was wondering how much you know about the War of Witches."

A deep sadness filled her eyes as she faced me.

"What do you want to know, Harlowe?"

"Why did it start?"

Everly sighed. "Unfortunately, the stories are all true on that account. Some witches were tired of serving monarchs and believed they were better suited to be rulers themselves."

"Is it also true that they turned to dark magic to wage their war?" I asked.

"It is," she confirmed. "Although, many suspect they were already experimenting with dark magic long before they made their play for power. Some say it was the dark magic that drove them to take over the realm in the first place."

I paused, appearing to contemplate her words. I knew all of this already, but I had to gain Everly's trust for my plan to work.

Everly resumed straightening my bedspread as she continued. "No single group of witches was involved. The truth-sayers played a big role in turning the minds of the kings and queens, of course, but witches of all magical abilities joined them. That's why all witches were cast out. The monarchs could no longer trust any of us. We'd all be dead or in hiding if the King hadn't allowed us to reside in Netheran."

"You sound as though you admire him."

"We know who and what the King is," she stated. "But we don't need to hide who we are here. Many would cling to that freedom, regardless of the cost."

"And you do? Cling to it, I mean?"

"If there was another place for me to truly be myself, I wouldn't have to."

I hummed as I tapped my fingers against my teacup.

"What do you know of the King's powers?" I asked.

Everly stiffened and let the blanket fall from her grasp. "What do you mean?"

She was clearly uncomfortable with my line of questioning, which meant she knew something.

"The King's powers are different from any other I have seen in the realm," I said hesitantly.

Everly turned to face me, and her eyes narrowed on me. "They are," she said and pursed her lips.

"Do you know why?" I pressed.

"Tell me what game you are playing, Harlowe." I opened my mouth to respond, but she silenced me with a single raised finger. "The truth. You don't survive in Netheran as long as I have without being able to discern when someone is trying to pry information from you."

I swallowed the knot of guilt lodged in my throat as I willed myself not to look away. "The King and I," I began, "have come to an agreement. He has agreed to release me from the marriage contract he made with my father if I can guess the source of his power."

"And you thought you could befriend me and get me to disclose it to you?" she accused.

"No Everly. You became my friend that first day we met. We only struck our agreement the day after he hosted that party."

"And yet, you would put me in such a precarious position knowing what would happen to me if the King discovered I had aided you?" She asked, the hurt clear in her tone.

Shame burned my cheeks, and I bowed my head.

"I'm sorry," I whispered in a broken voice. "It was wrong of me to place you in such a position." I met her gaze so she could see the truth behind my words. My eyes filled with tears that spilled over my cheeks before I could stop them.

"Oh Harlowe," Everly breathed, her resolve softening.

"I'm sorry, I'm being silly." I waved her off and dabbed at my cheeks.

"What happens if you cannot guess correctly?" she asked softly.

"Do not worry about it. It was wrong of me to ask in the first place," I said, forcing a smile.

"What happens, Harlowe?"

My smile dropped, and I looked out the nearby window, noting how the maze looked peaceful, almost inviting in the early morning glow.

"Harlowe?" Everly repeated.

"I am to submit to him. Give up my resistance and marry him willingly," I sighed.

"Was there ever another choice?" she asked gently.

"Probably not," I admitted.

"Then why does it trouble you so?"

"There are things... he needs... from me," I said evasively.

Everly remained silent, encouraging me to go on. I hesitated, not wanting to reveal too much and further compromise her. But something in my subconscious told me to trust her. That if she knew the truth, she would protect me at all costs. So I relented and said, "He wants to use me... to conquer the realm."

Everly gasped, and I glanced back towards her. She stared at me, as though encountering me for the first time.

Everly took a tentative step towards me before she rushed forward, closing the distance between us. She grasped my hands in hers as she whispered, "You're the Daughter of War and Peace, aren't you?"

"You know about the prophecy?" I asked, my brows furrowing. She nodded her head.

With a defeated sigh, I confirmed her suspicions. "Yes, I am."

It was the first time I had said it out loud.

"That is why he wants to marry me. So the blood oath binds me to him. I could never stand against him, even if I refused to aid him."

Everly's eyes shone in fear before settling into determination. "We must get you out of Netheran, Harlowe."

"What?" I blurted. "But you said..."

"Forget what I said. You are the one foretold to deliver the realm from tyranny."

"I don't think I would go that far," I murmured.

"I would," Everly said with conviction. "I have seen firsthand what happens when the balance of power is displaced within the realm."

"Do you mean... where you there... during the War of Witches?"

"Yes," she replied. "And I do not wish to see it repeated."

"Wait, how did you learn of the prophecy?"

"Those in power become so used to having the powerless servicing their every need. They often forget we are there, blending in with our surroundings," she said with a knowing glint in her eyes.

I grinned and then sobered. "Do you know his power's source?"

Everly swallowed nervously before answering, "I do."

Chapter Seventeen

Sweat coated my palms as I sat at the long dining table in the main hall that evening. My stomach was so twisted in knots that I could barely keep anything down. The goblet I had been drinking from remained full, however; liquid courage stilled the trembling in my hands. I chanced a quick glance in Everly's direction as she stood amongst the servers along the wall.

"Harlowe," Kieran said, pulling me back to the present.

"Yes," I answered before taking another long sip of my wine.

"Is everything all right?" His eyebrows knitted together and if I didn't know any better, I would think he was concerned.

"Fine," I said, in what I hoped passed as a bored tone.

Kieran arched an eyebrow. "You're distracted," he challenged.

I averted my gaze and took another swig from my goblet.

Taking a steadying breath, I replaced my goblet and turned to face him. I forced a sweet smile to my lips and his eyes darkened. "Actually, there is something I would like to talk to you about."

"Oh," Kieran replied in a tone both amused and intrigued.

"Yes," I said more confidently. "I have my final guess ready."

Kieran's eyes flashed with something I couldn't quite catch; excitement, victory, or was it a moment of fear?

Kieran leaned back in his chair, resting one arm over the back lazily, a small smirk playing at the corner of his mouth. He was the picture of ease and confidence. Whatever emotion had gripped him a moment ago was now very much under his tight control.

"Go on," he purred.

Exhaling, I began, "Did you," — I paused, needing a moment to collect myself — "did you strike a deal with the Original Witch? Did she grant you her power?"

The tension in the hall tightly enveloped me, making it feel like all the air had been sucked out of the room. The hairs on the back of my neck were raised in warning and a bead of sweat made its way down my spine. I didn't dare breathe while I waited for Kieran to respond.

Kieran sat unmoving, his eyes locked on me as he clenched his jaw. He narrowed his eyes in suspicion as he continued to study me.

In a voice alarmingly calm, he said, "Who did you speak to, Harlowe?"

"I-I'm sorry?" I stammered.

"Who. Did. You. Speak. To?" he repeated.

He spoke every word in a slow, deliberate manner, punctuating them with a growl that sent apprehension spiraling inside me. My heart rate picked up as I stared back at him, unable to quell the fear rapidly taking over.

"WHO DID YOU FUCKING SPEAK TO?" he roared as he pushed away from the table, toppling his chair.

Fury pulsed around him in waves as he stared at me, his eyes ablaze with the promise of retribution.

"Nobody," I said in a rush. "I figured it out on my own by reading the older texts in the library," I lied.

A cruel grin split his face as his eyes narrowed further; a predator locking onto his prey, readying for the kill shot.

"Try again, sweet Harlowe. I had every single tome in that library checked and triple-checked. Do you think me a fool?"

He stalked towards me, and before I could stand from my chair, he had me caged in, his palms gripping the armrests in a punishing hold. The wood groaned, and I swore I heard it splinter.

"Then you failed," I scoffed in response.

His massive hand darted out and wrapped around my throat. My own hands instinctively gripped his wrist in response, trying desperately to free myself. I was all too aware of how this scenario played out. Only this time, Misneach was nowhere close by to save me.

Kieran yanked me to my feet like I weighed nothing and pulled my face so close to his, our noses were almost touching. He leaned into me, burying his face in the crook of my neck.

"Do you know what I smell when I inhale your delicate scent, Harlowe?"

I swallowed but did not answer. He was playing with me, and my participation was not mandatory.

"I smell lies. Sweet, sweet lies." He kissed the side of my throat just below where his hand still gripped me. The move was anything but tender, and it stood in stark contrast to the punishing hold he had on me.

"Lies and... fear," he finished. He raised his head again and locked his eyes with mine. "You broke the rules, Harlowe," he said huskily. "You were forbidden from seeking help from any of my staff. Now tell me who told you."

He was not asking; he was commanding.

My gaze darted over his shoulder to where Lucinda sat, a victorious smirk on her blood-red lips.

Kieran followed my gaze and when he saw who I was looking at, he let out a feral snarl. He raised his free hand and sent shadows shooting out from his palm. They wrapped around Lucinda's neck and, with a jerk of his wrist, Kieran pulled her across the table, sending the remnants of the meal flying as he went.

When she was level with him, he rumbled, "I told you what would happen if you fucking interfered, Lucinda."

She tried to open her mouth to speak, but shadows filled the space, gagging her. "You were never going to sit on my throne, you worthless whore," he spat.

"Kieran, she didn't," I started to say, but it was too late.

With a slight twist of his wrist, his shadows tightened around Lucinda's throat, snapping her neck. Kieran let her body fall to the floor without so much as a glance back as he retracted his shadows.

He directed his gaze solely towards me.

"If it wasn't Lucinda, then who?" If Kieran was bothered by the fact he'd just murdered a woman without cause, he gave no indication of it.

"Not very chatty tonight, are you, Harlowe?" he mused.

My tongue darted out, and I wet my lips as I searched for something, anything, to say to defuse the situation.

"You will tell me who you consorted with, or I will murder every single person in this room," he whispered so only I could hear.

I tried to focus on Kieran and block out everything and everyone around me as I stared him down.

I really fucking tried.

But my treacherous body betrayed me, and my eyes darted involuntarily to the side.

Right to where Everly stood.

Kieran caught the infinitesimal movement and tracked it right to the one person who had shown me kindness in an otherwise bleak existence inside the walls of this palace.

When Kieran's sapphire-blue eyes locked with mine again, a vicious grin adorned his face. Without breaking eye contact, he thrust out his hand and let his shadows free. I heard Everly gasp, and I closed my eyes to prevent the tears now filling them from falling.

"Please," I whispered hoarsely.

"Please what, Harlowe?" Kieran asked, cocking his head to the side like I was something fascinating he couldn't wait to pull apart and study.

"Please don't hurt her."

Everly landed with a *thud* at my feet. Her ragged breathing was the only sound filling the hall.

"And why would I do that?" he purred, anticipation slipping through his carefully constructed mask of indifference.

He held all the power. He always had.

"What do you want, Kieran?" I asked, swallowing roughly.

"What I've always wanted," he hummed.

Me.

"You will spare her? Let her leave Netheran unharmed?"

"Harlowe, no," she breathed.

"She has committed treason against her King. That's a death sentence."

"Please," I repeated. "Let her leave unharmed and unobstructed, and..." — I took a deep breath — "and I'll do as you command me."

"I already have you at my mercy, Harlowe."

"What else do you want to strip from me, Kieran?"

His gaze heated, and I realized exactly what he would trade for Everly's life.

"I want to strip every single thing from you. I want to break you down and then rebuild you exactly as I dreamed. Piece by tiny piece."

"Harlowe," Everly pleaded, but I ignored her. I would not let her suffer for the situation I had put her in.

Kieran released his hold on my throat as he stepped closer and wrapped his arm around my waist, drawing me against him. He lowered his lips to my ear and said, "But most of all, Little Bride, I want you in my bed. I want to be buried inside you, so I can sate this unbearable need I have for you. And I know you want that too. I feel your desire humming under your skin, even though you deny it."

"How?"

The whispered confession escaped me before I could prevent it from slipping free.

"Because Harlowe, you were made for me, and there is no escaping fate."

Oh gods, it really was him.

I'd fought so hard against him. The rational side of me screamed I was repulsed by this man., I hated him for his viciousness and his casual disregard for the value of each individual life. And yet, my body had heated with every wicked word he whispered just for me.

The smirk lifting the side of Kieran's mouth told me he knew it too.

Kieran was my twin flame.

Chapter Eighteen

I crouched down in front of Everly and pulled her to me, gripping her in a tight hug.

"Thank you for everything you have done for me," I whispered so only she would hear.

"Harlowe, please don't do this. I made my choice, and I chose to protect you. You have others who depend on you," she begged, tears running down her cheeks in a torrent.

"And I've made mine. No one life is more important than any other."

"Harlowe..."

"Stop," I said, cutting her off. "You need to listen to me. Make your way to Valoren and seek refuge there. Tell them I sent you and that I will inquire after your treatment upon my return home."

Everly just stared, wiping the tears from her eyes, only to have more fall in their place.

"Everly," I barked. "Tell me you understand."

"I understand," she said, her shoulders slumping. "I'm sorry," she added, her voice straining.

"I'm not." I gave her a reassuring smile and rose to my feet. Everly quickly followed.

"You will leave immediately," Kieran commanded. "And if I were you, I'd make haste. If the Princess reneges on our bargain, I'll come for you."

I spun to glare at Kieran, narrowing my eyes to slits as my fury threatened to consume me.

He raised an eyebrow as if I were entertaining.

I returned my attention to Everly and gave her hand a gentle squeeze. "Go," I said and watched as she exited the hall.

Not a single soldier had moved a muscle during the entire ordeal. No one so much as flicked their gaze towards us. They feared Kieran's wrath too, I had to remind myself.

A hand snaked around my waist, and Kieran tugged me against his hard chest. The hair on the back of my neck lifted as he exhaled a breath.

"You have a promise to fulfill, sweet Harlowe," Kieran said in a low, husky voice; his lips pressed against the shell of my ear.

Before I could open my mouth to retort, shadows engulfed me and that feeling of weightlessness swept over me. We landed with a small *thud* moments later. When the shadows receded, I realized we were inside the King's chambers.

Kieran's chambers.

I tried in vain to swallow the lump forming in my throat. Kieran walked me towards his bed as apprehension and... anticipation filled me.

Shame colored my cheeks as I registered the second emotion.

When we reached the edge of the bed, Kieran turned me in his arms so that I was facing him.

"Take your clothes off and lie down," he commanded.

I put my hands against his chest, pushing him back a step. A low growl escaped him as he reclaimed the step I had forced him to concede.

"Changed your mind already, Harlowe? I am sure Everly is still on the grounds."

"I haven't changed my mind," I spat. I took a deep breath as I tried to control my mounting frustration.

"I haven't changed my mind," I repeated. "I just need to have some semblance of control," I confessed.

Kieran smirked. "Are you nervous?" he asked, his amusement plain to hear.

"No, I'm..."

Shit. Was I nervous?

A rational person would be nervous climbing into bed with a monster like Kieran. But I would be lying to myself if I said I was nervous about what he might do. I didn't fear Kieran in this way, even though I should. No, I was nervous because I was worried about who I would be once I'd crossed this line.

But more importantly, I was nervous because I feared I would enjoy it.

Kieran removed his tunic and tossed it to the floor. Rippling muscles etched the planes of his stomach, descending into an Adonis belt at his waist. The cords of sinewy muscles in his arms came alive as he flexed, highlighting the power that was barely contained beneath the surface. The bulging veins that ran like rivers across his thick forearms had me inhaling sharply at the sight.

Kieran's eyes locked with mine and he grinned as he slowly untied the laces of his pants. I watched with rapt fascination as he hooked his thumbs in the waistline of his pants and removed them. As he straightened, Kieran's hard erection sprang free, and I had to stop myself from reaching out to touch it.

"You're entirely too dressed for the things I have planned for you tonight, Harlowe."

My eyes snapped back to Kieran's and a knowing glint sparkled in his blue depths. Kieran moved back towards an armchair and lowered himself as he began stroking his cock leisurely.

"Undress, now," he demanded.

Regaining control of myself, I took a deep breath. I was going to do this, wasn't I? The heat banking in Kieran's eyes set off an inferno inside me, which only burned hotter with every stroke of his cock.

I reached for the hem of my dress and dragged it up my frame. Once I'd pulled it over my head, I tossed it to the ground where it joined Kieran's discarded clothes.

Kieran's gaze turned ravenous. "Come here," he ordered.

Stepping between his legs, I placed my hands on his shoulders to steady myself. Kieran gripped my hips and pulled me closer. His snow-white hair fell away from his face as he tipped his head back and peered up at me.

My breathing became heavy as our eyes met in a silent battle, each waiting for the other to make the first move.

With his gaze still locked on mine, Kieran gripped a fistful of my panties and tore them away from my body. I was now naked and exposed before him.

"Climb on my cock," Kieran said roughly.

I climbed into Kieran's lap, placing my knees on either side of his powerful thighs. Kieran watched every move I made, his hands never leaving my hips as he dug his fingers into my flesh.

I would definitely have bruises come morning.

"Kiss me," he said, his tone almost desperate. I leaned down and let my lips hover over his, tentatively acclimating to the feel of his mouth on mine.

Kieran wasn't prepared to wait, however, as he crashed his lips against mine in a bruising kiss. He forced his tongue into my mouth as he tasted me, leaving no area unclaimed.

Kieran reached between us and fisted his thick cock as he lined himself up with my entrance.

"I have wanted this for an eternity," he panted. Without warning, Kieran thrust inside me, and I threw my head back as I cried out.

"That's it, Bride," Kieran growled. "Scream for me!"

He pumped his hips as he plunged into me, his size creating a feeling of overwhelming fullness as he stretched me.

His lips found my breasts. His warm mouth took in one, and then the other, as he ran his tongue over my nipples.

A sharp sting erupted at the site, and I hissed in pain as Kieran sank his teeth into my swollen flesh. Looking down, I saw Kieran smirking as his tongue darted out and lapped up the blood he had drawn from his assault.

"Fucking ride me, woman," he commanded. I rose onto my knees before sinking back down on his cock, all the way to the hilt, before rolling my hips.

Kieran groaned, and the sound was guttural and arousing.

I did it again and again until I was panting hard, desperately chasing a release that would block out the rest of the world as I dove headfirst into oblivion.

"Look at me," Kieran snarled. My eyes darted to his, and I was startled when I saw the anger shimmering in them.

"You will look at me when you come undone on my cock," he demanded. "As your pleasure consumes you, you will know it was my cock that drove you to that edge. There is no escaping me Harlowe, not now, not ever."

Kieran snaked one hand into my hair as he held my gaze, locking me in place. His other hand reached between our bodies and his thumb began rubbing circles around my clit. I gasped at the intense pleasure that rocked through me.

"That's right. The only pleasure you will ever feel from now on will be at my hands," he snarled. "Now move."

I rocked my hips back and forward, unable to break eye contact as Kieran held my head in place. My mouth dropped open, a moan escaping me as I teetered on the edge. Kieran rammed his cock into me over and over until a scream tore from my lungs and my orgasm blazed through me like wildfire.

I slumped against Kieran's chest as I caught my breath.

Kieran rose to his feet as he slid his hands down my thighs, gripping my ass as he strode towards his bed. He dropped me unceremoniously, but before I could protest, he flipped me onto my stomach and pulled my hips back, raising my ass in the air.

His hand tangled in my hair, and he pulled it with such force that a whimper broke free. With his hold on my hair, he dragged me towards him, before he leaned in and placed a trail of kisses up my throat until he met my ear.

"Now I will take what you owe me," he hissed.

My heartbeat spiked at the hostility in his tone. I didn't have time to contemplate his words, however, as he plunged forward and pushed inside my body. He set a grueling pace as he slammed into me again and again, chasing his own release.

I met him thrust for thrust, refusing to relinquish control to him at this moment.

When he came, Kieran roared his pleasure before collapsing atop me, pinning me to the mattress beneath him.

We stayed like that, both catching our breath as our heart rates slowed.

Kieran rolled off me, pulling me with him as he curled his arm around me.

"I am going to enjoy stripping you down to your basic instincts and then rebuilding you into what you were always meant to be, Harlowe," he said through the thickness of sleep.

An involuntary shudder rolled through me at his words. His intentions were perfectly clear.

Kieran wanted to break me until there was nothing left of me to stand in his way.

Gods. I needed to escape him.

Chapter Nineteen

I grabbed the pack I had hastily thrown together and moved towards the window. The early morning sun taunted me as it shone brightly through the dusty glass, as if trying to illuminate my intentions to anyone passing by.

The frame showed signs of aging, with the paint peeling in places and tiny cracks peeking out through the timber. Centuries had passed since the Kingdom of Netheran had a queen. It was, therefore, unsurprising that the Queen's chambers had suffered with the passage of time.

The smooth, weathered texture of the wood felt stiff under my fingertips and I prayed the windowpane would not refuse to budge. Tugging on the latch, I threw all my strength into forcing the window open. The wooden frame groaned but did not relent.

"Come on," I begged. "Work with me."

I tugged on the wooden latch once more, and again the window protested with a loud groan.

I peered over my shoulder and waited with bated breath for any sign that someone had overheard my activities.

One.

Two.

Three.

No movement sounded outside the chamber. I released a controlled breath and returned my focus to the window.

"You will not deny me," I whispered to the window before me, only slightly alarmed at the intensity with which I communed with the inanimate object.

Trying again, I tugged at the latch and sagged in relief when I felt the resistance lessening.

"Thank you," I said breathlessly.

I pushed my arms upward, inching the window higher as I sent all my power into the movement to overcome the weight of the wooden frame. The friction between the frame and sash created a scraping sound that resonated throughout the empty chamber. Wincing, I paused just long enough to make sure that I had not drawn the attention of anyone lurking nearby.

Fresh air assaulted my senses, and I closed my eyes, inhaling deeply. The light breeze whipped the loose strands of my hair around my face and the sound of nature filled my ears. Birds chirped somewhere close by, and the scent of pine and damp earth engulfed me.

I opened my eyes, and my gaze darted around as I surveyed my surroundings. All I could see in any direction was the darkened confines of the maze.

I inhaled a steadying breath to stop the trembling in my hands and flung my pack into the maze before I could second-guess myself. I remained at the windowsill only long enough to capture the layout of the maze one last time in the hope it would be my salvation.

As I crossed the floor of my chambers, the soft, golden rug obscured the sound of my footfalls. When I reached the door, I gripped the knob tightly in my hand. Sweat coated my palms, and I commanded my body to not give me away. Turning the handle, I strode out into the hallway, relieved to find no one loitering nearby.

As I rushed down the deserted hallway, I couldn't help but long for my combat boots and tunic. The delicate slippers that adorned my feet were unsuitable for the task that lay ahead, and the dresses Kieran gifted me had already shown what a hindrance they could be should I need to defend myself.

As I reached the staircase to the palace's lower foyer, the sounds of people bustling about welcomed me. Soldiers stood on guard at the entryway, and I caught a glimpse of the kitchen staff as a door swung open and a flustered-looking maid hurried out.

My hand reached for the banister as I descended the staircase. My eyes remained focused, looking straight ahead as I made my way toward the front entrance. The sound of my beating heart filled my ears, and I was certain it would be audible to those around me. The soldiers showed no sign anything was amiss, however, as I passed by them. They kept their eyes downcast, as usual.

As I crossed the threshold of the maze, I immediately sensed something was different. A vibrant energy filled the air, as though the maze itself were alive. I stared down the rows of hedges that parted in the center, creating a narrow passageway, but there was nothing there. Putting everything out of my mind, I forced myself to take measured footsteps, making sure I didn't draw attention to myself by moving in haste.

Creeping through the maze, I navigated the twists and turns I just about knew by heart, making my way to the glass greenhouse, only stopping long enough to collect my pack and secure it to my shoulders.

I would not let myself be led astray. Today, I would make it to the end.

I repeated the mantra as I moved through the unknown part of the maze. For reasons I could not identify, I was confident I would find my way out today. It was as though some guiding force was leading me through every turn, protecting me as I traversed the labyrinth designed to keep me contained.

Either that or I was going mad and had become delusional.

That thought planted itself firmly in my mind when I came to the first dead end since entering the maze. Tall, thick vegetation blocked my path as if standing sentinel to the outside world. I cursed in frustration and retreated, only to be met with the same impediment time and time again.

"You need to get control of yourself, Harlowe," I chastised. "Panicking will not help you."

Closing my eyes, I let my feet connect with the earth beneath me, grounding myself in the here and now, and blocking out all outside influences. Once my breathing had returned to normal and I felt my frustration ebbing, I opened my eyes and surveyed my surroundings.

I could sense a faint hum coming from somewhere inside the maze.

I didn't know what it was, but I felt compelled to follow it. I let my feet lead me as I made several left turns before pitching right. With every step I took, the hum grew louder, and my skin prickled with awareness. I couldn't help continuously glancing around, monitoring my surroundings as the image of brilliant, golden eyes planted themselves in my mind.

As I rounded the corner, a faint glow caught my attention, emanating from the passageway up ahead.

I quickened my pace as I moved towards the source of the light, being drawn in like a moth to a flame. The humming sound became deafening, and I wondered why I had never detected it every other time I had entered the maze.

The surrounding air crackled with an eerie energy and my feet came to an abrupt stop as I inhaled sharply, taking in the sight before me.

A translucent barrier shimmered and glowed with ethereal luminescence; pulsing and humming with energy. It stood the same height as the hedges flanking it, blending seamlessly with the contours of the maze. Each radiant tendril danced across the surface of the barrier, with flickers of color in various shades of red and blue vibrating in sync with the hum coming from within the structure.

The towering, green trees of the surrounding forest, visible through the translucent barrier, drew my attention, and I remained transfixed as I studied the world beyond the labyrinth.

I stood at the very end of the maze. Beyond this barrier was... freedom.

My hand thrust forward of its own volition and connected with the barrier. A burning sensation assaulted my palm, and I pulled my hand back.

"Fuck," I hissed, peering down at my hand. Red, angry welts formed in the places where my flesh had connected with the barrier.

I slipped my pack off my shoulder, rummaging through the few items I had thrown in, and ripped a length of fabric from one of the dresses. Removing my water skin, I drenched the length of fabric before wrapping it around my palm and securing it tightly.

"That'll suffice," I muttered.

After I repacked my belongings, I returned my focus to the barrier, noting how the glow shifted in hues, transitioning from the calming shades of oceanic blue to the fiery shades of red that matched my burned flesh. The barrier was a tapestry of energy standing guard against those who would seek to leave this place.

"There must be a way through," I mused. "How else had Everly been able to leave?"

Unless she never left.

The thought rose, unbidden, to my mind and I had to shake myself or else my thoughts would spiral into dangerous territory.

"Fiery red," I muttered as I looked down at my palm. "Fiery red."

Inside the Forest of Nightmares, when I had called on the power within me, a raging inferno had engulfed me, burning everything that posed a threat to me while protecting Emmerson and me from harm.

Would it do the same now? Could I call on the flames to protect me from harm as I pushed through the barrier? But how did I pull it to the surface?

I hadn't been able to summon that power — dragon fire the Lost Witch had revealed — since that initial fight with the Harpy.

Still, it was worth a try.

Closing my eyes, I took a deep breath and blocked out everything else around me. I concentrated on my body, mentally exploring every inch of myself from my head to my feet.

The fluttering of my eyes behind my closed eyelids.

The steady beating of my heart as it pumped blood throughout my body.

The rise and fall of my chest as my lungs worked to inflate with oxygen.

The tingling in my fingertips as my body responded to the energy in the surrounding air.

The feel of my toes as they dug into the slippers encasing my feet, seeking the grounding influence of the earth beneath me.

I waited.

And nothing happened.

Frustration threatened to engulf me, but I blocked it out and tried again. I felt a slight warming in my fingertips and when I looked down, a faint red glow peeked back at me.

"Holy shit," I breathed. "It's working."

I threw all my mental energy into expanding that faint red hue, but again, nothing happened.

I wanted to scream but settled for a controlled exhale.

"You can do this."

Starting from my head, I worked my way down my body again, noting every movement, every rhythm, every sensation. I cracked one eye open and then the next. I gasped when I peered down and saw my entire arm ablaze as flames licked their way higher.

In nothing more than a blink, my entire body was covered in flames. They didn't burn me, however, just like when they first appeared.

"Here goes nothing," I mumbled. I took a measured step toward the barrier and raised my uninjured hand, tentatively pressing my palm against it.

Nothing happened.

There was no burning sensation, but the barrier did not yield either.

I pressed my hand further against the barrier, and this time, it moved with me. As much as I pushed, however, I could not break through.

"Fuck this," I seethed.

Throwing my entire body forward, I felt the barrier curl around me, trying to keep me contained within the maze as I desperately fought to escape it. One moment I was heaving with all my strength against the unyielding force, and the next, I was stumbling towards the ground.

On the other side of the maze.

"Fucking hell! I did it!" I yelled. A slow grin crept across my face as I looked back at the barrier. It had solidified once again and appeared as impenetrable as ever.

A tingling sensation crept along my skull, and I took a ragged breath.

"Misneach!"

Chapter Twenty

All around me, the group was discussing ways to penetrate the formidable fortress Kieran had built around his home. The soldier we'd captured had revealed that the palace was situated near a cliff and surrounded by dense forestry.

The most intriguing aspect, however, was the giant maze surrounding the entire palace, making it almost impregnable. If I wasn't relying on our ability to traverse the surrounding land undetected, I would admit that I was impressed. As it was, we were no closer to formulating a plan to extract Harlowe than we were yesterday, or even a week ago.

And it was fucking frustrating.

All I wanted to do was mount Caolán and fly directly over. We would lose the element of surprise, but I was beyond caring at this point. I needed my Little Menace back like I needed my next breath.

"You're not listening," Emmerson said, frustration seeping into every syllable.

"No, I heard you Em, it's just not as easy as you're insinuating," Cillian retorted.

"And... they're back at it," Zeke mumbled. When Emmerson and Cillian glared at him, he raised his hands in a placating gesture.

"Enough," I barked. "We've been going over this for days with no progress," I said, running a hand through my hair and gripping it tightly. The pain grounded me in the moment, preventing my wayward thoughts from carrying me away.

The truth was, I was barely functioning without Harlowe.

All my life I had been the one people could rely on to take control of a situation. I led the most fearsome collective of warriors in all the realm, and my men trusted me to make decisions that would preserve their lives and deliver victory.

And then in walks this gorgeous, fearsome, red-headed beauty with the heart of a dragon who brings me to my knees.

I'd met no one as enchanting as Harlowe in all my years; wise beyond her years, more courageous than any battled-hardened general, and a soul of pure goodness. And it was her goodness that floored me. Despite the privileges and comforts she had been born into, she never considered herself above anyone else. She regarded everyone as equals, regardless of their position in the hierarchy.

After all these years, she was exactly what this realm needed.

I returned my attention to the discussion in front of me. "What's the best plan we've devised so far?"

Emmerson narrowed her eyes on me as she rose to her feet and stalked towards me. "You'll recall this is my command, Silas," she hissed as she crossed her arms over her chest. "I meant it when I said I wouldn't let anyone risk my Queen. Get in line, or fuck off."

"I'm not trying to take over, Emmerson," I gritted out. "I just wanted to refocus the discussion."

Emmerson clenched her jaw as she studied me. Running a hand down my face, I growled, exhaustion chipping away at my patience.

A loud rustling noise sounded in the clearing across from us and our heads snapped in that direction. Misneach hastily rose from the ground, shaking out his wings before spreading them wide. He crouched low and then pushed off against the ground with his hind legs as he launched himself into the sky.

"Where the fuck is he going?" I asked no one in particular.

I watched Misneach's retreating form as he flew away at a dizzying speed, quickly disappearing from view.

"Something startled him," Emmerson whispered. "You don't think... you don't think something happened to Harlowe, do you?" she asked, fear flashing in her eyes.

"Misneach hasn't felt Harlowe ever since Kieran took her. If something happened," — I forced myself to swallow the lump in my throat — "he wouldn't know."

I refused to believe that any harm had come to Harlowe.

"Caolán, what's going on?"

"I don't know. He isn't responding to me. I suggest we follow."

"Fionn, Teller, remain at camp. Everyone else, follow Misneach," I commanded.

Nobody protested as we all mounted our dragons and launched heavenward.

"**Can you find him?**" I asked Caolán, scanning the skyline. I couldn't see Misneach anywhere.

"**I am not limited to sight,**" Caolán responded.

"**A simple yes would have sufficed,**" I grumbled.

The heavy beating of wings filled the air around me as we sped across the clouds, the ground merely an intricate design of interconnected elements from this height.

"**Misneach is descending,**" Caolán reported, after what felt like hours of traversing the skies.

"**Follow him.**"

We dipped below the cloud cover as Caolán dove towards the ground. The feeling of weightlessness was just as exhilarating today as it was the first time I flew. I felt at home in the sky.

Misneach landed a few hundred feet below us, with enough force to shake the surrounding trees. He threw his head towards the heavens and let out a sound etched in so much pain, it evoked a response so visceral, that I had to clamp my hand over my heart to make sure my chest had not split wide open.

"No. Don't let it be," I pleaded.

Before Caolán even landed, I jumped from my seat and sprinted towards Misneach. My footsteps faltered as I took in the crumpled body lying on the ground between Misneach's forelegs.

Harlowe.

Misneach's wings furled around her prone form, and he lowered his head towards her.

"HARLOWE!"

I pumped my legs as fast as they would carry me as I ran towards my girl and the dragon surrounding her protectively.

Please let her be alive. Please! I begged any god who would heed my prayer.

As I reached Misneach, I drew myself to an abrupt stop before I collided with the giant dragon.

"Tell me she's alive," I whispered.

Misneach unfurled his wings to reveal Harlowe — very much alive — clinging to his foreleg and sobbing uncontrollably. The dragon's snout was buried in her hair as they desperately sought the comfort only the other could provide.

"Little Menace," I breathed.

Harlowe's head snapped up and her swollen, red eyes locked with mine, both of us frozen as we just gaped at each other. Before I registered my movements, I stepped into her space and pulled her into my arms. She wrapped her arms around me as she trembled violently. I tightened my grip around her and smoothed her hair to reassure myself that she was here; she was really here.

"Shh, Harlowe, I've got you," I soothed. She only cried harder in response.

I could hear the others landing behind us, but I couldn't draw my eyes away from her disheveled, copper hair that had all manner of debris caught in it. She looked as though she had been through hell. I swallowed thickly at the thought of what she might have endured.

Her dirty, tear-streaked face tipped up towards me and she looked so pained, so vulnerable in that moment.

"Silas," she croaked.

I cupped her cheeks between my palms and lowered my eyes, so I was level with hers. "I'm here Harlowe. I won't let anyone take you away from me again."

Her eyes searched mine, and her resolve strengthened.

And gods, I meant it. There was nothing, absolutely nothing, that would come between me and this woman ever again.

Before Harlowe could respond, she was ripped from my arms and encircled in Emmerson's.

"Harlowe!" Emmerson said as she let out a shaky breath. "I was so fucking worried."

The usually stoic warrior tilted her head towards the sky, taking a moment to collect herself before returning her focus to Harlowe.

"I told you I would come for you. You couldn't wait for me?" she chided.

Harlowe let out a strangled sound; part laughter and part sob. Zeke joined the duo, wrapping his arms around both women, all three of them bowing their heads and taking solace in the fact that they were all here and all together.

"Gods Harlowe, it is good to see you," Zeke said, choking on the last word.

"You too, Zeke," Harlowe replied, and then asked, "What are you even doing here?"

"You know I can't resist a good fight," he grinned, and Harlowe laughed. A genuine, shoulder-shaking laugh.

I immediately wanted to stab Zeke for being the one to elicit it from her instead of me. However, I suspected that might upset Harlowe, all things considered. The last thing I wanted to do was cause her any more pain.

Cillian stood at my side, silently examining the friends as they held each other.

"She looks worse for wear," he whispered so only I could hear.

I clenched my jaw, fury washing over me at the thought of her being harmed.

"She needs to be examined for any injuries," he said. I nodded my head in agreement.

Cillian cleared his throat before continuing. "She might have been…" he trailed off when I turned my gaze on him, narrowing my eyes.

"I pray to the gods that nothing of the sort happened, Silas, but we'll still need to ask her to find out the extent of any injuries she may have."

I tore my gaze from Cillian and refocused on Harlowe, who was nestled protectively among her friends, speaking in hushed tones.

Stalking towards them, I paused just outside their circle and cleared my throat. "I'm sorry to rush you, but we need to get moving. We didn't canvas the area before we flew in."

"First, there's something we need to do," Harlowe said, raising her head and squaring her shoulders.

"What's that Harlowe?" I asked.

"We have to find Everly."

Chapter Twenty-One

"Who is Everly?" Silas asked in confusion.

"She was my chambermaid while I was in Netheran. She risked a great deal to help me, and she paid dearly for it. I won't leave her alone out here, unprotected. I owe her that much," I said, letting the guilt fuel me.

"Of course, Harlowe," Emmerson said softly, cutting Silas off as he opened his mouth to speak.

He nodded his head once in confirmation before heading towards Caolán. "We'll need to make it quick," he said as he seamlessly mounted the massive dragon in one fluid motion. "Where should we look first?"

I hesitated. I didn't have a clue what direction Everly may have headed.

"We will search every inch of this kingdom until we find her, Fire Heart," Misneach encouraged.

"I don't know," I said as I swallowed. "I was... otherwise occupied as she escaped."

Silas narrowed his eyes, and I held his gaze as he scrutinized me. Letting out a sigh, he darted his glance towards Cillian as he said, "We need to return for Fionn and Teller before setting off. Without knowing her direction, our search may take a while."

Everyone agreed and headed towards their dragons.

"What's Saoirse doing here?" I asked as Cian's massive black dragon stood at her full height.

A stab of pain jolted through me, and I worked to repress the emotions that were still so raw from his loss. We hadn't been close, but he gave his life to protect mine, and I would never fully forgive myself for that.

"It wasn't your fault," Misneach said as he nudged my shoulder with his snout. I placed my hand on his enormous head and let his comforting words soothe me.

"So?" I asked again when nobody answered me, seemingly lost in the same place my thoughts had taken me.

At my reminder, Misneach chuckled, and Zeke's face split into a wide grin.

Emmerson rubbed the back of her neck and smiled sheepishly. "She's mine," she offered with a smile somewhere between a grimace and a smirk.

"What?" I was certain my jaw had just hit the ground. "You hate flying," I reminded her. "How the hell did this happen?"

"She didn't really give me much of a choice," Emmerson mumbled, and Saoirse snorted.

"You are lucky I chose you to be my Cathal," a firm, yet feminine voice drifted into my mind. **"Besides, I know you find it exhilarating despite the pretense you insist on maintaining for everyone else's benefit."**

I whipped my head towards Saoirse, and the dragon's serpentine eyes locked on mine.

"I can hear you," I said breathlessly.

Honestly, I wasn't sure why this was still a surprise to me given Caolán and Niamh had both spoken to me previously, but it was.

The massive dragon simply lifted a shoulder and said, **"As it should be, Daughter of Fire and Flame."**

"You can hear her," Emmerson said in awe.

I returned my attention to the rest of the group, who were all gaping at me open-mouthed. No one seemed to be aware of what had happened back in Pyrithia with Caolán and Niamh.

"It was not our story to tell, Little One." Caolán's deep voice filled my mind, and I swung my head around until my gaze met his.

"Someone better tell me the story," Silas gritted out.

"Please do, before the General pops a blood vessel," a male voice drawled, and I turned to study the two remaining dragons.

Oisín stood tall, back straight, and awaiting Cillian's command. He was every bit the disciplined soldier his Cathal was. He huffed out a breath in annoyance, seemingly offended I would even consider such a comment could come from him.

"I will not dignify that with a response," a low, gravelly voice sounded inside my head.

Surprise lurched through me at the sound. Could a dragon sound... sexy?

Saoirse chuckled to my left and my cheeks heated as I realized they could all hear my thoughts just as Misneach could.

"Not as I can, Fire Heart. Our bond runs deeper than any... connection... you share with them."

Caolán chortled, and Misneach growled in his direction. Oisín rolled his eyes, telling us exactly what he thought of our antics.

I flicked my gaze towards Rónán. His colossal blue wings were spread wide, ready to leap into action at a moment's notice. The bronze scales that ran the length of his chest shimmered as the rays of the sun hit them, and he winked when our eyes met.

A dragon just winked at me.

It was all too much after everything with Kieran.

"Harlowe," Silas barked, pulling me back from my reverie.

I glanced in his direction, and I saw him take a steadying breath to calm himself.

"Can you explain the situation with the other dragons? I'm only hearing one side," he said, more gently this time.

The others muttered their agreement, and Caolán dipped his head in encouragement.

"You don't have to share your secrets, Fire Heart," Misneach soothed, sensing my hesitation. Oisín grumbled something unintelligible and Misneach snapped his jaws at the other dragon.

"It's okay, Misneach," I said, placing a hand on my bond mate and drawing on his strength.

I didn't know why I was hesitating. I knew I could trust Emmerson and Zeke with my secrets. Emmerson already knew everything I had learned in the Forest of Nightmares, and both she and Zeke would protect my secrets with their lives if the situation called for it.

It was Silas and Cillian I was hesitant to reveal the extent of my connection with the dragons too. While it appeared they had accompanied Emmerson and Zeke in some form of a rescue mission, they had still lied to me and Emmerson. Those lies could have easily cost us our lives and I would be a fool to trust them so easily a second time.

Yet, it was clear that I couldn't avoid giving them some insight.

I took a deep breath and said, "You already know that I share some sort of connection with the dragons."

Everyone nodded their heads and waited for me to continue.

"Well, that connection has grown, strengthened, I suppose. I first noticed it right before Kieran took me. I could hear Caolán and Niamh speak to me in my mind."

Silas narrowed his eyes and glared at his dragon. Caolán seemed unfazed and showed no reaction under the intensity of his gaze.

"I didn't know it had extended to any of the other dragons until just now," I finished with a shrug of my shoulders.

"How?" Silas asked. "How are you able to speak to them without a bond?"

"I don't know all the mechanics of it myself, Silas," I said. While technically true, I kept the part about me being a conduit of the dragon's fire to myself.

I could feel a tingling sensation on the side of my face, letting me know Emmerson was looking at me. I willed myself not to look at her, knowing that Silas would catch the movement, however brief, and know I was not telling him everything.

They all fell silent, lost in thought, attempting to make sense of it.

"Why not tell him everything?" Caolán asked.

"You know?" I asked as panic set in. I didn't want the dragons revealing anything to their Cathal until I could determine who was a friend and who was a foe.

"He has broken her trust once already, Caolán. You cannot expect Fire Heart to place her faith in him a second time," Misneach said, echoing my earlier thoughts.

Caolán huffed. **"To answer your question, Little One, we know. You practically shouted it at us during your internal debate just now."**

"Oh." I would need to figure out a way to keep my thoughts to myself.

"We will not betray your secrets, Little One," Caolán said, reassuring me.

Silas sighed, drawing our attention back to him. "Let's pause this discussion while we search for Everly. The Kingdom of Snakes is not the place to let down our guard."

His words sobered us quickly and Emmerson moved closer to me as if preparing to defend me from unseen foes.

"You'll tell me everything later, right?" Emmerson muttered while keeping her eyes trained straight ahead.

"Of course, but I won't trust them so easily a second time," I said, inclining my head towards Silas and Cillian.

Emmerson nodded in understanding and then headed towards Saoirse.

"Come, Fire Heart," Misneach said as he lowered himself down to the ground so I could climb on.

"Oh, there's an easier way to do that," Emmerson called out over her shoulder.

"Do what?"

"Get on the back of your dragon."

"Huh?"

Emmerson fully faced me this time. "The scales. You can use the divots between the scales like a ladder. No need to make a big show of things by launching yourself heavenward," she beamed. "Just like when we outmaneuvered Cillian that time and had to hold on to Misneach's scales while he threw us around... recklessly." She said the last word in accusation.

"It was her plan," Misneach grumbled while Cillian swore under his breath.

"I know Em," I chuckled.

"Just saying," she shrugged, before scaling Saoirse's foreleg.

I climbed onto Misneach's back and felt at peace for the first time in a long time.

"I am glad you have returned to me, Fire Heart," Misneach said.

"Me too, Misneach."

"I am sorry that I broke my vow to you." The pain in his words was unmistakable and a deep sorrow filled me as I registered his meaning.

"It was not your fault, Misneach. Kieran is powerful, and I doubt anyone can stand against him."

"One day, you will," he said with a confidence I did not feel.

"I'm not so sure about that," I said, giving voice to my fears.

"Well, I am. So let me be your strength until you recognize it in yourself. The fates chose you for a reason, Fire Heart. I understand you feel defeated right now, but you will rise from this day, and you will be stronger for it."

Gratitude swarmed my chest, and I quickly swiped at the tears that had spilled down my cheeks.

"Thank you Misneach. For everything."

"You are welcome, Fire Heart."

"Let's fly," Silas commanded, interrupting our private interlude.

The thunderous sound of beating wings filled the air surrounding us, and the familiar feeling of weightlessness welcomed me home.

Chapter Twenty-Two

After diverting to meet up with Fionn and Teller, we wasted no time in our search for Everly. By the third day, however, I was starting to lose hope. As the sky stretched endlessly before us, the warm oranges of the setting sun transitioning into the deep blues of twilight, I was about ready to call it a day.

We had searched every inch of the vast terrain, every forest, mountain, and river that was within the area Everly would have been able to reach on foot in the days since she fled the palace.

Still, we couldn't find any sign of her.

A gentle breeze tousled my hair and drew me from my musings as Misneach cut through the clouds with the pointed tips of his wings. The rhythmic melody of his wingbeats was a welcome distraction from the despair that threatened to overwhelm me.

I felt responsible for Everly. I'd used the trust we had developed and asked her to put herself in danger for me. She never would have been in this predicament if not for me.

"That's not your burden to bear, Fire Heart," Misneach said, interrupting my spiraling thoughts. **"From what you told me, Everly made a choice to protect you. You should respect her agency and honor her sacrifice by living the life she helped you secure."**

I sighed but did not argue the point. Misneach was right, but that didn't help ease the guilt I felt over Everly's whereabouts.

Turning my attention to the task at hand, I scanned my surroundings as Misneach soared over a mountain peak and dipped into the valley below us.

"Over there," Teller yelled, and I followed the direction his outstretched hand was pointing.

My eyes widened as I took in a slight figure marching with determined strides toward the forest just beyond the valley. The figure was clearly a woman with her blonde hair pulled tight on her head, and the skirts of her dress swaying around her feet with each step.

My heart raced, feeling both excitement and urgency as I tried to remember Everly's attire from our last encounter in the hall.

"Please let it be her," I muttered to myself as Misneach descended quickly, closing the distance between us.

If it wasn't Everly, this woman was about to get one hell of a shock when seven dragons swarmed her.

The thundering sound of wingbeats drew her attention, and the woman turned around to peer up at the imposing creatures. A delicate hand fluttered to her throat and an audible gasp escaped her at the sight. Her hazel eyes widened in shock as she swept her gaze toward me.

Everly.

Misneach had not yet landed before I was throwing myself to the ground and sprinting towards her.

"No need to get yourself killed, Fire Heart. She's not going anywhere," he grumbled.

But I was too focused on the woman in front of me to worry about his chastisement. Everly let out a strangled sound and threw her arms wide as I crashed into her, sending us both careening to the ground.

"Shit, I didn't mean to topple you," I murmured in apology.

"Harlowe," Everly breathed, as if not believing her eyes. "It is you, isn't it?" I nodded my head as tears sparkled in her eyes. She wrapped her arms tight around me and stroked my hair as we both sobbed.

Everly pulled back and grasped my face in her hands. "How did you escape, Harlowe? No one has ever passed through the maze without Kieran permitting it. It has been spelled by more witches than I care to count to ensure no one leaves the palace grounds without his approval."

Before I could answer, the ground beneath us vibrated and Everly swayed as the remaining six dragons landed with a *thud*.

"By the gods," Everly breathed. "They're all with you?" I grinned and pulled her to her feet.

Emmerson was at my side in an instant, and I could feel Silas's imposing form right behind me.

"I'm guessing this is her," he said, and I turned to face him.

"Yes. This is Everly. She helped free me from Kieran."

"Well, I tried. I'm afraid it was Harlowe who ended up freeing me." Everly returned her gaze to me, worry clear on her face. "What did Kieran do to you, Harlowe? In exchange for setting me free?"

I felt Silas stiffen next to me, but I kept my eyes locked on Everly as I answered. "Never mind that. I am so glad I found you. I have been worried sick that something might have happened to you."

Everly scoffed. "Of course you were. I was free, and you were being held captive, enduring gods know what, but you were worried about me."

I cringed at her words, knowing they would only arouse everyone's suspicions further.

Especially Silas.

I wasn't ready to talk about what happened in Netheran. Least of all what happened with Kieran.

Pasting a smile on my face, I put my arm around Everly and redirected the conversation.

"Where to now?" I asked Emmerson.

"The plan only went as far as getting you back, Harlowe," she grinned, and I couldn't help but return it.

"We need to find somewhere safe to make camp. Without Arabella's concealment spells, we are too vulnerable out in the open," Silas said, taking command.

I peeked a glance at Everly from the corner of my eye, but she was already speaking up.

"Concealment spell?" she asked.

"Yes. A friend gave me some before our last mission. However, we had to depart in a hurry once Harlowe was taken and I didn't have time to restock," Silas advised.

I noticed Emmerson bristle when Silas referred to my planned abduction as his 'last mission'.

"I can lay a concealment spell," Everly said brightly, oblivious to the tension unfolding.

"You're a witch?" Silas asked, cocking a brow.

"I am," Everly confirmed, not backing away from the title.

"Excellent. Give me a minute to confer with my group and we will find somewhere suitable to rest for the night." Silas stalked off in Cillian's direction.

Emmerson and Zeke sidled up next to me. "You all right?" Emmerson asked, nudging my shoulder.

"I will be. A lot happened in Netheran. I'm not ready to talk about it, but when I am, I'll find you."

Emmerson nodded her head in understanding, then turned her attention to Everly.

"I'm Emmerson. I can't tell you how grateful I am to you for taking care of my Queen when I could not." The grief in her voice had me reaching out for her hand, which she took eagerly.

"We took care of each other," Everly replied. "She is a very special woman, your Queen."

"That she is," Emmerson said. "She also happens to be my best friend, and I was bored half to death without her. These men are all too serious and incapable of taking a joke," she chuckled. "That one in particular," she said conspiratorially, pointing towards Cillian.

Cillian turned and glared at her.

Silas followed Cillian's gaze and when his eyes locked on mine, some emotion I could not decipher shadowed his features.

Was it suspicion? Worry? Regret? It was gone too quickly for me to determine which.

Silas returned his attention to Cillian, and the pair spoke briefly before he strode towards us. He stopped in front of me and said, "We'll camp in the forest tonight and then return to the ruins to plan our next steps."

"This is supposed to be my command," Emmerson muttered, but she didn't look too concerned. I was sure that had she truly wished to be in charge, Silas would know about it.

"What are the ruins?" I asked hesitantly.

Emmerson flashed me a mischievous grin. "It's an old, spooky castle, or what's left of it, anyway. It screams reckless danger. You'll love it!"

Chapter Twenty-Three

When Silas said we'd be staying at castle ruins, I had envisioned a dilapidated castle, yes, but mostly functional and most importantly, above ground. So when Silas handed me a vine and instructed me to climb down, I was a little more than apprehensive.

"This doesn't look very safe," I said, as I tugged on the vine.

"We've all been up and down plenty of times. They're sturdy. Trust me, Harlowe," he implored.

That was the thing though, I had trusted him. And it led to me becoming Kieran's prisoner and... a shudder ran through me at the thoughts forcing their way to the forefront of my mind.

"Are you all right, Harlowe?" Silas asked softly.

"Fine," I replied, snapping myself out of my ruminating.

I tugged on the vine before lowering myself to the large opening in the ground and wrapped it around my legs securely. Taking a deep breath, I let myself slip over the edge and down into the darkened belly of the ruins.

An eerie feeling settled over me when my feet connected with the earth below my slippers. The air was heavy with the scent of moss and decay, and as I peered around, I failed to identify the source of my unease. That did little to assuage my mind, however.

I took a tentative step into the darkness and let my eyes roam over the sight before me. Ahead, a derelict archway framed the path, and as I moved closer, I could make out small, intricate carvings that ran the length of the structure.

Below my feet, the labyrinth of weeds and shattered cobblestone groaned in protest at being disturbed after centuries of neglect. As I moved further into the ruins, the vast emptiness threatened to overwhelm me as something tugged at my mind, warning me against disturbing the secrets that lay buried here.

Trepidation formed a tight knot inside my stomach and the air surrounding me buzzed with an otherworldly energy. I could feel the small hairs on my arms lift as a prickling sensation settled between my shoulder blades and I had to fight to repress a shudder.

"You all right?"

I yelped and my body lurched forward at the sound of Silas's voice penetrating the silence from behind me.

"Easy," he said as he gripped my elbow to steady me.

A familiar jolt of lightning ran up my arm, originating from the spot where Silas's skin met mine. I peered over my shoulder to look at him and met his dark brown eyes that always managed to capture me in their warm depths.

As I studied his face, I could see the concern etched into his features. There were dark circles under his eyes and the corners were creased in a wariness that was all too familiar. This didn't detract from his godly good looks, however, and his sensual lips pulled up at the side in a sexy smirk as he watched me blatantly ogle him.

"Thanks," I said, clearing my throat.

"Any time," he purred.

My core tightened, and I clenched my thighs together as an uninvited wave of lust washed over me. No amount of time away from this man could diminish my desire for him.

But he had betrayed me, and that was something I couldn't risk repeating.

Silas and I had been in an awkward impasse of sorts since I had returned. He had sensed I needed space to reorient myself again following my time in Netheran. So I had spent the previous nights nestled between Emmerson and Zeke; the only safety I had found since leaving Pyrithia. Silas wasn't pushing me... for now. However, I knew he would eventually press me for answers to the many questions I saw reflected in his eyes every time he looked at me.

And this left me unsure of how to behave in his presence.

I could not afford to let him into my trusted circle again. Emmerson, Zeke, Everly, and I would need to plan our next move without Silas's overbearing presence derailing us.

That familiar sense of unease washed over me again, and I shivered as

I darted my gaze around. The feel of unseen eyes boring into me was suffocating; stealing the air from my lungs, choking me.

"What is this place?" I whispered, refocusing my thoughts on what was in front of me.

"We're not sure," Cillian answered from beside me, and this time I stifled the yelp that threatened to escape me at his sudden reappearance. Emmerson needed to put a bell on him.

"It's got to be centuries old," Zeke continued. "A casualty of one of the great wars," he muttered, as though to himself.

"It's spooky right?" Emmerson said as she joined me. Her wide grin told me she was enjoying this far too much.

"Why does that please you, Emmerson?"

"What's not to love?" she said, throwing her arms wide and turning in a circle. "It screams reckless danger! You know, that's the only thing that gets my blood pumping."

"Not the only thing," Cillian murmured, and Emmerson threw him her sauciest grin.

"This place feels..." Everly trailed off, unable to voice whatever she was feeling.

"Can you cast a concealment spell here?" Silas asked.

"Yes, I just need to check my supplies. I had to depart Netheran rather urgently, so I'm afraid I just grabbed whatever I could before fleeing." Everly gave me an apologetic smile, and I returned the gesture, reassuring her.

"What do you need?" Silas asked.

"I swept all my tonics and herbs straight into my pack, so I have all the ingredients. I just need to check on the state of my crystals though," she said as she removed her pack and started rummaging through it.

"We have crystals," Silas said as he indicated for Fionn to bring him something.

Fionn placed a small velvet pouch in Silas's hand, and he passed it to Everly. Her eyes widened in shock as she peered into the pouch before returning her gaze to Silas.

"These crystals are of the highest quality," she breathed. "Where did you come by them?"

"I told you, I have a friend in the same trade as you."

"Even so," Everly whispered.

"He is the Prince of Pyrithia, Everly," I said by way of explanation.

Silas's eyes darkened as they met mine. From what emotion, I could not say.

"W-What?" Everly stammered.

"I am the second-born son of King Leith of Pyrithia," Silas said, extending his hand to Everly.

She took it gingerly before whispering, "Shouldn't I curtsy or something?"

Teller barked out a laugh, breaking the awkwardness that had descended over the group.

"Please don't," he said between gasps. "His ego is big enough already."

My lips tugged up in a smile at Teller's antics. Truth be told, I had missed him. I had missed them all.

Silas grunted something unintelligible before returning his attention to Everly. "We are all very informal here, Everly. There is no need for any ceremony." The smile he gave her left her beaming, and a jab of jealousy tugged at my chest.

Everly regained her composure and said, "Right, well, let's get this place secured, shall we?"

As Everly gathered her supplies and began working, I found a piece of rubble that was large enough to serve as a seat. I made myself comfortable and watched as the others settled in as well.

"You don't happen to have any spare clothes, do you, Emmerson?" I asked, gesturing to the torn dress and slippers that I was still wearing.

Before she could answer me, though, Silas crouched next to me, placing a pack at my feet.

"I grabbed your things before we came after you."

Gratitude filled me, and I smiled up at him. "Thank you, Silas."

I dug into my pack and pulled out a tunic and some pants. When my hands landed on the boots tucked at the bottom of the pack, I couldn't contain the squeal of excitement that erupted from me. I pulled them out and clutched them to my chest. Silas chuckled to himself as he stood and moved away.

"I have missed you, my babies," I crooned.

"That," — Emmerson said pointing to my boots — "is something I can get behind."

"Of course you can, Em," Zeke chimed in as he sat beside me. "Didn't you wear boots to Harlowe's birthday ball?"

"It was to the welcome parade for the Netheran delegation, and I regret nothing," she said, jutting her chin out. Zeke just chuckled and pulled a knife out to cut up an apple.

My gaze wandered around our group, first to Teller, who was sitting beside

Fionn. The pair were engaged in some heated discussion, although neither of them could keep a straight face. Then my gaze fell on Silas, and I took in his profile as he stood with Cillian, hunched over a parchment of some kind. As though he could feel my eyes on him, Silas's head tipped up in my direction and our eyes remained locked for a moment before Cillian reclaimed his focus.

Shifting in my seat, I glanced in Everly's direction as she held the crystals in her hands before placing them in the concoction she had created earlier. She was chanting quietly to herself and that eerie feeling from earlier assaulted me once more, intensifying as my skin heated.

Everly's head snapped in my direction, her eyes wide with fear as she gaped at me.

"Everly, what's..." I began to say, but a heaviness weighed down on me, blanketing my senses with its oppressive presence.

"Harlowe?" I heard Emmerson call, but I couldn't answer her.

My eyes rolled into the back of my head, and I tried to scream, but no sound escaped me.

The world tilted around me, and then I was falling.

Chapter Twenty-Four

I struggled to open my eyes as a throbbing sensation pierced my skull. Lifting my hands to my head, I rubbed my temples to relieve the discomfort.

"Emmerson," I muttered, expecting her to be hovering nearby.

When she didn't respond, I lifted my head and glanced around me. I was lying on the ground beside the rubble I had claimed as my seat, but not a soul was with me. I pushed through the heavy fog that attempted to hold me in place as I scrambled to my feet.

"Emmerson," I tried again.

Nothing.

Not a single sound met my ears.

"Zeke?"

"Silas?"

"Where is everyone?"

The ruins were darker than I recalled. When I glanced behind me, I saw that the fire Teller had started had died down, with only embers remaining. A chill spread through me and I rubbed my arms in response.

"What the fuck is going on?" I whispered into the darkness.

I took a tentative step towards the archway that led back to the massive hole we had climbed down to reach the inside of the ruins. As I reached it, I peered up into the starless night sky that cast an ominous haze over the landscape.

"Misneach."

I tried reaching out to my dragon, and when there was no response, my heart rate picked up as apprehension and fear threatened to overwhelm me.

"Misneach," I tried again. Once more, a deafening silence greeted me.

"No, no, no. Not again."

I pushed my hands into my hair and gripped the strands tightly. The sharp stinging pain that followed confirmed my fears; this was not a dream. This was really happening.

As I fought off the impending breakdown that tried to smother me, I closed my eyes and kicked off my slippers. I focused on the feel of my feet as I connected with the earthen floor beneath me. My toes pushed into the dirt as I inhaled a deep breath and then released it. I repeated the process until I felt my heart rate slowing in time with my breaths and clarity returned to my senses.

My eyes fluttered open, and I looked around to take in my surroundings, trying to figure out my next course. I decided I couldn't just stand there waiting around, so I ventured further into the ruins in search of my companions.

The darkness grew suffocating as I made my way further into what remained of the halls. In the past, this place was likely bustling with life, laughter, and chatter. The stories of those who once thrived here, however, had since been lost to centuries of neglect, with their history consigned to oblivion long ago.

I ran my hand along the wall, feeling the intricate designs that had once been carved into the stone. They were now obscured by the canopy of overgrown vines that clung desperately to the remnants left behind. That feeling of unease returned and the pricking sensation between my shoulder blades sprang back to life.

I could feel eyes on me once more, and I glanced around, seeking the voyeur, however, the blackness looming around me prevented me from succeeding.

"Who's there?" I called out into the shadows.

When no one answered, I turned back the way I had been headed and quickened my pace. I reached a large door and pushed against it, eliciting a loud groan as I did so. The space ahead was brighter than the hallway. Moonlight seeped through the rubble, illuminating the area.

My footsteps were the only sound that could be heard as I stepped inside the room. The circular chamber housed a spiral staircase that once connected to higher floors. That staircase was now broken in places, damaged and falling apart as it fought gallantly against its demise.

A sudden burst of pain in the ball of my foot reminded me I had forgotten to put my slippers back on. I hobbled over to what remained of the staircase and took a seat, bringing my foot to my knee so I could examine my injury. Crimson blood smeared my skin, and I pulled a strip of fabric from my dress to wipe away the mess. A deep gash glared up at me, and the pulsing pain left me wincing.

"Shit."

I wrapped the length of cloth around the wound in a makeshift bandage.

"That'll have to do," I muttered.

A shuffling sound caught my attention, and I whipped my head in its direction. My breath caught as I locked eyes with intense grey-green ones that appeared to delve into the deepest part of my soul.

A woman stood across from me, her eyes rimmed in thick, dark kohl that almost reached her brows. A white powder had been applied beneath her eyes, with streaks of kohl appearing to emanate from the base of her bottom lashes before kissing her cheeks. Her lips were painted in a mix of black and white that extended to her cheeks and gave her a dangerous, sinister appearance. Her light brown hair, the same color as her complexion, was twisted and coiled into intricate knots that hung in individual strands past her breasts.

"Who are you?" I demanded with more confidence than I felt. I scanned the room, trying to find some kind of weapon to defend myself should the need arise.

The woman just stared at me, a cunning smirk on her painted lips that only enhanced the terrifying effect of the pattern adorning them.

"I asked you a question," I hissed as I continued my frantic search for a weapon. I was coming to the uneasy conclusion that I wouldn't find any.

The woman took a step in my direction, moving closer until she was standing right in front of me. She tilted her head to the side, her eyes carefully assessing me before she circled me in a manner that had bile rising in my throat.

I might have been unarmed, but if she intended to harm me, I wasn't about to make it easy for her. I pushed myself to stand, careful not to put too much weight on my injured foot, and casually took a stance that would allow me the most movement in my current state.

The woman narrowed her eyes at me before she threw her head back and cackled. Once she had regained herself, she returned her steely gaze to mine.

"Do you really think you can defeat me, child?" she asked in a mocking tone. "Especially in your condition," she finished, raising a brow.

My spine stiffened, and I let my anger block out everything around me, including the thrumming pain in my foot, as I squared my shoulders.

"I'm no easy prey, lady. If you think I'll lie down and allow you to do whatever it is you're planning without putting up a fight, think again."

Her lips pulled up in a grin and mirth twinkled in her eyes. Her expression should have been comforting. On anyone else, it would have been. On her though, it sent a wicked shiver racing down my spine.

"Now, now Harlowe. Is that any way to speak to the one person who holds the answers you seek?"

Chapter Twenty-Five

My whole body jerked at her use of my name and the insinuation behind her words.

"How do you know my name?" I asked, unable to hide the quiver in my voice.

The woman smirked and lifted a shoulder. "When you find yourself trapped in the void between realms, there is little else to do but watch and wait." A sinister glint shone in her eyes with her words.

"Void... between realms... what are you talking about?"

"Did you honestly believe Aetherian was the only realm out there?" she mocked.

Well, yes.

I didn't voice that thought, however. Instead, I asked, "What other realms?"

"That's not the purpose of your visit to the void, Harlowe," she chastised.

"The void... you mean... I'm in the void?" I stammered.

"Indeed," she purred.

I held a tight grip on the panic that wanted to break free and asked, "How did I get here?"

"I brought you here."

"You... brought me here?"

"Are you always this slow?" she admonished.

I blinked in surprise at her criticism and cleared my throat. "Why don't you tell me why you brought me here?"

"It's more accurate to say that your little witch friend created the opening that allowed me to drag you here, but semantics."

"Everly?" The woman rolled her eyes at me and tsked.

"Do you not know how witchcraft works, child?"

"No. Why would I?"

The woman sighed, lost in her thoughts.

"I forget they stopped teaching our history after the War of Witches," she muttered.

The witch returned her attention to me and said, "When a witch calls upon her power, she creates a tiny tear in the void. While the tear remains open, things can pass through the void and back out again. Once the witch releases her magic, the tear repairs itself, and the void is sealed off again."

"What. Why?"

"Because the void is the birthplace of the magic wielded by witches," she said with a lift of her shoulders.

"I'm not following."

The woman scowled at me. "My power was gifted to me by an entity that lives within the void. Whenever I drew upon my power, I was drawing upon that source, and to enable that, I needed to create a small tear in the void to allow my power to flow freely from here, to there," she said pointing off in the distance. "When my female descendants were born, they were born with the ability to do the same."

Realization knocked the breath out of me.

"You're the Original Witch, aren't you?" I breathed. She smirked at me and nodded her head.

"You're the one who gifted Kieran his power. Why?"

"For me to answer that question, I will need to start at the beginning."

She sat down on the crumbled stone floor and began arranging her skirts until she was satisfied. Once she was done, she looked up at me expectantly, and it took me a moment to realize she was waiting for me to join her. I lowered myself gently, so as not to jostle my injured foot as I settled in and waited for her to start.

"Decades before the War of Witches, I had been a healer of sorts, and provided care for the sick and ailing of my village." Her voice took on a light quality as she recalled her early years.

"One day, I was tending to a young girl who was very sick. She was not responding to any of my treatments. Her parents were beside themselves and

I was growing desperate to cure her of what ailed her." Her gaze flicked to mine and a moment of vulnerability passed between us.

She cleared her throat and continued. "I had grown quite fond of her, you see. So, every day when my remedies inevitably failed her, I returned home and prayed to the gods to spare her. And every day, they failed to heed my prayers." Anger contorted her features as she relived the tortured moments of her past.

"Then one day, an entity, not the gods, answered my call."

"What entity?" I asked, unable to help myself.

The witch's intense gaze met mine, and she tsked. "I can't tell you that, Harlowe," she said, swaying her finger.

"This entity," I prompted, waving a hand for her to continue.

"This entity," she repeated, "told me they could help me."

"They?" I asked, my curiosity peaked.

The witch ignored my question and continued her story. "They said that they could gift me with the power that could save the girl's life, but there was a catch."

"Isn't there always," I grumbled before I could think better of it, and the witch laughed.

"They told me that my power was to be used to help those who needed it. They instructed me to never deviate from that purpose, warning that if I did, my power would become distorted and darkness would slowly spread where the light had once danced."

"It didn't seem like a hard condition to meet, so I agreed, and this power was bestowed upon me. However, this entity failed to mention that my female descendants would also inherit the same abilities that I had been gifted with, and the same expectations would be placed upon them.

The witch paused for a moment before she sighed heavily. "You know," she said, looking up at me, "people once revered witches." I nodded my head, not wanting to interrupt the retelling of her history.

"People respected us and frequently sought our advice. Often, we acted as intermediaries between monarchs when conflict arose. That all changed, however, when a small but prominent contingent of witches turned their backs on their calling. No longer content with serving those around them, they instead sought to seize power and rule in their own right.

At first, I resisted them, but their influence grew, and more and more witches joined their cause. Then the reigning monarchs across the realm sought to shackle us all, keep us contained, while still draining us of our power," she spat.

The witch's eyes narrowed, and darkness spread from her irises until it drowned out all the color, leaving nothing behind except bottomless black. My spine stiffened, and I inhaled sharply as the witch continued.

"So, I finally relented. I abandoned my commitment to a people who no longer deserved my understanding and care. I joined with the witches who had already fled their positions and we waited, and we plotted until it was finally the right moment to make our move."

"The War of Witches," I murmured to myself.

"The War of Witches," she repeated, settling her dark gaze on me while a cruel smile marred her features.

"I'm guessing you know how that turned out," she said viciously.

I swallowed harshly and nodded.

"I died during the war, right here, in this stronghold which marked our final stand," she said as she peered around her.

Did she mean the castle ruins?

"Instead of moving on to my next resting place, I became trapped here," she snarled as she waved a hand about. "It was my punishment for breaking my oath to only use my power for righteous causes," she spat.

"Righteous for who, though? The people had already turned against us and thought they could tether us and use us at their will. They no longer deserved the gifts we bestowed upon them."

"So, how did Kieran end up with your powers?" I asked, hesitantly.

The witch's grin returned, something akin to triumph reflected in her expression.

"After the war, the young Prince had one of his witches create a tear in the void and bring him to me. He asked me to grant him the power that I had received many years before."

I didn't bother informing her that Kieran ascended his throne long ago and has been the ruler of Netheran for centuries.

"Why?" I asked, holding my breath as I awaited the answer that might reveal his intentions for me.

"He wanted to punish those who had wronged him and his kingdom during the war."

My mouth dropped open. "After all, you'd been through, you just agreed?"

Before I could blink, the witch was before me, pulling me to my feet roughly.

"Do not sit there on your sheltered throne and judge me, child," she growled, spittle landing on my cheeks as she seethed.

My breath hitched, and I frantically tried to summon the power that had been trapped inside me since I came through the maze.

Try as I did, there was no stirring, no tingling of awareness to answer my call.

"It was not only his enemies who would suffer. Inevitably, those who wronged me would also pay," she snarled.

The witch released me, and I sagged slightly. She began pacing in front of me, muttering incoherently to herself.

Steadying my breathing, I asked, "Why is Kieran's power so different from the witches?"

The witch stopped her pacing and glared at me. "The power I gifted the Prince was a distorted, twisted version of the power I had received. It was all that was left of me after the betrayal of my people and my ruination following the war."

The witch cocked her head in that unsettling way again and grinned maliciously. "There is no way of knowing the full extent of what the Prince can do, but rest assured, it is nothing good," she sneered.

"Why are you telling me this? Why help me?"

The witch threw her head back and laughed maniacally. The unhinged tenor reminding me too much of Kieran in his moments of madness.

The witch stepped forward, invading my space.

"Whoever said I was helping you?" she jeered.

The witch reached into her pocket and retrieved something, never once breaking eye contact with me. I glanced towards her hand, which was clenched in a fist, but I could see no weapon she could use to attack me.

Returning my eyes to her black ones, she smiled wickedly and exposed her palm to reveal some sort of powder that had been ground down to fine dust. The witch inhaled deeply and blew the powder into my face.

I reeled back, coughing and spluttering as I tried to extricate the noxious substance from my windpipe. I could hear the witch laughing mirthlessly as I struggled to recover from her assault.

A familiar heaviness settled over my limbs, dragging me down to the ground as my eyes once again rolled to the back of my head.

This time, when I screamed, the sound reverberated around me, filling my senses, and overwhelming me, until there was... nothing.

Nothing but never-ending blackness that swallowed me whole.

Chapter Twenty-Six

"Harlowe. Harlowe, can you hear me?"

A masculine voice sounded from above me, but it was indistinct, like I was hearing it from underwater.

"Harlowe," the male growled, as he tapped my cheeks.

I waved my hands in front of my face, intending to swat the offending hand away. Instead, I was pulled tight against a hard wall of muscle as Silas's scent filled my nose. There was a murmuring of other voices nearby, and I could hear Emmerson ordering me to open my eyes.

"Open your eyes before I claw them open myself," she demanded.

I peeled one eye open and then the other, blinking away the dark spots that danced in my vision.

"There she is," Emmerson crooned, but I could see the relief in her features.

"You gave us quite a scare," Zeke said as he came into my line of sight. Emmerson pushed him away, as she declared that she had best friend privileges, which meant she was taking the focal point.

I tried to sit and groaned as the throbbing pain from earlier returned with full force. Gripping my head between my hands, I focused on my breathing until the pain lessened.

"Here, drink this." Everly's soft voice drifted towards me, and I lowered my hands as I peered up at her. She stood above me, holding out a small vial.

"It will help with the healing," she encouraged.

Silas helped me into a sitting position, and I reached out, taking the vial from Everly. The bitter taste slid across my taste buds, and it was no less revolting than it had been the first time. Everly smiled in apology and took the vial from me once I'd finished.

"What," I croaked, before clearing my throat and trying again, "What happened?"

"You don't know?" Silas asked above me, and I craned my head back to look at him.

"Not exactly," I said, glancing in Everly's direction. Guilt distorted her features, and she looked to be on the verge of tears.

"I'm so sorry Harlowe. I had no idea that would happen. When I created the tear, I realized someone was waiting on the other side of the void, but it was too late."

"It's all right, Everly. It wasn't your fault," I said, squeezing her hand to reassure her.

"Fire Heart," Misneach breathed. **"You must stop doing this. You will speed up my aging process."**

"I wasn't exactly a willing participant, Misneach," I chuckled.

"What's funny?" Silas demanded, with an edge to his tone.

"Misneach," I said by way of explanation.

"Tell the General my importance in your life far outweighs his insignificant existence," Misneach grumbled.

"No." I was not in the mood to fan the flames of the next great war.

"I'll tell Caolán to relay the message," Misneach sulked.

"I am not sulking," he snapped, following my errant thoughts.

"You are, and Caolán will not play into the posturing that you and the Prince fall into," a stern feminine voice I had learned belonged to Teller's dragon, Grainne, chastised.

"Stop, all of you. One conversation at a time," I ordered. Misneach muttered something under his breath but did not interrupt further.

When I returned my gaze to those surrounding me, I realized every single one of them was watching me intently, with confused expressions.

"Sorry," I mumbled. Focusing back on Everly, I repeated, "It's not your fault."

"What's not her fault?" Emmerson asked as she subtly positioned herself between us.

I stifled the laughter bubbling up in my throat and asked instead, "What happened to me? To my body I mean?"

I was pretty sure that my body had remained behind while my subconscious was dragged into the void, given that I woke up with my head in Silas's lap.

"Your body?" Emmerson asked in a high-pitched voice, clearly fighting her mounting panic.

"What the fuck is going on?" Silas snapped, having exhausted his threshold for patience.

"Tell me what happened to me first," I repeated.

"You fainted, lost consciousness, and wouldn't wake up. Now tell me what the fuck happened," he demanded.

I gave Silas a withering look before recalling my encounter with the Original Witch.

"That's it, no more witches," Emmerson declared. "They have brought nothing but trouble, Harlowe, so I'm putting my foot down." Everly's shoulders drooped, and she lowered her head. "Except you, of course, Everly. I wasn't referring to you. You're fine, helpful even," Emmerson said with a strained smile.

Coddling was not something Emmerson could add to her repertoire.

Cillian chuckled behind his palm and Emmerson glared daggers in his direction.

"She didn't mean you, Everly," I said gently.

"What she said," Emmerson chimed in.

"Can we please refocus on what's important?" Silas growled. "Kieran's powers are untested, maybe even unlimited."

Silas's remarks sobered the room.

"What did you see him do in Netheran, Harlowe?" he asked.

"He could call the shadows to him. He somehow used them to transport us from Pyrithia to Netheran, and again from the dining hall to... to my chambers." Silas didn't miss my hesitation and his hold tightened around me.

"He could also direct them from his palm, as though they were an extension of his arm. That's how he killed Lucinda. He snapped her neck with his shadows, and..." I swallowed the lump forming in my throat, "and Cian too," I finished.

Silence followed my words before Fionn abruptly stood and left the room, Teller following him a moment later.

"I'm sorry," I choked. "I didn't mean —"

"You did nothing wrong, Harlowe. Fionn is just having a hard time coming to terms with Cian's loss. We all are." Silas said the last part so quietly I didn't think he meant for anyone to hear him.

Cillian mercifully broke the suffocating silence. "He also used the shadows to heal himself when you almost beat him to death, Silas."

My mouth dropped open, and I gaped at Silas. He just smirked and lifted a shoulder in a shrug.

"Wish you'd finished the job," Emmerson muttered, and Silas, Cillian, and Zeke all grunted in agreement.

Silas released a long breath before he rubbed his hands up and down my arms.

"Was the concealment spell cast, Everly?" Silas asked, making Everly startle in surprise.

"Yes. The spell had already been cast before Harlowe..." she trailed off, unsure how to categorize what had happened.

"Good. Then I suggest you all get a good night's rest, and in the morning, we'll plan our next move."

Emmerson's gaze darted towards Cillian, and she tilted her head to the side before striding in the same direction. Cillian pursed his lips before he let out a long breath and ran his hand through his hair. A moment later, he was trailing after her.

Hot breath fanned against my ear as Silas leaned in and whispered, "You better sleep, Harlowe. Tomorrow, we resume your training."

Silas curled his arms around me and lifted me effortlessly. He carried me towards his bedroll and placed me on the ground before curling his body protectively around mine.

Apparently, he had decided he'd given me enough space.

Too exhausted to fight with him, I closed my eyes and resolved to take it up with him in the morning.

Chapter Twenty-Seven

The next morning when I woke, it was to find that everyone, except Everly, had left the room we'd used for sleeping.

"Where is everyone?" I asked, rubbing my eyes.

"Emmerson insisted you sleep for as long as necessary to recover your strength," she said with a soft smile. "She is a good friend to have."

"The best," I agreed.

"So, where did they all go?" I asked, rising from Silas's bedroll.

"Up," she said, pointing her finger to the dilapidated roof.

I stretched my arms high above my head, relishing the feeling of my muscles coming to life.

"Do you know where Silas put my pack?"

Everly rose from her position by the pit we had used for a fire and collected my pack from across the room. She strode towards me, pack in hand, and a bowl of something she had been stirring earlier.

"Here," she said, first passing my pack and then the bowl.

"It's not much, but it's the best I could do under the circumstances."

"Thank you, Everly."

As I peered into the bowl, I could see she had made porridge. I settled on the ground and took a bite. Cinnamon and some other flavor I couldn't identify exploded on my tongue. It was positively divine.

"This is exceptional. What is that other flavor?" I asked with a mouthful of food.

I took another bite, trying to discern the unfamiliar flavor. "It's really good," I said.

Everly beamed. "It's pear," she said, answering my question.

Once I had finished my breakfast, I changed into the tunic and pants I had longed for while I had been in Netheran. When I pulled on my boots, I felt like myself again.

"I'm going to see what everyone else is doing. Do you want to come?"

"I'll come up in a bit. I just want to get started on the midday meal," Everly replied.

"You don't have to cook every meal, Everly," I said, furrowing my brows.

"It's no bother. I enjoy cooking," she said with a small smile.

"Well, in that case, I'll see you up there," I grinned.

When I reached the opening in the ruins that we'd used as our entrance, I grabbed a vine and tugged harshly. It seemed secure, but I still had my reservations.

After I secured it around my foot to prevent myself from slipping, I started to climb. Sweat beaded on my forehead and I realized I was out of shape. I'd missed training during my time in Netheran and it showed. I grumbled to myself the entire way up until I was almost within reaching distance of the edge.

A large, calloused hand jutted into the open space, and a moment later, Silas appeared at the entrance. I took his offered hand and let him pull me the rest of the way out of the ruins.

"Thanks," I said once I'd straightened.

He gave me a lopsided grin and tilted his head, beckoning me to follow. Before I could get far, a shuddering vibration disturbed the ground beneath me as Misneach landed behind me.

I threw myself at the massive dragon, and he chuckled at my antics. I still felt the acute pain of my forced separation from him.

"Come now, Fire Heart. None of that," he said, having heard my thoughts. **"I wanted to check on you before I left to go hunting."**

"I'm fine. Go, don't worry about me," I said, waving a hand in encouragement.

"It seems all I do is worry about you, Fire Heart," he grumbled, before launching himself into the sky.

Turning my attention back to Silas, I asked, "Where are you taking me?"

"Training," he replied simply.

We walked in silence, going deep into the forest.

My mind wandered to last night, and the way Silas had crushed me to his chest as I slept. He clearly thought things would go back to how they were before.

Too much had passed between us for that to be the case, so I needed to establish some ground rules.

Consumed by my thoughts, I didn't realize when Silas stopped abruptly, and I walked straight into his rigid back.

Scanning my surroundings, I saw we had come to some kind of clearing. Silas stalked to the center of the open space and beckoned me forward.

"I need to test your capabilities. I assume you didn't train much while you were away."

I shook my head. "Before we start, I want to discuss something."

Silas straightened, his eyes narrowing as he marched towards me. He planted himself in front of me and said, "You forget yourself, Little Menace. I command, you follow," he growled.

"That was before you revealed yourself to be a lying, cheating —"

Silas interrupted my tirade by reaching out and sweeping my feet out from underneath me. Landing on the ground with a *thud*, my breath left me in a whoosh as Silas pinned me to the ground beneath the hard planes of his body.

"First of all, I never cheated," he growled. "And second, I've already apologized for lying to you. You know my intentions were not malicious, Little Menace, so you need to let it go."

"Let it go," I scoffed.

"Yes, let it go," he gritted out.

"Sure Silas. The next time I kidnap you, hold you captive in my kingdom against your will to be used as a pawn in the schemes of others, I'll be sure to remind you it wasn't malicious and that you need to let it go."

Silas's lips curved up in a wicked grin. "Don't threaten me with a good time, Little Menace."

"You're unbelievable," I grumbled as I bucked against him. "Get off me."

Silas groaned. It was then that I realized I'd positioned myself so that my core was rubbing against his very erect cock as I tried to buck him off me.

I immediately stilled, and Silas chuckled darkly.

"Soon, Little Menace," he purred.

"In your dreams," I scowled.

"Every night." His grin was downright predatory.

"Just burn him alive already," Misneach snarled.

"I thought you were hunting. Stop listening in on my private

conversations."

"Again, it's not listening in when you're blasting your every thought down the bond," Misneach sneered.

I chose to ignore him and focused my attention back on Silas. "What do you mean you didn't cheat? Sienna told me all about your night in her bed, where you confessed your plan to use me, and how you had me playing your dirty little slut!" I spat.

Silas's jaw clenched, and he said, "What are you talking about, woman?"

"S-I-E-N-N-A," I drawled.

"I didn't fuck Sienna. Well, not after you, anyway." I renewed my efforts to push him off me, but he remained in place, not giving an inch.

Silas's eyes widened and then twinkled with amusement. "Are you jealous, Little Menace?" he asked huskily.

"What? No. You can fuck whoever you want, Silas, just leave me out of it."

"You are," he said, overly gleeful. "And here I thought you'd never stake your claim."

"Get off me," I huffed.

Silas laughed and lifted himself off me before offering me a hand to help me up. I swatted it away, but this only made him laugh louder.

"You're an asshole, you know that," I said as I stood and straightened my tunic.

"I do actually," he grinned.

"Let's just get on with it."

Silas wasted no time in taking the offensive. He had me defending every time as I tried to deflect blow after blow. I was a little stiff and slower than I'd like to admit, but in my defense, it had been weeks since I'd had to push myself.

"Come on Harlowe, hit me," he taunted.

"Take him down, Fire Heart," Misneach growled.

"Not helping," I snapped.

Silas moved in fast, throwing a punch that I dodged. He aimed another at my ribs, but I darted sideways, avoiding the connection. Silas was still turning to face me when I raised my fist and launched it straight for his mouth. My hand met flesh and Silas's head snapped to the side. When Silas faced me again, I could see a small trickle of blood running down his chin, and he swiped at the red substance in... satisfaction?

"Finally," Misneach howled.

"Go away," I hissed.

Silas looked me up and down, taking in every inch of me, as his eyes darkened with lust. A sexy smirk lifted the corner of his mouth as he continued to assess me.

"Silas," I warned, holding up a hand.

"You'd better run Little Menace, because when I catch you, I'm going to fuck you raw."

I didn't hesitate.

I turned and sprinted towards the tree line.

Chapter Twenty-Eight

My pulse was hammering in my throat and my breaths were coming out in rapid pants as I fled into the forest, seeking refuge in the vegetation. It was a stark contrast to the last time I had traversed the twists and turns of the green labyrinth of the maze. This time, I welcomed the never-ending shrubbery.

An undercurrent of fear sparked at the nape of my neck and shot downwards, running the length of my spine. I shivered with the unsettling feeling it left in its wake.

But there was another feeling coursing through me, delving into every corner of my body, and settling low in my abdomen.

Desire.

I could not deny the anticipation that collided with my fear, sending a thrill rushing through me at the thought of the unknown.

A chorus of crunching leaves and snapping twigs followed in my wake, and I pumped my arms harder, willing my feet to follow suit.

The deeper into the forest I ran, the darker it became. The towering trees created a high canopy, which blocked out the sun, only allowing fleeting bursts of sunlight to penetrate the darkness below. A light breeze tousled my hair, and every step I took pulsed with excitement and trepidation in equal measure.

An upturned root brought my efforts to an abrupt halt as I careened towards the ground. I threw my arms out in time to soften my fall. My breath left me in a rush, and I rolled onto my back as I inhaled sharply.

"Caught you, Little Menace," Silas said roughly as he peered down at me.

Pushing off the ground, I quickly stood and faced Silas.

"Go find Sienna to fuck, Silas."

He smirked and stepped closer.

"I already told you I didn't fuck Sienna. Whatever poison she whispered in your ear was only her attempt to rile you." Silas cocked his head to the side. "Looks like it worked," he purred.

I adamantly refused to acknowledge the warmth that spread across my chest with his words.

"So what's this really about, Little Menace?"

"You lied to me, Silas. You fucking betrayed me!" I shouted.

Silas clenched his jaw and studied me. "I've already told you —"

"I know, I know. You didn't mean it, or you did it to protect me, or whatever other bullshit excuse you came up with to make yourself feel better. But that doesn't change the fact that you betrayed me, and that cost me, Silas. For weeks I was at Kieran's mercy, and you and I both know he has none."

Silas stalked towards me with purpose and reached his hand up to cup my jaw. He forced me backward until I slammed into a tree, his gaze never leaving mine. Lightning struck my skin where he touched me and traveled down my body, settling in my core. Liquid fire stirred inside me, soaking my panties.

Silas's nostrils flared as he said, "Tell me what he did to you."

I averted my gaze, but he drew my attention back to his with the harsh grip he still held on my jaw.

Silas was not letting this go.

"I fucked him to spare Everly's life," I said in a clipped tone. I raised my chin, daring him to challenge me.

His eyes narrowed to slits, and a vein bulged in his forehead. Just when I thought he was about to unleash his fury, his eyes softened as they roamed over my face.

"Fuck, Harlowe. I'm sorry," he said with a ragged exhale.

That had me seeing red. The absolute last thing I wanted from him was his pity.

"Don't be. I didn't say I didn't enjoy it," I purred.

Silas's eyes narrowed again in an instant, and his hand moved from my jaw to my throat. "Is that so?" he said in a deadly whisper.

I refused to cower under the weight of his stare or the dangerous energy emanating from him in waves. I continued to stare at him, waiting for him to make the first move.

"Did you forget who you belonged to, Little Menace?" he snarled. "Tell me, did your pussy weep for him as it does for me? Did his cock stretch you and own you as mine does? Did he hear the sweet melody of your moans as you came undone? Tell me, Little Menace?"

"You don't own me, Silas."

"Don't I?" he mocked as he raised a brow. "I bet you're already wet for me, aren't you?"

Without warning, Silas pulled the ties of my pants open and slipped his fingers below the waistband of my panties. He dipped a finger inside me, finding me soaking wet.

"Mmm, that's what I thought," he growled.

"I might want your cock, but I don't want you, Silas," I taunted.

Silas smirked. "It's a start."

"I hate you," I said breathlessly.

"No you don't," he grinned.

"I don't trust you."

"You don't need to trust me, to fuck me," he said huskily.

We stared at each other for a beat, and then our lips crashed against one another in a hungry kiss, full of desperation. Silas bit my bottom lip and I gasped. He took advantage of the moment and thrust his tongue inside my mouth.

I wrapped my arms around his neck as I deepened the kiss. As I kicked off my boots, Silas reached down, pulling my pants from my body. His large, calloused hands found my ass as he lifted me, and my legs snaked around his waist. He pressed me further into the tree for support as he reached into his pants, freeing his cock.

His cock slid along my entrance, and he groaned. "Fuck, Little Menace. Your pussy is fucking dripping for me." I rubbed myself against him, beckoning him inside.

"I need to be inside you right now, Little Menace. I'm going to fuck you hard and fast. It's been too long, and I need to feel you coming undone around my cock."

Silas thrust inside me in one fluid motion, filling me to the brim. A moan escaped me, and Silas buried his head in my chest.

"Fuck, you're so tight." He lifted his head and locked his eyes with mine. "Do you see how well you take me, Little Menace? This pussy was made for me, wasn't it? No one else. Now tell me who fucking owns it," Silas demanded.

"Just move," I snarled, and Silas chuckled darkly.

Rocking his hips against mine, Silas kept his word, fucking me raw as he drove himself inside me.

"Oh, gods," I breathed.

"That's it, Harlowe. Take my cock. Take. Every. Fucking. Inch."

"More," I panted, and Silas became merciless as he impaled me on his length. I threw my head back as I felt my orgasm creeping to the surface.

"Look at me, Harlowe," Silas demanded. I lowered my head and met his feral gaze. "I want to see your eyes fill with tears as your pleasure unravels you."

And just like that, I came undone. I screamed Silas's name as he continued his brutal assault.

"Yes, Little Menace, scream my name. I'm the only one who will ever give you this kind of pleasure," Silas growled. "Fuck, Harlowe, your pussy is strangling my cock."

And then he was coming. His seed filling me and mixing with my own release.

We were both panting heavily as we came down from our shared orgasms.

"I still hate you," I panted.

"And I still don't believe you," Silas breathed.

Silas leaned in and placed a tender kiss on my lips as he whispered, "I'm going to fucking kill him for touching what's mine. I don't care if I have to destroy this entire realm to get to him. His end is coming."

I glared up at him, fiery hot anger coursing through my veins. "You're a fucking bastard. I'm not your anything," I seethed.

Of course, he would be pissed that Kieran had challenged his ownership of my body. He spared no thought to what I had been through or the toll it had taken on me as a human being.

Silas just stared at me, saying nothing.

I pushed against him, and he lowered me to the ground as he said, "Let's get back."

Chapter Twenty-Nine

When we returned to camp, we found the others sitting around the clearing surrounding the ruins, watching Cillian and Fionn, who were sparring.

As soon as Emmerson caught sight of me, she made a beeline straight for me.

"Where did you two come from?" she asked a small smile on her lips and a single brow raised.

"We were training," I said nonchalantly.

"Uh-huh. So, why is your hair telling me you're freshly fucked?" She leaned in and sniffed me. "And you smell like sex," she grinned.

"Emmerson! You don't just go around sniffing people," I hissed.

"I do when they're full of shit," she laughed.

"First, that's gross. And second... I'm going to go... over there," I said, pointing in Teller's general direction.

As I walked away, I could hear Emmerson chuckling as she followed me. We settled down with Teller to watch the fight, and Zeke soon joined us.

"How's he holding up?" I asked Teller, tilting my head towards Fionn.

"We've all felt Cian's loss, but none harder than Fionn."

I swallowed roughly, and said, "I'm sorry."

"Shit, Harlowe, I didn't mean to make you feel bad. Cian made his choice and honestly, it's a choice every single one of us would have made without thinking twice, Fionn included. It wasn't your fault."

Tears filled my eyes, and my vision swam in front of me.

"Fuck," Teller barked before he pulled me into his chest for a bone-crushing hug.

"Don't cry, Harlowe. I didn't mean to... I just... fuck, I'm not good at this."

I let the tears fall, hidden within Teller's embrace. When I regained control of myself, I wiped my eyes and lifted my head.

Every single person was staring at us.

Laughter bubbled up inside me and I was almost certain I was a hair's breadth from falling into hysterics.

Instead, I pushed the feeling down and waved a dismissive hand, saying, "Don't worry about me. It was nothing."

Cillian and Silas shared a look before the latter gave a brief nod and Cillian resumed his sparring with Fionn, bringing everyone's attention back to the pair.

"Is there any way I can help?" I asked Teller.

"We're just keeping him busy. I'm trying to fill that space for him. Become some kind of mentor to him. I fear I'm a poor substitute, however," he chuckled awkwardly.

"I'm sure that's not true. You're helping more than you realize. Sometimes, all we need is for someone to just be there for us, so we don't feel so alone." My gaze danced to Everly, and she gave me a knowing smile.

"Thanks, Harlowe." I squeezed Teller's arm and then returned my attention to the match.

Cillian wasn't going easy on Fionn. To be honest, I wasn't sure the Cathal understood the concept. Cillian spent the next twenty minutes taking Fionn to the ground while offering him tips and correcting his stance.

It was all very reminiscent of the way Silas had trained me.

"Harlowe, you're up," Silas barked.

I whipped my head towards him and glared. He just pointed at Fionn as though that was discussion enough.

"I'd love to, Fionn, but I'm spent."

"Bet you are," Emmerson whispered in a conspiratorial tone.

"Harlowe," Silas growled.

"Silas," I growled right back.

"**And here we go again. The General is on the verge of bursting that blood vessel**," Rónán chortled.

"**No one's in the mood for your foolishness today, Rónán**," Niamh chastised.

"Where are you? I can't see any of you?"

On cue, the thundering sound of beating wings permeated the air surrounding us and seven colossal dragons descended in unison. Everly still wasn't used to the way these beasts just appeared, and she let out a small squeak in surprise.

"Good hunting?" I asked Misneach.

Oisín scoffed and Misneach snarled in his direction.

"Changing the subject noted."

"How was your training, Fire Heart?" Misneach asked, and my cheeks heated.

"I wasn't referring to *that* type of training," Misneach grumbled, and my face heated further.

Silas cocked his head to the side as he studied me, his brow furrowed as he took in my flustered expression. Then he turned his head slightly, angling himself in Caolán's direction. When his gaze returned to mine, a smirk tugged at his lips, and I knew Caolán had informed him about the topic of discussion.

I lowered my head, refusing to engage further.

"From what I understand, she doesn't need any training," Rónán chuckled, clearly not getting the message.

"For the love of the gods," I muttered.

"Don't even think about relaying this conversation to your Cathals," I said as I glared at each of them in turn.

"Why are the dragons chuckling?" Emmerson asked. "It's... unsettling."

Silas's smirk grew into a broad smile and that was when I'd decided I'd had enough.

"All right, fine. Fionn, you and me," I said, pointing my finger between us.

Fionn grinned and jumped into the center of the clearing.

"Come on, Harlowe. Show me what you've got," he teased.

I walked towards Fionn, stopping a short distance from him. Taking a moment to shake the stiffness out of my limbs, I rolled my shoulders and stretched my neck.

"Ready?" Fionn asked, and I nodded my head, taking my stance.

We circled each other for a moment, weighing up the other, searching for weaknesses. I made the first move, having realized that being forced into defense against any Cathal was the quickest way to get yourself killed.

My fist darted forward, aiming for Fionn's kidney, but he avoided the hit effortlessly.

"You'll have to do better than that if you want to take me out, Harlowe," Fionn grinned.

"Don't get cocky," Teller warned from the sideline.

Fionn glanced towards him, and I took advantage of his distraction, sending my fist into the side of his head.

Fionn stumbled back. "Damn, Harlowe. That was a cheap shot," Fionn grumbled.

"Told you," Teller smirked.

"Should have been paying attention," I teased.

Fionn shook it off and redirected his entire focus back on me. I gulped, recognizing the ruthless determination I saw reflected in his eyes.

This is what set the Cathal apart.

Fionn moved with a fluidity that had me gaping at him in awe... before he thrust a fist out with lightning-fast speed and connected with my hip.

Fuck, that really hurt.

Another fist cut through the air towards me, but this time, I managed to evade the contact. Fionn didn't hesitate as he followed up with a series of punches and kicks that almost had me beat.

"Come on, Harlowe. Kick his ass," Emmerson hollered.

My vision narrowed to the one obstacle in front of me, blocking out everything else around me until it was nothing more than background noise.

Fionn came at me again, and this time when he kicked his leg out, I grabbed it in a tight hold and brought my elbow down on the tender flesh behind his knee.

Fionn cried out and stumbled to the ground.

Pressing my advantage, I followed him down and jumped on him, pinning him in place with my forearm across his windpipe.

"Do you yield?" I asked in a sickly sweet tone.

"Shit Harlowe, you're ruthless," Fionn breathed. Then a huge grin split his face as he said, "It's fucking hot."

I laughed down at him before large hands gripped my shoulders and pulled me off Fionn. Silas was glaring at the young Cathal as he remained sprawled on the ground. I rolled my eyes and threw out a hand to help Fionn up, but Silas knocked it away and replaced it with his own.

Caveman.

"See if Everly can give you something to help with the knee," Silas grunted, as he helped Fionn to his feet.

Turning to me, a sinister smile lit up Silas's face as he said, "Are you ready for the real training to begin?"

Chapter Thirty

"**No**," Misneach snarled for what felt like the hundredth time.

"**He said no,**" I informed Silas.

"Then you can train with me on Caolán," Silas retorted... again, and Misneach snarled... again.

Silas had declared that I needed to elevate my training so that I was capable of aerial warfare. Misneach had been all for it until Silas insisted he would have to accompany me on Misneach so that he could conduct the lesson.

Misneach was vehemently opposed to the suggestion, hence the current standoff.

"Look, I'm not getting between you two. I'll just fly with Misneach, and you and Caolán can fly nearby," I said as I rubbed my temples.

Silas just glared at me. Obviously, that was not a suitable solution.

"**Are you ever going to get past your issues with Silas?**" I asked Misneach.

"**Are you?**" he challenged.

"That's different. He betrayed my trust. He didn't do anything to you, Misneach."

"Didn't do anything to me," he scoffed. "You and I are bonded. You are mine as I am yours. Any infraction against you is an infraction against me. The General thought he knew what was best for you, which makes him an idiot considering your intellect is far superior, and as a result, he put your life in danger. I don't take kindly to such things. But most importantly, Fire Heart, his actions *hurt* you, and for that, I will never forgive him."

I couldn't help the overwhelming sense of gratitude and love I felt towards my dragon.

"**As you should,**" Misneach said.

"**Way to ruin the moment,**" I muttered.

"**Are you two done with your little private discussion while the rest of us wait patiently in the background,**" Silas grumbled, and Misneach bared his teeth in his direction.

"**Enough,**" Caolán sighed. "**This is important, Little One. You must be ready for what lies ahead. Surely you don't want her to be at a disadvantage, do you, Misneach?**"

"**Guilt, it really is the best motivator,**" Rónán chuckled.

"Does your dragon ever take anything seriously?" I asked Zeke.

"Not really. But he's one badass dragon, so I'm fine with it." He shrugged his shoulders as though bored.

"**Badass,**" Rónán repeated with pride.

"**Children,**" Grainne sighed.

"**Caolán has a point, Misneach. Not that long ago you were insisting I train in aerial combat.**"

"**I never suggested the General had to accompany you, only teach you,**" Misneach interjected.

"Like it or not, Silas is the expert when it comes to these things. He's been training Cathal for many years. I'm willing to put my anger aside so that I can learn the skills I will need to survive. Can you do the same? Please Misneach," I begged.

"**Fine,**" Misneach grumbled.

"See," Rónán said. "**The best motivator.**"

The other dragons groaned, which had Rónán chuckling again.

"Misneach is agreeable to you accompanying us," I informed Silas.

"About time," he muttered.

"**The General better improve his attitude or else he might have an unfortunate accident,**" Misneach growled.

"**Misneach!**" Caolán and I snapped at the same time.

The dragon just rolled his eyes as though we were the unreasonable ones.

"Let's just get this moving before he changes his mind," I mumbled.

I climbed onto Misneach's back and Silas followed. When he settled behind me, the hard planes of his muscular chest enveloped me, and a shiver of desire rushed through me.

"Careful Harlowe, you could tempt a saint. And you and I both know I'm far from saintly," Silas purred.

Misneach huffed, which pulled me out of my lust-induced haze. Then Silas settled his hands on my hips and my desire immediately sparked to life once again.

"Do you touch all your trainees this intimately?" I said in challenge, but it came out far too huskily to hit the mark.

"Only when they've been riding my cock, as I fucked them mercilessly up against a tree."

I scoffed. "Do that often, do you?"

"Your jealousy is quite adorable, Little Menace," Silas chuckled.

"If you two don't stop, I'll throw you both off," Misneach growled.

My face heated, and I cleared my throat. "What now?" I asked.

"You know the fundamentals of flying. Now all you need to do is extend those same principles. As always, the key is to trust your dragon and allow your body to move in sync with his. Let him lead you," Silas said, returning to general mode.

"Everyone, mount up," he barked, and the others complied, eager to get on with the lesson after the earlier delay.

"Take a moment to connect with Misneach, and when you're ready, let him know."

I inhaled a deep breath, letting the oxygen fill my lungs, and then exhaled. Misneach's heartbeat was steady, and his muscles were coiled, ready to launch heavenward.

"I'm ready."

A moment later, we were airborne and soaring among the clouds that stood out against the brilliant blue of the sky. The wind roared in my ears as Misneach's wingbeats sliced through the air as he climbed higher.

I peered down at the vast expanse of the world below, each divergence in the landscape barely distinguishable from our height. We were soaring through the endless sky, and I felt the most at peace since escaping Netheran.

"Level out, Misneach," Silas instructed, and the dragon huffed, but complied.

Gripping my hips tightly, Silas said, "I want you to rise from your sitting position until you're standing."

I hesitated, nerves quickly flooding my system.

"Caolán is right below us. If you fall, he will catch you," he encouraged.

I peeked over the side of Misneach's broad wings and caught sight of the grey-green scales that belonged to Caolán.

"I am here, Little One."

In slow, deliberate movements, I rose from my position until I was standing at my full height. Silas quickly followed, and I turned to face him.

"Good. Take a moment to find your center," he instructed.

When I felt I was ready, I nodded my head, signally for him to continue.

"Now, I want you to take up a fighting stance. Be sure to plant your feet firmly along Misneach's back, but be careful not to catch the tip of your boots in his scales. If you trip from this height, you'll likely fall off."

"That's not very reassuring," I said.

"I've got you, Little Menace. And if you slip by me, Caolán is there," he reminded me.

Taking my stance, I planted my feet, making sure to avoid the divots in Misneach's scales as Silas had instructed.

"Now I want you to come at me. You're working in a confined space with not a lot of room for movement, so you're going to want to keep things nice and tight. You'll be fighting in extremely close quarters."

I nodded once and then advanced. My footsteps were small and measured, never taking larger strides that would risk losing my balance. I aimed my first jab at Silas's ribcage, which he deflected with ease.

"Good. Go for the parts of the body that are easy to reach and don't overextend yourself," Silas praised.

I took another step closer and unleashed a combination of hits on Silas's face, abdomen, and hip.

None connected.

"You're doing really well, Harlowe."

"I haven't hit you once," I pointed out.

"I'm not an easy opponent," he smirked.

"The ego of this male," Misneach interjected, and I grinned.

I tried to land another hit, this time feigning left and striking right. For a moment, I thought Silas would fall for it, but he corrected at the last second and deflected the blow.

"I'm going to start hitting back now, Harlowe," Silas advised.

I wasn't sure if I was ready for that, but I nodded in agreement anyway. Silas bent his knees in a low crouch and sent his fists flying. His jabs were delivered at a breakneck speed, and he had withdrawn before I even registered I'd been hit. My hip and upper ribs both protested in pain.

Ignoring the throbbing in my sides, I darted forward and landed a blow to

Silas's kidney before he'd retaken his stance.

A wicked smirk curved his lips. "Very good, Little Menace. Let's see if you can do it again."

Silas advanced, and his towering frame loomed over me as he swung his fist in my direction. I ducked and narrowly missed being hit. This close to Silas and in my crouched position, I realized the limited range for movement was an advantage with my shorter frame.

Darting under Silas's arms, I landed a combination of blows to his kidneys, ribs, and sternum before darting back out of reach.

"You're learning," he grinned, but it was far from friendly.

"Balance and coordination are vital, Little Menace. You're quick, which will work to your advantage, but first, you need to make sure you can adapt to your conditions. Misneach, I want you to employ a series of alternating dips and Harlowe, you'll need to tailor your movements so you're moving in harmony with Misneach."

"This male," Misneach gritted out. **"I'm not some pet he can call out to perform tricks at his leisure."**

I didn't have time to reply before Misneach tilted his wings to the left, throwing me off balance. I thought I was going to fall, but Silas steadied me as he'd promised. When Misneach evened out, I reclaimed my footing and waited for the next dip.

When it came, Silas charged forward, landing a kick to my upper thigh. Somehow, I maintained my balance, but it came at the cost of my stance, which Silas used to his advantage as his fist connected with my shoulder.

A growl of frustration escaped me, and Silas smirked in amusement. He beckoned me forward, and I let my anger drive me.

A novice mistake.

I lost track of my footwork as I charged towards the arrogant male and my boot got lodged in one of Misneach's scales. My body lurched forward, and Silas flung his hands out to grab me. Just as he did, however, Misneach tilted his wings into another dip, and I felt myself falling to the side.

A panicked scream escaped me, and Misneach immediately straightened. This only jostled me further, and I lost my grip on the dragon.

"Harlowe!" Silas shouted as my fingers slipped out of his reach.

My heart was hammering wildly in my chest as I slipped over the edge of Misneach's body and began free-falling into the abyss of clear blue skies.

"FIRE HEART," Misneach roared.

My hands fruitlessly scrambled for purchase, only to be left wanting. Then my back collided with a hard surface that stole my breath. For a moment, I wondered if I had crashed into the landscape below, but I soon realized I was still moving.

Chancing a glance beneath me, the grey-green color of Caolán's scales greeted me, and a sigh of relief left me.

"Did you really have such little faith in me, Little One?" Caolán asked, amused.

"To be honest with you, Caolán, my brain could not process anything outside of the fact that I was falling, likely to my death," I said breathlessly.

The dragon chuckled and I just lay there, thanking whatever gods were listening for letting me live to see another day.

"The Prince is rather agitated and wants us to return to the ruins," Caolán advised.

"Uh-huh," I agreed, very much ready for the lesson to end.

"Before either Misneach or the Prince does something stupid," he added, under his breath.

I spun on Caolán's back until I was sitting nestled between his wings. As I looked out at the others, I could see they were all further along in their training.

"They had the benefit of time while you were away," Caolán said, in answer to my unspoken question.

An irrational sense of hurt washed over me as I thought about my friends spending their time together while I had been locked away in Kieran's palace.

"You cannot blame them for continuing to live their lives, Little One. They were determined to bring you home, but sometimes that meant being patient," Caolán counseled.

I sighed, knowing he was right. "I don't begrudge them, Caolán. It's just... I guess I'm struggling to find where I fit in now that I'm back. A lot happened in Netheran, but I'm the only one who experienced it."

"Then share it with them. Maybe your burdens will feel a little lighter if you do. The Prince wishes to understand," he said pointedly.

"Stop pushing her, Caolán," Misneach snapped.

But as we sailed through the sky, catching the updrafts that carried us effortlessly toward our camp, I had to wonder if Caolán had a point.

Chapter Thirty-One

Caolán landed with skilled precision when we arrived back at the ruins. Moments later, Misneach followed. His landing, however, was far less graceful as he all but tossed Silas from his back. Silas reached me in three strides, his large hands coming to my face as he cupped my cheeks.

"Are you all right, Harlowe?" he asked with concern etching his tone.

"I'm fine." I looked over Silas's shoulder to peer at Misneach. "Are you?"

Silas chuckled. "Worried about me, Little Menace?"

"She should be," Misneach grumbled. **"I'm going hunting. I trust you'll be safe here, Fire Heart?"**

"I'm fine. But didn't you hunt this morning?"

"I did," Misneach replied before he launched himself into the sky.

I pulled away from Silas's hold as I headed towards the entrance of the ruins.

"I'm going to find Everly," I called over my shoulder. "Do you mind telling Emmerson and Zeke I'm looking for them when they return?"

"Harlowe," Silas barked. My footsteps halted, and I turned back to look at him.

Silas was running a hand through his hair, his face a mask of frustration. When our eyes met, he stared at me for a long while before releasing a controlled breath.

He nodded once, and I hesitated for a moment before continuing on my way.

I found Everly fussing over the fire as she prepared our next meal.

"Good lesson?" she asked when I entered.

"I fell," I said, shrugging.

Everly gasped, and I quickly reassured her that Caolán was there for that purpose. That seemed to calm her nerves, and we continued chatting as we worked on the meal preparation. Although, I'm not sure that I was much help given I had never actually cooked anything before.

"Something smells amazing," Teller said from behind us, and we both jumped, not having heard his approach.

"Gods Teller, announce yourself or something. My heart just about flew out of my chest," I said, still shaking. He just grinned and took a seat.

"You were looking for me?" Emmerson asked as she entered the room.

I cast a quick glance in Everly's direction, and she gave me a small wave of her hand, indicating for me to go.

When I reached Emmerson, I grabbed her hand and pulled her to a quiet corner of the room.

"Where's Zeke?"

"He's coming," she replied. "Ready to tell us about Netheran?" I nodded once, and she squeezed my hand.

Zeke arrived a few moments later and joined us.

Directing my gaze to Zeke, I said, "Emmerson already knows this part of the story."

"All right, Harlowe. You can trust me," he encouraged.

"I know I can," I said as I smiled back at him.

I recalled what happened in the Forest of Nightmares and the Lost Witch's message to me. I told him about the prophecy and that I was created to counteract Kieran's power. How Kieran had orchestrated the Skirmish of Power just so he could get to me. And about me being the conduit of dragon flames.

I told him everything.

"Shit," he said as he released a breath.

"There's more," I continued.

The others had all arrived back now and were settling in as the night descended. I could feel Silas's eyes on me, but I ignored him as best I could.

"Kieran knows I am his other half. He knows I was created to balance out his power. That's why he wanted to marry me. In Netheran, marriage vows are exchanged with a blood oath that binds the couple together, preventing them from harming their spouse. He wanted me to join my power with his, but if I refused, he wanted to be sure that I couldn't stand against him," I said.

"Of course he did, the sadistic prick," Emmerson grunted.

"I'm still not entirely sure what his plans are, save for the fact that he wants to take revenge against those he feels harmed him and his kingdom during the War of Witches. The specifics, however..." I trailed off, shrugging my shoulders.

"All right, but you escaped him before you could be forced to marry him. Now what?" Zeke asked.

"While I was his captive, I repeatedly made it clear to him I would never join with him. He told me he would kill me if I posed a threat to his plans."

"Like fuck he will," Emmerson shouted.

"Shh, Em," I said, glancing around.

Sure enough, every set of eyes inside the room were trained on us. I had to stifle a groan of frustration. My eyes flicked to Silas, and I found his narrowed on me, trying to decipher the nature of our discussion. I quickly returned my attention to Emmerson and Zeke.

"Sorry," Emmerson mumbled.

"Yes, well, it gets worse, so please try to temper your reaction," I chided.

I quickly ran through the rest of my time in Netheran, including the man with the golden eyes who tried to murder me.

"Fuck Harlowe, this is bad," Zeke said, as he scrubbed a hand over his face. "Kieran's hunting you and maybe trying to kill you. And there is also an unnamed assassin in the mix, which I don't understand, by the way. Why would anyone, aside from Kieran, be hunting you? It's not like this fire power... or whatever it is, is common knowledge."

"Remember what I told you about the Lost Witch?" Zeke nodded once in confirmation. "She said not everyone would allow me the chance to choose. That, they wouldn't want to take the risk that I would choose to stand with Kieran instead of standing against him. And we already know of a few people who know of this prophecy," I said pointedly, and Zeke glanced over my shoulder.

"Also, I'm almost certain that the attack on our palace in Valoren was about me. I don't think the man with the golden eyes was the first to try to remove my choice. Did my father ever hear back from Vidyaa?" I asked, needing some kind of certainty out of this mess.

"I'm not sure. I followed you almost immediately. Once I'd regained consciousness that is," he said sheepishly.

Emmerson snorted and said, "Not predictable," as she pointed her finger toward her chest.

"Emmerson, really?" I scolded. She just smirked and lifted one shoulder in a shrug.

"There's one more thing I need to tell you," I said nervously.

Emmerson and Zeke both sat up straight, their spines stiffening as they waited for me to continue.

"So, I explained how I escaped," I started.

"Your cool ass fire power, yes," Emmerson grinned.

"Before that, Kieran proposed a deal - guess his power's source, and I'd be free. However, I was only given three guesses, and he forbade me from asking those inside his palace for help. If I did, he wouldn't honor the agreement." My eyes darted towards where Everly sat, peering into a pot as she hummed to herself.

"This is what you meant when you said Everly paid dearly for helping you, isn't it?" Emmerson asked as she followed the direction of my gaze.

I nodded once, swallowing the lump forming in my throat.

"Everly knew the origins of Kieran's power source, and she shared that information with me." Before I could lose my courage, I continued, "Kieran discovered the truth and was going to execute Everly. However, I intervened and offered myself in her stead."

"When you say offered yourself..." Emmerson began.

"He wanted me to submit to him. He... he wanted me to give myself to him willingly. My body, I mean."

Emmerson sucked in a breath, and Zeke stared at me. The air crackled with tension around us, and Emmerson's eyes filled with tears.

"Em, don't —" I started to say, but Emmerson stood abruptly.

"I need a minute," she muttered and walked out of the room.

Feeling dejected, I hung my head, fighting the overwhelming feeling that I had let her down.

"Hey, Harlowe," Zeke said as he lifted my chin. Seeing the tears threatening to spill down my cheeks, he lifted me to standing and led me out of the room with his hand pressed gently at the small of my back.

"I thought you might like some privacy," he said, once we were outside.

"She's disappointed in me, isn't she?" I whispered.

"Is that what you think?" The surprise in Zeke's tone made me lift my head to meet his gaze.

"Harlowe, Emmerson is more loyal to you than she is to herself. She will always put your needs before her own. If you asked it of her, she would lay down her life for you. You could never disappoint her. Right now, she feels like she let you down. She's disappointed in herself."

A sob wrenched itself free with Zeke's words and before I could stop it, a torrent of tears spilled down my cheeks. Zeke pulled me into his arms and wrapped me tightly in his embrace. I had been feeling so alone all this time, worried about what everyone would think of me once they learned I had surrendered to Kieran. And yet, I'd only been met with compassion. I let this knowledge center me and my tears slowly dried up.

"Am I interrupting something?" Silas asked from the entryway.

I glanced up at him. He was standing with his arms folded across his chest, his jaw clenched and pulsing with anger.

"You need to reign in whatever alpha male urge that is currently overriding your senses and give Harlowe some space," Zeke warned, as he clutched me tightly to his chest. "She's been through enough."

Silas took a step in our direction but halted when a feminine voice barked, "Not another step, Silas. I mean it." Emmerson strode down the hall, dagger in hand, as she joined us.

"If Harlowe needs a minute, you'll give her a fucking minute," Emmerson snarled.

Her expression looked wild; crazed even. Her eyes were rimmed in red, and her features were contorted into a feral snarl. In all the years I had known her, I had never been frightened of Emmerson.

Not once.

At this moment, however, I was seriously considering the possibility that I might be capable of such a reaction.

If her wrath had been directed at me, instead of Silas, that is.

Silas's eyes narrowed on Emmerson as he glared at her. He must have seen the same thing I did because he gave her a curt nod and glanced back in my direction before heading back inside.

Emmerson turned to face me. "I'm sorry," she said in a broken voice.

"Emmerson, you have nothing to be sorry about," I said, trying to soothe her.

"Just let me say this," she pleaded, hand raised. "I'm sorry I couldn't stop Kieran from taking you, and that you had to go through all of that on your own. And I'm sorry for not being more supportive when you came back."

"Em, it wasn't like you knew."

"Still, I should have seen the truth behind the careful appearance you put on for everyone else. I'm your best friend. I should have seen that you were struggling." She choked out the last part.

"You're being too hard on yourself, Em," I said gently.

"She's right, Em," Zeke added. "As much as we might hate it, bad shit is going to come our way from time to time. All we can do is be there for each other when that time comes."

Emmerson and I shared a look, and then we pulled Zeke into a tight hug. He protested slightly, but his efforts were disingenuous.

"What scares me the most about the whole thing is that I was attracted to Kieran. I may have slept with him to spare Everly, but I desired him. What does that say about me? Am I attracted to his darkness? Will I eventually choose him?" I said as I let my hands fall to my sides.

Since departing Netheran, this had been my greatest fear. If I felt a pull towards Kieran, was I destined to succumb to it?

"Fuck, no!" Emmerson said confidently. "The pull you feel towards him is just a byproduct of fate's twisted game. You're bound to him, so it's natural that you would share some kind of connection. But you're nothing like him, Harlowe."

"How can you be so sure?"

"Because I know you. You saved Everly, and you fought like hell to escape him. You are the personification of good, Harlowe."

"What she said," Zeke added.

"I'm hardly the personification of good," I snorted.

"All right, all but that last part," Zeke chuckled. Emmerson and I both pushed him, but he only laughed harder.

"Let's eat," Emmerson said as she squeezed my hand.

We all headed back in the direction we had come, and I was feeling much lighter for having confided in my friends.

As we sat and ate the meal Everly had prepared for us, I could feel Silas's gaze on me. He never diverted his attention, not even momentarily.

When it came time to sleep, he tried to insist that I share his bedroll again, but I refused.

On the cusp of sleep, I felt strong arms wrap around me and lift me from the spot I had claimed for the night.

Moments later, I was nestled beneath strong arms and enveloped in a very familiar scent.

Chapter Thirty-Two

I awoke with a start as a cool breeze prickled my skin, causing goosebumps to rise on my exposed flesh. The nightgown I wore covered very little and I couldn't find the blanket as I moved my hand across the mattress.

A bed. I was in a bed.

Sitting bolt upright, I scanned the room and could hardly make out my surroundings as the black color scheme of the room blended in with the shadows.

"No, no, no," I whispered.

"Something wrong, Bride?"

I couldn't move, afraid of the truth I knew awaited me if I turned around.

"I expect you to look at me when I'm talking to you, Harlowe," Kieran snarled.

My fingers trembled as I slowly shifted my position until I was facing him.

"There she is," he crooned.

Kieran was sitting in the same armchair he had fucked me on only days prior.

"Where am I?" I asked, not yet ready to face the situation.

Kieran tsked. "You know where you are, Little Bride."

Kieran rose from the chair and strode towards me. I jumped to my feet, not wanting to be trapped on the bed by this monster. When my back met the wall, however, I quickly realized there was little I could do to protect myself from him at this moment.

My gaze returned to Kieran, and I caught sight of the metallic object he held, its tip shining in the moonlight.

I swallowed roughly when I realized it was a dagger.

"I must say," Kieran purred, "I'm very disappointed with you, Harlowe."

"Is that so?" I asked, trying to project the confidence I was not feeling.

Kieran tilted his head to the side, his wide grin and intense eyes making him appear deranged; unhinged. With one hand, he twirled the dagger while the other toyed with its tip.

When he reached me, Kieran caged me in with his body as he planted his hands on either side of my head. He was wearing loose pants and nothing else. His broad, muscular chest was on full display, with his tattoos that always drew my attention.

"My, my, my, Little Bride. Are you done fucking me with your eyes?" he said huskily.

My attention snapped back to his face and to the cocky smirk he wore as he raised a single brow.

"How did you find me?" I asked, changing the subject.

Kieran chuckled, well aware of what I had done. "I haven't... not yet," he said with a dangerous lilt.

My brows furrowed in confusion, and Kieran's smirk only grew wider.

"What do you mean?" I asked, finally breaking the tension.

"I mean," he drawled, "you're not actually here," he said as he waved his knife around the room. "You're dreaming."

"I don't understand," I said, confused.

"I know," Kieran grinned. "There are many things you do not know about me, Little Bride." He ran the tip of the dagger down my chest until it reached the juncture between my breasts. "And that should terrify you," he purred.

My heartbeat picked up speed as sweat beaded on my forehead.

"Why am I here, Kieran?" I demanded.

"I wanted to give you one last chance."

"A chance for what?"

"A chance to submit to me. Return to me willingly, become my bride, and I will forgive your past transgressions. You can stand at my side where you and I both know you belong."

His voice lowered menacingly as he said, "Make me come and find you, though, and I will be forced to eliminate the risk you pose."

There was no mistaking the threat behind his words.

"I will never —"

My words were cut off when Kieran crashed his lips against mine in a punishing kiss. His hand snaked into my hair as he deepened the kiss, spearing my lips with his tongue until I opened for him.

Kieran lowered his hand to my breast and cupped it in his large palm. He thrust his hips forward so I could feel the hard outline of his erection as he ground himself into my core.

"One taste of you wasn't enough," he growled against my lips.

I sank my teeth into Kieran's lower lip hard enough to draw blood. The copper taste exploded on my tongue, but Kieran only chuckled darkly. I pushed against his chest, but he was as immovable as stone.

"Careful, Little Bride. I might just take offense to your antics," Kieran purred.

"What does it matter? This is only a dream, remember?" I taunted.

The sharp tip of his dagger met the delicate skin of my throat. "Go ahead," I challenged. "I'll eventually wake from this nightmare, no matter what you do to me as I sleep."

Kieran pressed the blade further against my throat and a sharp stinging sensation erupted from the site. I could feel the warmth of my blood as it trickled down my throat.

"Did I forget to mention this is no ordinary dream?" Kieran asked as he smirked wickedly.

I gulped, audibly.

It was at this moment that I remembered his words from earlier.

There are many things you do not know about me, Little Bride. And that should terrify you.

Was this one of those things?

"I see you have finally realized the predicament you are in."

"What is it you want, Kieran? What do you truly want? What is all of this about?" I asked, gesturing between us.

"You want to know my secrets, do you, Bride?"

"I want to know the truth. You want me to join you? Why?"

He seemed to consider my question for a moment before he shook his head. Kieran opened his mouth to speak, but before he could, the room started to shift around me.

Kieran growled low in his throat and the room distorted further.

"This is not the end of this discussion, Little Bride," Kieran hissed.

"What's happening?" I asked, unable to conceal my growing panic.

"Do not fret. No harm will come to you... yet."

Darkness crept in around the edges of my vision, and my pulse hammered wildly. But my eyes remained locked on Kieran's as I watched the determination settle within them.

He would come for me and this time, there would be no escaping him. Of this, I was sure.

"Soon," Kieran whispered, as the darkness ensnared me.

Chapter Thirty-Three

Someone was shaking my shoulders as they called my name.

"Harlowe, Harlowe, can you hear me?"

The scene playing out around me was all too familiar. My head was perched in Silas's lap, and I could hear Emmerson nearby demanding he stop shaking me. I groaned and rolled to my side as I pushed myself up.

A small bite of pain hummed at the base of my throat and my hand instinctively flew to the site. I could feel warm liquid beneath my fingers and when I pulled them away to inspect them, they were coated crimson.

"Oh gods," I whispered. "It was real."

"What did you say, Harlowe? What was real?" Silas asked.

I straightened, suddenly alert. "Kieran," I whispered.

Silas stiffened, and Emmerson narrowed her eyes. Casting a glance around the room, I could see everyone was awake and had been observing Silas's efforts to rouse me.

"Why is everyone awake? And why are you all staring at me?" I asked, as my cheek heated.

"You were thrashing in your sleep and moaning as though you were in pain," Silas answered.

I glanced around and realized I was, indeed, sprawled out on Silas's bed roll.

"Why am I in your bed?" I demanded as I glared at him. "I distinctly recall going to sleep over there." I pointed toward my abandoned bedroll.

Silas merely shrugged and grinned unapologetically, eliciting a growl of frustration from me.

"What happened, Harlowe? Why are you bleeding?" Zeke asked, concern evident in his tone.

"Kieran somehow pulled me into a dream. I don't understand the mechanics of it, so don't ask," I said as Emmerson opened her mouth to do just that.

"But why are you bleeding?" Zeke pressed.

"He held a dagger to my throat."

Silas released a feral snarl behind me at the same time Emmerson swore under her breath.

"What did he want?" Cillian asked, redirecting the conversation.

"Same thing as before. He wants me to marry him and bind myself to him."

There was a collection of muttering, and Emmerson swore again.

"Marry me," Silas said, as he pulled me closer to him.

Deafening silence met his words as everyone stopped talking to gape at him.

I slowly turned to meet his gaze. "What did you just say?" I asked, sure I heard him wrong.

"You heard me. Marry me."

"You're being serious, aren't you?" I asked, bewildered.

"You know I don't play around when it comes to you, Little Menace," he replied.

"And pray tell, why the hell would I do that?" If Silas was surprised by my outburst, he didn't show it.

"If I marry you, then Kieran won't be able to use you in that way," he said.

"Oh, right," I said sardonically. "While we're at it, we can send your father an invitation to let him know that his son married the bride he intended for his brother, just so August couldn't," I mocked.

"August was never going to marry you," Silas growled. "In any case, it kills two birds with one stone."

Cillian winced and Fionn retreated a step. Emmerson wore a grin that was pure mischief, and Zeke's shoulders shook with quiet laughter.

"Two birds, with one stone," I repeated slowly.

"Yes," Silas replied simply.

"Oh, that's how every girl dreams of being proposed to," Emmerson snorted. "Will you accept my lifelong commitment of convenience?" she taunted.

"That's not what I meant, Emmerson. I'm simply offering an easy solution to a persistent problem. There can be no grand schemes to force Harlowe into a marriage against her will if she is already married to me."

Emmerson burst out laughing, and Zeke shook his head. "Just stop."

"What?" Silas asked, sounding genuinely confused.

Standing from my position, I strode towards the door as Silas called after me. As I turned the corner, I heard Zeke say, "Good luck. You're going to need it."

I was at the entrance to the ruins and climbing up the vine before Silas caught up to me.

"Just wait a minute, would you?" he growled.

Slipping free of the entrance, I stalked towards the forest as my anger consumed me.

"Harlowe," Silas called again, but I ignored him. "Harlowe, stop." Strong fingers curled around my arm as Silas pulled me to a halt.

He turned me to face him as he said, "That came out all wrong."

"Wrong," I scoffed.

"Yes, wrong," Silas gritted out. "I didn't mean to upset you. I was just thinking of the practicalities."

"Practicalities," I repeated, as I crossed my arms over my chest.

Silas exhaled roughly as he ran a hand through his hair. "Marrying you has always been the goal, Harlowe. And I'd decided that long before I knew of Kieran's plans or my father's misguided attempt to have you wed August."

"Oh, really? And did it ever occur to you that I might, I don't know, want a say in all of this?" I asked, throwing my hands up in the air.

"Stop taking everything I say and twisting it. I'm not the enemy, Harlowe. You need to stop fighting me."

"You are the fucking enemy, Silas!" I shouted. "You betrayed my trust," I continued as I stepped towards him and jabbed him in the chest with my finger.

"You lied to me." I jabbed him again, this time poking him hard enough to make him stumble back.

"And even if none of that had occurred, I wouldn't just marry you to avoid a shittier offer. When I marry, it will be because I need my husband as badly as I need air in my lungs. It will be because I can't imagine spending a single day, let alone a lifetime, without seeing his face or feeling his touch. But most importantly, it will be because he feels the same way about me."

I was breathing hard now, and when I attempted to thrust my finger into Silas's chest for a third time, he captured my wrist and pulled me to him. We remained like that, both glaring at each other as we fought to reclaim our senses.

"You're killing me, woman," Silas groaned, and then his lips were crashing against mine.

The kiss was a collision of teeth, tongues, and lips. Each of us vying for dominance. Silas broke the kiss and spun me in his arms. He marched me forward, his hand wrapped around my chest until my front was flush against a tree.

His hot breath fanned the shell of my ear as he whispered, "I'm going to need you to be a good girl and do as I say. Can you do that for me, Little Menace?"

My body trembled with anticipation, and Silas chuckled darkly. "I want you to keep your hands flat against that tree. Don't move them until I say you can," he purred.

My breathing hitched as one hand snaked below the waistband of my pants and the other wrapped around my neck.

"When I touch your pussy, am I going to find you dripping wet for me, hmm?" He didn't wait for me to answer as he curled a finger inside me.

"You might lie to yourself, Little Menace, but your pussy tells me exactly how much you want me."

Silas pushed another finger inside me, and I groaned at the pleasure he created. "I never want to hear you talk about marrying another man again," he snarled as he thrust into me. "Do you hear me, Harlowe?" I ignored him as I rode his hand with abandon.

"I own this body, don't I, Little Menace?"

"Silas," I whimpered.

"Yes, Little Menace?"

"Shut up and fuck me."

Silas snarled but increased his pace, moving inside me with a frenetic energy. I could feel my orgasm building and my movements became wild and desperate. Silas tightened his grip around my throat, and I gasped.

"You like that, Little Menace? You like my hand wrapped around your throat as my fingers fuck you without mercy?"

His hand became tighter and dark spots coated my vision. I struggled to suck in a breath and Silas snickered.

"Are you going to come for me, Harlowe? Are you going to show me just how much you hate me?" Silas taunted.

The hand on my throat squeezed even tighter, cutting off my air supply completely. Just when I thought I couldn't take anymore, Silas released his hold slightly and my orgasm tore through me with an intensity that left me shaking. If it wasn't for Silas's grip on my throat, I would have collapsed in a heap on the ground.

Unimaginable pleasure coursed through my body, and I moaned as I muttered incoherently. Something pierced the skin of my shoulder, and it took me a moment to figure out that Silas had bitten me. I barely registered the pain as Silas continued to thrust his fingers inside me as I rode out my orgasm.

When I finally came down from my high, I peered over my shoulder to find Silas grinning victoriously. He leaned down until his lips brushed the shell of my ear.

"Spread your legs... wide," he commanded. My brows furrowed in confusion and Silas laughed.

"I'm nowhere near done with you, Little Menace."

I turned to face forward and did as he instructed. "That's my good girl," he praised.

Cold air assaulted me as Silas pulled my pants past my knees. His hands moved leisurely up my calves and continued their upward exploration until they met the juncture of my thighs.

"Is my pussy ready for more punishment?" Silas asked huskily before he sank his teeth into the flesh of one of my ass cheeks before doing the same to the other.

"Now, every time you sit down, you'll be reminded who owned this ass." He emphasized his words with a slap to the tender flesh.

"You have a filthy mouth," I said breathlessly.

"A mouth that's explored every inch of your body," he countered. "Lift your ass in the air because I'm about to nail you to that tree."

I did as he instructed, eagerly anticipating what was to come next.

"You're a glutton for my cock, aren't you, Little Menace," he said roughly.

And then he was entering me, his massive length stretching me, and tearing me apart from the inside. The delicious burn reminded me just how ruthless Silas was when he fucked me.

His fingers dug into the flesh of my hips, his bruising grip holding me in place as he pounded into me.

"Fuck Harlowe. Your greedy pussy was made to be filled by me. See how well you take me. I could watch my cock sliding in and out of your weeping hole for the rest of my life and die happy."

His lewd words had arousal slickening my thighs, and I moaned as his thrusts became hurried. I could tell he was close to coming, so I reached a hand down and pinched my clit.

A hard slap connected with my tender ass, and I yelped. "Did I give you permission to move your hands?" Silas snarled.

I growled in frustration but moved my hand back to the tree.

"Good girl," Silas crooned.

Just when I thought he would deprive me, Silas reached a hand around my waist and rubbed my clit. It only took two strokes of his masterful fingers before I was coming hard. Silas continued to thrust wildly before he grunted and spilled himself inside me.

We were both panting hard; Silas's cock still sheathed inside me. When my breathing evened out, I tried to step away, but Silas pulled me by my hips until I was flush against his chest.

"Tell me you're still mine. Tell me I can fix this," he whispered.

"It's not that simple, Silas."

"Say the words, Harlowe."

"I can't. Not tonight," I whispered. His hands tightened on my hips before he relaxed his grip.

"Maybe with time," I said, barely audible.

The featherlight kiss he placed on the nape of my neck was the only sign he had heard me.

Chapter Thirty-Four

The rest of the week followed a similar pattern; I trained every day, oftentimes while flying on Misneach. I had only fallen off one other time, so I was considering the training a success.

Yesterday, Silas had introduced weaponry, and I quickly realized I favored a dagger over my short swords when flying. Even though my balance and coordination had improved from that first lesson, my short swords were heavy enough to throw me off. Misneach and I had also found our rhythm and I could now anticipate his movements before he made them.

Our sessions quickly became my favorite part of the day.

Since asking Silas to give me time to move past his betrayal, our interactions had also improved. We were both making an effort to be more amicable towards one another, and the tension surrounding the group had lessened considerably.

Despite this progress, however, he still waited for me to fall asleep every night before he lifted me from my bedroll and carried me to his.

I was conveniently ignoring this, however, as I felt safe when I was wrapped in his arms, and his reassuring presence each night kept the nightmares at bay.

I was getting ready for my daily flight lesson when Emmerson approached me, pulling me from my ruminating.

"What's up, Em?" I asked as I tied the laces of my boots.

"I want to know what the endgame is, Harlowe," she said, sounding unusually serious.

I lifted my head to meet her gaze. "What do you mean?"

Her gaze flicked to Cillian for a moment before settling back on me.

"Are we staying with them?" she asked, tilting her head in Cillian's direction. "Or are we making our own way?"

I blinked in surprise, and then realization hit me. "Holy shit," I breathed, my eyes widening.

"What?" Emmerson asked, looking about confused.

"You love him, don't you?"

"What? Who?" I gave her a pointed look and her cheeks reddened.

A wide grin split my face. "You do," I said, the astonishment clear in my tone.

Emmerson groaned. "All I want to know is if we are sticking with the Cathal or cutting them loose."

"Uh-huh," I grinned.

"Harlowe," she growled. "What's the plan?"

I sighed, the excitement from my discovery evaporating as I struggled to answer the same question I had been asking myself all week.

"I don't know, Em. Kieran's planning something, and I know we'll all be dragged into it at some point. I'm unsure what to do for now. I'm still struggling to decide if the Cathal can be trusted. Ideally, we would all stay together as we make our preparations for Kieran's inevitable attack, but..." I trailed off, unable to give voice to my inner conflict.

"But... you can't trust that Silas won't turn on you again," she finished. I gave a curt nod in confirmation.

"If it helps, I think he may have learned his lesson."

My eyes widened and my mouth dropped open as I gaped at my best friend.

"I know. It was a surprise for me too," she chuckled. "Believe me, defending Silas with everything he has done was the last thing I ever thought I'd be doing. Don't get me wrong, he's still a dick and made stupid decisions based on his dick tendencies."

I couldn't help but chuckle at her apt descriptive skills.

"But watching him as he searched for a way to get you back from Kieran... I don't know Harlowe, there was just something there." Her expression turned pensive, as though trying to find the right words.

"It was like he would slay every monster and burn every kingdom until he got you back. He was a madman, deranged, his every thought consumed by you. To be honest, he was kind of unbearable to be around," she deadpanned.

My eyes darted to the man in question as he discussed something with Cillian. As though he could sense my eyes on him, he glanced toward me, and his face brightened as our gazes locked. He threw me a sly wink, and I rolled my eyes before redirecting my attention back to Emmerson.

"So, you're saying that I should cut him some slack?" I asked.

"Definitely not," she snorted. "But I no longer think he's the enemy. He still deserves to be led around by his balls for the shit he pulled, for deterrence purposes only, of course." Emmerson's eyes twinkled with mischief, and I got the impression that she very much enjoyed Silas's fall from grace.

Emmerson stood and extended her hand to me. "Come on. It's time to train. I want to test your reflexes again," she said as she pulled me to my feet.

"You're like a dog with a bone sometimes, Emmerson. I'm still sporting the bruises along my ribcage from your 'testing' two days ago," I grumbled.

"Better that than a blade, Harlowe. And since when have you been such a whinger?" she teased as she bumped me with her shoulder.

"I'm not a whinger," I muttered. "I just don't think it hurts to have a day of respite, that's all."

"No rest for the wicked, kid. Now let's go."

"Kid!" I said, aghast.

Emmerson winked and yelled, "I'll race you," before she took off sprinting towards the entrance. I immediately followed suit, and she hollered behind her, "Knew that would get you going."

Once we'd reached the surface, I found Misneach waiting for me.

"Ready for another lesson, Misneach?" I asked as I approached the colossal dragon.

The dragon huffed. **"Today we are going to eviscerate Rónán and his Cathal. Am I clear, Fire Heart?"**

"Eviscerate? That's a bit... intense, Misneach. Even for you. Don't you think you two are taking this competitiveness too far?" I asked, genuinely concerned. **"Plus, I happen to like Zeke, remember?"**

Yesterday, the two male dragons had spent the lesson trying to outmaneuver, outfly, and generally outshine the other. Given Zeke has had more training than I have, he and Rónán were ultimately victorious. Something Misneach did not stop berating me about for the entire journey back to camp.

"You can have no friends when it comes to combat, Fire Heart. Remember, he is the enemy, and we *will* prevail."

Ignoring his antics, I scaled Misneach's foreleg until I was seated comfortably between his wings. Not bothering to wait for the others to be ready, Misneach crouched low and launched himself into the sky.

"You could have waited," I grumbled.

"I will not forfeit an advantage for good manners, Fire Heart."

I rolled my eyes but didn't press the matter, knowing full well that Misneach would not be swayed. He was a formidable dragon, and that did not come without an edge.

We were soaring high above the clouds as Misneach assessed the surrounding skyline for any hidden threats. The wind tousled the small wisps of my hair that had escaped my braid, and I closed my eyes, allowing myself to enjoy the sensation.

"Pay attention, Fire Heart. You are half of this partnership and I rely on you as much as you rely on me," Misneach snapped.

"Yes, sir!" I quipped.

Misneach banked left before leveling out, allowing the air currents to carry him. In my periphery, I spotted a glint of blue as it streaked through the clouds.

"Over there," I said, pointing in the direction I had seen the beast.

"It was either Rónán or Oisín," I added.

Misneach darted in the direction I had indicated, and I readied myself for the collision.

This had been the routine all week; the dragons would break away in pairs or groups of three and would simulate aerial warfare. Each dragon and their Cathal were considered an enemy combatant, and it was up to each Cathal to take down the other. The dragons increased the stakes by trying to throw the other dragons off course.

For obvious reasons, the dragons refrained from breathing fire, much to Misneach's dismay.

As we got closer, I could see that it was Rónán and Zeke that we had locked on to.

"Remember Fire Heart, evisceration!" Misneach snarled.

Misneach flew in a direct line towards the pair, and I could see Zeke rising from his seat. Adrenaline coursed through me, building the anticipation. Misneach beat his imposing wings, and I stood from my seat before he dipped low, gliding right under the pair.

Misneach banked right, pulling off an impressive curve, and using the altitude to even out. He then let himself drop back down until he was once again level with Rónán. Flying at a dizzying speed, Misneach headed back towards the dragon and his Cathal, coming at them from the side. Misneach extended his claws, using the momentum to thrust himself forward as he gripped Rónán's midsection.

The dragon snarled in anger, but I was already moving.

I darted forward, using Misneach's neck to bring myself closer to Zeke. He was waiting for me, an affable grin plastered on his handsome face.

"Come on, Princess. Show me what you've got," he teased.

I jabbed my fist forward, landing a hit to his side, which I followed up with a jab to his abdomen.

"You know I hate it when you call me that, Zeke," I huffed as I ducked a wide punch to my right side.

"I do," he grinned.

Zeke shot his leg out, connecting with my upper thigh, and I stumbled back. I wasn't adept enough to use kicks in my attacks from this height, so it pissed me off when the others did it. It highlighted my lack of progress compared to theirs.

"Cheap shot," I muttered, but Zeke was unperturbed.

"Drop now!" Misneach shouted, and I dropped onto all fours as I wrapped my arms around his neck.

He released his hold on Rónán, and kicked off from the other dragon, sending Rónán pitching sideways. I caught sight of Zeke as he dropped back into place, retaking his position between Rónán's wings.

Misneach climbed higher until we were well above the clouds once more, before leveling out, allowing me to scramble back into position.

"That was better, Fire Heart," Misneach said, and a feeling of pride swelled inside my chest.

"Thanks, Misneach."

We drifted lazily for a moment before Misneach dove back down in pursuit of Rónán.

A dark wing caught my attention, and Misneach immediately changed course in pursuit.

"Ready, Fire Heart?"

"Ready."

Chapter Thirty-Five

"**Above or behind? Your pick, Fire Heart.**"

"**Let's go above,**" I instructed.

Misneach had been teaching me the best strategies for executing an attack during our sessions this last week, and this was one of my favorites.

He beat his massive wings as we climbed higher, using the altitude to our advantage, concealing us from our target below. Misneach used the element of surprise to maneuver into a better position until he was flying directly above the dragon, although some distance still separated us.

"**He looks so small from up here,**" I remarked, and Misneach chortled.

Misneach dipped lower, closing the distance between us.

"**I love these sneak attacks,**" I said, giddy with excitement.

"**When we get closer, I want you to drop onto Rónán's back and pull his Cathal over the edge.**"

"**What!**" I screeched, my heart rate increasing with my rising panic.

"**Don't worry, Fire Heart. I'll dip low until I'm beneath you. I'll catch you, I promise.**"

"**I don't know, Misneach, this sounds kind of risky,**" I said hesitantly.

"**It's not risky when you're as skilled as I am,**" he scoffed. "**And Rónán would never see the move coming.**" I could hear the excited anticipation in Misneach's tone. He really wanted to do this.

"**All right. But don't drop me,**" I warned.

"**Don't be ridiculous,**" Misneach huffed. "**Get into position.**"

I stood from my position and moved to the base of his wing, crouching low as we descended upon our prey. My muscles were coiled with tension, ready to spring into action at any moment. As we continued to close the distance, a feeling of unease settled over me.

"**Misneach, are you sure that's Rónán?**"

Fear prickled at the base of my spine as I made out the unmistakable feathers lining the creature's wings.

"**Roc!**" I screamed, sending the message down every connection I could feel pulsing within me.

"**Where?**" Caolán responded. The lethal tone of his voice heightened my fear.

Before I could answer, a high-pitched, ear-splitting shriek cut through the air, and it felt as though sharp claws were scraping along the inside of my mind. My hands flew up to cover my ears as I tried to block out the sound.

The enormous, feathered creature turned its head to stare at us and quickly corrected its course until it was flying straight toward us. On its back sat a cloaked warrior, and my heartbeat became erratic as I studied him.

"Please don't be him," I prayed. I had held my own against the golden-eyed man when we were on the ground, but I'd wager he was far more proficient in aerial warfare.

"**Where are you, Little One?**" Caolán demanded, and I realized that I'd forgotten to answer his earlier question in my shock.

As I glanced around, I could make out the mountains that were situated east of the ruins and relayed the information to Caolán.

"**We're coming.**"

But so were the roc.

"**I'll incinerate them before they harm you,**" Misneach snarled.

With a deep, guttural growl, Misneach arched his neck and opened his mouth wide as a low hum emanated from his throat, steadily growing louder. The surrounding air shimmered with heat, and small embers sparked from his nostrils. With an explosive roar, Misneach unleashed a torrent of deadly flames.

The roc dipped sideways, rolling into a defensive spiral, and narrowly avoided being caught in the crosshairs of Misneach's fiery exhale. I lost sight of the creature as it disappeared into the clouds, and I desperately searched the surrounding sky.

Another horrifying shriek penetrated the air, and I looked up just in time to see the underbelly of the creature as it rapidly descended upon us.

They had used my favorite maneuver against us.

I jumped to my feet and unsheathed my daggers, gripping them tightly in my hands. The warrior executed a precise leap from the back of its roc and landed with a gentle *thud* in front of me. Azure blue eyes peered out at me from the confines of the warrior's hood as they withdrew their sword.

A small mercy.

Given the warrior's stature, I was almost certain that it was a man. He charged forward, never faltering as he swung his heavy blade towards me. I ducked low to avoid the hit, and thrust my dagger out, slashing his thigh.

The man stepped back, and if the wound I had inflicted pained him, he showed no sign of it.

The roc flew close to Misneach, the dagger-like bones protruding from the tip of each wing as it angled them toward the dragon.

"**Misneach,**" I screamed as I dropped low, anticipating the dip he performed to avoid the hit.

Misneach snarled as he curved upwards, now pursuing the roc as it fled towards the heavens. I rose from my crouched position as Misneach leveled out and I glanced around, searching for my attacker.

My eyes locked with azure ones as the man stood and stalked towards me. He kicked his leg out and his foot connected with my stomach before I could defend against the hit. My breath left me in a rush as I swayed backward.

Pressing his advantage, the man jumped on top of me, pinning me beneath his heavier frame. He plucked both my daggers from my grip and tossed them to the earth below.

"**Hold on, Fire Heart,**" Misneach commanded.

"**I can't.**"

"**Then I'll catch you,**" he promised.

"You have been difficult to find, Princess," the man snarled.

"**Wait,**" I yelled as I felt Misneach leaning into a roll.

"**Fire Heart,**" Misneach growled.

"**I need to find out who sent him.**"

Misneach roared in frustration but leveled out.

"Why are you looking for me?"

A small grin lifted his lips as he said, "I think you know why. It's nothing personal," he added with a shrug.

"If I knew why you were searching for me, then I wouldn't have asked the question," I gritted out.

"The risk you pose to the realm is too great to leave things to the fates," he said.

"I'm not a risk to the realm. I would never join with the King of Netheran."

The man stared down at me intently for a moment and I used the opportunity to slide my hand down my side, retrieving the dagger I'd hidden beneath my tunic.

"I wish it were different, but we can't take that risk," he said, as he pressed the blade of his sword against my throat.

My pulse spiked and my hands trembled as the bite of steel pressed against my flesh. I willed myself to calm down and clenched my dagger tighter in my fist to stop my hand from shaking.

"Who's we?" I asked.

"The Kingdom of Vidyaa," he answered simply.

"So the attack in Valoren was sanctioned by the King of Vidyaa, then?" I pressed.

"He'll deny it. There is only a small group of us who know of the prophecy, and we were sworn to secrecy under the punishment of death."

"Why are you telling me all this?" I asked, already aware of his reasoning.

"You can't reveal my secrets when you're dead," he grinned without mirth. "Now, I need to know what the King of Netheran is planning. If you tell me, I'll make it painless, I promise," he said, tilting his head towards his blade.

Heat kissed my cheeks when Misneach sent searing fiery flames soaring over his shoulder as he tried to incinerate the man threatening my life.

"What the hell, Misneach? You could have killed me," I screamed.

"You need to have more faith in my abilities, Fire Heart. I would never endanger you. Besides, flames cannot harm you."

"That is an untested theory, Misneach! MY flames can't harm me, but there is nothing to say yours won't," I said, my voice taking on a slight note of hysteria.

Misneach rolled his eyes.

He. Rolled. His. Fucking. Eyes.

Returning my attention to the more pressing matter of the man trying to kill me, I caught sight of him clinging to Misneach's side at an awkward angle.

I didn't waste the advantage that Misneach created for me, as I jumped to my feet and dashed towards the man before he had the chance to recover his footing. I drove my dagger into his side all the way to the hilt, hoping to puncture his kidney.

A groan left the man, and I felt his blood drench my hand.

The wound would be fatal.

The man tried to pull himself upright, but he staggered back, collapsing in a heap on Misneach's back. A shriek disturbed the tense silence, and I whipped my head up to see the roc flying at speed, straight for us.

"**Drop**," Misneach ordered, and I followed without hesitation.

Misneach soared upwards, flying in the direct path of the roc. The man tumbled from his spot on Misneach's back until he reached his tail and slipped over the edge into the void below.

My attention snapped back to the impending collision as another ear-splitting shriek sounded. The roc was not diverting its path, and neither was Misneach.

"**Misneach**," I screamed, but he ignored me.

Just as the roc was coming into range, Misneach tilted his wings, adjusting his trajectory and avoiding a direct hit by mere inches.

Everything seemed to slow down around me as the roc glided by us. Misneach opened his enormous mouth and snapped his jaws around the creature's neck. A pain-filled screech left the roc before it ended abruptly as Misneach closed his jaws, snapping its neck.

The roc's lifeless body plummeted towards the ground as everything sped up again, the sound of the rushing wind blocking out the rapid beating of my heart as it pounded in my ears.

"**Don't you ever ask me to stand aside as you put your life in danger again, Fire Heart**," Misneach said in a tone so calm that an involuntary shudder ran through me.

The quiet fury behind his words made me pause, however.

"**I'm all right, Misneach**," I said in an attempt to soothe the dragon.

Whatever retort he had planned to deliver faded away, as a dozen more roc broke through the clouds, flying directly towards us.

Chapter Thirty-Six

"Oh gods," I breathed.

I darted back to my spot between Misneach's wings and scanned the horizon to see how many of the creatures made up the attacking force. I exhaled a shaky breath when I detected no more roc beyond the dozen already headed our way.

"**Where are you, Caolán?**" I asked, unable to hide the desperation in my voice.

"**Beneath you,**" he said in a measured tone.

"**Thank the gods,**" I breathed as I glimpsed his wings flying below us.

The others had come too.

Teller and Grainne appeared on our right, while Cillian and Oisín were flying close by Emmerson and Saoirse off to our left. Fionn and Niamh were flying in an attack formation with Zeke and Rónán down the center.

Up ahead, the roc broke apart, forming into pairs and scattering in all directions.

"**They're going to try to draw our attention to the lead group while the others circle us out of our line of sight,**" Caolán informed us. "**Be vigilant.**"

With that, he lurched forward, leading the charge towards the roc, flying straight at us. When he was within firing range of the winged beasts, Caolán opened his gaping maw and sent an inferno of flames sailing towards them. I could feel the intensity of the heat, even from the considerable distance that separated us, as Caolán's fiery breath roared through the air like a blazing storm.

The roc screeched as they dove and spun, desperately trying to evade the burning wind intent on ending their lives. One creature failed to react quickly enough and the destructive wave of heat caught it, turning it to ash right before my eyes. The acrid smell of burning flesh that permeated the air surrounding us told me that its rider had met with the same fate.

I didn't have long to marvel at the magnificence of the terrifying display I had just witnessed, as more roc descended from the clouds above us, just as Caolán had predicted.

I hadn't stowed as many daggers as I normally would, given our flight today was supposed to only be a training exercise. Instead, I unsheathed my short sword, conserving my remaining daggers as my last defense, and rose from my seated position on Misneach's back as I readied myself for the battle rapidly approaching.

Two roc sped in our direction, signaling that we were their intended target. Careful to avoid Misneach's muzzle, they moved into formation, one flying low while the other remained above us, intent on boxing us in.

Misneach roared, and the roc released a battle cry of their own as they moved in to attack. The roc flying low dipped its wings, and it was then that I realized it was not carrying a rider. It spiraled into a roll as it glided beneath Misneach, flying inverted as it reached its claws out, finding purchase in his flank. The dragon roared in pain and my heart hammered widely as fear for my dragon threatened to consume me.

My distraction cost me.

The roc flying above me had been carrying a warrior who now stood before me, slashing his weapon in my direction. I twisted my upper body in time to avoid the full impact of a direct hit, but the blade sliced through the flesh of my shoulder as I deflected the blow. Pain ignited at the site as blood flowed from the gash down my arm.

"Fuck," I hissed as I breathed through the pain.

"Fire Heart," Misneach shouted, just as he locked his powerful jaws on the feathered beast, trying to tear him apart, and ripped it from his body before sending it careening towards the earth.

Not wasting his advantage, the warrior thrust his sword forward, slicing it through the air as he came at me again. This time I raised my blade and repelled the strike, but the blood coating my palm made it difficult to maintain a tight grip on my short sword.

"**Drop,**" Misneach ordered, and as I did, he dipped into a roll and looped upwards as he maneuvered our position, so we were behind the remaining roc.

I glanced around for my attacker, but he was nowhere to be seen.

"**Are you all right, Fire Heart?**" Misneach asked, concern coloring his tone.

"Yes," I breathed. "**I think the warrior fell when you rolled us.**"

"**Good, that was my intention,**" Misneach huffed.

Misneach's nostrils flared, and a familiar rumbling sound started in his throat. His cavernous mouth opened and on a powerful exhale, he released a stream of searing flames that danced wildly across the sky before reaching their target.

The roc didn't even have time to wail as the heat of Misneach's flames consumed it, leaving no trace of the feathered creature in its wake.

"**How badly are you injured, Fire Heart?**" Misneach asked as he leveled out.

"**It's not too bad,**" I said. "**I just need to wrap it to stem the bleeding.**"

I removed a dagger and cut a strip of fabric from my tunic and placed it over the wound in my shoulder. With one end between my teeth and the other in my hand, I tightened the cloth to make a tourniquet. Satisfied that it would hold, I cut another strip of fabric and used it to clean up the blood that had caused my grip on my short sword to falter.

"**All right, I'm ready,**" I informed Misneach once I was done.

Misneach dove through the clouds in search of the battle that was unfolding nearby. As we cut through the clouds, Emmerson and Cillian came into view, the scales of their dragons reflecting the light of the sun. Emmerson fought off an attacker who was wielding a dagger while she remained unarmed.

My breath hitched in my throat as fear for my best friend coursed through me.

Emmerson easily deflected the hit her assailant attempted to deliver as she gripped his arm and twisted. The dagger fell from his grip and his arm fell limply to his side, clearly broken.

Without hesitation, Emmerson gripped his head between her hands and pulled it into an unnatural position. The snapping of bone reverberated around us as the warrior fell lifelessly at her feet.

Emmerson nudged him with her boot, and his body fell over the edge of Saoirse's colossal wings and plummeted to the ground below.

Cillian, who had been fighting off his own enemy, swiftly buried his blade in the midsection of his opponent before withdrawing it. The warrior swayed on his feet and then tumbled off Oisín's back. Cillian turned to face Emmerson and shouted something indiscernible to her. A broad grin was her only reply.

Out of nowhere, another roc carrying a rider flew towards us, the sound of its flapping wings my only warning.

Moving swiftly, the warrior flung themselves free from the creature's back, then rolled and landed in a crouch at the base of Misneach's neck. As the hood of the warrior's cloak slid down, a woman's rounded face peeked out. Her ash-blond hair became tousled as the wind whipped it around her head.

In a graceful motion, the woman stood up from her crouched position and retrieved the sword from behind her back. I extended my hands around the middle of my back and retrieved two daggers, deciding to forego my short sword.

"You don't look like much," sneered the woman. "How can you possibly be capable of bringing destruction to the realm?"

"Let's find out, shall we?" I challenged, and she smirked.

With agile movements, the woman closed the distance between us and swung her sword in a sweeping arc toward my head. Steel met steel as I raised my daggers, and my hands trembled with the force of her blow.

The woman pulled back, only to charge at me again. This time, she struck low as she sliced her sword through the air. Unlike her previous hit, this one found its way into the flesh of my thigh, and I hissed in pain as I retreated.

A series of precise and calculated strikes followed me as the woman sought to push her advantage. The next hit was so brutal, she dislodged a dagger from my death grip.

I didn't hesitate as I reached for my boot and gripped the hilt of the dagger that was hidden there.

With a flick of my wrist, I sent the dagger sailing through the air towards her, and it landed with a wet *thud* in her abdomen. The woman inhaled sharply, and her hand instinctively went to her wound. She gripped the hilt of the dagger that was protruding from her body and grimaced as she tugged on it.

"Now, Fire Heart," Misneach ordered, and I darted forward.

I lifted my leg and kicked out, my boot connecting with the dagger, and a sickening tearing sound met my ears as the blade penetrated deeper, butting through muscle and tissue. A choked cry left the woman's lips, and she staggered back.

"**Drop,**" Misneach yelled, as he tilted his wings and sent the woman flying into the open sky.

I took a moment to catch my breath before scrambling back into position between Misneach's wings.

"**All right, Fire Heart?**"

"**Yes,**" I said with a ragged exhale.

Glancing out over the horizon, I caught sight of Silas and Caolán. They were fighting off two roc while another circled behind them.

"**Get to Silas now!**" I screamed, and Misneach dove with lightning speed as he barreled towards them.

"**I'm going to drop onto Caolán's back, so move in close Misneach,**" I instructed.

Misneach flew up beside Caolán and leveled out.

I sprang from my seat and ran towards Misneach's flank, where I took a running leap and launched myself through the air. I landed with a *thud* and straightened as I turned to face the fighter attacking from behind.

Without thinking, I released a vicious battle cry and raised my hands. Flames burst free from my palms, sailing towards the roc and its rider, who thought to take advantage while Silas was distracted.

As the flames receded and I lowered my hands, I was panting heavily, sweat coating my forehead from the exertion. When I turned around to see where the two remaining roc were, stunned silence greeted me.

There was no sign of the roc who had been engaging Silas and Caolán moments before.

Silas was staring at me; his mouth agape as he took me in, but thankfully, untouched by my flames.

"Harlowe," he breathed. "What the fuck was that?"

Chapter Thirty-Seven

The realization of what I had just done slowly caught up with me.

The secret I had revealed.

I swallowed the knot forming in my throat as I turned to face Silas.

"Later," I said. "We have to eliminate the others."

"The others," Silas said. "What others?" He spread his arms wide and peered around.

I did the same, not finding any more roc surrounding us.

"What the fuck?" I muttered to myself.

"You incinerated them," Misneach said with pride. **"All of them."**

"You took them all out, Harlowe," Silas said, voicing what Misneach had already revealed.

Nausea churned in my stomach, and I fought the urge to vomit. "Oh," I said weakly.

"Oh," Silas repeated, somewhere between awe, confusion, and anger.

Or maybe all three.

Emmerson saved me from having to think of something else to say when she and Saoirse approached us, Cillian in tow.

"Fucking fire power, Harlowe!" she hooted, pumping her fist in the air. "Did you see that?" she asked Cillian from the seat of her dragon. He grunted in confirmation.

"Now I understand what you meant, Emmerson," Zeke said with a broad grin as he joined us. "That was amazing."

I didn't need to see Silas's face to sense his anger beginning to win out over all his other emotions.

"Harlowe," he growled.

I wasn't about to get into an argument with him while airborne, so I marched towards Caolán's flank and said to Misneach, **"Catch me."**

I stepped from the side of the massive dragon and Misneach darted forward. I landed with a light *thud* before standing and making my way back to my seat.

"A little warning next time," Misneach huffed.

"Shit, that was badass," Fionn called out to me, as Teller added, "And hot."

I wasn't in the mood for joking, however. As soon as we returned to camp, I knew Silas would demand answers.

"You don't have to tell him your secrets, Fire Heart," Misneach said in a tone intended to reassure me.

"It's a little late for that, I think, Misneach," I laughed without mirth.

I always knew I would have to tell Silas and the others about the true extent of my connection to the dragons. However, I wanted it to be on my terms, and only when I was sure they could be trusted.

We flew in silence as I stewed over the situation and what I would be forced to disclose. When Misneach started to descend, I was surprised to realize that we had made it back to camp already.

"I will stay by your side, Fire Heart," Misneach growled.

"It's all right Misneach. I'd prefer not to have an audience for this conversation, anyway."

"Harlowe," Silas barked as Caolán landed with a *thud*.

Misneach curled his enormous body around mine, his head coming to rest beside my shoulder as he bared his teeth and snarled at Silas.

"Tell the General to watch the way he speaks to you, Fire Heart," Misneach said, venom dripping from his every word.

"I can handle Silas," I said, really hoping that was the truth.

Silas was pacing in front of me, his agitation emanating from his every pore.

As the others reached camp, they promptly excused themselves until there was only Silas, me, and the dragons remaining. I gave Misneach a pointed look, and he leveled Silas with a parting snarl before launching himself into the sky. The other dragons quickly followed, leaving me alone with the man on the verge of exploding.

I pulled my hair free of my braid and raked my fingers through the copper strands as Silas glowered at me.

"Say whatever you have to say, Silas," I sighed.

"Tell me what's going on," he gritted out.

"I can manifest flames," I said simply.

"Yes, I got that, thank you, Harlowe. I want to know how. More importantly, I want to know why this is the first time I am learning about it."

Silas's words were measured, but I could hear the undertone of fury he was trying very hard to contain.

Sighing, I gestured towards the woods, knowing I could no longer stall this discussion.

After finding a rock that looked comfortable enough to use as a seat, I waited for Silas to join me. He crossed his arms over his chest as he leaned against a tree, waiting for me to start.

"Kieran started the Skirmish of Power," I said.

"What are you talking about? He aided your father in defending Valoren."

I recalled the conversation I'd had with Kieran where he revealed he had been the one to manipulate the other kingdoms into attacking Valoren.

"He was that desperate to wed you?" Silas sneered.

"There's more. He'd learned of a prophecy that suggested I would be his equal in power, and that my power would strengthen his own if I joined with him. It's why he wanted to wed me so badly. He wanted the marriage vows to be fortified by a blood oath so that I could never use my power against him."

"That's a bit of a stretch. How could he be sure it was you?" Silas asked.

"The prophecy referred to the Daughter of War and Peace, my parents' kingdoms," I said, glancing up at him. His jaw was clenched, but he waved his hand, indicating for me to continue.

"After meeting me, Kieran was certain I was the one he needed."

"Why?"

"When we met, we had an instant connection. Something in him called to me and it was the same for him," I explained.

Silas growled as he pushed off the tree and stalked towards me. He crouched down in front of me, so he was at eye level with me.

"An instant connection," he said harshly.

"Yes," I said, lifting my chin in defiance. "It was like a tugging sensation, drawing me towards him."

"Is that so?" Silas said darkly. "Even though you were already tethered to me?"

"What are you talking about?" I asked, narrowing my eyes at him.

"Don't fucking play games with me, Harlowe. You know what I'm talking about," he snapped.

Silas inhaled a calming breath before he continued. "When you tried to extinguish my life by thrusting your little dagger into my throat on that very first day, I felt it then," he said, as his gaze raked over me with hunger.

"That sensation of lightning racing over my flesh where our bodies made contact. It was there from the very first touch, and I know you felt it too," he said as his eyes darkened. "It was written all over your face as your pretty, green eyes widened and filled with awe."

I inhaled sharply.

He had felt it, too.

Silas smirked at my reaction. "It made me ravenous for you, and I felt compelled to be near you, to touch you, to claim you, to make you mine," he purred.

Heat flooded my core, and I squeezed my thighs together to relieve the tension. An action that did not go unnoticed by Silas if the wolfish grin splitting his gorgeous face was any indication.

"It's why you can't get enough of me, either. Why you're a glutton for my cock."

I cleared my throat and said, "We're getting off topic."

Will I go back and scrutinize every interaction we've ever had?

Absolutely.

But the sex fiend standing in front of me didn't need to know that.

Silas chuckled darkly and leaned in to whisper against my ear. "Don't you ever claim to share a connection with another man again. If you do, I will take you far away where no one will ever find us. I'll tie you to my bed and fuck you senseless until the only thing you can remember is my cock, and how much you love it filling your holes."

I knew I should be outraged by Silas's threat, one which I didn't doubt he would follow through.

However, my body didn't quite get the message as all my brain cells abandoned logic and reason as they filled my vision with filthy images of Silas and the ruthlessness with which he'd own me.

"You're vile," I chastised, but it came out breathy, wanton, betraying the current state of my arousal.

Silas grinned, and then he pushed up from his position, retaking his spot against the tree.

"Continue," he ordered.

I needed a moment to regain my focus. "It's why I fled into the Forest of Nightmares," I eventually said. "To search for the Lost Witch. I heard she was a powerful truth-sayer, and I needed to verify Kieran's prophecy."

"And?" Silas pressed.

"When Emmerson and I were attacked by that Harpy, we were losing, and badly. That was until I burst into flames and incinerated her," I said, exhaling a long breath. "So, I figured he was onto something."

"You've known about this fire power since then?" Silas asked in a dangerous tone.

I lifted my head to meet his gaze. "Yes."

"Don't think I missed how Emmerson and Zeke were both up to date with what's been going on with you either," he said, his anger returning.

"I trust them," I said, shrugging my shoulders.

"For Fuck's sake, Harlowe," he growled. "When will you let go of this?"

"Who said I will?" I challenged.

Silas resumed his pacing. "I've already apologized to you, Harlowe," he barked. "I've tried giving you space. Hell, I've even tried fucking it out of your system. Tell me what it will take for you to get over this because I'm a hair's breadth away from stealing you away and forcing the issue," he bit out as he tugged roughly on his hair.

"Yes, that'll help," I scoffed.

"Harlowe," he said through gritted teeth. "Things need to change. You and I," — he said gesturing between us — "are it for each other. You know it, just as I do. And I'll never let you go, so why don't we skip the sulking and stop being so fucking miserable all the time," he scowled, his chest heaving as he tried to keep a hold of his anger.

"And what? I have no say in the matter?" I asked as I folded my arms over my chest.

"Sure, so long as the end result remains the same," he deadpanned.

"For fuck's sake Silas! You can't just command someone to love you again."

I took a sharp breath as the impact of my words sank in. Silas appeared momentarily stunned, then a wicked grin slowly appeared on his face.

Well, fuck!

I was not ready to unpack the word vomit that had just escaped my mouth.

"That's not what I... I didn't mean... I..." I couldn't form words with the way Silas was looking at me. It was masculine pride mixed with ravenous hunger and it made me incoherent, apparently.

Heat stained my cheeks, and I averted my gaze. "Let's get back on topic," I mumbled.

"Of course. Go on," Silas said, the smirk clear in his tone.

"Emmerson and I eventually found the Lost Witch, and she told me the prophecy was true, and that I was made to balance out Kieran's power."

"What do you mean, balance out his power?" Silas asked, all traces of his earlier amusement gone.

So I told Silas everything.

I told him how the fates created me because nature required balance. And how I would either side with Kieran and bring about the ruination of our realm or stand against him and somehow stop it. I told him how I was the conduit of dragon's flames, which was why I could communicate with them all despite not sharing a bond.

I let it all spill from me, and it was surprisingly liberating. I still did not know if I could trust Silas, but keeping this secret from him and the others had been taxing.

Silas remained quiet after I had finished, which had me fidgeting as I waited for him to say something.

"So?" I asked, impatience getting the best of me.

"So," he drawled, "you need to practice. You need to incorporate wielding into your training regime until you have complete control over your power."

"That's it?" I asked as I gaped at him.

"What else is there to say?" he asked.

"You heard the part about how I might join forces with Kieran and destroy the realm, right? It's kind of why people are trying to kill me."

"That won't happen," Silas said confidently.

"Why not?"

"First of all, I know you, and at your core, you're a good person. You'd never willingly hurt others. You refused to allow Misneach to harm anyone in Pyrithia so that you could escape, despite not owing them anything."

"You were holding Emmerson prisoner, remember?" I scowled.

"Yes, and you wouldn't leave her, even if you should."

"And second?" I asked.

"And second," he purred. "You belong to me, Little Menace, whether or not you're ready to acknowledge that. I will never let another man have you. I will never give up what is mine. So no, you won't join forces with Kieran, because I'd never allow it."

Exasperated, I stood from my seat and stalked away from him. "You're incorrigible," I muttered as I passed him.

His low chuckle followed me as I headed back to camp.

Chapter Thirty-Eight

Silas had become unbearable ever since he decided I needed to incorporate wielding into my training regime. Despite my insistence that I could not call up my flames on demand, he had been forcing me to take part in lessons all week. Everyone, including Everly, had been trying to coax my flames free, but their efforts proved unsuccessful.

Silas had been unwilling to accept that whatever power I housed was unlike anything else in the realm, and conventional teachings were not the answer. Hell, Emmerson, and Zeke had been training me the same way for years in the hope I would be able to manifest fórsa.

However, even I had to admit that I was becoming concerned about my inability to manifest my power. I had tried to replicate the process of grounding myself with the earth and finding my center, just as I had done to escape the maze, but even that had failed me.

The current experiment consisted of having the dragons try to guide me. However, it became clear very early on that they had no idea what to do, either.

"**Do you call it from your belly?**" Rónán asked. "**Maybe if you open your mouth wider and put your full force behind your exhale, something will stir.**"

"She is not a dragon," Misneach huffed.

"Obviously," Oisín mumbled.

"Oisín," Cillian snapped. "That's not helpful."

The dragon had the good grace to look chastised. He had not forgiven me for assuming he had been the one mouthing off the first day I had heard them all speak instead of Rónán.

The dragon was close to redefining the term 'grudge'.

"Let's try this again," Cillian said with an encouraging smile. "What did you feel each time you have called on your flames previously?"

I considered Cillian's words for a moment before answering. "Fearful, desperate, and... anger," I shrugged.

Emmerson snorted. "Maybe try picturing one of the many stupid things that Silas has done since you met him and see if that ignites a murderous inferno."

Misneach chortled, and Teller laughed outright. The others were sensible enough to conceal their amusement as Silas glared at Emmerson.

"Em," Cillian warned.

"What? It's not like she hasn't got plenty of material to draw on," she said, batting her eyelashes at him.

Silas cursed under his breath and ran a hand through his hair. My lips pulled up in a small smirk that threatened to break out into a full-blown grin. It was always entertaining to see Emmerson baiting Silas. It was quickly becoming her favorite pastime.

"Little One," Caolán said, redirecting my attention. **"Focus on your breathing and clear your mind."**

I closed my eyes and inhaled deeply, doing as he suggested. As air filled my lungs, I concentrated on the sounds around me. There was a slight breeze, and I could hear the leaves on the trees rustling as they swayed in time to the dance of the wind.

As I exhaled, I let the noises of the forest-dwelling creatures penetrate my senses. Small creatures were scurrying about on the forest floor, likely foraging for food. The melodic sound of birds singing was the next thing to reach me. Bright, uplifting music played in the air as the birds welcomed the day and basked in the warmth of the early morning sun.

A low growl greeted me next, followed by a low whine as one of the predators that called the forest home asserted its dominance.

Feeling much more settled now, I opened my eyes to see everyone had gone quiet and was watching me expectantly. My cheeks flushed under the intensity of their gazes, and I shifted nervously.

"Ignore them," Saoirse encouraged. **"Just focus on the task at hand."**

My hands trembled at my sides, and I clenched them into fists as I closed my eyes once more. I exhaled a controlled breath and let my mind search every recess of my body for the power lying dormant within me.

The air crackled with tension around me as I felt the weight of the eyes on me.

"Concentrate," Grainne said in a hard tone.

"It is easier said than done," I gritted out.

"Leave her be," Niamh interjected before Misneach could snap at the amber dragon.

A soft hum stirred within me, and to my horror, it was coming from my belly as Rónán had suggested.

"Please don't let this power emanate from my mouth. My hands really would suffice," I pleaded to any god listening.

I really didn't want to go around breathing on my enemies in order to end their lives. It was awesome when the dragons did it... if I did it, however... I couldn't imagine it having the same effect.

The dragons chuckled around me as Rónán said, **"Told you."**

The humming intensified and yet, I still couldn't grasp the power it was trying to offer me. Frustration crept in, and I furrowed my brow as I doubled my efforts. Sweat beaded on my forehead and my limbs trembled under the exertion.

"Harlowe?" I heard Silas ask, and Misneach snarled at him, not wanting him to divert my attention.

I pushed forward, desperately seeking to connect with the well of power vibrating to life inside me.

"Come on," I said as I gritted my teeth.

It was as if an invisible barrier stood between me and the power source, hindering the free flow of magic that remained stubbornly out of reach.

My breathing became labored as I continued the internal war I was waging, once again delving into the recesses of my body and mind for any sign that my efforts would prove fruitful.

"Fire Heart," Misneach breathed, and I snapped my eyes open to see a small flame flicker to life in my palm.

One moment, the flame was glowing brightly, dancing in the wind as it reached towards the sky. And the next, it flickered once, twice, before fizzling out and receding into my palm. Something strained against my chest, clamping tight, as I struggled to draw in a breath.

My hand flew to the site, and I stumbled backward. A figure darted towards me, but I couldn't make out who it was as my vision blurred and

I fell to the ground.

"Harlowe? Harlowe, can you hear me? Just breathe, Princess." Zeke's comforting words floated to me and I inhaled, forcing air into my starved lungs.

Misneach's enormous head came into view above me, snarling at everyone as a sense of helplessness coursed through him.

Zeke continued to encourage me to breathe as he rubbed soothing circles on my shoulders. The tightness in my chest slowly ebbed and my breathing returned to normal. I lifted my head, and my eyes clashed with rich brown ones and the storm churning within their molten depths.

Silas's gaze dipped to where Zeke was still stroking me, and his upper lip curled into a snarl.

"Fuck off, Silas," Emmerson barked. "She was ours first asshole."

Sensing the impending explosion that was brewing between the pair, I sat up, gaining their attention.

"How are you feeling?" Emmerson asked.

I took a moment to assess my body before answering. "I think I'm all right."

There was a collective exhale of breath and my heart warmed at the concern etched on the faces of those who surrounded me.

"What happened?" Silas asked gently.

"I'm not sure exactly," I muttered. "I could feel the power, sense it thrumming to life as I called it to me. But something was preventing it from reaching me." I furrowed my brows, not understanding what had happened myself.

"Like a shield or something?" Cillian asked.

"I guess. Whatever it was, it blocked me from reaching my power and manifesting my flames."

"You had a tiny baby flame for a minute there," Teller said in encouragement, and everyone turned to scowl at him.

"What? It was supposed to be a compliment," he defended.

"Thanks, Teller," I chuckled, and the others relaxed. Teller grinned at me, looking satisfied with himself.

Silas helped me to my feet, and I straightened my tunic.

"I don't know what else to try," Silas said, scrubbing a palm down his face. He looked tired, defeated even.

"**There is always the Ancient,**" Oisín muttered to himself.

"**No,**" Misneach growled. "**It is too dangerous.**"

K.J. JOHNSON

"Misneach," Caolán said gently.
"I said no," Misneach snarled.
"What is the Ancient?" I asked.
And all eyes turned to me.

Chapter Thirty-Nine

I hadn't meant to say that out loud.

I'd hoped to keep the discussion contained to the dragons. However, judging from the gazes fixed on me, that choice was no longer available.

"What did you say, Harlowe?" Silas asked, his eyes narrowed on me.

"The dragons," I said and gestured towards them. "They seem to think they have a solution."

Silas tilted his head in Caolán's direction, which told me he was now communicating with his dragon.

The rest followed suit shortly after.

"It is too dangerous, Fire Heart. I will not risk your life for such a reckless feat. With time, you will learn to wield your flames on your own. You just need to be patient," Misneach implored.

"Shouldn't I at least have all the information before making my decision?" I asked, raising a brow. "And it will be *my* decision, Misneach, not yours."

My dragon huffed in frustration but did not challenge me further.

Caolán straightened, and I felt the weight of Silas's eyes on me.

"The Ancient," he started, "is a dragon who lives within the most isolated area of the Mountains of Dragonia. We believe he is the first of our kind and is extremely powerful. If anyone can help you access your dragon flames, it will be him."

"That doesn't sound very dangerous," I mused. "What's the catch?"

"The catch," Misneach snapped, "is that he no longer lives among dragonfolk. He's become a recluse; few who've sought him out survived to tell the tale."

"Oh," I mumbled.

"Oh, indeed," Misneach snarled in Oisín's direction. He was definitely on Misneach's shit list for suggesting this.

"When you say he's a recluse..." I murmured.

"I mean, he lives in an area so inhospitable that even other dragons cannot reach it. We can only take you part of the way, then you must continue on foot. And that, Fire Heart, is where the true danger lies," Misneach said ominously.

"How can he, a dragon, live in an area inaccessible to other dragons? That makes little sense," I mused.

"No one knows," Caolán said. "All I can tell you is that he lives high in the mountains where dragons can't perch."

"He is the first dragon. The full extent of his power is unknown," Saoirse added.

"We can bring you to the rocky outcrop lower on the mountain, where it is still safe for us to land. From there, you will have to scale the rest of the mountain without our aid," Caolán said.

"And what dangers lurk beyond the outcrop?" I asked Misneach.

"The terrain, for one. I mentioned the area was inhospitable, did I not?"

"You did. What else is out there?"

"Therein lies the danger, Fire Heart, the area is unknown to us," Misneach finished

I released a long breath.

"Say I could reach the Ancient without getting myself killed," I started.

Misneach snarled, his agitation clear.

"How would he be able to help me access my power?" I asked, ignoring Misneach's antics.

I knew he was only trying to protect me, but I wasn't feeling too confident that my power would manifest on its own. Whatever was blocking me from accessing it had nearly killed me.

"We can't answer that, Little One because we simply do not know. Like Saoirse said, the extent of his power is unknown. If it can be done, it is he who can do it," Caolán finished.

"This whole one-sided conversation thing is really annoying," Emmerson said. "Can someone fill in the gaps for the rest of us? Who is the first and what power is unknown?" she said, placing her hands on her hips.

"Sorry," I said, and quickly caught them up.

"So what are you thinking, Harlowe?" Teller asked.

I cast a glance in Misneach's direction. His anger was still thrumming strongly down the bond and there was no mistaking what he wanted me to do.

"I'm not sure we have the time to wait around while I try to figure this out on my own," I confessed. "Kieran is coming for me, and Vidyaa is clearly not a fan."

Emmerson snorted and Silas stiffened, his eyes turning hard and unforgiving.

"If I can't gain control soon, it may be too late," I said. I ran a hand through my hair, suddenly exhausted.

Misneach crouched low before he launched himself into the sky. Pain erupted behind my ribcage at the thought I had disappointed him.

"He is not disappointed," Niamh soothed. **"He fears for your safety. That is not the same thing."**

"All right, when do we leave?" Emmerson asked. I gave her a small smile of gratitude.

The dragons shifted uncomfortably, and I tensed, sensing I would not like what they said next.

"It's a journey you will need to make on your own, Little One," Caolán said, breaking the tension. **"It's been over a century since anyone reached the Ancient. He might not react kindly if a group of Cathal swarmed him. There is a reason he removed himself from the company of others."**

Just... Perfect.

"No fucking way!" Silas seethed, obviously having heard Caolán's last comment.

He stormed towards me, eyes narrowed and fixed on me. Anger radiated from him in waves, and I took an involuntary step back before I caught myself.

Silas planted himself in front of me, his jaw clenched and his chest heaving. "There is no way I am letting you go without me," he hissed.

"It's not exactly up to you," I spat, pissed at myself for my moment of weakness.

Silas quirked a brow. "Try again Harlowe, and this time mean it."

"You heard what Caolán said —"

"And you heard me just fine. It's. Not. Fucking. Happening."

"Silas," I whined. I was beyond frustrated with him and honestly, I felt like I was on the verge of a breakdown, he had worked himself under my skin so deeply.

Exhaling a controlled breath before I made a fool of myself, I lifted my chin and leveled him with a challenging glare. "It is not your place to intervene, Silas."

"Not my place," he chuckled, without amusement. He took a step closer to me until we were chest-to-chest. "You. Are. Mine. Little Menace. Mine to protect. Mine to own. Mine," he said in a tone so rough liquid heat pooled between my thighs.

"Umm," Cillian said, clearing his throat. "Should we leave?"

I sucked in a breath and took a step back, creating some distance between us. Silas had the infuriating ability to block out everything else around me, making him the center of my focus. His lips curved in a seductive smirk as if he sensed where my thoughts had traveled.

"Not before someone tells me what the fuck is going on. Harlowe?" Emmerson demanded.

Diverting my attention from the sinfully delicious man before me, I flicked my gaze to Emmerson.

"Caolán says I have to make the journey on my own and Silas is insisting he accompany me," I sighed.

"Ah, I don't think so. If anyone is going with Harlowe, it'll be me," she said, pointing her finger towards her chest.

"Hey!" Zeke protested, but Emmerson just ignored him.

"Not happening," Silas said, folding his arms.

"Oh, really?" Emmerson drawled as she withdrew a dagger.

And then utter chaos erupted.

Chapter Forty

As soon as Emmerson had withdrawn her dagger, I'd stepped to the side, fully aware of her intentions. I was certain she wouldn't actually impale Silas.

Well, almost certain.

Luckily for Silas, he appeared to have deduced her plan too, as he easily deflected her shot with a dagger of his own.

I hadn't even seen him unsheathe it.

Now Teller, Fionn, and I were watching on as Cillian played the intermediary. Zeke, who knew better, was relaxing by a tree, enjoying the show.

"Should we do something?" Fionn asked.

There was a moment of silence before Teller and I responded at the same time. "Nah," we said, and all three of us burst out laughing.

"Why did the dragons have to agree that one person could accompany you," Fionn muttered, as he pulled out his blade to sharpen it. "Surely they have spent enough time with this pair to know that wouldn't help the situation." Teller grunted in agreement.

"Em, you need to calm down," Cillian said, frustrated.

Emmerson stilled before rounding on Cillian. Zeke and I shared a brief look before we both scrambled to our feet and raced towards Emmerson.

"All right Em," Zeke said as he reached her, pulling her towards him by her waist. "You will definitely regret it if you murder Cillian."

"Me? What the hell did I do?" Cillian asked as he threw his hands in the air.

"Actually, I think it would be extremely satisfying," Emmerson hissed.

"Em, you're being unreasonable," Cillian huffed. Zeke and I both glared at him. The man had a death wish.

"Let's all take a moment," I suggested, attempting to calm things down. Zeke and I led Emmerson back over to the others, putting as much distance as possible between her, Silas, and Cillian.

"For someone as intelligent as Cillian," Teller murmured, "he sure can be stupid."

"Even I'm not that stupid," Fionn added.

I glanced back toward Silas and Cillian, who were in the middle of an animated discussion.

The sound of beating wings filled the clearing, and I knew without having to look that it was Misneach.

"I'll be back," I said.

Misneach settled on the ground, and I sat between his forelegs, resting my back against the hard scales of his chest.

"Are you all right?" I asked my dragon.

"Define all right?" he grunted.

"I know it's not what you wanted, Misneach, but I have to try. Kieran is only getting stronger and if I am to stand a chance against him, I not only need to have access to my power, but I need to master it as well."

Misneach sighed. **"I understand Fire Heart. I just can't stand the thought of you going anywhere I cannot protect you. The last time that happened, you were betrayed, and I could not shield you."**

I placed my hand on Misneach's leg, offering what comfort I could.

"What have I missed?" he asked, changing the subject.

I gave Misneach a quick run-down of what Caolán had said and how Emmerson and Silas were now vying for the role of my companion.

"I loathe to admit it, but the General might be the better choice here."

Surprise flittered through me, and I turned to face my dragon.

"Don't look at me like that. As resourceful as the hellion is, the General has been training Cathal in the ways of dragons for many, many years. If anyone can guide you through a meeting with the Ancient, it's him."

I considered Misneach's words and quickly realized that he was right. Groaning, I ran my hands through my hair, knowing Emmerson would not take this well.

"Good luck," Misneach chuckled.

"Where are those protective instincts now?" I grumbled as I stood. This only made him laugh harder.

I walked towards Emmerson, nervous tension settling heavily in my gut.

"Em," I squeaked.

Clearing my throat, I tried again. "Em, Misneach, and I have been speaking, and he just made a valid point."

"Don't make me the scapegoat," he groaned.

"It *was* your suggestion," I hissed.

From my peripheral vision, I could see Silas and Cillian making their way toward us, having realized something of importance was being discussed.

"He suggested maybe Silas might be the better option on this occasion."

Emmerson's mouth dropped open and Silas grinned as he sidled up next to me.

"Hear me out," I continued when I saw she was about to argue. "He suggested that because of Silas's experience training Cathal in dragon bonding and how to interpret different dragon behaviors, he might be best placed to guide me should the Ancient not be inclined to help me. And you know how much he dislikes Silas, so it's not something he would suggest lightly."

Silas cocked a brow and folded his arms over his chest.

I shrugged. "It's hardly a secret."

Emmerson tilted her head to the side, contemplating my words.

When she returned her gaze to mine, I knew she had come to the same realization I had.

"All right Harlowe, he makes a valid point."

Cillian's jaw dropped, clearly shocked by Emmerson's concession.

"That is literally the same argument I made, and you bit my head off," he growled.

"Really?" Zeke asked. "Do you want to die today?"

"You," — Emmerson said, pointing towards Cillian — "were not very polite about it." She leveled him with a withering glare before tossing her chocolate-brown hair over her shoulder.

Cillian muttered something incoherent but did not press the issue.

Rounding on Silas, Emmerson leveled him with a glare that promised death. "If you fail to keep her safe, I will find you, and I will kill you. If she is returned with even a single hair out of place, I swear to the gods, Silas, your end will follow."

Silas just chuckled before bowing low. "I give you my word, Emmerson. On my life," he said, his fist clenched over his heart.

"I'm glad we understand each other." Turning to me, Emmerson asked, "So, when do we leave?"

"I guess there is no point in delaying." I glanced toward Misneach, who gave me a small nod.

I turned back to the group, seeing their expectant faces.

"Tomorrow."

Chapter Forty-One

Three days had passed since we'd left the ruins and began our journey towards the Mountains of Dragonia. We'd had to make a detour along the way as the others would be staying at a campsite the Cathal were familiar with while they waited for Silas and me to return. The camp was situated between the border of Elysara and Pyrithia, which provided some comfort that the others would be safe until our return.

If we returned, I reminded myself.

"You will return, Fire Heart," Misneach growled. **"Your story does not end here."**

"Remember what I said, Silas," Emmerson warned, for what had to be the hundredth time.

"How could I forget when you have been reminding me incessantly?" Silas grumbled.

"What was that?" Emmerson snapped.

"I said you have my word, Emmerson."

I stifled a laugh. It was good to know that even the mighty Cathal was not immune to Emmerson's wiles.

"If he gives you any trouble, send word through Misneach," she whispered in my ear.

"I'll be fine," I said, reassuring her.

"Ready?" Silas asked once Emmerson had triple-checked my pack.

"As I'll ever be."

Silas extended his hand toward me, and I hesitated a moment before placing my own in his.

"This should be interesting if nothing else," Misneach chortled.

Silas led me around to Misneach's side and held my pack while I climbed on his back. Settled between his wings, I reached down and accepted the slight burden from his outstretched hand. The familiar tingling sensation that always coursed through me whenever our bodies touched sparked to life and I quickly withdrew my hand, muttering my thanks.

Silas shook his head as he chuckled. Once he was seated between Caolán's outstretched wings, both dragons crouched low before launching themselves into the sky.

We had been soaring through the clouds for hours when Misneach finally dipped his wings, signaling our descent.

"Caolán says we will make camp here for the night," Misneach advised.

I sighed in relief. I was more than ready to stretch my legs.

When my feet connected with the earth, however, I struggled to stay upright as my muscles locked, protesting the long flight.

Groaning, I looked about, detecting the sound of rushing water nearby.

"I'm going to find a place to bathe," I told Silas.

"Don't wander too far away," he said, voice stern.

I rolled my eyes, not bothering to answer.

I meandered through the woods, inhaling the smell of pine cones as I hummed to myself. It was the first time I had been alone in days. Emmerson had been hovering around me constantly as she struggled with the knowledge that she would not be accompanying me on this journey. I loved her for it, but it was nice to have a moment for myself.

As I stepped through the tree line, a glistening pool came into view. It looked inviting and promised my aching muscles some much-needed relaxation. A short distance away, a small waterfall cascaded over the edge of a peaked hill, not quite large enough to be considered a mountain. I could see an opening nestled beneath the shimmering curtain of water, and it immediately piqued my interest.

Eager to explore my surroundings, I quickly discarded my clothing and waded into the refreshing depths of the pool. The water was biting against my heated flesh, but the further I strode in, the warmer it became.

I kept going until my entire body was completely submerged up to my neck, allowing my muscles to gradually relax. I sighed in contentment. This was pure bliss.

Dipping my head below the water, I sliced through the pool toward the waterfall. As I emerged, my wet hair clung to my forehead, and I ran my hands through it, brushing it out of my face.

The waterfall before me was like a silken veil, flowing gracefully from the hillside, creating a beautiful contrast to the rugged rocks and earth that made up the landscape.

As I crossed through the natural screen concealing the cavern beyond, the subtle scent of moss and earth filled my nostrils, and my skin pebbled as the cool, damp air of the cave caressed my flesh. The sound of rushing water became softer, creating a serene ambiance that enveloped the darkened space.

Tiny insects glowed brightly along the walls of the cave, giving the space an ethereal feeling. The cavern expanded into a chamber of breathtaking beauty as hundreds of stalactites hung like crystalline chandeliers from the ceiling, their tips capturing droplets of water that shone like tiny diamonds.

I stood in awe, taking in the majestic beauty of nature before my curiosity got the best of me and I ventured further into the cave. The clear waters around me formed a natural mirror, capturing the light from above and reflecting it around the cavern.

A small alcove peeking out from the stones surrounding the pool caught my attention, and I swam towards it before seating myself on the bench it housed.

This place was truly stunning.

"Exquisite," I mumbled to myself.

"Yes, it is," a gravelly male voice reverberated around the space.

I had been so caught up in the magic of the cavern that I had failed to detect Silas entering the cave. When I turned to look at him, however, he was not looking at the enchanting spectacle surrounding us.

His gaze was locked on me.

My cheeks heated, and I diverted my attention, only to realize that my breasts were on full display as I sat above the water's surface. I slipped off the bench and submerged myself below the water. Not that it did much good, considering the crystal-clear water that surrounded me.

Silas chuckled darkly as he waded through the water towards me.

When he reached me, his hand darted out, gripping my waist as he tugged me to him.

"What's wrong, Little Menace? It's not like I haven't seen it all before," he purred against the shell of my ear.

An involuntary shiver escaped me, and it was then that I realized Silas was completely naked as his erect cock strained against my stomach.

"You're naked," I hissed.

"Very astute observation, Harlowe," he said, cocking an eyebrow as his eyes twinkled with mirth. "Like what you see?" he whispered huskily.

My gaze raked down his body greedily.

I did. Very much so.

Swallowing audibly, I asked, "What are you doing here?"

Silas lifted a shoulder in a lazy shrug. "Same as you."

"You couldn't wait until I was done?" I challenged.

"Why would I do that when the view is so much better when you're present?"

My cheeks flushed again, and Silas lowered his lips until they were hovering above mine. "You're a temptress, Little Menace. Especially when your cheeks heat with need," he said roughly.

"And what about your need, Silas?" I whispered against his lips.

"My need for you will never be satiated, Little Menace. Whenever you are near, my cock throbs, begging me to take you and bury myself so deep inside you, you'll never get rid of me."

I inhaled sharply, his wicked words going straight to my core.

Silas pressed his lips against mine, tentative and gentle at first. When I kissed him back, Silas growled low in his throat before devouring me. His kiss was devastating in its dominance. Silas sought to own me, and his unyielding tongue demanded my submission.

I whimpered, and Silas slid his hands down my hips, until he gripped the back of my thighs, lifting me. My legs wrapped around his waist and his cock nudged at my entrance.

"It's only sex," I breathed harshly.

"Never," he growled. "When are you going to stop fighting this?"

I didn't answer him, and Silas growled again before plunging his length inside me, sheathing himself to the hilt.

My head tilted back as I cried out. The burning sensation quickly gave way to pleasure as he rocked his hips against mine.

"Your pussy takes me so well, Little Menace," he groaned as he ground himself into me. "Every. Single. Time."

Silas's muscles flexed underneath my fingertips, and I moaned as he rotated his hips, planting himself deeper inside me.

"Eyes on me, Little Menace," Silas demanded, and I returned my gaze to his hungry one.

Silas slammed into me before withdrawing to the hilt and pushing forward once more. I moaned and my eyes rolled to the back of my head.

"You're such a greedy whore for my cock, aren't you, Little Menace?"

My eyes widened at his words, and he chuckled darkly.

His words should have felt degrading.

But the molten heat emanating from my core was evidence to the contrary.

My body trembled with an involuntary shiver as Silas latched onto the base of my throat, sucking my pulse point into his mouth. I arched my back, pressing my breasts against the hard ridges of his chest.

That was going to leave a mark.

His lips kissed a path from the base of my throat, all the way to my earlobe. Silas nibbled on it as he whispered, "Hold on tight, Little Menace. I'm going to fuck you so hard, you'll be begging me to stop because you can't take it for a single moment longer."

And then he did just that.

Silas lifted my ass, so my body was sliding up his chest before he slammed me back down on his cock... repeatedly.

I was a blubbering mess as I came undone around him for the third time. Tears streaked my face as my pleasure overwhelmed me. My orgasm was so intense, I was begging him to stop, just as he promised.

"Please Silas, I can't take another one." My body was spent, and every inch of my flesh felt as though I had been struck by lightning.

"You can, and you will. You're not done yet, Little Menace," he said huskily. "Did you really think I would continue to indulge this distance you keep creating between us? You can't get rid of me, and I'm about to show you just how much I'm under your skin."

Chapter Forty-Two

Despite my earlier pleas, my body flared to life with his promise of more. Silas walked me backward until we reached the alcove. He then dropped me unceremoniously into the cool water, a sexy smirk pulling up the corner of his mouth.

The arrogant prick!

I stood, snarling at him as I did so. The water was shallower here, and my full body was on display for his perusal. Silas reached out, cupping a breast, and squeezing roughly. He took a step closer, lowering his head until he sucked my hard nipple into his hot mouth.

He released me with a loud pop, a feral look on his face that had apprehension and anticipation thrumming through me in equal measure.

"Get on your knees," he commanded.

When I didn't move, Silas placed a hand on my head, pushing me down. I glared up at him in defiance, and he chuckled as he fisted his cock in his hand.

"You look so pretty when you're on your knees, waiting for my cock to stuff that bratty little mouth of yours," he purred. "Open," he demanded, as he tapped my cheek with his free hand.

I narrowed my eyes on him, but I couldn't deny the pulsing need that was building between my legs.

I parted my lips and opened my jaw wide.

"Mmm, that's my good girl," he praised.

He moved closer, his cock standing erect. "Suck," he said pointedly.

My tongue darted out, lapping up the bead of pre-come glistening on the tip. Silas groaned, and that was all the encouragement I needed. I sucked him into my mouth until he hit the back of my throat. I gagged, drool dripping from my chin, but I didn't stop. The power I felt at that moment was intoxicating.

Silas fisted my hair, holding my head in place as he fucked my face without mercy. He was moaning and panting above me, chasing his release as he used me. I cupped his balls in my palm, tugging on them, eliciting a snarl of approval.

I felt Silas stiffen, and he withdrew, spilling his seed as he came over my breasts.

Once he had drained every drop, Silas smeared his come all over me, marking me as he claimed me as his. When he was satisfied, he reached down and gripped my arms.

He pulled me to my feet and ran his thumb over his masterpiece. Silas lifted his eyes and met my gaze as he pushed his thumb inside my mouth. I cleaned it up greedily as he watched me with a burning hunger blazing in his eyes.

Without warning, Silas spun me around, bending me over the bench as he pressed his hard length against my ass. Despite having just had an orgasm, Silas was erect and ready for more.

"You're insatiable," I breathed.

"When it comes to you," he purred, "always."

He pressed the tip of his cock at my back entrance, and I froze.

"I need to claim every inch of your body, Little Menace. This raging beast inside me demands I show you just how much you are mine." His breathing was labored, as though it was a struggle to contain himself.

"You're too big, Silas," I said, anxiety coating my words.

"Relax," he whispered as he lowered himself over me.

His hand reached between us, finding my clit. He rubbed slow, languid circles around my swollen knub and I whimpered. His other hand wrapped around my breasts as he coated his fingers in his come. Silas rubbed his fingers up and down his length, drenching his cock with his release. When he was done, he pressed a slick finger to my back entrance.

"Have you ever taken a cock inside this tight hole?" he asked roughly.

"No," I whispered, as trepidation filled me.

"Good," he growled as he pushed a finger inside me.

A burning sensation assaulted me as he stretched me from the inside. A moment later, he added a second digit, spreading me wide.

I gasped, feeling unbearably full as he fucked me with his fingers.

Silas continued to massage my back hole as he readied me to take him there. Once he was satisfied with his efforts, he removed his fingers from inside me.

"This may hurt at first, but I promise you'll enjoy it by the end," Silas said, and then he pushed the tip of his cock inside me.

Searing pain erupted at the site, and I whimpered.

"Shh, Harlowe," Silas said in a soothing tone. He didn't move, allowing my body to adjust to the intrusion.

"Focus on me."

"I am focused on you. That's the problem. You're fucking huge," I said through gritted teeth.

Silas chuckled, but a moment later, his strong, calloused hand rubbed soothing circles over the base of my spine, and I relaxed slightly. The pain ebbed, and I inhaled a shaky breath.

"There, you see," Silas cooed.

"It's only the tip, Silas," I groaned.

"Trust me," he implored.

Silas resumed his ministrations of my clit, dipping a finger inside my core, and I moaned. At the same time, he thrust his hips forward, filling me to bursting, and I cried out in pain as tears filled my eyes. Silas increased his pace as he fucked me with his fingers, slipping a second digit inside me as he did so.

"You're so fucking tight, Little Menace," he groaned, and I could tell it was taking all his self-restraint to not move inside me like he wanted to.

A tingling sensation spread throughout my core, and I moaned as the pleasure overtook the pain. Silas rocked his hips against me in a slow, gentle rhythm.

"Are you all right, Harlowe?" Silas panted, but I couldn't answer him. I moaned in pleasure as I writhed beneath his touch, completely consumed by the new sensations assaulting me.

"I can't hold on any longer, Little Menace," Silas said with desperation. "I need to fuck your ass."

"Do it," I panted, not recognizing the sound of my voice from the lust coloring it.

Silas let out a feral snarl as he snapped his hips forward, fucking me without restraint.

"Silas," I moaned.

"Gods, Little Menace," he said, sounding pained. "You're fucking perfect.

You're taking my cock in your tight little ass, and it's... Just. Fucking. Perfect." He punctuated each word with a thrust of his hips.

My orgasm built inside me, slowly making its way to the surface before it crashed through me with the fury of a storm, leaving no corner of my body unaffected. Silas shuddered above me and his movements slowed as he came down from his own release.

Both panting hard, we stayed like that as we caught our breath.

Silas placed soft, gentle kisses along my spine until he reached my ear. "Are you all right?" he breathed, and I nodded my head, not capable of words at that moment.

Silas stepped back from me, withdrawing himself from my body, and I winced at the slight discomfort. He bundled me up in his arms and settled me against his broad chest. My arms wrapped around his neck instinctively, and he placed a chaste kiss on my temple.

That slight gesture sent butterflies fluttering in my stomach, and I couldn't help the sigh that escaped me.

Silas carried me back towards the entrance of the cave, settling me in the water between his legs as he retrieved something from the ledge. Pulling my hair away from my face, he started lathering something through my copper strands.

"What are you doing?" I asked hoarsely.

"Washing your hair."

"Have you ever washed a woman's hair before?" I asked skeptically.

"I wash my hair," Silas replied.

"I'm not sure that's a valid comparison," I chuckled. "Our standards are definitely higher."

Silas's movements stilled. "You're probably right... but I'm still doing it," he said, biting my shoulder playfully.

I allowed Silas to wash my hair, his gentle ministrations a complete contrast to the brutality with which he fucked me. A small moan left me as he massaged my scalp, tension unfurling from me in waves.

"Don't tempt me, Little Menace. Your sounds are so delicious they make me want to fuck you again, and your body is not ready for that right now," he said, his tone low and rough.

I muttered something incoherent as he continued massaging my scalp. I could die right now and be perfectly content.

All too soon, it was over, and Silas was ordering me to rinse the suds from my hair under the cascading flow of the waterfall. He then washed every inch of my body before doing the same to his.

This side of Silas was new to me. He was rarely ever gentle and never to this extent.

"Why are you doing all this?" I asked, giving voice to my musings.

"Do you really have to ask?" he said, a lazy grin on his face. "I fucked you raw, Harlowe, and now I'm taking care of you while you recuperate."

"Oh," I replied, still confused. Silas had always been a savage lover, but he had never felt the need to tend to me like this before.

As if sensing my thoughts, Silas chuckled. "I took you every way possible tonight, Harlowe. That's not something you're used to. I expect you're sore, and if you aren't yet, you will be."

"Oh... Oh," I said, finally catching on. My cheeks heated in embarrassment, and I ducked my head so he wouldn't see.

Silas being Silas, however, nothing escaped him. He gripped my chin, tilting my head until I was facing him.

"You never have to hide from me, Little Menace," he said softly, before placing a light kiss on my lips.

Warmth spread throughout my chest and that familiar tingling sensation followed his touch. I felt the hard exterior I had constructed around my heart crack infinitesimally.

We exited the cave in silence, making our way back to the shore where our clothes were. After we got dressed, Silas took my hand and guided me back to camp.

A small fire was glowing brightly in between our bedrolls, and some kind of animal was roasting over it.

"When did you have time to do this?" I asked, surprised.

"I'm efficient," he said, winking at me.

We ate in comfortable silence and when it was time for sleep, Silas dragged me towards his bedroll, cocoooning me in his warm embrace.

And this time, I let him.

Chapter Forty-Three

Hot breath fanned my face and something wet slid down my cheek. I brushed it away, mumbling to myself when it happened again. I cracked one eye open and then the other, only to be greeted by Misneach's colossal head as he peered down at me.

Drool, I realized. The wetness was drool.

"Misneach," I screeched as I scrambled upright. "That's disgusting!"

Silas chuckled from the ground behind me, and Misneach snorted.

"Bad dragon!" I huffed.

I stormed towards the water, desperate to wash all remnants of my dragon's saliva from my face. When I returned, Silas had already packed up our makeshift camp.

He was efficient, indeed.

Silas passed me an apple as he took a bite of his own. I sat on my bedroll, wincing slightly as I gently lowered myself.

Flying was going to be absolute hell today.

A coy smirk lifted Silas's lips, letting me know he had noticed the movement. I tossed my apple at him, and he caught it deftly, laughing as he did so.

His laughter was infectious, and I found myself joining in against my better judgment. Silas returned my apple, and I took a large bite, savoring the sweet taste of the juice as it hit my tongue.

"How far away are we?" I asked Misneach, as I munched on the fruit.

"We will reach the lower outcropping by the afternoon. It's all up to you from there."

I didn't miss the wave of apprehension spiraling down the bond.

As soon as we had finished breakfast, we headed out. I didn't want to delay the inevitable while dwelling on all the things that could go wrong.

I regretted that decision almost immediately. The reminder of what Silas and I had done last night, once again, flared to life the moment I slid into place on Misneach's back.

I did my best to ignore my discomfort as we traveled throughout the day, but I could not contain my relief when we reached the outcropping.

Misneach, however, had become increasingly agitated as the day wore on.

"I'm not sure this is the right path for you to take, Fire Heart," he said hesitantly.

"I know you're worried Misneach, I am too. But I'm also worried about what will become of the realm if I am forced to face Kieran at a disadvantage," I said, trying to soothe him.

"You know this is the only option, Misneach," Caolán added, earning a snarl in his direction.

"Ready?" Silas asked, oblivious to the tension between the dragons.

I nodded once in confirmation.

I walked towards my dragon, meeting his lowered forehead with my own as his wings encircled us, giving us privacy. We stayed like that for a while, drawing comfort from the other and gaining strength for the task ahead. Neither of us enjoyed being separated from the other, especially considering every time we were apart, something awful happened.

"You are fierce. You are powerful. You are a Daughter of Fire and Flame. Never underestimate what you are capable of, Fire Heart. No matter what you face out there, remember that you are my destiny, and I am yours. Our story is not over yet."

Tears pricked my eyes at Misneach's words, and a small sob broke free of my throat.

"Hush, Fire Heart," Misneach soothed.

"I just don't want to leave you," I said through a choked sob.

"Nor I you. But you must. As much as I hate it, Caolán is right."

A strangled laugh escaped me, knowing just how much it must have pained him to admit that.

"Go now, before I change my mind and carry you away from here," Misneach ordered.

I swiped at my eyes, clearing all traces of my tears from my face. When I had regained my composure, Misneach lowered his wings.

"Harlowe," Silas said gently. I turned towards him and grasped his proffered hand.

Snatching up my pack from the ground, I settled it over my shoulders before glancing in Misneach's direction one last time.

He inclined his head in a small nod of encouragement.

I squared my shoulders and took my first step toward answers.

Silas and I had been walking for hours under the warm afternoon sun. The trail winding up the side of the mountain had more shrubbery than I expected, making it difficult to navigate. Thick, towering trees lined the narrow path and my feet kept getting tangled in the dense undergrowth. Silas had stopped me from falling over the mountainside more than once.

The air was thick with the scent of decaying leaves and the higher we climbed, the more difficult it was to breathe. Our progress was painfully slow, and I grew increasingly agitated as the day wore on. We would need to stop and find shelter soon, despite our lack of progress.

"You all right, Harlowe?" Silas called to me over his shoulder.

"Yes," I panted.

"We'll need to stop and find shelter soon. I don't want to risk getting caught out in the dark."

Silas didn't sound the least bit out of breath. He could have been having a leisurely stroll in the garden for how at ease he sounded.

Meanwhile, sweat soaked my tunic, and I was panting heavily enough for the both of us.

"You... saved... his... life... don't... forget... that... he... might... have... more... endurance... than... you... but... he... would... be... roc... chow... if... it... wasn't... for... you," I wheezed in encouragement.

"What was that?" Silas asked, turning to face me.

"Nothing," I huffed.

The smirk playing on his lips told me he knew exactly what I'd said.

Prick.

A subtle rustling in the underbrush drew my attention, and I glanced around, trying to locate the source of the noise. Silas stopped walking and tilted his head, listening intently, indicating that he had heard it too.

The noise began again, and I spotted two glinting yellow eyes. They shone with a feral intensity and they were trained wholly on Silas.

"Silas," I cried out.

The piercing, savage snarl that tore through the air drowned out my warning, as a streak of brown fur and black stripes sprang toward Silas.

The creature struck with primal ferocity as it sank its claws into Silas's side, dragging him to the ground. It opened its deadly jaws, filled with razor-sharp teeth, before it latched onto Silas's shoulder, tearing flesh. The sounds of deranged growling filled the surrounding space, and I clawed for my dagger as I darted forward.

The frenzy with which the beast attacked had adrenaline flooding my veins, and I didn't hesitate as I launched myself at the animal.

My dagger plunged into the tender flesh of the creature's flank, and the coppery tang of blood flooded my senses. It did nothing to deter the beast, however, as it shook its head wildly, consumed by its bloodlust.

Silas wrenched the creature's jaw free and pushed it away, landing a hard kick to its head. Its large, pointed ears tucked back against its skull were the first sign it was in any kind of distress.

Silas didn't waste the advantage he'd created as he lifted the beast and slammed its body into the side of the mountain. A low, guttural growl emanated from the creature, and it threw all its remaining strength into one last attack as its visceral need to survive took over.

Silas lifted the beast once more and slammed it against the mountainside; its head hitting the rock with a sickening crunch. This time, the creature did not stir, and Silas dropped its lifeless body to the ground.

Silas doubled over, panting hard as he placed his hands on his knees. Blood trickled down his arm from the bite on his shoulder and I raced towards him, needing to reassure myself that he would be all right.

"How badly are you hurt?" I asked, fear holding me in a tight grip.

Before he could answer, a harsh, groaning sound spilled down the mountainside, moments before the earth trembled under our feet, and a wall of enormous rocks came careening straight toward us.

Chapter Forty-Four

"HARLOWE," Silas roared as he lunged for me.

Strong, muscular arms encircled my waist as I was tossed through the air.

The sound of grinding rocks and cracking stones warred with the rumble of the mountain that seemed to roar in protest.

The noises collided in a horrifying symphony, echoing off the surrounding peaks, and amplifying the terror clutching at my chest.

A cloud of dust billowed after, sending debris hurtling down the steep slope towards us. It was as if the earth itself was in motion, seeking to destroy anything in its path, and at this moment, that was Silas and me.

My back hit the ground with a punishing force, pushing all the air from my lungs and dragging me harshly back to the present. The power of Silas's body propelled us forward, and he ducked his head over mine, shielding me with his frame.

It wasn't enough, though. Or maybe it was too much.

My body slipped over the edge of the mountainside as Silas desperately tried to claw me back.

My chest rammed against the hardened side of the mountain and my eyes moved of their own accord, peeking down at the vast open space below my dangling feet.

Scattered amongst the sheer mountainside were trees and other rock formations that would only make my fall more destructive rather than offering any form of help in slowing my descent.

"Hold on to me, Harlowe," Silas shouted as he tightened his grip around my forearm.

My gaze flew to his. I hadn't realized he was clutching me in my dazed state.

The fear I saw reflected in his stare sent an avalanche of dread crashing through me. Something dripped on the exposed flesh of my arm where my tunic had ridden up, and to my horror, I realized it was blood.

Silas's blood.

The only thing standing between me and certain death was Silas's injured arm.

He must have seen the panic in my eyes, because Silas squeezed my wrist as he said, "Look at me, Harlowe. How many times do I have to tell you I will never let you go?"

The determination that pulled at his features made me believe Silas might just be capable of anything at this moment. That fantasy was abruptly shattered, however, when a torrent of smaller rocks followed the first strike, becoming dangerous projectiles as they flew through the air at speed.

Silas swung my body hard against the mountainside, shielding me as best he could from the lethality of the advancing force. I wrapped my free arm around my head, and I saw Silas do the same.

Not that it would do him much good.

Silas remained in place as he held me tight, unable to spare himself as he lay sprawled out and exposed to the onslaught.

A large stone struck Silas's outstretched hand and his grip loosened on my wrist as he cried out in agony. I felt my arm slipping from his grasp, but the moment was over before it began as Silas's iron hold clenched around me once more.

"Silas," I screamed, as my feet tried to find purchase in the grooves of the mountain.

A moment passed before Silas responded. "I'm here, Harlowe," he panted.

"Are you all right?"

"Not really," he chuckled. "I'm going to pull you up now. I need you to listen to me, all right, Harlowe."

I nodded my head.

"Harlowe, I want to hear you say the words," Silas commanded.

"Yes, I understand," I said, letting out a shaky breath.

"Grab hold of my wrist with your other hand."

I did as he commanded and wrapped my free hand around his forearm.

Silas's muscles tensed under my hold, and I knew he was straining to keep his grip on me.

"I need to get a better grip, all right," he said, as if he could hear my thoughts. "I'm going to release my hold a fraction so I can slide my palm further up your arm."

"W-What?" I asked, fear clogging my airway, making it hard to breathe.

"Focus, Harlowe," Silas said in a soothing tone. "You're holding on to me, remember? You're strong enough for this. It'll only take a second."

My eyes darted below me once more and I clutched Silas's hand tighter.

"Little Menace," Silas cooed. "Don't look down. Eyes on me."

Slowly and with great effort, I pulled my gaze from the death promising to consume me and locked my eyes on piercing brown ones.

"Good girl," Silas praised. "Do you trust me, Harlowe?"

I stared intently into Silas's captivating gaze, and a sense of warmth and safety washed over me. Despite everything I had tried to convince myself to the contrary, I did trust Silas. I knew at this moment he would protect me and keep me safe.

It was only then that I noticed Silas's palm was slick with blood. The wound on his shoulder was bleeding profusely, making it difficult for him to maintain his grip. Soon enough, my grip on Silas would be the only thing preventing my fall, and I wasn't sure how much longer I could hold on.

"Y-Yes," I stuttered.

A satisfied grin curved his lips. "That's my girl," he said. "We'll go on three, all right."

My heart thundered in my chest and my palms grew sweaty. Despite my fear, I nodded my head and said in a strained voice, "All right."

"One," Silas counted, and I took a deep breath.

"Two."

I closed my eyes and exhaled slowly.

"Three."

Silas relaxed his hold on my arm, and I felt my stomach drop as the sensation of falling lurched through me. My lips parted, and a scream was wrenched from me, but before my terror could truly seize me, Silas's rough hand wrapped around my forearm. His fingers dug into my flesh with a bruising force, and my breath left me on a whimper.

Silas's broad grin met me when I returned my gaze to his. "See, nothing to worry about."

A hysterical laugh burst free of my chest, and I struggled to calm myself.

"Harlowe," Silas said. It was a command and my body responded immediately, rejecting my mounting hysteria.

"Good girl. I'm going to swing you a short distance across the face of the mountain so that I can reach you with my other arm, all right?"

Silas's body was positioned at an unnatural angle, his right side almost hanging off the edge of the mountain while his left side was further back.

"Can't you just shift a bit until you can reach me with your free arm?" I pleaded.

"Little Menace, if I move even a fraction, I will pull my foot from where it is ensnared in the undergrowth, and we'll both be tumbling over this mountain," he said with a harsh exhale.

"Oh," I replied shakily.

"Are you with me?" Silas asked, and I nodded.

Without warning, Silas flung my body to the side and then swung it in the opposite direction. His free hand darted out, catching my other arm in a firm grip.

"I got you," he panted. "Dig your feet into the side of the mountain and climb with me as I pull."

I wiggled the toes of my boots into the grooves along the rough edge and secured my grip on Silas's arms.

"Ready?"

"Ready," I breathed.

Silas began to lift me, the sinewy muscles of his forearms bulging with the effort. My feet crept higher as I supported myself against the mountain.

Inch by inch, Silas drew me up until his hands moved to beneath my arms and he pulled me free of the treacherous drop behind me.

We were both breathing hard, and my pulse hammered wildly at the base of my throat. Silas sat up, pulling me into his lap as he wrapped his arms around me tightly.

I glanced around my surroundings as I caught my breath. Trees had been uprooted; their branches snapped like mere twigs. The acrid scent of freshly exposed earth and dirt filled the air, and debris scattered across the undergrowth.

Returning my gaze to Silas, I took in the injury to his shoulder; he had deep gashes that tore into his flesh where the creature had locked its jaws. As my eyes tracked lower, I saw that shallower gashes marred Silas's sides from the beast's claws.

We had escaped death not once, but twice today.

That reality struck me hard, and my eyes filled with tears as I stared at Silas. We could have died today.

"Hey," Silas soothed as he brushed my hair away from my face. "I've got you, Harlowe. You're safe. With me, you'll always be safe."

His words tore open the floodgates, and I could no longer contain my tears as they spilled down my cheeks.

Chapter Forty-Five

We abandoned the idea of traveling any further and instead found a cave to see us through the night.

Once I'd made a small fire, I ordered Silas to remove his tunic so I could check his injuries.

"If you wanted me naked, Little Menace, all you had to do was ask," Silas said, a smirk playing on his lips as he shed his tunic.

"Don't worry, I'm well aware of how easy it is to get you naked, Silas. This is purely for medical purposes," I teased.

"Are you calling me easy, Little Menace?" he asked, arching a brow.

"Are you denying it?" I quipped.

A moment passed as our gazes met, then laughter erupted from both of us.

"Let me see," I commanded, jutting my chin towards his side.

Silas lifted his arm, giving me a better view. I tentatively prodded around the swollen flesh, careful not to aggravate the shallow gashes left by the beast's claws.

"These aren't too bad," I murmured.

Once I'd cleaned and wrapped the wounds on his side, I moved on to the deeper gash on his shoulder. I gasped when I took in the full state of the injury.

"How the hell did you hold on to me, let alone pull me up with this injury?" I asked Silas incredulously, unable to pull my gaze away from the gaping wound.

"I told you Little Menace. You belong to me, and I'll never let you go. I'd sooner throw myself over the edge than watch you slip through my fingers."

Silas's eyes darkened with each word, and I felt a warm flush creeping up my neck and settling on my cheeks.

I returned my attention to Silas's shoulder, needing to escape the intensity of his penetrating gaze. Prodding the flesh around the wound, I checked the depth of the gashes. There were two deep cuts, and it appeared as though the beast had torn the flesh from the bone.

My stomach turned queasy at the sight, and I had to inhale a long, controlled breath to settle the nausea.

I had to surmise those came from the creature's canines. The surrounding teeth had also left two more shallower gashes amidst the deeper ones.

"Ow, Harlowe," Silas hissed.

"Don't be a baby," I teased. "You have two rather nasty gashes that need stitches. Unfortunately for you, I'm not very adept at needlework." I flashed him an apologetic smile.

I wasn't lying; I was terrible at needlework, and Silas would probably end up with one hideous-looking scar.

I returned to the fire and retrieved my pack. Emmerson had prepared some medical supplies for me and I fished them out before going back to Silas. I'm sure when she was packing them, however, she had envisioned it would be me needing the medical attention and not Silas.

Silas watched me with rapt attention as I pulled out the rubbing alcohol, needle, thread, and bandages. He seemed to pale slightly when I struggled to push the thread through the fine needlepoint.

"You really aren't adept at needlework, are you?"

"I already pointed that out," I mumbled, as a blush crept over my cheeks.

"You have done stitches before though, right?" Silas asked with increasing discomfort.

"Not exactly," I muttered.

Silas groaned. "You could have just lied to me, Harlowe."

"Stop whining or I'll tell all the Cathal how much of a sook their big, bad general is," I said in a threatening tone.

"If they knew just how bad you were at this, I think they'd consider me heroic for letting you near me at all," he muttered under his breath.

"I heard that," I said, and Silas flashed me a dazzling smile.

If he thought a smile was all it took to divert my attention, he was sorely mistaken. A sick satisfaction filled me as I lifted the rubbing alcohol to the wound and poured generously. Silas winced, hissing through gritted teeth. A slow smile spread across my lips, and he narrowed his eyes at me.

"You don't need to enjoy it quite that much, Little Menace."

I just shrugged my shoulders and started cleaning the wound, smile still in place. I was standing between Silas's thighs as I worked, and I felt the hardening of his impressive length the longer I stood there.

"Is this a turn-on for you, Silas?" I asked, raising a brow. Given his penchant for delivering pain with my pleasure, I shouldn't be surprised.

"Your perfect tits are pressed right in my face, Harlowe. I know you may consider me a god when we are in the bedroom, but I assure you, I am only a man."

When I glanced down at him, his heated gaze was trained on my breasts, and I rolled my eyes.

"Pervert."

"Only for you, Little Menace." Silas wrapped one hand around my waist as he pulled me closer. His other hand reached up, plucking the ties of my tunic open.

"What are you doing?" I asked, narrowing my eyes at him.

"I'm about to let you attempt to stitch me back together. Given you've already admitted your lack of experience, the least you could do is offer me a distraction," he said huskily, and the sound went straight to my core.

"The least I can do, huh?" Silas just nodded, not peeling his eyes away from the exposed flesh of my breasts.

"I could always just leave your injury as is, wrap it, and hope for the best. The flesh might knit itself back together, but then again, it might not," I said sardonically. "I'm sure a gaping wound like that is no more likely to facilitate dirt and germs getting into your bloodstream either, right? Infection shouldn't be a problem."

"Are you done?" Silas asked as he re-tied my tunic.

"Are you?"

"I'll keep my hands to myself," Silas said with a grin, his hands raised in surrender.

I smiled before grimacing.

"This will hurt," I said as I raised the needle to Silas's shoulder.

Silas gritted his teeth as I pierced the needle through his skin. I tried to distract him by prattling on non-stop about this and that, avoiding any subject of substance. Silas dutifully played along, asking questions, and feeding me his own tidbits.

"There, all done," I said as I finished the last stitch.

Silas glanced at the mess I'd made of his shoulder, and then at me.

I smiled sheepishly and lifted my shoulder in a shrug.

"At least you won't get an infection and die," I said, laughing nervously. "Probably won't... hopefully."

"You need to work on your bedside manner, Little Menace," Silas chuckled.

He stood and reached out, wrapping his arm around my waist as he pulled me flush against his hardened chest.

His naked chest.

Silas placed a soft kiss on my temple. "Thank you, Harlowe," he whispered.

My heartbeat became erratic at his closeness and the intimacy of the simple gesture.

"You're welcome, Silas."

He took my hand in his and pulled me to his bedroll, tugging me down with him as he lowered himself to the ground.

"You should sleep. We have a long day ahead of us come morning," he murmured against my hair as he draped an arm over me.

For the first time in a while, I fell asleep feeling content.

Chapter Forty-Six

We departed early the following morning to regain the lost ground from the previous day. I strained my neck for a better view of the mountain peak, trying to convince myself of our progress.

I had no such luck.

The low cloud cover cast everything in various shades of grey and obscured the peak of the mountain. The journey ahead felt ominous, to say the least. With the events from the previous day, the task ahead seemed downright perilous.

The air was thick with the scent of rain, and I shuddered beneath my cloak as a cool breeze prickled my skin. The faster we get off this mountain, the better.

"Ready?" Silas asked, startling me.

I turned to face him and caught the wince he tried to hide as he settled his pack on his shoulders.

"I can carry your pack for you. That wound on your shoulder doesn't need any added pressure. You'll probably open your stitches."

Silas gave me a look that told me I hadn't a hope in hell of separating him from his pack.

"Stubborn male," I muttered.

A hard swat landed on my rear, and I yelped in surprise.

"What the hell was that for?" I asked, indignation burning my cheeks.

"Muttering is rude, Little Menace. Especially when it's about me," he teased.

"I wouldn't need to mutter if you were capable of being reasonable," I countered.

Another hard swat landed on my backside, and I jumped out of Silas's reach.

"Silas!" I screeched, but one look at Silas and the brow he had raised in a challenge had me picking my battles. I didn't need to add a sore ass to my troubles.

Swallowing my pride, I headed towards the path, stomping my feet a little more than necessary.

We walked in companionable silence for a time, and I couldn't help but marvel at the lethal beauty that surrounded us. The rocky terrain of the mountain was treacherous and unforgiving. While the wildflowers that flourished in the undergrowth offered a stark contrast. The same undergrowth that snagged my boots with every step and threatened to send me careening over the edge with every stumble.

The untamed wildness of the place only amplified its beauty.

As I rounded the corner, I halted abruptly. I forgot my earlier musings as I peered at the sharp incline of the mountainside. A narrow ledge, just a foot wide, was our only path across.

"Harlowe?" Silas asked from behind me.

I stepped aside, letting him take in the problem at hand.

Silas released a low whistle. "This should be fun," he said as a wicked grin split his handsome face.

"Fun," I scowled.

"Yes, Princess, fun. Ever heard of it?"

I shoved him away and then immediately reached out to steady him, remembering just how high up we were.

"Careful Harlowe, you'll have me believing that you just might care for me after all," Silas said in a husky tone.

"Be serious for one minute, Silas. What are we going to do about that?" I asked, pointing to the narrow ledge behind me.

"Climb it," he said casually.

"Seriously?" I asked, unable to hide the panic in my tone.

"What else can we do?" He shrugged and added, "It's the only way across."

I sank my teeth into my lower lip as I peered over the edge. I hadn't thought I was afraid of heights, but I was quickly reassessing that. A nauseous feeling settled in my stomach and my palms became clammy.

"I'll go first," Silas said, sensing my mounting fear.

Silas removed his pack and placed it at my feet. Then he stepped onto the ledge, flattening his torso against the side of the mountain. His hands found purchase in the small imperfections of the rocky surface. Silas took a tentative step forward, followed by another, and then another. In no time at all, he had scaled the incline and was on the other side of the ledge, smiling like an idiot.

"Easy," he said as he indicated for me to toss him his pack. Silas caught it with ease.

"Now yours," he said. I removed my pack and sent it sailing through the air into Silas's waiting arms.

I approached the ledge, tucking myself snugly against the mountainside, and gripped the rocking surface just as Silas had done. Sending a quick prayer up to any gods that might be listening, I stepped onto the ledge. I didn't glance down, instead fixing my gaze on each groove as I used them to guide my steps.

The wind howled in my ears and whipped loose strands of my hair around my face, restricting my vision. The first drops of rain hit my forehead, and I groaned.

"You couldn't hold out just a few minutes longer," I said, glaring up at the darkening clouds.

The rock beneath my fingertips became slippery, and I struggled to get a good grip. Lightning flashed across the sky, illuminating the sheer drop below, and the booming sound of thunder quickly followed.

I inhaled sharply, willing myself to not let my fear gain a stronghold.

"You're doing great, Little Menace," Silas cooed. "Just focus on the next step, nothing else."

I nodded my head frantically and took a steadying breath. The rain was hammering down now, but I listened to Silas's soothing words as I made my way across.

Strong arms enveloped me, and Silas's familiar scent filled my nostrils.

"I've got you."

I stepped off the ledge and let out a breath I didn't realize I was holding. Silas nodded once, and I returned the gesture. Without another word, he slipped my pack onto my shoulders and continued on the path.

The rain was relentless, cutting through my clothing and stinging my flesh. It made for a miserable journey as we climbed higher. The wind was deafening, and the height only intensified the sound as it reverberated off the surrounding stone.

When we finally made it to the top, I was a soaking, trembling mess.

But all of that quickly fell away as the darkened entrance ahead drew my attention. Spiderwebs covered the entrance and an involuntary shudder crept up my spine at the thought of going anywhere near the horrid creatures.

"You're not afraid of the dark, are you, Little Menace?" Silas asked, amusement plain in his tone.

"It's not the dark, but more the things thriving inside it," I said, pointing to the silken threads of the spiderwebs.

Silas chuckled, and I had an irrational urge to set him on fire.

"It's not funny," I seethed. "Those little monsters are demons from hell whose only purpose is to terrify and traumatize," I huffed.

When Silas made no further comment, I glanced in his direction and found him red-faced, his shoulders shaking with quiet laughter. I narrowed my eyes on him, and he burst out laughing, no longer able to contain it.

"Demons from hell?" he wheezed. "The best part is that you're serious."

"I should have brought Emmerson," I muttered.

"You wound me, Little Menace," Silas said, still chuckling.

Silas rummaged through the undergrowth until he produced a thick branch. He stalked towards the cave entrance and promptly cleared it of all traces of the web.

"Better?" he asked as he turned to face me.

"Better," I grumbled.

When I reached the threshold of the cave, Silas gripped my hand in his. The opening was just wide enough for us to stand together. We stepped into the pitch-blackness of the cave and I let Silas lead me. I pointedly refused to place my hands anywhere near the cave walls, since I couldn't make out what might be lurking there.

A small orb of light emerged on Silas's free palm as he drew upon fórsa.

"Won't that drain you?" I asked, furrowing my brows.

"I'm only using a small amount. Just enough to help us see by." I squeezed his hand in thanks.

The cave's entrance sat at the very top of the mountain peak and slowly traveled deeper into the core of the mountain, becoming wider as it wound its way back down.

I had no idea how a dragon was supposed to fit inside the space.

We walked for what seemed like hours, the echo of our footfalls the only sound as they vibrated around the cavern.

The damp air that filled the cave shifted suddenly, tingling with tension as the hairs on my nape stood to attention. We made a sharp turn that led into a wide, open chamber and a low rumbling sound erupted in the silence.

Silas pulled me to his side, shielding me from what lay ahead.

A rough masculine voice cut through the mounting tension, sending a tremor of awareness shooting through me.

"I have been waiting for you, Daughter of Fire and Flame."

Chapter Forty-Seven

All around us, light flooded the chamber as dozens of sconces fired to life. I peered around Silas's broad shoulder and gasped as I took in the magnificent beast before me. His dark red scales shimmered like molten gold in the light as he stood tall and imposing inside the cave. The immense beast dwarfed the chamber that once seemed endless.

His massive frame was all sinewy muscle that radiated power, and I wondered how such an enormous creature could navigate the small entrance and passageways of the cave.

Grey, serpentine eyes locked on mine, and I felt a pull towards the primordial intelligence I saw reflected there. The dragon stepped closer, and I spotted a ridge of spines along his back that looked as lethal as any dagger.

The air seemed to hum around us, almost as if in deference to the dragon's might. There was also an enigmatic beauty to the creature that stood in contrast to his menacing exterior. I felt like this was as close as I'd get to standing with the gods.

"But how do you even get inside this cave when you're so... huge?" I thought to myself.

The dragon chortled.

Did I just say that aloud? Please tell me I didn't say that out loud. I glanced at Silas who looked at me with an amused yet slightly stunned expression.

I slapped a hand over my mouth. I definitely said that out loud.

I risked life and limb to traverse this treacherous mountain, nearly plummeted to my death taking Silas with me, all to meet the Ancient dragon, the one who could see inside me and unlock my powers, and the first thing I ask is how he navigates his living space.

I glared at the ground, cursing its audacity for failing to open up and swallow me whole.

"Fret not, daughter. Your curious nature is somewhat refreshing," the dragon chortled.

I winced. It appeared that I had a similar connection to this dragon, just like the others.

"Indeed," the dragon rumbled.

"What is your name?" I asked.

"I am Drakkon," he said as he lowered his head in a slight bow. I mirrored the action. "My name is Harlowe."

"Yes daughter, I am aware."

"Why do you call me daughter?" I asked, my curiosity winning out.

"I am the premier dragon, brought forth by the fates and intertwined with the fabric of time. Every creature that houses fire and flames carries a small piece of me inside them, including you, daughter."

"Is that why the other dragons call me Daughter of Fire and Flame?" I asked.

"Every dragon is a daughter or a son of mine, as they too house my flames. I imagine they sense your connection to the flames they, themselves house and recognize you as one of their kin. It is why you can commune with any dragon, not just your bond mate. Your flames speak to theirs. You are a Daughter of Fire and Flame, just as they are children of the same."

"Misneach won't appreciate hearing that our bond is almost identical to the one I share with all other dragons," I muttered to myself, recalling how he liked to remind me of the fact that our bond differed from the others.

"To the contrary, daughter. The bond you have with your dragon is unparalleled. The fates created him especially for you. He is your anchor," Drakkon said.

"My anchor? What does that mean? And what do you mean, the fates created him, especially for me?"

My head was spinning. Without even broaching the point of my visit, I already felt overwhelmed.

"No other being was meant to house dragon flames. They are too powerful and could easily consume you if you let them."

Unease settled low in my stomach at the image that information conjured.

"There is no need to worry, daughter. As I said, your dragon was created by the fates to be your anchor. He will keep you grounded and will know if you dance too close to danger."

"So, Misneach will help me control my powers... so I don't combust, I mean, right?" I asked, making sure I understood.

Drakkon chuckled but nodded in agreement.

I heard Silas shuffling behind me, and I glanced over my shoulder to where he was making himself comfortable as he took a seat against the cave wall.

Returning my attention to Drakkon, I inched closer, settling myself before him as I crossed my legs. Drakkon lowered himself until his head perched on his forelegs in front of me.

"Why do I house dragon flames?" I asked. Drakkon's eyes softened as if recalling a fond memory.

"You were created to counteract the power imbalance that had arisen in the realm," he said in a faraway tone.

"Kieran's power," I nodded.

"Yes. The Serpent King came to possess a power that was never intended for him. A power that was never meant to be forged into the darkness it became."

I remembered the Original Witch and her remarks about her powers. She had given up helping those who turned against her. Betraying her promise to the fates, she used her powers for darkness, not light.

"I met the Original Witch. She told me about what happened and why she made the choices she did."

"Choices I am sure she is now regretting given the high cost," Drakkon mused.

I wasn't so sure she did regret her decisions. She was unhinged, still clinging to her bitterness all these centuries later.

"So why flames?" I asked, redirecting the conversation.

The sound of rustling once again drew my attention, and I peered over my shoulder to see what Silas was doing. He had retrieved an apple and was busy using his dagger to peel the skin off as he whistled quietly to himself.

"Don't mind me," he said with a wide grin. "Watching you two sit in silence as you both stare at each other is rather dull."

I rolled my eyes, but a small smile pulled up my lips despite myself. When

I returned my gaze to Drakkon, he was studying me intently.

"So, why flames?" I repeated.

"Dragon flames are the only force within this realm powerful enough to overcome the shadow. When the fates asked me for an offering so they could create you, I could hardly refuse. Nature demands balance. Allowing an imbalance to remain would have seen the end of us all."

I swallowed hard, recalling the Lost Witch's warning that I would either be the salvation or ruination of the realm.

"How can you be so sure that I won't bring about our ruination, anyway?" I asked, my voice sounding small even to my ears.

"How can I be sure that the sun will rise tomorrow?" Drakkon said as if that was answer enough.

"The Lost Witch told me I would have to choose. That I would either side with Kieran and bring about the destruction of our realm, or I would stand against him, and be its salvation."

"Ah yes, free will. It is always about free will with them," Drakkon muttered.

"Who are they? The fates?" I asked, suddenly desperate for information. Drakkon ignored my question.

"You can indeed choose your fate, daughter, but I am the giver of fire and flames, and a part of me is inside you. I know your mind just as I know mine. Before you were even created, I knew that your goodness would prevail. It is why I agreed to share myself with you," he said.

"You just said you couldn't refuse the fate's request," I said, doubt coating my tone.

"I said nature requires balance and I could not let an imbalance corrupt our realm. If I had any doubt that a daughter of my flames would stand with the darkness instead of against it, I would have refused the fates," Drakkon said. "**You must learn to listen with your heart instead of your ears,**" he added cryptically.

"I don't know what that means," I mumbled. Drakkon just gave me a pointed look.

"Tell me why you came to my mountain," Drakkon encouraged.

I took a deep breath and exhaled slowly.

"I can't access my powers. I mean, I can, just not on command," I clarified.

"Can't you?" Drakkon asked with an underlying tone I could not identify.

"No," I said simply.

"Let me ask you this, daughter. Why do you think you can't access your flames?"

"I have no idea. It's why I'm here," I said, shrugging my shoulders.

"Try again," Drakkon commanded. "Look inside yourself and tell me what you see."

Look inside myself? What did that even mean? And yet, as I sat there, confused and directionless, a sense of understanding slowly crept over me.

I was afraid of my powers.

"I am afraid of the flames," I said softly, ashamed of my weakness.

Drakkon hummed. "And why do you think that is?"

Because they wrought destruction.

But they had also saved those I loved as well.

I had only destroyed those who had threatened me or those I cared about. I had harmed no one who didn't harm me first. I had even somehow managed to protect those I loved from the power of my flames.

So why was I so scared to wield them?

"There, now you see, daughter," Drakkon said, having followed my internal musings.

I didn't see it. Not exactly.

"When you have needed your flames, they have been there, have they not?" Drakkon asked.

"Yes."

"But you weren't able to summon them when there was no threat, correct?"

I nodded my head.

"What is the difference?"

"When I need them, I don't even think about it, they just appear."

And that's when it hit me.

"Are you saying that I am... somehow blocking myself?"

Drakkon dipped his head in confirmation.

"But how? And why would I even do that?"

Drakkon's eyes drifted to Silas before he returned his gaze to me.

"It comes back to why you fear your flames," Drakkon said.

"I already told you, it's about the destruction they could unleash if I let them."

"And why would you let them?" Drakkon pressed.

"**Because...**" I trailed off.

I feared what I was capable of if I sided with Kieran.

Drakkon gave me a knowing look.

"**I am blocking myself from fully manifesting my powers out of fear I will eventually side with Kieran,**" I said, letting out a ragged breath.

"**It appears you are,**" Drakkon replied sagely.

"**How do I stop it?**"

"**How do you stop blocking yourself, or how do you stop yourself from siding with the Serpent King?**" Drakkon asked.

"**Both.**"

"**The answer is simple; don't,**" Drakkon said.

I barked out a laugh. "**If only it were that easy.**"

"**It's not?**" Drakkon asked pointedly.

"**No. There is this pull I feel towards Kieran. I felt it from the very first moment I met him. I think he is my twin flame, and because of that, I fear I will eventually give in to him,**" I admitted.

It's why I was no longer willing to trust freely. I couldn't even trust myself.

My thoughts drifted to Silas. I also felt inextricably connected to him. Something I was reminded of every time our bodies shared even the briefest of touches.

"**He is not the only one you share a connection with,**" Drakkon said as if reading my thoughts. On second thought, he probably did just that.

The dragon chuckled, confirming my suspicions.

"**How do I know which connection to follow?**" I asked tentatively.

"**It is like I said, you must learn to listen with your heart instead of your ears. You were told about twin flames, and you surmised the Serpent King was yours because of the pull you felt towards him.**

You listened with your ears.

Did you ever consider it may have been the pull of his magic? That the power inside you recognized the power inside him?"

That's what Emmerson had told me. However, I had been unwilling to believe her, convinced of the inevitability of my demise.

"**What are you saying?**" I asked cautiously.

"**I am saying listen with your heart. Your twin flame is someone whom you share a profound connection with. A connection so deep that it sparks to life, coursing through your entire body with a simple touch. Whose name does your heart whisper, Daughter? For he is your twin flame.**"

"**It can't be that simple,**" I said hoarsely.

"**It is. The choice was always yours. You only need to choose him.**"

My gaze flicked to Silas, and my heartbeat grew more erratic the longer I stared at him.

"**Hmm,**" Drakkon said. "**It appears your heart has spoken.**"

Chapter Forty-Eight

I pondered Drakkon's words for what felt like an eternity. The dragon remained silent beside me, allowing me the space to process everything that I had learned.

Lost to my musings, I did not hear Silas approaching.

"The day is growing late. We will need to go soon, Harlowe."

Pain erupted in my chest at the thought of leaving Drakkon behind. Maybe it was irrational since I'd only just met him, but he made me feel like I wasn't alone in all this.

"You could never leave me behind, Daughter of Fire and Flame. You carry me with you, always."

"Will I ever see you again?" I asked, already feeling the loss of his presence.

"We shall see what the fates have in store for me," Drakkon said thoughtfully.

I rose to my feet and placed a hand on Drakkon's muzzle. **"Thank you Drakkon, for everything,"** I murmured.

"You are most welcome, daughter."

"Wait! You never answered my question about how you navigate such small spaces," I said, waving my arms around me.

While I knew it was not the most pressing question, considering everything I had learned today, I couldn't help that my curiosity had been peaked.

Drakkon stood from his position on the ground, his impressive frame once again dwarfing the space. I stared expectantly, narrowing my eyes when Drakkon said nothing.

The colossal dragon standing before me seemed to vibrate, and then he began to... shrink.

Drakkon kept getting smaller and smaller until he was only a foot tall. He trundled over to me, rubbing his scales against my leg before he extended his wings, lifting himself until he settled around my shoulders.

I could only gape.

The magnificent beast was reduced to, what, a baby dragon?

Drakkon snorted. **"I'm hardly a baby. I'm merely... adaptable."**

"But how?" I had never heard of, let alone seen, a dragon possess power such as Drakkon's.

"I was the first dragon. You could say I'm... unique," he chuckled.

I turned to look at Silas, who was standing still, shock clear on his face as he gaped open-mouthed at Drakkon.

It was a relief to see I wasn't alone.

The small dragon made a purring sound as he rubbed his head against mine. Then he fluttered to the ground, where he grew in size once more.

"Incredible," Silas whispered.

"Yes, it is," I agreed.

Silas had sensed my need to be alone.

Well, as alone as possible while walking alongside one another.

He hadn't pushed me to reveal anything that I had learned, even though I could tell he was itching to ask what Drakkon and I had discussed.

Every few minutes he would glance in my direction, studying me, before returning his gaze to the path ahead.

When we finally found a cave for the night, my nerves were completely frayed.

Could I have been wrong? Could the pull I feel towards Kieran be no more than a recognition of power?

Like calling to like.

Where did that leave me and Silas?

Even if he was my twin flame, he had betrayed me for his father, and there was no avoiding that truth.

He chose you in the end by going against his father. My inner voice seemed to whisper.

But she was a harlot who only cared about getting dick.

Silas had intended to take me away from Pyrithia once he learned of his father's plans. But had the King's interests not changed, what would've happened? Would Silas have kept me prisoner in some misguided attempt to keep me safe from Kieran?

No matter his intentions, Silas needed to recognize that I was my own person, and he could not make decisions on my behalf. If he couldn't accept that, then twin flame or not, I had no space in my life for him.

I was a grown-ass woman, and he could either stand beside me or step aside.

Once we were done with our meal, I broached the subject.

"Silas," I said tentatively.

"Yes, Little Menace?" he said, his voice as smooth as velvet.

Silas lifted his gaze to meet mine, and his piercing brown depths instantly captivated me.

After taking a moment to compose myself, I cleared my throat and said, "Drakkon told me why I couldn't access my power."

Silas stopped sharpening his sword, giving me his full attention. I both loved and loathed the weight of his gaze upon my skin.

"And?" he pressed when I failed to continue.

"He said that I was blocking myself."

"Blocking yourself?" Silas asked, the confusion clear in his expression. "Why would he think that?"

I explained to Silas how I was fearful of the power I possessed, as it had been created to complement or counter Kieran's.

"You're afraid you will choose Kieran," he said through gritted teeth.

"I was," I replied.

"Was?" I didn't miss the heat banking in Silas's eyes as he studied me.

"For a while, I thought Kieran was my twin flame. I believed he and I were inevitable because of the pull I felt towards him. Then Drakkon suggested an alternative interpretation," I said.

"Which was?"

"That it was the power I housed recognizing an equally powerful opponent."

When Silas remained silent, I glanced in his direction from beneath my lashes. He appeared to be deep in thought.

"Drakkon also knew that I shared a connection with another."

This time Silas stiffened, his entire focus fixating on me.

"He told me it had always been my choice. That I had the power to choose my path and with it, the man who was my true twin flame."

Silas's throat bobbed as he swallowed roughly.

I let out a measured breath. I didn't realize until this moment just how much this knowledge settled me. It was as though a weight had lifted from my chest. One that had been slowly crushing me to death.

"And who do you choose, Harlowe?" Silas asked, his voice sounding low and rough in the silence.

I met his gaze, and I am sure he could see the resolve reflected there.

"That depends, Silas."

"On what?" If I didn't know any better, I would think Silas was holding his breath as he waited for me to answer.

"On you."

Silas released a ragged breath. He lowered his head for a moment, before he returned his gaze to mine, his eyes burning with an intensity that both terrified and excited me.

"I acknowledge I've made mistakes, Harlowe, but I've been trying to be the man you need me to be. I've been trying to prove myself worthy of you because you are the only thing that matters to me anymore. I abandoned my King and my home for you, Harlowe, and my only regret is that I didn't do it sooner before I had the chance to wreck us. I. Chose. You. And every day we were apart, a little piece of me died. Every. Single. Day. I know what it is to live without you, Harlowe, and I'll do anything to fix this, so I never have to feel that pain again. So tell me what to do," he pleaded.

"Do you want me to get down on my knees and beg, because I'll gladly do it if it means you'll be mine again? Anything you want, ask it of me, and it will be yours." His chest was heaving with the emotion behind his words.

I studied him for a long moment. I could see the truth of his words and the vulnerability he always tried to hide.

"What if I asked you to let me go? Would you do it?"

Silas clenched his jaw, his sinewy muscles poised as if ready to attack.

Would he stop me if I tried to leave him?

Everything came down to this. I needed to know if he would continue to hold me back.

Would Silas stand beside me, or would he stand in my way?

We stared at each other for the longest moment. Then Silas rose from his seat and prowled towards me.

My eyes fluttered closed. My heart breaking into pieces.

This was it.

This would be the moment Silas vowed to never let me go.

I would never be free as long as I was with him.

A traitorous tear spilled down my cheek as I tried to hold myself together.

Silas's calloused hand gripped my chin, and the pad of his thumb wiped away my tears.

"Look at me, Harlowe," Silas said in a pained tone.

I shook my head, unable to face what this meant.

"Look at me," he growled.

I felt a cold object being pressed into my palm, which startled me and drew my attention.

My eyes flicked open.

Silas had thrust his sword into my waiting hand.

Confused, I glanced at Silas. His jaw remained clenched, but I saw the pain in his eyes where determination had once shone.

"If you want to leave me," he whispered thickly, "I will not stand in your way. However, I have one request of you."

"And what is that?" I asked, breathless.

Silas picked up my free hand and placed it over his heart. It was beating wildly inside his chest as if fighting to get free.

Then he lowered his forehead to mine.

"You are my beating heart, Harlowe. From the moment you tried to end my life, I knew it was you. All it took was one touch, and I fell completely under your spell. I gave you my heart that day and I don't want it back. So, if you want to leave me, do it. But take my sword and cut my heart out. It belongs to you, so take it with you. It won't beat if you're gone."

With that, Silas stepped back, creating distance between us, and giving me the space to choose.

His expression conveyed so much pain and agony that it caused my heart to clench in sympathy.

I let the sword fall to the ground with a loud clatter.

And then I ran to Silas, throwing myself into his embrace.

Chapter Forty-Nine

I smashed my lips to Silas's in a bruising kiss.

"Not that I'm complaining, but what's going on, Little Menace?" he asked when we came up for air.

"All I've ever wanted was to be given a choice, Silas," I said, breathing heavily. "You kept taking all my choices away, not listening to me when I told you what I wanted."

Silas opened his mouth to speak, but I continued before he could. "I'm willing to leave all that in the past and start anew if you can promise me you'll never pull anything like you did in the Forest of Nightmares again," I said, before adding, "Even if you think it's in my best interests. And I expect you to treat me as an equal. I want you to stand at my side, not in my way."

"Done," he said as he lifted my tunic over my head. "Except inside the bedroom," he added with a sexy smirk.

"Just like that?" I asked, not able to hide my surprise.

"Just like that," he answered.

"But —"

"I told you, Harlowe, I know what it is to live without you, and fuck me if that wasn't the hardest thing I've ever done. I will never, ever, betray your trust again. You have my vow."

My lips found his again as I untied the laces of his pants. A small whine escaped me when Silas pulled his tunic off, breaking the kiss. He chuckled darkly and then peppered my face with soft kisses.

"I'll stand beside you, Harlowe. I'll protect your back. And I'll be there every step of the way when you bring the realm to its knees."

I slipped my hand beneath the waistband of his pants and gripped his hardened length.

Silas groaned. "Is this a bad time to ask you to marry me?"

"Don't push your luck, Silas," I said as I freed his cock.

"I was being —" Silas cut off abruptly as I pumped his length. He moaned, and the sound had my thighs clenching, desperate for some friction.

I was no longer averse to the idea of Silas's proposal, but I was content to let him sweat about it for a little while longer.

"That's cheating, Little Menace," Silas growled.

"And what do you intend to do about it?" I purred.

Silas picked me up and threw me over his shoulder. I shrieked in surprise as he carried me over to his bedroll.

"You better pray to the gods for mercy, Little Menace, because when it comes to the things I want to do to your body, I have none to offer."

As if to emphasize his point, Silas landed a harsh slap on my ass and tossed me down on his bedroll. My indignation was short-lived when Silas placed his knees on either side of my frame as he glided his hands up my body until he reached the waistband of my pants.

I gave an involuntary shudder when his fingertips dipped below my leathers. Silas tore the rest of my clothing from my body, and I flinched as the frigid air teased my bare pussy.

His heated gaze roamed over my naked flesh, and my thighs became slick with arousal. Silas removed the last of his garments, exposing his powerful body to my hungry gaze. When he fisted his cock in his hand, my tongue darted out, tracing my lower lip.

Silas smirked, and then with the intensity of a predator watching their prey, he kept his gaze locked on mine as he crawled his way up my body.

Gooseflesh erupted in his wake, and my breath hitched. Silas hovered his lips over mine and flicked his tongue out, tasting my lower lip just as I had.

I let out a shaky breath, running my fingertips up his sides, reveling in the feel of his muscles as they contracted.

Silas's large hand gripped my throat as he fell back, pulling me with him. His grip tightened as he lifted me, placing me on his lap.

"Sit on my face," he commanded.

"W-what?" I asked breathless, sure I had heard him wrong.

"You heard me."

"I can't," I said incredulously.

"You can, and you will. Don't make me repeat myself, woman."

Silas's hands moved to my hips, pulling me forward until my thighs straddled his head.

"Silas," I panted. "What if I somehow smother you?"

"Then tell everyone I died eating my favorite meal."

Any protests I might have made disappeared as Silas's tongue parted my folds and thrust inside me. A low moan escaped me, and my hips rocked forward of their own volition.

Silas devoured me. His tongue moved in and out of me as he sucked my swollen knub into his mouth and bit down.

"Oh gods, Silas," I moaned as I reached for my nipple, tugging gently. "I-I'm going to come," I whimpered.

Silas increased his pace, fucking me with his tongue as if it was his cock.

I was right on the edge, shamelessly fucking his face as his fingers tightened around my hips. A powerful orgasm tore through me, sending stars dancing in my vision as I continued to rock my hips.

Struggling to keep myself upright, I fell back as I caught my breath. Silas sat up, making a show of licking his lips as he cleaned my arousal from his face.

Fuck! Why was that so... hot?

Silas lifted my leg, kissing a path towards the juncture of my thighs before lowering it and repeating the action on the other. I fixed my gaze on him, watching him closely as the heat began banking in my core once again.

Silas's hand drifted to my folds, teasing me before he plunged a finger inside me.

"Silas," I moaned.

"Tell me you're mine," he said as he thrust another finger inside me, filling me and stretching me.

"I'm yours," I moaned.

Silas's eyes heated as a wild, almost unhinged gleam shone from his brown depths. "Say it again," he demanded.

"I'm yours Silas, only yours."

He increased his rhythm, fucking me with his fingers like a man possessed. "Whose cock turns you into a wanton whore?"

"Yours," I whimpered.

"This greedy pussy is clenching around my fingers, Little Menace. Do you want me to make you come?"

"Yes," I said breathlessly.

"Beg me," he growled.

"Please, Silas. Please make me come."

A feral possessiveness contorted Silas's features as he ruthlessly plunged his fingers inside me. His thumb reached up, rubbing circles around my clit, and my hips bucked up off the ground.

I was panting hard, meeting him thrust for thrust as he brought me to the edge of oblivion for a second time.

His name was on my lips as I crashed over, my body slick with sweat and my heart hammering rapidly inside my chest.

Silas continued to pump his fingers in and out of me as I came down.

But he didn't stop.

"Silas," I gasped. "I can't... I can't go again just yet," I said, my tone pleading.

"Remember that mercy I don't have, Little Menace," he said huskily as he curled his fingers inside me.

I wiggled my hips to move away, but Silas placed his free hand on my stomach, holding me in place.

It felt like every nerve ending in my body was alight. My core was so sensitive it bordered on pain.

"P-please, Silas," I begged.

"You can do one more."

I shook my head from side to side, tears streaking down my cheeks.

"Come for me, woman," he said, gravel filling his tone as he pushed down on my clit.

A scream tore from me as Silas wrenched another orgasm from my body. I slumped against the bedroll, struggling to inhale as my body trembled violently.

Silas lowered himself atop me as he claimed my mouth with his.

And that's exactly what it was, a claiming. A demonstration of ownership. Silas was telling me without words exactly who I belonged to at this moment.

This time, I didn't mind it one bit. I felt safe, treasured even, in Silas's arms. His promise to stand beside me had resolved my doubts about the man I craved more than the air in my lungs.

Silas pulled back as he rose to his knees. His hands gripped my waist as he flipped me over and pulled me to my knees with his iron-clad hold on my hips. Silas threaded his hand into my hair, wrapping it around his wrist as he yanked me up and onto all fours.

His cock nudged my entrance before he jutted his hips forward, plunging inside me.

Silas set a brutal rhythm as he fucked me mercilessly. This was about him. My body was merely a vessel through which he chased his pleasure.

Placing a hand on the small of my back, he forced my spine to arch as he tugged on my hair. My breathing became ragged, and I struggled to hold on as he repeatedly impaled me on his cock.

Silas's movements became frantic as he raced towards his climax. He let out a low groan as he spilled himself inside me.

He released his grip on my hair, and I fell forward, utterly spent. Silas followed, pulling me to his side as he wrapped his arm around me.

We just lay there, catching our breath as we came down from our shared euphoria.

I was just about to drift off to sleep when Silas placed a soft kiss behind my ear.

"I love you, Harlowe. And one day, I am going to make you my wife."

A smile spread over my lips as I gave into the pull of sleep.

Chapter Fifty

A quiet moan slipped from my lips, and I rocked my hips, seeking more of the pleasure emanating from between my thighs. Soft kisses were placed on my shoulder and gradually traveled up my neck, inciting a need in me that went straight to my core.

"Good morning, Little Menace," Silas purred seductively. His voice was thick with sleep and the sound was so fucking sexy.

"And what do you think you're doing?" I teased, a smile pulling up the corner of my mouth.

"Taking my fill," he said and emphasized his point with a thrust of his hips.

"Silas," I moaned.

"It's been too long since I've had you at my leisure, Harlowe," he said, as he reached around and pinched a puckered nipple.

I ran my hand up the side of his neck and speared my fingers through his hair, pulling him closer.

I understood Silas's sentiment all too well.

Silas chuckled and rocked his hips against me once again.

"Silas," I whined.

"Yes, Little Menace?"

"Move faster," I demanded.

A low growl of approval made its way up his throat as he increased his rhythm. My pulse beat rapidly as my orgasm built to a crescendo inside me.

"I'm going to come," I panted.

"Come for me, Harlowe. Come all over my dick and show me just how badly you want me."

His sinful words were my undoing as I cried out, his name falling from my lips like a prayer.

Silas followed me over the edge before our bodies slumped towards the ground, both of us panting hard.

"I could get used to being woken up like that," I sighed, content.

"Good, because that's how I plan to wake you up every morning." Silas tilted my face towards him and planted a soft kiss on the end of my nose.

"I don't think that idea would thrill our companions, given our current sleeping arrangements," I joked.

"Let them watch."

"You would too, you heathen." A wide grin split Silas's face, reaching all the way to his eyes. It was such a beautiful sight, I forgot how to breathe.

"Come on," Silas said, breaking the spell. "Caolán and Misneach are meeting us back at the bottom of the outcropping. We should be able to make it by midday."

Excitement coursed through me at Silas's words. It had been too long since I'd seen my bond mate and I wanted to tell him everything I had learned.

I was still reeling from the knowledge that he had literally been created for me.

I also knew Misneach would feel vindicated, knowing that we did, in fact, share a unique bond that surpassed the one I shared with the rest of the dragons. A bubble of laughter had my shoulders shaking at the thought.

We packed our belongings and ate a simple breakfast of fruit and cheese before setting out.

The sun was high in the sky by the time we reached the outcropping. It hadn't been a difficult trek, especially compared to the journey up the mountain, but I was more than ready to rest my feet.

"Where are you?" I asked Misneach, unable to hide the excitement in my tone.

"I see you, Fire Heart," the dragon rumbled.

Craning my neck, I scanned the skies to search for him.

The sound of deafening wingbeats was the first sign of the massive beasts, followed by a disturbance in the air surrounding us.

Misneach's dark grey wings, which were splintered by indigo hues that shone as they captured the sunlight, came into view, and I beamed when his gaze met mine.

He was a sight to behold, my dragon.

His powerful body and air of authority were not uncommon among dragonkind, even if he was on the larger side.

However, it was the deft way he executed every maneuver he made, every stroke of his wings, and his inherent ability to adapt to any situation that set him apart. Despite his young age and the fact that he was mostly untested in battle, he possessed the skill set and wit of a seasoned warrior.

The ground shook beneath my feet as Misneach, and then Caolán landed on the rocky outcropping. I wasted no time as I ran towards my dragon, throwing myself at his foreleg and hugging him tight.

Misneach chuckled. **"I guess it's safe to assume you missed me, Fire Heart."**

"Very much," I beamed, stepping back to gaze up at him. **"I have so much to tell you."**

Misneach stiffened, his eyes narrowing as he peered down at me.

"What?" I asked in confusion.

Misneach's head rotated at an unnatural angle as he leveled a vicious snarl in Silas's direction.

"What? What is it, Misneach?" I asked frantically.

"The General harmed you," he growled.

"What? No, he didn't. What are you talking about, Misneach?"

Misneach returned his gaze to me.

"Then explain the bruises covering your entire throat?"

"Bruises?" I repeated, baffled by whatever was going on.

Caolán chortled, and a moment later Silas grinned, a satisfied expression on his face.

"Will someone tell me what the hell is going on?" I yelled.

"It appears Misneach may have mistaken your... ahh... love bites, as evidence of foul play," Caolán chuckled.

"Love bites?" My eyes widened in realization and my cheeks flushed with heat as I rounded on Silas.

"What did you do?" I said as I pointed an accusatory finger in his direction.

"I might have been overly enthusiastic last night," he confessed, attempting to hide his grin.

I wasn't sure if he was more entertained by my reaction, or that of the dragon, who was seething right over my shoulder.

"Tell him to keep his unworthy extremities to himself next time," Misneach scowled.

"Oh, my gods! Can we not have this conversation?"

Caolán snorted and Silas howled with raucous laughter. It was then that I realized I had said that last part out loud.

I climbed onto Misneach's back and left the other pair of idiots to find their own way back.

As we flew, I filled Misneach in on everything Drakkon had told me.

"I knew what we shared was far more significant than the mere connection felt by the others," he scoffed as soon as I had finished telling him about my encounter.

The satisfaction was rolling off him in waves.

"That's your takeaway from everything I just told you?" I chastised. I knew it would be.

"It is an important fact to understand, Fire Heart. The other dragons will know of it."

"What about the part where you were literally created for me so that you can anchor me to the present and not let me draw more power than I can contain?" I asked.

"It goes without saying that I will be an excellent anchor," Misneach huffed. **"There's no need for further discussion on the topic."**

I just rolled my eyes. What could I possibly say to that?

"It's a relief to understand why I'm connected to the other dragons. I mean, I knew being the conduit of dragon flames was part of it, but knowing we are kin and that is why we can all communicate has helped settle my unease," I said.

"Does this mean you will start training your powers?" Misneach asked.

"Yes. Now that I know I'm not destined for evil, and that you will be there to help me and guide me, I'm no longer afraid of my powers."

"I have always been there for you, Fire Heart."

"Of course, I know that Misneach. I just meant that I didn't realize you could help me with this."

"We will navigate this path, together," Misneach declared.

"Together," I repeated.

And for the first time since fleeing my kingdom, I felt... hopeful.

Chapter Fifty-One

After spending two days traveling, we finally arrived back at the camp, where everyone was eagerly awaiting our return. I had hoped the love bites Silas had given me would have faded by the time we made it there.

It seems that was not the case.

As soon as I had dismounted, Emmerson was on me. "What the fuck are those?" she asked as she pointed toward my neck.

No hello, I'm glad you're safe and I'm happy you've returned, I thought in irritation.

"Nothing," I said, trying to pull my collar up higher. At this point, I wasn't sure if I was more annoyed at Emmerson or Silas.

Misneach huffed, and Silas grinned.

All right, I was definitely more irritated at Silas.

"Those are love bites," she crooned.

"Shut up," I hissed.

"By the gods, Silas, did you leave any part of her unscathed?" Emmerson teased. "I don't know whether to make good on my threat to end your life for letting harm come to her, or congratulate you on a job well done."

I groaned.

Without fail, my best friend took every opportunity to embarrass me.

Silas, however, was grinning like a fool. The other men snickered, demonstrating they lacked any basic manners between the lot of them.

Glaring at Emmerson, I said, "If you're done."

She grinned mischievously, and I knew I hadn't heard the last of her taunting.

"I have rather pressing information to impart. Or did you forget the purpose of our journey?" I chided.

Emmerson sobered, prompting the others to do the same.

I walked over to the makeshift eating area and then settled down on one of the logs. Emmerson took the seat next to me, and Zeke sat on my other side.

Silas frowned at Zeke, and I ducked my head to hide my smile.

After everyone was seated, I told them everything Drakkon had shared with me.

"So, you're a dragon?" Fionn asked, not understanding Drakkon's explanation that I was the dragon's kin.

"No fool," Teller said with a smile as he pushed Fionn playfully.

"I'm not a dragon," I confirmed. "However, I originated from the same source as all other dragons. In a way, they are all my brothers and sisters. That's why I can communicate with them all."

Fionn rubbed his forefinger and thumb over his chin for a moment before he said, "I guess that makes sense."

"And Misneach was made specifically for you?" Cillian clarified.

"As Drakkon explained it, dragon flames were never meant to be wielded by a human. From what I understand, the fates knew Kieran would become extremely powerful. So, they sourced the most lethal magic they could and instilled it in the one they created to serve as a counter to his powers," I said, pointing my thumb at my chest.

"Lucky me," I muttered to myself.

"Since I was never intended to possess this level of power, Misneach was created as my anchor. He can lend me his strength, which will ground me in the present, and he'll also know if I draw on more power than I can hold."

When I glanced in Misneach's direction, I found him already looking my way. He bared his teeth, in what I think was supposed to pass as a reassuring smile.

If so, it required significant improvements.

Misneach snorted, seemingly displeased with my observations. **"Ungrateful fiend,"** he huffed.

"Now that's more like it, Misneach. Your insults and sarcasm are the balm for all my worries," I grinned.

Misneach rolled his eyes, but I caught the chuckle he tried to conceal.

Cillian blew out a breath, drawing my attention back to the group. "That's a lot. I'm glad it's you and not me, Harlowe."

Emmerson threw the apple she had been carving, and it hit him in the head.

"Ow, Em! What was that for?" Cillian howled.

"For being insensitive," she growled.

As Cillian's gaze flicked to mine, a sheepish smile crossed his lips. "Sorry Harlowe, I didn't mean it like that."

I waved him off. "Don't be. If the situation were reversed, I would feel the same way."

"See," Cillian said to Emmerson.

The dagger she had been using to cut her apple went sailing through the air. Cillian narrowly avoided being struck by the blade as he lunged sideways.

"Somebody is a little too fond of violence," Zeke chuckled.

"Getting back on track," I said before Zeke could become Emmerson's latest victim.

I happened to like my friend as he was; breathing.

"So, it turns out there was never any block on my powers. Not in the way we all thought, anyway." No one said anything as they waited for me to continue.

"I was blocking myself," I said in a rush.

"What?" Emmerson asked.

"I was fearful of what I might be capable of, so every time I tried to summon my flames, I was unable to manifest them."

"But you used your flames on the Harpy and then when you roasted all those roc. So what's the difference?"

"Drakkon said that when I didn't think about it, I acted on instinct and so my flames responded. But the minute I tried to call them to me if I wasn't being threatened... nothing happened," I said with a shrug of my shoulders.

"Why didn't you tell me, Harlowe? I would have helped you work through it," she said.

"You know you can rely on us," Zeke added.

The others pointedly looked in any direction but ours, giving us the illusion of privacy. Although, I knew better. They all strained to listen. Hell, they were barely even breathing.

Bloody gossips.

"I didn't realize that was what I was doing," I admitted. "Drakkon sort of led me to the realization by asking me all these questions until I discovered it on my own."

I might not have told them, even if I had known. I thought I was destined to turn to the darkness, and the pull towards Kieran filled me with so much shame I didn't give it the attention it deserved. Maybe I would have realized there could be more than one explanation for my feelings if I had.

I wouldn't repeat that mistake, though.

"I'm still terrified by the idea that I could one day summon too much power that I might incinerate myself," I said, chuckling nervously.

"That won't happen," Emmerson said with determination.

"How can you be sure?"

"One, you have Misneach. That grumpy bastard would never let you self-destruct. Hell, it will be hard for you to even test your limits before he freaks out and starts dragging you away without even scratching the surface."

Misneach's head rotated towards us and this time when he bared his teeth, I knew his snarl promised violence.

Emmerson just bared her teeth and snarled right back.

"And two," she said, grinning, "we'll train you. Isn't that right, Z?"

"Of course we will," Zeke said enthusiastically. "How exactly will we do that?" he added after a beat.

"Simple. Trial and error," Emmerson beamed.

Chapter Fifty-Two

When Emmerson said, 'trial and error', convincing the others to let me throw flames at them was not exactly what I had in mind.

From the looks on their faces, it wasn't what they thought would accompany my training, either.

"Can't we start with the basics?" Teller asked. "You know, let's get Harlowe to conjure her flames and practice wielding them first."

Emmerson snorted and a delicate chuckle came from Everly's direction as she prepared herself a cup of tea.

"If you're too much of a coward, Teller, feel free to stand down," Emmerson purred.

"It's got nothing to do with being a coward, Emmerson," Teller grumbled. "I just think it makes more sense to focus on helping Harlowe control her power before offering life and limb."

He had a point.

I tuned out the bickering pair and closed my eyes, focusing on my breathing. The only other time I had managed to conjure my flames was when I escaped the maze. My life was in danger, so I wasn't sure if I could replicate the process, but it was worth trying.

As I cleared my mind, I focused on the ground beneath my boots and visualized myself connecting with the earth. I imagined my energy flowing from my body into the dirt before the earth returned its energy to me.

A small tugging sensation formed in the pit of my stomach the harder

I pushed. I kept repeating the process, pushing my energy down and welcoming it back on its return.

My palms heated, and I cracked one eye open and peeked down. A flame flickered in my hand, and a smile spread across my lips.

The flame flickered once before dying out.

I closed my eyes again, not wanting to get distracted and lose whatever connection I had established with my power. This time when I visualized sharing my energy with the earth, my flames responded. My palms burned, and I knew without looking that they were both alight.

Clasping my hands together, I visualized a sword with scorching, red embers, and let my energy flow freely from me.

The clearing fell silent, and I quickly snapped my eyes open.

Everyone was staring at me.

Peering down at my hands, I saw the most incredible sight.

In my hands was a sword; its blade was made of fire with flames that flickered and danced in hues of crimson, gold, and orange. The handle of the blade reflected molten steel as it glowed brighter than any ember. I could feel the heat emanating from the sword like a raging inferno, but it did not burn me, as if it yielded to my touch.

I lifted the blade higher, moving it through the air as I tested its range. Unlike a typical sword, it was light in my grip, and yet, it was as solid as if forged from the same metal. The blade pulsed with a controlled ferocity, ready to follow my every command.

I needed to test the sword's durability to see how it would hold up against a physical weapon.

"Zeke, spar with me?" I asked eagerly.

Zeke hesitated for a moment, but one glance towards Emmerson had him retrieving his blade and squaring up against me.

"Gods, Harlowe. The heat coming off that thing is insane," Zeke said as he raised his sword.

The moment our blades collided, a sizzling sound filled the clearing and sparks flew in a wide arc. I could feel the power of the sword thrumming in my palms as though it were an extension of me. As if reading my thoughts, the blade was already moving before I recognized the strikes I was making.

The sword was not merely a weapon; it was a conduit of my will.

Zeke and I went blow for blow as we sparred, each thrusting, slicing, and parrying in equal measure.

When we finally called a halt to the demonstration, I was a sweaty, panting mess. I glanced in Zeke's direction and saw he had fared no better.

I leaned over, placing my hands on my knees, and recalled my flames to me. Once the last ember died out, I flopped to the ground for some much-needed respite.

"That was amazing, Harlowe," Zeke panted as he dropped down next to me. "I think that sword improved your skills."

I sent the back of my hand sailing in his direction, and it landed on his stomach, eliciting a grunt from Zeke.

"Are you telling me I've been lacking?" I huffed.

"No, you vicious little harpy. All I meant was the sword seemed to hone your skills. It was as if it responded to you rather than being controlled by you," he said.

"That's exactly how it felt too," I panted.

Emmerson's gleeful expression filled my vision as she peered down at us.

"That was fucking awesome," Emmerson said, a wide grin splitting her features and making her look somewhat maniacal.

"Look at Zeke's sword," Fionn said, and we both rose onto our elbows as Fionn inspected it intently.

"There are small chips in the steel," Teller said as he joined Fionn.

"What?" Zeke hissed as he scrambled to his feet.

He wrenched the blade from Fionn's grip and studied the sword, his face falling.

"That's my favorite sword," Zeke said, and he sounded like he was in actual pain.

I got to my feet and ambled over to him. As I peered over his shoulder, I saw the reason behind his distress.

The blade, once honed to perfection, now bore the unmistakable scars of steel meeting unyielding resistance. Irregular, jagged edges lined the blade to the hilt. It was as if every point of contact with my blazing sword had left a mark on Zeke's blade.

"That's..." I trailed off. I had no idea what that was. "I'm sorry Zeke. I'll get you another blade, I promise."

"No need, Harlowe. I brought a half dozen with me when I left Valoren."

"Is that what you're hiding in that enormous pack you insist on carrying around, but won't let me peek inside of?" Emmerson asked from his other side.

"None of your business, woman," Zeke snapped. "They are my weapons, and you can keep your grubby little hands off them."

Emmerson stared at Zeke with a blank expression and then pivoted on her feet and bolted in the direction of his belongings.

Nothing, and I mean nothing, excited Emmerson more than the sight of weapons. She is one bloodthirsty little hellcat.

"Emmerson," Zeke bellowed before sprinting after her.

I shook my head in sympathy with Zeke, knowing all too well his weapon stash would be lighter by day's end.

A hand snaked around my waist, and I was pulled against a hard chest. "That was the hottest thing I have ever seen," Silas whispered against my ear so only I would hear.

"Is that so?" I asked.

Silas thrust his hips against my backside, letting me feel the hard outline of his erection.

"I suggest finding a quiet corner to take care of that, because there is no way Emmerson is done for the day," I purred.

Silas tightened his grip on my hip. "You tease."

A cry of victory had everyone turning toward where Emmerson and Zeke had disappeared. Emmerson ran over to me, something glinting in her hand.

"Harlowe look," Emmerson said as she thrust something towards me.

It was a beautiful obsidian dagger, with a large midnight-colored sapphire in the center of the pommel. Smaller clusters of diamonds and emeralds surrounded the larger stone. The blade itself was equally stunning with its intricate patterns. I looked closer at the patterns, realizing that they were protection runes that curved with the blade until they reached the pointed tip.

"Do you know how long I have coveted this dagger?" Emmerson asked, the awe unmistakable in her tone.

"You have to give it back, Emmerson," I said.

"What? No way," Emmerson said as she clutched the dagger tight against her chest.

"My father gave Zeke that blade. He had it custom-made for him in recognition of his bravery during the Skirmish of Power."

Emmerson's face fell, and I felt Silas stiffen against me. I sometimes forgot about Silas's history and how he fought against my kingdom in the war.

"Fine," Emmerson grumbled, heading back in the direction she came. "Don't think we're done," she called over her shoulder.

"Don't worry, I was under no such illusions," I muttered to myself, and I heard Silas chuckle.

Emmerson declared that my demonstration with the sword was enough practice at wielding and we could now move on to practicing using my flames as a shield as I had done in the Forest of Nightmares.

When no one volunteered to be my test subject, she berated them all and even invoked some nonsense about cursing their descendants for their cowardice.

"Looks like it's you and me, Harlowe," she said, grinning. "I had hoped to observe because I really want to see what it looks like from the outside. But seeing as they are all COWARDS," she hollered and lifted her shoulder in a shrug.

"I'm not sure what to do," I confessed as we stood facing each other.

"What did you do to conjure the sword?" she asked.

"I visualized it."

"All right, then visualize yourself on fire and expand that image to include me," she offered.

I raised a brow at her description. "Visualize myself on fire?"

"Oh, don't give me that look. You know what I mean," she said, waving me off.

I chuckled to myself as I closed my eyes and did as she instructed. Again, my flames responded, starting in my palms, and working their way up my arms until my whole body felt warm.

"Great," Emmerson said, and I opened my eyes. As I peered down at myself, I could see that I was, indeed, on fire. I would be lying if I said the sight wasn't a little nauseating.

"Now me," Emmerson said eagerly.

"I don't know, Em," I said, fear slowly working its way up my throat.

"I trust you, Harlowe," Emmerson said with determination.

She nodded once, and I closed my eyes once more, as I imagined my flames spreading from my body to hers.

"Anything?" I asked, not breaking my concentration.

Emmerson inhaled sharply, and I threw my eyes open, fearing the worst.

With a broad grin, Emmerson ran her fingers along the flames that were encasing her body.

"This is incredible, Harlowe," she breathed. "You're incredible," she added as she raised her gaze to mine.

Her grin was infectious, and I couldn't help but return it.

"Cillian," she called out, peering over her shoulder.

Cillian strode in our direction until he reached her side.

"Yes, Little Viper?"

My eyes darted to hers, and she flushed.

"It seems to be a Pyrithian thing," she muttered. I barked out a laugh and Cillian smirked, obviously enjoying her embarrassment.

"See if you can touch me," she said to Cillian, redirecting the conversation.

Cillian reached his hand towards her but immediately jerked it back.

"Fuck," he hissed.

"What is it?" I asked, letting the flames fall away.

Cillian was clutching his hand and when he laid it out flat, small blisters were forming all over his palm.

"I thought you said Harlowe's flames don't harm you," Cillian said as he glared at Emmerson.

Emmerson just grinned. "They didn't," she said, gesturing up and down her body. "But you weren't inside the bubble, Cillian. You were the one trying to get past its defenses." Her saccharine tone was dripping with satisfaction.

Cillian shook his head, but a smile pulled up his lips all the same. "You're vicious, you know that," he said to Emmerson, but there was no bite to his tone.

"Come on," Emmerson said, linking her arm with his. "Let's see if Everly has anything for this," she said, tilting her head towards Cillian's palm. Lowering her voice, she purred, "Then I'll kiss it all better for you."

Cillian's footsteps faltered and then quickened as he rushed towards Everly.

Emmerson threw me a saucy smile over her shoulder and winked.

I had to wonder if Cillian realized just how tightly she had him wrapped around her dainty fingers.

Chapter Fifty-Three

The last few days had been brutal.

Emmerson had given me little reprieve from training, and she had been pushing me to go further with every lesson.

She was also correct in her prediction that Misneach would struggle to sit by and watch as I tested my limits. The first signs of fatigue had him cursing and trying to spirit me away.

And my dragon never cursed! No, he was too refined for such vulgarities.

I had to talk him down each time it happened. I'd convince him I was fine, only to repeat the cycle with the next huff of breath.

Managing Misneach was almost more draining than the actual training.

That's how I ended up scrambling in the grass, playing dodge with Misneach. He refused to move out of my way until he was satisfied my strength had been replenished.

May the gods have mercy on me because I wasn't sure I would survive his form of compassion.

Conceding defeat, I grabbed my waterskin and sat down on the ground.

Somebody dropped to the ground next to me and I turned in their direction, expecting to find Silas. Only it was Teller's serene smile and relaxed aura that met me.

"How are you hanging in there?" he asked, with a subtle tilt of his head towards Misneach.

I snorted, forgetting about the water I had just gulped, forcing its reemergence through my nostrils.

How the hell could cool liquid burn?

I coughed and Teller thumped me on the back as I tried to recover my breathing.

"Sorry Harlowe," he said with a sheepish grin.

"All good. I'm the idiot who forgot how to breathe," I said, waving off his concern. "To answer your question, it's a little... suffocating," I whispered so as not to let Misneach overhear.

"You forget Fire Heart, I do not need my ears to hear what you're saying," he grumbled.

Shit. Of course not.

"Sorry," I said in a sweet tone as I peered over at him, offering him a smile.

Misneach huffed but said no more. I took that as a sign I was forgiven.

Teller followed my line of vision and chuckled in understanding.

We both turned our attention to the sparring session before us. Zeke was teaching Fionn a few new moves, and he was adapting rather quickly.

Zeke was a formidable warrior, and it showed with how deftly he fought whenever sparring with the Cathal, the most feared warriors in all Aetherian.

"How is Fionn going? He seems better lately," I asked Teller as I studied Fionn.

"He is. I think I have seen him through the worst of it," Teller replied.

It still hurt to be reminded about the fallen Cathal. Cian's death still haunted me, knowing I played a role in his demise.

"I think you're selling yourself short, Teller," I said, nudging him playfully with my shoulder. "Fionn was struggling, we all saw it. From where I'm sitting, I'd say you dragged him out of the darkness and back into the light."

Teller's ears heated at my praise, and he cleared his throat awkwardly.

"Yes, well, he's like a little brother to me and I'd do anything within my power to help him. Besides, the hard stuff was all him. He was the one who had to decide to keep moving forward, to keep living."

I nodded in agreement.

Watching Fionn mourn the loss of someone he considered a brother and drag himself back out of that despair had been harrowing. Teller often disappeared with him for hours at a time so he could work through his emotions; his anger, his grief, and his fear. At one point, he seemed hell-bent on cutting himself off from everyone, fearful to get too close in case he lost them, too. I was glad to see him returning to his joyful and fun-loving self, little by little.

"And how are you doing with everything? From your time in Netheran, I mean?" Teller asked cautiously.

I took a deep breath, mulling over my answer.

"I think I'm doing better as well. For a time, I felt so... I don't know how to explain it exactly. Ashamed maybe. I was scared too. Scared about my future, or what I thought would inevitably become my future.

But after meeting Drakkon and learning more about my purpose and how I was created, I feel more settled. More in control of my life. And that was something Kieran desperately tried to take away from me, my control."

I glanced in Teller's direction as my cheeks heated. "I'm rambling, sorry," I muttered.

Teller threw his arm over my shoulder and pulled me tight against his side. "You never have to apologize for being yourself with me, Harlowe," Teller said affectionately.

"Thanks, Teller," I said, hugging him back.

"So, once you've figured all this out," — he said, gesturing towards the training field — "what's next?"

"Well, we can't stay here," I said, stating the obvious. "While we were away, Silas mentioned an old manor house that his family owned, but no longer used."

"Which one?" Teller asked. "The one that borders Elysara, or the one that sits alongside the Forest of Nightmares?"

"There's two?" I asked, surprised.

"Yes."

"And they're both unoccupied?"

"When the Queen died, the King consolidated his estates. He didn't enjoy being too far away from his sons and no longer stays away from the palace unless he's traveling for court business."

I pursed my lips. The King sounded like a caring, reasonable man when described like that. Nothing like the man who tried to coerce me into a marriage with his deranged son for personal gain.

"He may not have given you the best impression when you met," Teller said as if sensing my thoughts. "But he has always been a good king to his people."

I had nothing to say to that, so I remained silent. I didn't disbelieve Leith was loved by his people, but that did nothing to assuage the anger I felt towards him for how he treated Emmerson and me.

"So, which one is it?" Teller prompted.

"The one near the Forest of Nightmares," I said absentmindedly.

"Ah. It's a fair way from the forest, but I must admit, I was secretly hoping for the other," Teller chuckled.

"I wasn't too keen on the idea myself, Teller, so you're not alone."

We sat in silence for a time, both watching the sparring session, lost in our thoughts.

"War is coming, isn't it?" Teller asked, not pulling his focus from Fionn and Zeke.

"It is," I said, and that reality filled me with sadness. "Kieran has been planning this for centuries and he's not about to put his grievances aside simply because I escaped him."

Teller nodded, his shoulders straightening with his acceptance.

"We will need allies," Teller said. "And a plan beyond releasing you on the realm and hoping for the best." Teller flashed me a cheeky grin and I couldn't help but laugh.

"I certainly hope that's not the extent of our plans, Teller," I joked.

"We also need to deal with whoever is hunting you. Aside from Kieran, I mean."

The thought of the golden-eyed man sobered me immediately.

Before I could dwell on it too much, a dark shadow fell over us, and I craned my neck to see who it was. Silas's rich brown eyes studied me before a small smirk tugged up one side of his mouth.

"Are you ready?" he asked.

"Ready for what?"

Without answering me, Silas thrust his hand out to me, and I tentatively placed mine in his.

"You'll see," Silas said as he led me to the center of the clearing.

Chapter Fifty-Four

Silas stood across the clearing, his hands hanging by his sides as he watched me.

Everyone else was a safe distance away as they formed a semi-circle around us.

My heart was hammering in my chest, and I was certain I was on the verge of emptying my stomach.

I did not want to be doing this.

When Silas suggested we spar, I was all for it. That was, until he mentioned I would wield my flames, and he would summon fórsa.

The stakes were far higher than when I practiced with a flaming sword or used the dragons as targets while I tossed fireballs at them.

At least they were fireproof.

Silas was not. And I most definitely was not immune to the destructive power of fórsa.

Sweat coated my body as I stared at Silas, and I hadn't even started yet.

"I still think this is a terrible idea," I yelled at Silas.

"Show me what you've got, Little Menace," Silas hollered back.

One of us was definitely dying today.

"Make sure it's him and it will serve him right," Misneach scoffed.

Misneach also wasn't fond of this idea.

Everly almost fainted when Emmerson suggested she could simply heal either of us if things got out of hand. Everly politely pointed out that someone still had to be alive to be healed.

Small wisps of light danced around Silas's fingertips as he summoned fórsa to do his bidding. I took a deep breath and let flames form in my palms as they licked their way up my arms.

I could see Silas's satisfied smirk from across the clearing.

The bastard was enjoying this.

"**Eviscerate him**," Misneach growled.

"Misneach," I snapped. "**We aren't playing around. One of us could get hurt.**"

"**Who said I was playing?**" he retorted.

For the love of the gods, these two.

Silas released an orb of energy that sped across the field toward me, and I sent a fireball flying back.

The distance that separated us was supposed to act as a buffer of sorts. In theory, it should allow us enough time to get out of the way if either of our defenses failed. That thought did nothing to calm my raging nerves, however, as the two power sources converged.

A deafening explosion filled the air, and I clapped my hands over my ears. What happened next can only be described as a display of chaotic beauty. Embers sparked and danced upon impact, and the searing heat of the collision sent rippling waves through the air that shimmered and glowed as they went.

The remnants of the two power sources swirled around each other, fusing together, before they dissipated and fell to the ground. The scent of scorched earth assaulted my nostrils, and I lowered my gaze, taking in the destruction of the charred landscape at the point of contact.

"That was fucking amazing," Emmerson hooted as she threw her fist into the air.

At least someone had enjoyed the show.

I, on the other hand, promptly turned away from everyone, lowered my palms to my knees, and dislodged the contents of my stomach. Now that I had purged the adrenaline from my system, I became a shaking, nauseated mess.

Misneach winced.

If I wasn't so sure I was about to heave again, I'd have sent a rude gesture his way. Someone placed a palm on my lower back and started rubbing soothing circles as I continued to heave and gag.

When my tender stomach finally relented, I straightened and was surprised to find Cillian standing behind me.

"Sometimes they forget there is a person behind the power, but they mean well," Cillian said as he tilted his head towards the others, still caught up in their celebrations.

"Thank you, Cillian," I said as I gave his hand a light squeeze. He produced a waterskin, and I took it eagerly, washing away the foul taste still coating my tongue. Cillian gave me a curt nod and then rejoined the others.

"Harlowe," Silas called out, cupping his hands around his mouth. "Are you all right?"

I gave him a thumbs up and he acknowledged Cillian with a nod of thanks.

"Now, erect that shield of yours, and once you're ready, I'll attack it with fórsa," he yelled.

I let out a shaky breath but nodded once and called up my flames. They climbed up my body until they completely covered me.

It still amazed me how rapidly they responded to me now that I was no longer blocking my powers.

While focusing on extending the reach of my shield, I pushed my flames further out until I felt satisfied that I had built a large enough buffer.

"Ready," I called, and then added, "Don't aim head-on all right. Make sure I can escape the crosshairs if necessary."

"Little Menace, have I ever endangered you?" Silas crooned.

"Debatable," I shouted right back, which had our spectators chuckling.

Silas shook his head, but when he met my gaze a moment later, all signs of amusement had disappeared from his features. All that remained was steely determination.

Silas's hand shot out, releasing another orb of energy. I planted my feet and tried not to give in to the urge to flee. When Silas's power collided with my fiery shield, it exploded, the same as before. This time, though, no trace of the orb passed the point of impact.

My shield held.

Silas grinned and I let the flames recede. He jogged across the clearing, reaching my side in seconds.

"You did it, Little Menace," Silas said, a wide grin splitting his face.

His palms cupped my cheeks, and he pulled me towards him for a scorching kiss. Loud cheers erupted and this time, I sent a rude hand gesture flying their way.

They then started calling out random numbers, and I had to ask Silas what the hell they were doing.

"They're either rating your impressive skills or my kissing abilities," he said, grinning against my lips. "Knowing that lot, it's probably the latter. They are incapable of taking anything seriously."

"Five," Fionn yelled, and I laughed.

"Looks like you better up your game," I taunted.

Silas gripped me by the nape of my neck and lowered me into a dip as he kissed me with barely restrained need. His tongue assaulted mine as we battled for dominance in a clash of lips, tongue, and teeth. When we came up for air, I was panting heavily.

"A solid nine-point five," Emmerson howled.

Silas grinned. "Much better."

"Aren't you curious how you lost the point five?" I asked.

Silas shrugged. "I got all the confirmation I needed when you were tasting me as if your life depended on it."

Cocky bastard.

Pulling me upright, Silas said, "Come on. Let's see if you can do that again, but this time, let's add someone else inside your shield for you to protect."

I groaned.

Any hope I had for a reprieve just evaporated with Silas's eager grin.

This day was far from over.

Chapter Fifty-Five

We remained at our camp for another week while I practiced wielding my flames and improving the strength of my shield. I could now extend my shield to ten feet in every direction. I had even protected both Emmerson and Zeke while being attacked by the others. Neither fórsa nor steel had penetrated my shield, and I was feeling more confident by the day.

That's why we decided to progress to the next phase in our plan and were heading to Silas's family manor. We'd packed up early this morning and had been traveling all day. By the time we picked a place to camp for the night, I was relieved to be back on the ground.

I found myself lost in thought, wondering about what we'd find at the manor.

Would a younger, carefree Silas still linger in the halls, or had he been a stoic child, like the man he was now? It was hard to picture Silas growing up as a pampered prince given the rigidity he employed when training the Cathal. I couldn't see beyond the formidable Commanding General.

He was nothing like his brother, August. I shivered with disgust at the thought of that animal.

While I hadn't known August for long, I couldn't help but notice the hint of sadism that twinkled in his eyes. After all, what man would try to take the woman his brother is obsessed with, only to break her to cause him pain?

The woman his brother loves, I corrected.

That thought sent a burst of warmth straight to my chest.

"What are you thinking about?" Silas whispered against the shell of my ear. A startled squeal left me, and I turned around to glare at him.

"Do not, do that!" I growled.

Silas laughed and pulled me to his chest before placing a small kiss on the top of my head.

"Do you want to come hunting with me?" Silas asked, his eyes glinting with mischief.

"By hunting, you mean..." I let my words trail off, recalling the last time he hunted me in the forest.

"Don't tempt me, Little Menace," Silas growled. "I meant hunting for dinner."

My whole body lit up, excitement and adrenaline flooding my veins. I loved hunting. And I was damned good at it, too.

"Absolutely," I said, unable to hide my eagerness. "Let me get my bow."

I knew Silas hunted in close quarters, relying on his dagger as his weapon of choice. It took skill and more stealth than I probably possessed.

However, there was something about having an arrow pulled taut, blocking out the rest of the world, and living and breathing in the same moment as my prey, that never failed to humble me. Those moments always reminded me of the fragility of life and how it was truly a gift.

With my bow and quiver secured to my back, Silas grabbed my hand and led me into the woods surrounding the camp.

As we delved into the woods, we found traces of wildlife and Silas suggested we separate to increase our chances of catching a meal. Most times, I hunted alone at home, so I had no concerns about trekking through the woods by myself.

The sun was rapidly fading as I moved silently through the underbrush, tracking the small hoofprints of what I guessed was a deer. The sound of a twig snapping drew my attention, and I moved towards it as the smell of moss and damp soil filled my nose.

I inhaled deeply. I loved the earthy scents of the woods after the rain.

A rustling of leaves told me I was getting close now. It only took five more steps before a large deer, grazing peacefully in the vegetation, came into view. I crouched low, concealing myself against the base of a thick tree. I lifted my bow, my arrow already nocked and waiting.

Inhaling deeply, I released a controlled breath as I steadied my hand and pulled the arrow taut. The deer raised its head as if sensing the threat lurking nearby.

The sound of my arrow shattered the stillness of the woods as it raced through the air toward its target. My aim was true, and the deer fell to the ground with a loud *thump*.

Rising from my crouched position, I moved towards my kill, and a small pang of guilt tore through me when I found the creature struggling in the dirt.

"I'm sorry," I whispered. "I'll make it quick."

I retrieved my dagger and placed it at the deer's neck. When I moved the blade over the creature's throat, I felt the flood of warm liquid pour over my hand as the animal's life force left its body. All the while, I stroked the deer's head, offering what comfort I could.

When it was over, I reached down and lifted the deer before throwing it over my shoulders. I was making my way out of the woods when the sound of dirt and leaves crunching under boots reached me. Silas emerged at my side, carrying half a dozen rabbits.

He looked at my deer, and then down at his rabbits before scowling.

"Don't be a bad sport," I teased.

"Easy for you to say. You're not the one who is about to be ribbed by your subordinates for the rest of the evening," he grumbled.

I laughed at his sullen expression, which only deepened in response.

Silas was right to worry. The others taunted him mercilessly the whole time we were preparing our meal. It was only when he threatened to withhold their portions that they relented.

The atmosphere around the camp was peaceful, jovial even. In usual form, Teller serenaded us with tales of his bravery, skill, and conquests. The last was a topic of heated debate as his companions argued against his version of events in his retelling.

My stomach muscles ached from laughing so hard, I had to beg him to stop just so I could get a moment of reprieve.

"Fire Heart," Misneach said, drawing my attention.

"Yes, Misneach?"

"The other dragons and I are going hunting. Don't wander from camp while I'm gone."

"All right, Misneach," I said, barely preventing myself from rolling my eyes.

"I find it incredible you still think you can hide things from me, Fire Heart. You might not have rolled your eyes at me, but you thought about it... hard," Misneach scolded.

"All right, all right. I'll stay put. Go have fun," I implored.

"We do not hunt for fun, Fire Heart. We hunt for sustenance."

"Speak for yourself," Rónán added.

"Except Rónán, but he's an idiot," Misneach said, eliciting a snort of agreement from Oisín.

Rónán grumbled something unintelligible as the sound of wingbeats disturbed the quiet night air.

"The dragons are going hunting," I told no one in particular.

By the time Silas came to ask if I was ready for bed, I was barely keeping my eyes open.

I was ready to surrender to the pull of sleep when Silas's large palm skirted under my tunic and settled on my stomach just above the waistband of my pants.

When his fingers dipped below my leathers, I froze.

"What are you doing, Silas?"

"Shh," he whispered, as he trailed kisses along my throat.

"Everyone will hear," I hissed.

"Not if you're quiet. Can you be quiet for me, Little Menace?"

Silas's finger dipped inside me, and a soft moan escaped me.

Silas chuckled. "They'll surely hear you if you keep that up."

"I can't help it," I said, breathless.

Silas dipped another finger inside me, and I moaned again. This time, Silas tipped my head towards him, capturing the sound with his lips.

He pumped his fingers in and out of me roughly. Just as I was about to come, he curled his fingers inside me, sending stars dancing behind my eyes.

Silas continued his ministrations as I came down from my orgasm.

"Relaxed?" Silas asked with a prideful smirk.

"Very."

He kissed the tip of my nose as he pulled me tight against his chest.

"Sleep," he commanded, and my body obeyed.

Chapter Fifty-Six

I startled awake, my pulse pounding rapidly as I peered around me. For a moment, I didn't recognize my surroundings until I caught sight of the tattooed arm draped over my waist.

I was with Silas and the others at our camp.

My dreams had been vague; flashes of dark shadows contrasting against vivid colors. Whenever I thought they'd form into something tangible, the image was lost against the warring shades again.

An uneasy feeling crept over me in the aftermath of my dream. I didn't know what it was exactly, but it was unsettling all the same.

As I peered around, I noticed the dragons had not returned from their hunting trip. This knowledge only served to further disturb me. I always felt safe around Misneach, whether or not that was rational.

The fire we started earlier still shone, assuring me it wasn't too late. The others must have only recently gone to bed.

Unfurling Silas's arm from around me was a more challenging task than I had expected. Every time I tried to tug it away, he moved closer, tightening his hold. Once I was free of his iron grip, I walked around the perimeter of the camp, peering into the woods as if it would reveal its secrets to me.

A prickle of awareness started at the base of my skull and traveled down the length of my spine. Even straining, I still failed to detect anything amiss. However, I had learned the hard way to trust my instincts.

I moved back towards my bedroll, slipping beneath the blankets, and prodded Silas awake.

"Harlowe," he said roughly, sleep thickening his tone.

"Shh," I said against his lips as if we were two lovers stealing a kiss beneath the stars.

Silas responded immediately, so in tune with my body he could tell something was wrong.

"What is it?" he asked as he pushed his fingers into my hair as if deepening our kiss.

"Something feels off, but I don't know what."

Silas reached between us, silently unsheathing his dagger. He placed it into my palm before he retrieved another.

"I'm cold," I said, loud enough to disturb the others.

We had all agreed this would be the phrase we'd use to alert the others that something was amiss.

Well, the others had agreed to it as I was in Netheran at the time, but semantics.

Zeke muttered something under his breath, but he rose from his bedroll and stalked towards the fire, picking up his sword as he went.

When he reached Teller, he gave him a stiff kick, mumbling something about being on watch. Teller grumbled in response, flicking Fionn's ear as he rose to join Zeke.

Cillian and Emmerson were both wide awake, darting glances around the clearing while they remained huddled close together. I had no doubts they were both heavily armed.

"Do you think Everly has any of that tonic left, the one she gave me for my headache earlier?" I asked Silas.

"Why don't you wake her and see?"

I rose from my position, making my way over to Everly, who was the only one of us still sleeping. Grabbing her shoulders, I shook her gently as I leaned in to whisper in her ear.

"Everly. Everly, you need to wake up."

Everly moaned and rolled to her other side, away from my intrusions.

"Everly, I need you to wake up," I said, more urgently this time.

"Harlowe?" she asked, still subdued by sleep.

"Do you have any more of that tonic you gave me earlier?" I asked. Then more quietly, I added, "Something is wrong. Don't look around or act suspicious. Say yes, then go find a hiding spot. Nod if you understand me."

Everly nodded once and said, "Yes."

A DAUGHTER OF FIRE AND FLAME

I pushed Silas's dagger into her hand, and she rose to her feet. "I'll retrieve it for you."

"Thank you," I said before returning to Silas.

I sat on the bedroll, not bothering to lie back down. Silas pushed yet another dagger into my hand, and I had to wonder where he was keeping them all, considering I never noticed them when we went to bed. The bulk of his weapons lay in a pile beside him, well within reach, should he need them.

In the distance, a branch breaking shattered the silence of the night, reverberating around the open space.

That was all the confirmation I needed.

"Sounded about 30 yards away and to the left," Silas said as he rose to a sitting position behind me.

He wrapped an arm around my waist and nuzzled the side of my neck. As I turned my head in his direction, I caught the silent communication that passed between him and Cillian.

Cillian stood, pulling Emmerson with him, and she let out a high-pitched squeal. He then lowered his lips to hers and claimed her with a passionate kiss. With a grin that promised wicked delights, he pulled her by the hand towards the woods and she squealed once more.

If it were not for the seriousness of the situation, I would have laughed and teased her for her poor acting skills.

A shadow danced between the trees, and I leaned into Silas, nipping at his earlobe. He wrapped both his arms around me, pulling me against his chest.

"Twenty yards," I said. "Any idea how many?"

"None," Silas said. "Cillian and Emmerson will circle to the rear and then push forward."

A commotion erupted at the campfire as Fionn and Teller bantered about some sparring session where they both believed themselves to be the victor.

"I've got to take a piss," Zeke declared and headed towards the woods.

For someone who had been sleeping not too long ago, I didn't miss the sword slung over his shoulder or the dozen daggers that caught the light of the glowing embers, sheathed about his person. He cast a quick glance in our direction and gave a subtle nod to Silas.

"Have you all done this before?" I asked, impressed by the way they all worked seamlessly together.

"When you were in Netheran," Silas said.

"Can you reach Caolán? Misneach is still too far away."

I tried to reach Misneach once I knew there was activity in the woods, but

269

I was unable to.

"No, but they should return soon."

I cast my gaze around the tree line once more, and this time, my eyes landed on glowing amber ones.

I sucked in a harsh breath, and Silas stiffened beside me.

"Five yards," I whispered to Silas.

"NOW!" he roared.

And then all hell broke loose.

Chapter Fifty-Seven

I sprang to my feet and summoned my flames, my palms burning with the need to release them. Fighters emerged from the tree line, swords, axes, and bows all raised as they ran straight for us.

There had to be dozens of them.

Those glowing golden eyes remained locked on me as he remained within the protective embrace of the woods.

What was he waiting for?

I was right here.

He told me he would find me, and now that he had, he just stood there, watching me intently as if I intrigued him.

That was more unsettling than the horde screaming furious battle cries as they descended upon us.

"Hold," Silas commanded.

I flicked my gaze to Teller and Fionn, who both held swords in one hand and had summoned fórsa with their other. The light from the small orbs swirled and tangled around their outstretched fingers, creating a mesmerizing display.

"Harlowe," Silas barked, and I followed his unspoken command as I pulled up my shield, encircling us all.

The first wave was too close to halt their advance, their bodies colliding with the fiery wall I had erected between us and them. Their skin sizzled and melted upon contact before they erupted into flames and were incinerated in mere seconds.

Mere seconds.

That's all it took for me to kill a dozen people.

The acrid smell of burning flesh hit me, and I forced myself to breathe through my mouth as my stomach revolted against me.

"Now," Silas yelled.

I dropped my shield and Silas, Teller, and Fionn released the radiant orbs of energy they had called to their fingertips. Fórsa tore through the air, a whistling sound following in its wake as each orb headed straight for those in the second wave.

Blast after blast illuminated the dark clearing, tearing limbs from bodies and painting the ground crimson as each orb found its target, decimating them.

Just as quickly as I had dropped my shield, I pulled it back up, locking it in place.

My eyes were drawn to the woods where the golden-eyed man stood. He tilted his head as he studied me. A small smirk played on his lips beneath his cloak, and he reached into his pocket and retrieved something.

I couldn't discern what the object was from this distance. However, his expression suggested I wouldn't like to find out.

When I redirected my attention to the battle in front of me, I was shocked to see just how many bodies littered the ground. With two demonstrations of power, we had already eliminated around two dozen fighters.

And yet they were still coming.

I had underestimated their numbers. They'd learned from their last attempt on my life and now sought to snuff out my existence with overwhelming force.

Just as I had expected, the attacking fighters retaliated with brute strength, sending their own orbs of fórsa sailing through the night. When they collided with my shield, a spectacular display of fire and light erupted as the two elements fought for supremacy. Embers burst to life around us and the heat from my flames intensified as they dispersed the assault.

The advancing wave slowed, surprise mingling with fear as they registered that their blasts of energy had failed to penetrate my blazing shield.

Sweat coated my forehead and a single droplet made its way from my temple down the side of my face. It was growing hot behind my shield, uncomfortably so, and I wasn't sure how much longer I could hold it for.

The resounding clang of metal meeting metal reached my ears, drowning out the sounds of the horde, and relief washed over me at the thought of Emmerson, Cillian, and Zeke entering the fray. A moment later, fear threatened to strangle me as I realized just how many fighters were out there and they were up against them all alone.

As if sensing my trepidation, Silas said, "They are the most capable fighters I know. They understand when to advance and when to withdraw. Trust in their abilities."

I swallowed the lump forming in my throat but nodded once.

"Get ready to change things up," Silas said to Fionn and Teller. "Harlowe will drain herself if she keeps this shield in place for much longer."

"About time," Teller said with far too much excitement for someone facing overwhelming odds. By the broad grin on his face and the deft swing of his blade, he was completely unfazed.

When I glanced in Fionn's direction, he, too, wore an eager expression. It was no wonder Emmerson got along with them all so well.

They were all bloodthirsty and a little unhinged.

Silas nodded once, and I grabbed two daggers before I lowered my shield. My palms remained alight with flames, causing my daggers to appear as if their blades were made of fire. But the small reprieve allowed me the chance to rebuild my reserves.

We all darted forward as one, and I didn't hesitate as I thrust my blade into the soft flesh of the first warrior I encountered. My blade landed with a *thud* as it carved its way through the internal organs of the man before me. I forced my dagger higher, ensuring the wound would be fatal before retracting my blade.

The rustling of fighting leathers sounded behind me, and I dropped to the ground, only narrowly avoiding a direct hit from a wicked-looking blade. The sword curved in a dramatic arc, and its sharpened edge glinted whenever it caught the light. At the tip was an acute point, made for thrusting and eviscerating an enemy.

A massive beast of a man with wide shoulders and arms as thick as tree trunks gripped the hilt of the sword as he sneered down at me. Without hesitating, I kicked out at him, my boot connecting with his gut, which elicited a grunt in response.

As I tried to stand, an enormous hand sailed through the air and collided with the side of my face. The force of the blow sent me crashing back to the ground. The pain was immediate, and it felt as though he had cleaved my jaw free with the sheer power behind the hit.

If I survived the night, my face would bear the marks of that blow for days.

The coppery tang of blood filled my mouth, and I rolled to my side, spitting it out on the ground as I tried, and failed, to regain my footing. Realizing both my daggers had slipped from my grip during the assault, I moved my hands over the dirt as I desperately searched for them.

A sharp tug on my hair had me crying out in pain and my hands instinctively reached up, gripping the wrist of the man pulling me to my feet by my roots.

"So, you're the little bitch we've been searching for," he sneered.

Before I could answer, a vicious snarl echoed through the air, vibrating with the fury of the one behind it.

My lips tugged up the corners of my mouth and the cut on my lip throbbed as my face split into a broad grin. A low chuckle escaped me, sounding deranged, even to my own ears.

"What's so funny, bitch?" the man seethed.

"You're a fucking dead man," I laughed, throwing my head back.

"What the fuck is wrong with you?" he demanded, shaking me roughly.

His movement stopped abruptly as his gaze slid down his frame. My eyes followed the same path until I reached the pointed tip of the sword jutting out of the man's midsection. The sword disappeared, only to reappear in the center of the man's chest.

Blood poured down the front of his fighting leathers and he coughed, the crimson liquid spilling from his mouth and landing on his chin. He released his hold on my hair, and I dropped to the ground.

The man continued to make a gurgling noise that was interrupted by pained moans. He fell to his knees with a loud *thud* and his eyes locked with mine. His features contorted in agony, but his eyes still reflected his shock.

He hadn't seen his death coming.

I darted my gaze above his head and met piercing brown eyes that were alight with fury.

Silas was panting heavily. His face, his chest, and his arms were all smeared with blood as he held his sword at his side.

Silas lifted a foot and placed a hard kick to the center of the man's back, never breaking eye contact with me.

He fell, face-first, into the dirt.

I inhaled a sharp breath upon seeing the many slashes on his flesh. His tunic lay in ribbons, and he appeared as though someone had whipped him.

Silas stormed towards me, his wrath pulsing around him as though a living entity. He reached me in three strides and lowered himself to his knees in front of me.

"Harlowe, are you all right?"

The battle continued to rage around us and I wondered how Teller and Fionn were holding back the throng of fighters on their own.

"Harlowe," Silas said gruffly.

"I'm all right," I said, coming back to myself.

Silas's gaze danced between my eyes as if assessing the truth of my words. He rested his forehead on my own and released a harsh breath.

"When I saw you fall..." he trailed off, swallowing roughly. "I thought I was about to lose you," he said.

I gripped his face with my palms and pulled his lips to mine. I winced when his lips met my damaged ones, but I didn't move away. Silas threaded his fingers in my hair, deepening the kiss.

I pulled back, breaking the kiss, and said, "You didn't lose me, but we have bigger issues to deal with right now."

Rising to my feet, I saw that Emmerson, Cillian, and Zeke had made it back to the camp. The attacking force had dwindled, and I saw some warriors retreat to the tree line for safety.

I wasn't foolish enough to think it was over, however.

The man with golden eyes came here with a purpose. And he hadn't made his play yet.

I scanned the woods but found no sign of his presence. As I spun around, I searched the rest of the area, but he was nowhere in sight.

Chapter Fifty-Eight

"They're retreating," Cillian called, and Teller hooted.

"They're not retreating," I mumbled. "They're regrouping."

"What's that, Harlowe?" Silas asked.

"They're regrouping. It's the same man from Netheran. The one who tried to kill me in the maze. I'm certain he was behind the attack with the roc too. He hasn't made his play yet, so they're not retreating, they're regrouping."

"Circle formation," Silas shouted, and everyone moved into position, forming a circle around the clearing so no one's back was exposed.

"Call your flames, Harlowe," Silas instructed.

I was still drained from maintaining the shield for so long, but my flames flicked to life at my fingertips when I beckoned.

Tension filled the air, turning it stifling as we waited for the next attack. We were too few that we couldn't afford to bring the fight to them. Not if we hope to make it to daybreak, at least.

"Misneach," I tried again, but he was still beyond reach.

"Where are your daggers?" Silas hissed.

"Lost them when the giant oaf threw me down," I said, shrugging.

Silas clenched his jaw and then lowered himself to the ground. He retrieved a dagger from each boot and then rose, pushing them into my hands.

"How many more of those could you possibly have stashed?" I asked incredulously.

Silas just smirked and winked at me.

The shuffling of feet amongst the undergrowth of the woods had my spine straightening.

I knew they'd be back. They weren't done yet.

The rhythmic sound of steel banging against steel filled the clearing, creating an ominous atmosphere that I had assumed was done to intimidate us.

And it was fucking working.

I had to forcibly repress the tendrils of fear fighting to twist and contort my resolve.

"Hold," Silas yelled. "If our deaths are what they seek, they will have to earn them. Let them come to us!"

Shouts and jeers erupted from our group, but their disciplined training kept them rooted in place, their stances never faltering.

At Silas's words, an eruption of howling surrounded us, and the stomping of feet cut through the air as our assailants advanced.

When they broke through the tree line for the second time tonight, their sheer numbers once again overwhelmed me.

Where the fuck were they all coming from?

Despite the valiant effort we had made in diminishing their ranks, they still had the numbers to bring about our demise.

I scanned the faces of the advancing warriors, but found no sign of glowing amber eyes beneath their hoods.

Still, I felt his gaze on me, biding his time and waiting for the perfect moment to strike.

I was pulled from my musings when a distinctive swishing sound cut through the night. Sidestepping, I evaded the blade aimed at my head. Not sparing my near death a second thought, I threw a fiery inferno in the direction it had come, ending the one who had sought to claim my life.

And then they were on us.

They Sliced and hacked their weapons through the air as they sought purchase in our flesh. All they found was the unwavering resistance of steel.

A warrior squared off in front of me. A woman if her slight stature was any indication. With all their hoods pulled low on their heads concealing their faces, it was difficult to identify at first glance.

The woman raised her short sword and charged. I steadied my daggers in my hands and released my flames to conserve my energy. Just as she reached me, the woman swept her sword downwards as she attempted to slash me with her blade. My hands darted forward, both my daggers rising to block her advance. The metallic clash of blades was sharp, echoing around us.

I lowered my daggers and spun away from her, before thrusting my blade low as I sliced the sharpened tip across her lower abdomen. The woman hissed in pain and danced out of the range of my weapons. She placed a shaky hand on her stomach, her palm coming back covered in blood and she stared at it in disbelief.

I didn't wait for her to regain her composure. I sent my dagger sailing towards her. It flew through the air, end over tip until it landed with a dull *thud* in the center of her chest. Her eyes widened in surprise, her mouth forming a perfect 'O'.

She lifted her gaze to meet mine, utterly unprepared for her rapidly approaching demise. She took a tentative step back before her knees gave out and she stumbled to the ground.

I stalked towards her. As I reached down to retrieve my blade, I saw the life leaving her eyes as she stared up at me, unblinking.

I didn't have time to feel guilty as another fighter appeared at my side. Another woman. She kicked out at my hip, sending me hurtling to the ground. I used the momentum of my fall as I rotated my shoulder, digging it into the hardened earth, and rolling, pushing myself upwards into a crouch.

The woman removed her hood, revealing shoulder-length brown hair and an eager smile.

"Let's see what the so-called bringer of destruction is capable of, shall we?" the woman sneered.

The bringer of destruction? That was a terrible moniker.

"By all means," I said, curling my fingers in a come-hither motion.

The woman lunged as she thrust her sword forward and I ducked, moving to the side and avoiding the hit. I kicked out and my boot connected with her hip, returning the favor for her earlier jab. Like me, she used the momentum to her advantage and avoided colliding with the ground.

"How original," she taunted as she stood.

"Originality doesn't spare one's life when on the battlefield," I said in a bored tone.

The woman grinned and then cut her sword through the space between us in a wide arc. I barely had time to deflect the blow as I pivoted away from the sharpened tip of the blade.

The pulsing sound of clashing blades sang all around me, but I didn't have time to check on my companions as the woman advanced again.

She feigned left, and I fell for it.

A burning sensation erupted in my side, and I inhaled sharply, the metallic scent of blood filling my nostrils.

My blood.

I breathed through gritted teeth as I tried to block out the pain.

Seconds.

I had seconds before she would be upon me again.

Sure enough, the woman sent another devastating blow in my direction, this time striking low, disorienting me. Another burst of pain shot forth as I registered the cut to my calf and I staggered back, almost buckling under the weight of my injuries.

Almost.

The woman tsked. "I must say, I'm unimpressed," she said, as she slowly advanced on me again, taking pleasure in watching me struggle.

"Well, I'd hate to disappoint you," I grit out, summoning my flames to my palm.

I thrust my hand forward, releasing the fireball I had conjured. It sped through the air, colliding with the woman's sternum, tearing a gaping hole in her center before continuing its trajectory and hurtling into a second fighter, killing them instantly.

The woman's body fell forward as she landed in the dirt.

I limped over to her and pushed her onto her back with the tip of my boot. Her lifeless gaze stared back up at me.

"What about now? Impressed yet?"

Chapter Fifty-Nine

Searching the battlefield, I still couldn't locate the man with glowing amber eyes.

It was unnerving me.

What was he waiting for?

My body was screaming in pain, my injuries leaking my energy reserves with every drop of blood that seeped from my wounds.

I brushed a bead of sweat off my eyebrow with the back of my hand as I caught my breath.

I could see Emmerson engaged in a fight with three other warriors. Despite the odds, I could tell she was only playing with them. She could easily defeat them, despite letting them believe they had the upper hand.

Being a woman made it easy for them to underestimate her.

No sooner had I thought it, and Emmerson released a battle cry, swinging her blade around her in a tight formation. At first, it seemed like nothing had happened.

Then all three men dropped to the ground.

Well, their upper limbs fell to the ground and a moment later, their lower bodies followed. The crazy hellion had cleaved all three men in half with one precise blow. And now she was standing amongst their mutilated limbs, covered in their blood, and laughing like a maniac.

I wasn't terrified of my best friend. Definitely not.

Movement caught my attention, drawing me away from the sight of

Emmerson. Fionn was battling a large warrior, trading blow for blow with the skill of a well-practiced fighter. The warrior wrenched his sword back before advancing again, striking fast and hard.

Fionn parried, his arms trembling with the effort required to push the larger man back. The lingering sound of vibrating steel permeated the clearing.

But that wasn't what had my heart pounding as if it was trying to break free of my chest. Another warrior was sneaking up behind Fionn, his sword raised and glinting in the moonlight.

My feet moved of their own accord, racing towards Fionn even though I knew there was no way I would reach him in time. I summoned my flames, and then released them, realizing there was no way I could take out the incoming assailant without hurting Fionn.

My throat closed painfully around a sob, but I forced my voice out as I did the only thing I could.

"FIONN," I roared.

His gaze danced to mine and seemed to register the crippling fear reflected in my eyes. Slowly, too slowly, as if time was standing still, Fionn rotated, his sword glancing across the blade of the opponent he had been engaging as he cast a look over his shoulder.

Realization hit him, and he returned his gaze to mine. I saw resignation spread over his features as he accepted the knowledge that his time had come to an end. The sob I had been trying desperately to bury burst free.

"NO!"

A furious battle cry rend the air and a figure darted forward. Just as quickly as it had slowed, time sped up again with nauseating efficiency.

Fionn screamed, his features contorting in agony as he pushed back at his attacker with a pained roar. He thrust his blade forward, impaling the warrior on his sword, and spun, slicing through the neck of the man who had been trying to sneak up on him.

But it was too late.

I crashed to the ground at Fionn's feet, confusion washing through me as I peered down at Teller. Blood coated his throat, soaking his braids in the crimson liquid as he tried to swallow. A deep, red gash ran from the base of his ear, down the side of his throat, and all the way across his torso until it reached his hip.

I placed my hands on either side of his face, angling him towards me.

"Teller," I choked. "Teller, can you hear me?"

Teller reached a bloodied hand towards my face and stroked my cheek.

"It's all right, Harlowe," he gurgled, blood seeping from the side of his mouth.

Tears filled my eyes as Fionn dropped to his knees beside me, his hands cradling his head as he rocked back and forth.

"Tell Fionn," he coughed, blood spilling onto his chin, choking him.

"It's all right, Teller. Fionn is right here. It's all going to be all right," I said as I smoothed his hair. I didn't know if I was trying to convince him or me at that moment.

My tears spilled down my cheeks, and Teller used his thumb to brush them away. The tender act momentarily shocked me as Teller used his last moments to comfort me as I drowned in despair.

"Tell Fionn," he said again. "Tell him it wasn't his fault. Tell him... he is strong enough to survive this."

Fionn's gaze locked on mine, tears flowing freely down his face as he watched on in horror. Emotion clogged my throat as the heavy weight of grief settled on my chest, crushing me, and making it difficult to breathe.

"Tell him all he has to do —" Teller coughed again, blood hitting my face as he spluttered and fought to inhale. "All he has to do... is choose to live," he finished.

I nodded my head, unable to form words as sobs wracked my body.

"Don't... cry," Teller mumbled. "You... are more courageous... than any person I know, Harlowe. It... has been an honor... to stand beside you."

Pain as I had never experienced before lanced my chest deeper than any blade could ever penetrate. Teller couldn't die. He was the light on dark days. His carefree, jovial nature, his enthusiasm for life, his compassion for others. How would any of us ever feel whole again without his presence?

Desperation clawed at me.

"Teller please," I begged, although I had no idea what I was begging for. For him to conserve his energy, to hold on ... to live?

"It's... all right... Harlowe. Everything... will be all right." Teller gave me a weak smile, blood coating his teeth in a macabre display of his mortality. Through my tears, I did my best to return it.

Teller's hand dropped from my face, his eyes rolling to the back of his head as his lids shuttered closed. An ache erupted behind my ribcage, building until it was so acute, so debilitating, that every inhale was pure agony.

"Teller!" I screamed as the pain of his loss hit me like a physical blow. "Teller, wake up!"

I shook his shoulders roughly, willing him, no pleading with him to open his eyes.

I lowered my forehead to his, my tears pouring down my face in a torrent of paralyzing sorrow.

"He's gone," Fionn said gruffly, unable to look at him.

Fionn rose to his feet and turned his face towards the heavens. He let out a soul-crushing scream, his whole body vibrating with his anguish as he fought to purge it from his body. When he lowered his head, his eyes were dark as night and he let his rage flow through him.

"Fionn," I called, but he was beyond hearing me.

He took determined strides, throwing himself back into the fray like a man possessed. He swung his sword without mercy, cutting down anyone who dared to enter his path. I prayed to the gods to protect him. To not let his grief and recklessness get him killed.

The battle was still raging around me, and I knew I was exposed and vulnerable, but I couldn't bring myself to pull away from Teller.

He had become so much more than a friend. He had become family. I knew I would carry his loss with me every day.

"Touching," a voice said from behind me.

I frantically searched for my daggers, having dropped them to the ground when I reached Teller. Gripping them in my hands, I stood, rising to face the newest threat.

A man stood before me, his hood pulled forward, concealing his face in the shadows. He smiled when recognition lit up my features.

His smile was full of menace, and it reached all the way to his glowing golden eyes.

Chapter Sixty

"FIONN," Harlowe roared, and my eyes scanned the battlefield until I found him.

He was facing off against a much larger warrior, but he could still hold his own. Fionn was a strong fighter. He showed dedication and discipline, and I trusted his ability to protect himself.

However, the battle he was currently engaged in was taking all his focus and energy as he fought to overpower a man twice his size.

And it was this single-minded focus that another warrior was seeking to exploit as he snuck up behind him.

I caught a glimpse of fiery red hair as Harlowe raced towards him.

"Harlowe, no!" I yelled, but she couldn't hear me above the sounds of clashing metal and agonized screams.

If Fionn fell, Harlowe wouldn't stand a chance against the two men preying on Fionn. Fórsa sparked to life in my palm, and I gripped the closest fighter by the face as I released it. They dropped to the ground, unmoving. I didn't spare them a second glance as I engaged the next attacker.

A sharp stinging sensation flared on my bicep, and I glanced down, seeing tiny crimson droplets rush to the surface of my skin. A woman smirked back at me, the dagger she held in her hand glistening with my blood.

A male warrior joined forces with the woman, and they both encircled me as if I were easy prey.

Frustration and anger roiled inside me, fueled by my desperation to reach Harlowe.

"Let's finish this," I snarled.

They didn't hesitate, both coming at me at once. The man wielded a wicked-looking axe, and the woman held a short sword in one hand and the bloodied dagger in her other.

The man went high while the woman went low. I deflected the man's blow with my sword, as I swung my leg out hard, connecting with the woman's shoulder and sending her flying before her short sword could get within striking distance.

I angled myself back towards the man and landed another hard kick to his gut. He grunted and retreated a few steps. Exploiting the momentary advantage I'd created, I followed the man, forcing him to defend before he got his bearings.

My blows were precise and powerful, and I didn't let up as the warrior struggled to parry.

"Teller!" Harlowe screamed, and I lost focus as I frantically searched for her. The pain in her voice filled my chest with dread, and my need to reach her only intensified. Another pained scream filled the clearing, but it wasn't Harlowe's. I wasn't sure who it belonged to, but I knew something was very, very wrong.

The female warrior used my distraction to her advantage, her blade piercing the flesh of my thigh, and I hissed in pain.

I gritted my teeth as I swung my sword in a wide circle, and she met my blade with her own. It was clear she was the more capable fighter, using her size and speed to move quickly and without detection.

In contrast, the male relied heavily on brute force, lacking strategy or precision. He just flung his axe around wildly and hoped it connected with muscle and bone. When it did, however, I was certain it would be effective.

I kicked out once more, aiming for her gut, but she'd learned her lesson and danced out of range on agile feet.

As I brought my palm up, I shot an orb of fórsa straight at her, and she ducked, deftly avoiding the strike.

I could hear the heavy breathing of the male fighter as he attempted to sneak up on me. Without looking, I spun, landing a kick to his flank, and sent fórsa sailing towards his midsection.

He fell to the ground with a loud *thud* that vibrated beneath my feet. He didn't get back up.

The woman stared at her fallen comrade, stunned and frozen in place. Then anger contorted her features, and she released a ferocious snarl as she came at me like a feral animal. Her blades worked in unison, slashing and thrusting as she tried to land a blow. Small sparks erupted where our blades clashed as she let her bloodlust dominate her movements.

And that was her undoing.

She was so fixated on her blades and mine that she didn't take notice of the small sparks of light that were gliding along my fingertips. I reached my hand up and grabbed hold of her head, my fingers digging into her temple.

When her gaze locked with mine, her bloodlust abated, her eyes brimming with fear, and then... acceptance. I released my power, and it crashed into her skull, sending her head flying back as she careened toward the ground.

I didn't wait to see her fall.

Instead, I ran in the direction I had last seen Harlowe.

When I reached her, the scene before me pulled me up short.

Teller lay lifeless on the ground; an enormous laceration ran from his ear to the opposite hip. The wound exposed the underlying muscle of his chest cavity and a rib bone protruded from the site. A dark substance soaked the ground beneath him, and the coppery smell of his blood overwhelmed me.

My heart tightened painfully, and I wanted to fall to my knees with the agony tearing me apart from the inside.

Teller and I had grown up together. All of us had, except for Fionn, but we had adopted him into our group as though he was our annoying little brother.

We had spent years of our lives training alongside one another. Together, we faced every challenge, always ready to protect each other, no matter the cost. That's why we were so in tune with one another and could communicate with just a look.

But now Teller was gone. Dead. And I had failed him.

I didn't protect his back when he needed it the most.

Just like Cian.

We had spent a lifetime together, and now I had lost two of my brothers in the span of months.

Harlowe's panicked voice reached me, pulling me from my spiraling thoughts.

"What the fuck was that?" she shouted as she wiped something from her face.

"It's a nullifying powder," the man standing before her said smugly. "It puts a stop to your pesky little fire powers," he chuckled.

I swallowed my grief and closed off all my emotions, becoming numb to the pain until there was only a single feeling left.

Rage.

Chapter Sixty-One

Whatever was in the powder the golden-eyed man had just blown into my face, it fucking burned. My eyes watered and tears streaked down my cheeks as my body fought to purge the substance from my sockets.

"A nullifying powder?" I asked as I coughed on the potent mixture coating the back of my throat.

"Indeed. It is offensive magic used by the witches during the war. Of course, it has been outlawed for centuries. Desperate times and all that." He waved a hand dismissively.

"Why are you doing this?" I asked, feeling exhausted by everything that had happened. Not only tonight but since the very beginning, when everything shifted.

When the Cathal first arrived on my kingdom's doorstep.

"It isn't personal, Princess. We can't take the risk that you will become an even greater threat to the realm should you choose to do so."

"I'm taking it pretty fucking personally," Silas bit out and I swung my head towards him.

He stood tall and imposing on the slight hill at the edge of the clearing. At this moment, his face shrouded in darkness, the small glimmer of moonlight glinting off his weapons magnifying the threat they posed, he appeared otherworldly.

He was the personification of death, ready to unleash his vengeance as his body trembled with his barely contained wrath. The sinewy muscles of his forearms flexed as he tightened his grip on his sword. His whole body seemed to be covered in blood, a testament to the lethality of his power.

He was mesmerizing. Beautiful. Terrifying.

The man with the golden eyes lowered his hood and smirked up at Silas.

"If it isn't the prodigal son of Pyrithia," he hummed.

Silas clenched his jaw, but I couldn't tell if it was in recognition or irritation at the taunt.

Before I registered he had moved, the golden-eyed man had reached beneath his cloak and retrieved a dagger. He flung it at Silas, and it landed near his collarbone with a thump, sending him staggering backward.

"Silas!" I screamed, but he didn't respond.

Golden eyes turned their full attention back to me, and I tried to summon my flames, but they failed to respond.

He really cut me off from my power.

In my moment of panic, I'd completely blocked out the world around me.

A sharp pain exploded in my lower abdomen, the abruptness of it shocking me. As I glanced down, I saw the end of a sword protruding from my body. Blood soaked through my tunic at an alarming rate, and I glanced back up at the man with golden eyes who was still gripping the hilt in his grasp.

He smiled at me, but it was far from friendly.

We just stared at each other for a moment. His face reflected smug victory and I'm sure mine was frozen in surprise. As I studied his face, his smile dropped, his lips thinning into a straight line. My mind struggled to make sense of it until a low growl sounded from behind him.

Silas stood at his back; his gaze locked onto my injury, which I was almost certain would be fatal. My eyes dipped lower, and I saw another sword protruding from my assailant's stomach.

I burst out laughing at the sight.

We had twin injuries. Maybe golden eyes had been my twin flame all along.

I couldn't explain why that thought made me chuckle uncontrollably. Perhaps the pain that was drowning me was also loosening my grip on reality.

"Find Everly," Silas barked as he rushed to my side.

I swayed on my feet, but Silas caught me.

"Easy, Little Menace," he said in a soothing tone, as he lowered me to the ground.

I watched as the man with the golden eyes fell backward, further impaling himself on Silas's sword as he did so.

If he wasn't dead already, he soon would be.

The thought wasn't comforting since I was about to join him in the afterlife.

"Where's Everly?" Silas barked again, and I heard the pounding of feet as someone approached us.

"Teller," I whispered.

"Shh, don't talk, Harlowe," Silas said as he pulled my blood-soaked hair away from my face.

Emotion twisted Silas's features, his eyes flared wide, and a tick pounded in his jaw.

I heard a gasp to my right seconds before Emmerson came into view.

"Harlowe, oh gods, Harlowe," she sobbed, unable to contain her mounting despair. Cillian wrapped an arm around her, and I blinked.

I hadn't even noticed him standing there.

My vision swam, and I shook my head, clearing the fog, trying to descend upon me. Zeke appeared next to Emmerson, his face paling as he stared down at me.

"All right, so I've looked better," I tried to joke, but it came out sounding pained as I wheezed with the effort it took to speak.

"Where the fuck is Everly?" Silas screamed as his panic seeped into his tone.

"Here," Fionn said as the pair appeared beside me.

Everly gasped, hesitating only briefly before she started rummaging through her pack.

"Save her," Silas barked, and Everly flinched at the severity of his tone.

I tried to speak, to chastise Silas and comfort Everly, but my thoughts were interrupted by the arrival of another.

"FIRE HEART," Misneach roared, and I felt the telltale vibrations in the earth beneath me as my dragon landed somewhere nearby.

"About time you showed up," I teased.

Misneach's colossal head filled the sky above me and he released a ferocious snarl before turning to face the heavens and letting loose a torrent of blazing fire.

The heat kissed my cheeks and everyone except Silas moved back.

"Is the fighting over?" I asked, concerned for my friends as they sat unprotected around me.

"We incinerated any who remained upon our return," Misneach growled. **"It was too quick. They deserved a far more painful death for what they have done to you, Fire Heart."**

I chuckled and then winced as the movement jostled my injury.

"Try to remain still, Harlowe," Silas pleaded, as he supported my weight against his chest. He was careful not to obstruct the blade that remained lodged within my body.

"Fire Heart," Misneach said, emotion clogging his tone.

I gazed up at him, surprised by his moment of vulnerability. He had always been strong; an impenetrable force that nothing or no one could harm. And even when he wasn't, he pretended for my benefit.

Fuck! I really was about to die.

"No, you will not," Misneach seethed. **"I forbid it."**

"That's not really how it works, Misneach," I laughed and immediately regretted it.

"Can someone please ask the extremely large, rather intimidating dragon to move back so I can look at Harlowe's wound?" Everly's sweet voice shook with trepidation, as she glanced in Misneach's direction.

Misneach snarled before retreating a step.

A single step.

"Really? You're huge. You'll have to back up a bit more than that."

Misneach snarled again, but he retreated further.

A heartbreaking keening sound broke through the tension, and I rolled my head to the side trying to locate the source. Pain tightened my throat and tears filled my eyes as I took in the sight of Grainne standing over Teller's body. With her head lowered to his, the dragon nudged her fallen Cathal as if willing him to wake up.

The pain radiating down the bond was unbearable and I ached to reach out to her. To comfort her in some way.

"You have to go to her, Misneach," I pleaded, as the tears filling my eyes spilled down my cheeks.

"I will not leave you, Fire Heart," he stated firmly, although I could sense how much it pained him.

Before I could argue, Caolán's voice filled my mind. **"Fret not, Little One. I will go to her."**

With one last agony-filled cry, Grainne launched herself into the sky, and a moment later, Caolán followed.

Everly's tear-stained face came into view, returning my attention to the dire situation I found myself in. She scanned my body, looking for any other wounds before returning to the one in my abdomen.

"I have a healing elixir. It's the same one I gave you in Netheran. I made a few batches while you and Silas were away," she said sheepishly.

"Excellent forethought," I said, trying to ease the tension.

"Your wound is more severe than last time. I'm going to give you one dose before we remove the blade, and one immediately after, just to be sure. I'll need you to stay conscious for the second dose to ensure it's effective," she said apologetically.

This would not be pleasant.

"Will she be all right?" Silas demanded.

"That'll be up to Harlowe," Everly said, sending an encouraging smile in my direction.

I nodded once in understanding. I might not survive this.

Everly brought the first vial to my lips. The bitter taste filled my mouth, and I resisted the urge to spit it out.

Once I had swallowed it, Everly turned to the others.

"Can someone help me?" she asked, gesturing towards the sword.

Zeke nodded and came closer.

"I'm sorry about this, Harlowe," he said, a painful attempt at a smile gracing his lips.

Misneach growled low in warning.

"Remind your dragon I'm only trying to help, will you?" Zeke said as he cast a cautious glance in Misneach's direction.

"On three, all right?" he said, and I nodded once.

Silas tightened his hold around my shoulders, rubbing small circles in a soothing pattern.

"One," Zeke said, and a blinding pain shot through me.

The intensity of it made me vomit.

Black dots danced in my vision and my eyes closed of their own volition.

"Hey, hey, Little Menace. Open your eyes," Silas commanded, desperation clinging to his tone.

I opened my eyes, taking in the fear swimming in Silas's chocolate ones.

A rancid taste filled my mouth once more, and I realized Everly had administered the second dose. She closed my mouth, encouraging me to swallow.

"Stay awake, Harlowe. Just a little longer," she said.

"You said on three, you bastard," I croaked as I closed my eyes.

Zeke chuckled. "It wouldn't have made it hurt any less."

I made some sound, not even I recognized and opened my eyes.

"The man," I said, angling my head towards Silas.

"What?" he asked, confused.

"The man who was hunting me. The one with the golden eyes. Who was he?" I asked.

Silas's frame stiffened around my body and for a moment, I didn't think he was going to answer me.

"The Crown Prince of Vidyaa," he finally replied.

Holy shit!

So, the monarchs of Vidyaa had sanctioned an assassination attempt on my life.

Attempts, I corrected bitterly.

"We just started the war," I breathed.

That was the last thought I had before I succumbed to the pull of unconsciousness.

Chapter Sixty-Two

Familiar black drapes were the first thing I saw when I opened my eyes. My hand darted out instinctively, seeking a weapon, but the only thing I could grip was the silken sheets between my fingers.

"And here I thought you were going to sleep our time away." Kieran's rough voice filled the chamber and I sat up, wincing as pain tore through my stomach.

I carefully lifted my shirt to see my lower abdomen covered in bandages with spots of crimson bleeding through.

As I lowered my top, I realized just how big it was. Was I wearing one of Kieran's tunics?

"That's a nasty wound you've got there, Bride," Kieran mocked. "Had you stayed with me where you belong, you wouldn't be in this predicament."

My gaze found Kieran's as he slouched lazily in a chair by the window. I tried to swallow, but my mouth was so dry it felt like I was swallowing sand.

"What am I doing here?" I asked.

Kieran glanced towards the side table and then back at me. I followed to where he had been gazing and saw a glass of water. I looked back towards Kieran who smirked and raised a brow as if challenging me.

Tentatively, I lifted the glass and took a sip. The cool liquid soothed my burning throat. I took another sip before placing the glass back on the table.

"Better?"

"Yes, thank you," I said, reluctantly.

"As to your question," he said, rising to his feet and striding towards me. "I have brought you here to impart some rather pressing news, I'm afraid."

"What do you mean, you brought me here?"

Kieran smirked, and he sat down on the bed. "You're dreaming sweet, Harlowe."

Relief washed over me, and I could breathe a little easier.

Kieran must have noticed my reaction because his next words had me stiffening again. "Even in a dream, I can do terrible things to you, Bride."

He lifted his hand to stroke my cheek, and an involuntary shudder raced over my body, leaving gooseflesh in its wake.

Pleased with the effect he had on me, Kieran chuckled, the sound raising the hairs on the nape of my neck.

"Now, as to why I brought you here," he said, all amusement vanishing from his tone. "I wanted to let you know in person that I am coming for you."

"Coming for me?"

I guessed he would try to reclaim me, but he hadn't given me a warning last time. He just showed up, leaving death and destruction in his wake. My unease grew with every moment Kieran remained silent.

"I had great hopes for you, Harlowe," he said, as if he was speaking to himself. "I wanted this to work. I truly did."

"Wanted what to work?" I asked, confused.

"You and I, of course."

I snorted, and Kieran narrowed his eyes on me.

"You were never interested in me, Kieran. All you wanted was my power."

"I may not care for you in the traditional sense, but make no mistake, I do want you, Harlowe."

Kieran's eyes darkened, and I shifted uncomfortably.

"Not enough to treat me with respect or abandon your foolish plan to conquer the realm," I retorted.

Kieran sprang forward, wrapping his hand around my throat and squeezing roughly.

"Do not make the mistake of thinking you know me, Bride," he spat.

I tried to suck in a breath, but it was no use. I would only breathe if Kieran allowed it.

He watched me for a moment, his head tilted to the side as if my impending death intrigued him. When he released my throat, I gulped down air as I greedily filled my lungs. I scooted further up the bed, putting distance between us.

My hand snaked around my throat as I prodded the tender flesh.

"Of course, I don't know you," I wheezed. "You've never let anyone in."

Kieran cocked a brow. "What is it you would like to know about me, Bride?" he purred.

"I want to know why you're doing this," I said, gesturing toward myself.

"It's not about you, Harlowe. You're only a means to help me achieve my goals."

I already knew that. I wanted to know why he was hell-bent on destroying the realm and I said as much.

Kieran looked out the window, his expression pensive as he considered his answer.

"By the time I was born, my mother had already been living under the tyrannical rule of my father for close to a century. Everyone said that my birth changed her whole life. She was more outgoing, she smiled again and for a time, she was happy." A small smile tugged at Kieran's lips as if recalling fond memories. "My father, however, was not pleased that she was one way with me, and the complete opposite with him."

He turned towards me, his stormy ocean-blue eyes filled with fury.

"They hated each other, my parents," he said, pursing his lips. "One day, my father decided he could no longer stand the look of happiness on my mother's face whenever she saw me. So, he took it upon himself to make sure he would never see it again."

I held my breath, waiting for what I knew would be a horrible end.

"He took her to the cliff edge on the western side of the palace and threw her into the sea," he said in a nonchalant tone. The turmoil roiling in his azure eyes betrayed his true feelings, however.

"Kieran, I'm sorry," I said, reaching a hand out to comfort him before I could think better of it.

Kieran jerked away from my touch, and I let my hand drop to the mattress.

"I'm not telling you this so you can feel better about how you perceive me, Bride. I am a monster, but I choose to be one," he snarled.

He stood then, returning to his chair by the window.

"I grew up under the harsh treatment of my father. He wanted to punish me for gaining my mother's love when he never could. So, the years went by and when I reached adulthood, the War of Witches was brewing. My father, being the fool he is, chose the wrong side, hoping to gain more power than he deserved. When the war ended and he was forced to surrender some of his lands as part of the peace treaty, he became withdrawn. He was but a shell of his former self."

There was a glint in Kieran's eyes as he recalled his father's failure. He enjoyed watching his downfall.

"Not one to waste an opportunity, I saw the chance to overthrow him, and I took it."

"You killed your father?" I asked.

Kieran turned his whole body towards me. His lips kicked up in a smirk that had knots forming in the pit of my stomach.

"I never said that," he replied menacingly. "I overthrew him, yes, but I never killed him. Death would have been a mercy that he did not deserve. No, my father continues to rot below our very feet. He has his own private dungeon, and he has lived there for over four hundred years. Being the dutiful son that I am, I visit him frequently," he hummed.

I swallowed, not wanting to think about the kinds of things he did to pass the time when he was in his father's company.

"You asked me why I'm doing this," Kieran said, his gaze locking on mine with such intensity I forgot how to breathe. "I'm doing this to show my father that I am the better man, the better leader, the better king. I always have been. When I have achieved what he could not, then I will kill him, but only then."

"Kieran," I whispered, my mind reeling. "That's madness."

Kieran just shrugged, as if the conquest of an entire realm was insignificant.

"Now that you understand what's at stake, Harlowe, you'll have to forgive me for what must come next."

"Kieran, you don't have to do this," I pleaded. "It's not worth it. He's not worth it."

"It's not a matter of having to, Harlowe. I want to do this."

And I saw it then. His need for absolute power, absolute supremacy. It wasn't only about his father or getting revenge.

Kieran wanted to destroy. To rule. To conquer.

"Now you see me as I truly am, Bride," he said, grinning maniacally.

"What comes next?" I whispered, afraid that I already knew the answer.

"Ah," he said. "I'm afraid you're a threat to my plans, Harlowe. If you had joined me, this situation could have been avoided. But now you've forced my hand. When I see you next, it won't be to bring you home, Bride. It will be to end your life and the threat you pose to my ambition."

I inhaled sharply, a hand flitting to my throat.

Kieran rose from his seat and crossed the space between us in a few short steps. He leaned down, cupping the back of my head as he placed a gentle kiss on my forehead.

"Sleep well, Harlowe, for tomorrow, I start hunting you."

Chapter Sixty-Three

When I woke, I was drenched in sweat and shivering violently. Silas's large arm was wrapped around my body, and he looked exhausted, even in sleep. Careful not to disturb him, I lifted Silas's arm and moved out of his hold. It was an arduous task as every movement threatened to reopen my wound and searing pain flared at the site.

I slipped out of bed and looked around for my clothing. I was, in fact, wearing a man's tunic, one of Silas's if I had to guess. It was large enough to double as a nightgown.

Wait, what?

Why was I on a bed?

The last thing I remembered was being in the woods.

As I glanced around my surroundings, I found myself in an unfamiliar room. The panic that had been building inside me abated somewhat when I realized I wasn't in Netheran.

For a start, the room was painted a light green, the color of freshly sprouted leaves in spring. It cast a soothing ambiance, reminding me of days spent playing in the forest as a child. The rest of the decor was a muted, earthy shade of green that also showed hints of brown and grey.

The room had a masculine feel, although the combination of colors and tasteful furniture scattered about gave the room an understated elegance that was aesthetically pleasing.

I crept towards the window, pulling the drapes aside just a sliver.

No maze.

I had been almost certain I was no longer in Netheran, but the lack of a maze surrounding every inch of the palace's exterior confirmed it.

Had we made it to the manor already? I didn't remember traveling here. I remembered nothing after my encounter with the Prince of Vidyaa.

Anxiety turned my stomach as I remembered we had killed the Crown Prince of Vidyaa. If the Kingdom of Vidyaa had been hunting me before, extinguishing my life would soon become their sole focus when they found out their prince was dead.

Deciding I needed a distraction, I hunted around the room until I found some pants. When I reached the door, I eased it open, not wanting to disturb Silas. Once outside the room, I found a long hallway with doors lining either side.

This must be the guest wing.

I headed further down the hall until I found a beautiful staircase with wooden banisters, displaying intricate floral carvings that were polished to perfection.

I thought the manor had been abandoned. Someone obviously still cared for the place.

Meandering through the many rooms, I eventually came to a dining hall, where I found Fionn sitting at a long banquet table, alone and staring out the window, seeing nothing.

"Fionn," I said gently as I approached him.

He whipped his head around and surveyed me. I wasn't sure what he was looking for, but he let out a shaky breath and nodded to himself.

"Harlowe," he breathed, as he stood from his chair and strode towards me.

He gripped me in a tight hug, and I fought the wince that tried to slip free as my wound was jostled. Fionn needed this moment of comfort, and I wouldn't deny him. When he released me, his eyes were misted, and he quickly scrubbed the evidence away.

"How do you feel?" he asked, taking my hand in his as he led me back to the table.

"I'm all right, Fionn," I lied.

Physically, I was, or I soon would be. Mentally, however, that was a different story altogether. I willed myself to banish the tears I could feel forming in my eyes. I didn't want to think, I didn't want to feel. I just wanted to sit with my friend and take solace in the fact we were alive.

"Liar," he said, and nudged my shoulder playfully.

"Where are we?" I asked, changing the subject.

"We're at Silas's family manor. We've been here for just under a week."

"A week!" I screeched.

"You've been unconscious for the entire time," Fionn said.

My brows furrowed as I tried to make sense of everything.

"The last thing I remember was fighting with the Prince of Vidyaa," I said. "Well, he fought. I sort of just stood there gaping like an idiot and let him stab me. Not my finest moment," I mumbled.

"Don't be so hard on yourself. You fought bravely, Princess. Fuck, if it wasn't for you, I'm not sure any of us would have made it out alive. That little fire shield is one handy defense."

Despite Fionn's attempt at providing comfort, my mind was fixated on the one who didn't make it. He seemed to sense the change in me as we sat in silence, lost in our crippling misery.

"It should have been me," Fionn said, breaking the silence.

"What?" I asked, turning to face him.

"It should have been me. Not Teller," he clarified. "When I noticed the warrior behind me, it was too late to defend against his hit. I was only able to finish him because Teller spared me from the hit that was meant for me."

His voice trembled, and I could tell he was fighting the urge to break down. So, I wrapped my arms around him tightly and drew him to me.

"Would you have died to save Teller's life?" I asked.

"Of course," Fionn answered without hesitation.

"What about the others?"

"Without a second thought. They are my brothers."

"Would you have begrudged them for your sacrifice?" I pressed.

"No. I would have been honored to die while protecting the ones I care for the most," Fionn stated, straightening up.

"Then why are you taking that away from Teller?" I asked gently.

"I..." Fionn opened and closed his mouth a few times, but when words escaped him, he hung his head.

"I don't say this to hurt you, Fionn. I know Teller would make the same choice again, given the chance. He loved you, and he wouldn't want you to blame yourself for his death. He only wished for you to live, so don't disappoint him."

"I don't know how to push through all this pain," Fionn whispered. "It fucking hurts," he choked. "Right here." Fionn balled his hand into a fist as he pounded his chest just above his heart.

I closed my eyes, as the tears I had been holding at bay finally fell, cascading down my cheeks like a gentle waterfall. Each drop carried the weight of my unspoken anguish that tightened around my heart like a vise.

"I know," I said, my voice quivering. "I feel it right here too," I said, placing his palm over my heart.

Fionn met my gaze, his face awash with agony as silent tears slipped down his face.

"How do we make it stop?" he asked, his eyes pleading.

"We can't. Because that's how much Teller meant to us. His absence hurts because there is now a void where he once stood. Over time, the pain will lessen. Eventually, we'll learn to live with the pain of his loss. And when that day comes, we'll be able to look back on the moments we shared with fondness. We'll remember how much joy Teller brought to our lives, even if only for a time," I promised.

A sob wrenched itself free from Fionn's throat and I pulled him to me, placing his head on my chest as he sobbed freely. I stroked his hair, humming quietly as he let everything out.

A shuffling sound came from the door. I glanced back and saw Silas standing there. His pain was clear on his face as he watched Fionn. When his eyes locked with mine, he gave me a small nod before he turned and left the room, giving Fionn his privacy.

Fionn let out a shaky breath and raised his head. I reached my palm up to his face and wiped away his tears.

"We'll do it together. One day at a time," I said.

"Together," Fionn repeated before standing from his seat.

He leaned down and planted a chaste kiss on my forehead. "Thank you, Harlowe," he said.

Then he turned on his heels and left.

Chapter Sixty-Four

Silas returned a short time after Fionn departed.

"Are you all right?" he asked, concern etching his features.

"Honestly, I've been better," I admitted.

"I think we've all seen better days," Silas said as he scrubbed a hand down his face.

"Harlowe!" Emmerson screamed as she sprinted into the dining hall, Cillian, Zeke, and Everly on her heels.

I stood from my seat; arms outstretched as she barreled into me.

"Gods, Harlowe," she breathed as she hugged me tight.

Zeke joined her, and the three of us stood there for a long time.

"Let me look at you," Emmerson said, taking a step back.

She ran her gaze up and down my body, seeming satisfied with what she found.

"You had me scared there for a minute. I would have had to slaughter half the realm to avenge you. Starting with Vidyaa," she spat.

"Only half?" I teased, cocking a brow.

"You're right! Let's burn the whole realm down."

"I love you too, Emmerson," I said through my laughter.

"You love me too, right Harlowe?" Zeke asked.

"Of course," I said brightly, and Zeke beamed.

Silas growled behind me, but I ignored him.

Emmerson pulled me back into a hug and held me for a long time. So long,

I wondered if she'd ever let me go.

"Ah, Emmerson?" I asked.

"Just one more minute," she said, squeezing tighter.

I laughed, patting her lightly on her back until she finally released me. When she did, Silas pulled me down by my arm until I was sitting in his lap.

Emmerson bared her teeth at him, and he smirked back at her.

"Children," Misneach muttered.

"Please, like you're any better," I said, smiling like an idiot, knowing he was close by.

"I never left, Fire Heart," Misneach said gently. **"I even let that insufferable man ride with you as I carried you here."**

My smile widened further. **"And you don't even sound the least bit resentful,"** I teased.

He grumbled something unintelligible, and I chuckled to myself.

My thoughts drifted to Grainne and my mood immediately plummeted. **"How is she?"** I asked Misneach, afraid to hear the answer.

"She's... struggling," Misneach sighed, and I closed my eyes to regain my composure as my grief threatened to cripple me.

"We are all there for her," Misneach assured me, and I swallowed the lump forming in my throat as I nodded my head.

"Now that we're all here, what's next?" Zeke asked, redirecting my attention.

I hesitated, not wanting to add to our troubles.

But I had little choice.

"Kieran dream walked with me again last night," I said.

Silas's grip around my waist tightened.

"What did he want?" Emmerson said through gritted teeth.

I took a deep breath and then released it. "He said he's coming for me."

Emmerson scoffed. "Can't the guy take a hint? You don't want to marry him," she said, throwing her hands up in the air.

"He's no longer interested in marriage," I said quietly. Silence filled the room as everyone's gaze focused on me.

Silas growled again, and this time, Emmerson joined him.

"Like fuck he will!" Emmerson shouted.

Cillian wrapped a hand around her waist, pulling her close to his side. It seemed to settle her down somewhat.

"We need to start making bolder moves," Silas said.

"Like what?" I asked.

"We need allies," Emmerson interjected.

"Vidyaa is out, obviously," Zeke muttered.

"We should appeal to your father," Cillian said, directing his gaze towards Silas who nodded in agreement.

"That leaves Elysara and Zarinia," Fionn said as he strode back into the room.

"Elysara is out," I said, huffing out a breath.

"Not necessarily," Silas mused. "They might be the Kingdom of Peace, but that does not mean they are without arms. They have some of the most fearsome warriors I have ever trained with."

"You've trained with warriors from Elysara?" I asked, stunned.

The reclusive kingdom rarely entertained other dignitaries, nor did they often visit other kingdoms on court business. The fact that they had allowed Silas to train with their soldiers was truly remarkable.

"I have," he smirked. "And just because they don't allow troublemakers to enter their kingdom, does not mean they won't defend their kingdom if a threat is headed their way."

"But they've never joined any wars before," I pointed out.

"We've never faced a threat like Kieran before, either."

"He has a point," Misneach grumbled.

"What about unbonded dragons? Do you think they would help?"

"There is only one way to find out, Queen of Fire and Flame."

I balked. **"What do you mean, queen?"** I asked nervously.

"If you ask it of them, they will follow, Fire Heart. Dragons protect our own, and you are one of us. And while you may not hold the title in your kingdom, to us, you have proven yourself worthy to be called queen," Misneach said with pride.

My cheeks heated, but I accepted the sentiment.

"We can ask the dragons," I said to the group, filling them in on my discussion with Misneach, omitting the part about being their queen.

Turning to Everly, I asked, "Do you know anything about the powder the Prince used against me to nullify my powers? He said it was dark magic used by witches in the past."

"I don't, I'm afraid. I have never dabbled in offensive magic," Everly said sheepishly.

"Arabella," Silas said, although I'm not sure he meant to say it out loud.

"Good idea," Cillian agreed.

"What's a good idea?" I asked.

"Arabella, the witch you met in Pyrithia," he said, and I nodded. "Her mother knew about offensive magic. I'm sure she passed on some of that knowledge to Arabella."

"Is she still in Pyrithia?" I asked.

"I don't see why she wouldn't be," Silas answered.

"So, we start with Arabella and your father, and then move forward from there?" I asked.

Everyone in the room either nodded or grunted in agreement.

"So, we have a plan," I said, fear warring with determination.

"We have a plan," Silas echoed.

Chapter Sixty-Five

I rolled onto my back, sweat coating my body as I caught my breath. Sienna snuggled close to my side as she traced her fingers idly over my chest.

Being inside that woman was my definition of heaven. She was a wild one, eager to please, and knew moves that would make an experienced whore blush.

Fuck! My cock was getting hard again at the thought.

I wasn't foolish enough to think she wasn't using me just as much as I was using her. Or using her body to be more precise.

Every. Fucking. Hole.

"August," she purred.

I was impressed she could even speak, given what I'd done to her throat. I glanced over at her, my gaze snagging on the bruises surrounding her neck.

"Yes, Sienna?" I asked absentmindedly, studying her body.

Her skin was covered in bruises. An artwork of my making.

"Now that Harlowe is no longer around," she said tentatively.

I stiffened. I had been furious when that little bitch had escaped me, taking with her any chance I had to expand my kingdom, but more importantly, the chance to crush my brother in the process.

"Now that she's gone," Sienna continued, "you no longer have to wait to take your crown," she said.

"What are you talking about?" I bit out.

"Well, your father had intended to abdicate once you married Harlowe.

Now that's no longer an option, what's stopping you from succeeding him?"

I gave a harsh laugh. "He is, woman."

My father made it clear that he would only step aside if doing so would benefit the kingdom. Marrying Harlowe had presented me with an opportunity to expand our lands, and had I been successful, my father would have made me king upon our union.

But Silas and his bitch had to fuck it all up.

There was no telling how long father would make me wait now.

"Have you thought about pushing the issue?" she asked in a sultry tone.

I narrowed my eyes at her. "Speak plainly, Sienna. You know I despise your riddles."

She hesitated for a moment before an erotic smile pulled up her plump lips.

Lips that were wrapped around my cock as I forced her to take me all the way to the back of her throat, I thought smugly.

"You could always force him to stand down," she said huskily.

"And how would I do that?" I asked.

"You could force him to retire to one of the manors your family used to frequent," she suggested with a small shrug.

"That wouldn't work," I mused. "He would refuse, and I'd have no leverage to force his hand. The soldiers wouldn't follow my command if he remained on the throne. A more drastic approach would be required."

"More drastic," she laughed. "Why August, it sounds like you're plotting his death," she teased.

Plotting his death?

Could I really kill my father?

On the other hand, would he ever consider me worthy of the throne?

He had always favored Silas. Maybe he was biding his time until he could give the crown to him instead of me. He had the Princess of Valoren's favor, after all.

My vision turned red as anger assaulted me. My hands balled into fists, and I stood from the bed as I paced.

Had this been the plan all along?

Had father been playing games with me?

I mulled over everything, calculating my chances of convincing my father to stand down despite not securing an alliance with Valoren.

The answer to that question was simple.

Zero.

To seize the throne, I had two choices; I could wait until my father died and potentially face Silas in a battle of succession.

Or...

I could end that battle before it ever began.

A glint caught my attention, and I stopped my pacing. Sienna was playing with a bejeweled dagger I had placed on my bedside table.

I marched over to her and snatched it out of her hand. The tip was sharp, and a small droplet of blood pooled on my fingertip when I pressed it into my flesh.

Silas was off, doing who knows what. If father was to perish, news of his death would not reach him right away.

I could be crowned king and secure on the throne before he even knew what had happened.

If I were to do this, there was no time like the present. Every piece aligned perfectly, as if the gods were encouraging me.

If I waited, they may not remain that way.

A smirk tugged at my lips as a plan took shape in my mind.

I glanced down at Sienna, and she peered up at me from under her lashes. The picture of demure innocence.

I scoffed at the thought.

Dressing quickly, I tucked the dagger beneath my cloak as I strode towards the door.

"Where are you going?" Sienna asked in a sickly sweet voice.

"Stay here, Sienna. I mean it. If I return and you're not naked on my bed offering me that cunt of yours to do with as I please, well, let's just say you won't like the consequences."

Sienna glared at me.

"What's wrong, sweetheart?" I crooned. "Don't enjoy being reminded of the fact that you're my fucking whore?"

Sienna opened her mouth to argue, but thought better of it.

Pasting on a broad smile, she said, "Whatever you say, August."

My cock hardened painfully beneath my pants at her submission, and I grunted, contemplating if I shouldn't just bend her over and fuck her ass once more before executing my plan.

I shook my head to dispel the lust coloring my mind. There would be plenty of time for me to wreck that whore later.

I exited my chambers and quickly navigated the hallways until I reached my father's wing. His guards were stationed outside, as expected.

"Your Highness," one guard said. "His Majesty is sleeping."

"I have urgent business to discuss with my father. Step aside," I commanded.

They hesitated for a moment before complying.

I moved silently through my father's chambers, making my way to the side of his bed without rousing him.

"Father," I whispered, as I shook his shoulder.

My father's eyes fluttered open, and he looked up at me, confused.

"August," he said, his voice thick with sleep.

I wrapped my hand around his mouth, and his eyes widened.

"I'll make it quick," I promised.

I slid my dagger beneath my father's ribcage and thrust upwards, piercing his heart. A soft gasp escaped him, and he just stared at me for the longest moment.

"I'm sorry," I murmured. "It shouldn't have come to this."

The light in my father's eyes dimmed as his life drained out beneath him. When his eyes finally drifted closed, I pulled my dagger free.

"Long live the King," I whispered, as I retrieved my crown.

Acknowledgments

To everyone who read A Heart of Fire and Flame - Thank you! Thank you for taking a chance on a debut indie author who really had no idea what she was doing but somehow got there anyway. Your support means the world to me and the fact that you came back for more is truly humbling. I hope you enjoyed the second installment of Harlowe's journey as much as I enjoyed writing it!

To my sister Sherrin - Thank you for being my biggest cheerleader! Thank you for being a whole street team wrapped up in one individual. Thank you for the encouragement when imposter syndrome threatened to derail me. And thank you for saving my characters from facial injuries by patiently explaining the complexity of archery to someone who clearly had no idea. Thank you!

To my Husband Luke - Thank you for your love and support and for always encouraging me to pursue what makes me happy. I'm so thankful for the help you provided in reviewing this project for me and I'll always be grateful for the time you invested despite not having much to spare.

To Billie and Nalannah - Thank you for being such fantastic beta readers, even though I broke your hearts. Your help in shaping this story to make it the best it can be is truly appreciated!

To my ARC readers - Thank you for taking the time to review my work. Without you, my story would struggle to find its audience and I hope you know how much I appreciate each and every one of you! Thank you!

To my children - Thank you for inspiring me every single day. I love you.

I hope you can all join me for book three, and the conclusion of Harlowe's

story, A Queen of Fire and Flame, later in the year.
Happy Reading!
K.J.Johnson

About the Author

K.J. Johnson is a fantasy and romance indie author who writes about headstrong heroines and morally grey men.

K.J. Johnson's debut novel, A Heart of Fire and Flame, is book one of the Fire and Flame series.

After a lifelong obsession with reading and escaping into different worlds where anything is possible, she decided to let her imagination run wild and

K.J. JOHNSON

penned her debut novel - A Heart of Fire and Flame.

K.J. Johnson enjoys writing romance of the darker persuasion and you can expect plenty of spice, but check your morality at the door because it won't survive the ride.

In her downtime, she still enjoys getting lost in a good book and experiencing the world through the eyes of her favorite authors.

Also by K.J. Johnson

Fire and Flame Series

A Heart of Fire and Flame, Book One of the Fire and Flame Series
A Daughter of Fire and Flame, Book Two of the Fire and Flame Series
Coming Soon...
A Queen of Fire and Flame, Book Three of the Fire and Flame Series

Social Media Links

Follow me on:

TikTok/Instagram/Threads: @authork.j.johnson
Facebook: Author K.J. Johnson

Or sign up for my newsletter to keep up-to-date on all new releases and receive exclusive behind-the-scenes content at, https://kjjohnsonbooks.com/newsletter.

Milton Keynes UK
Ingram Content Group UK Ltd.
UKHW031318271124
451618UK00007B/265